A SONG OF SHADOWS

A SONG
OF SHADOWS

A CHARLIE PARKER THRILLER

WITHDRAWN

JOHN CONNOLLY

EMILY BESTLER BOOKS
—
ATRIA
NEW YORK   LONDON   TORONTO   SYDNEY   NEW DELHI

ATRIA BOOKS
An Imprint of Simon & Schuster, Inc.
1230 Avenue of the Americas
New York, NY 10020

Copyright © 2015 by John Connolly

Extract from *The Master and Margarita*, by Mikhail Bulgakov and translated by Michael Glenny. Copyright © Michael Glenny & Mikhail Bulgakov, is used by kind permission of Vintage Classics—an imprint of Random House Group and Andrew Nurnberg Associates.

Extract from *The Sirens of Titan*, by Kurt Vonnegut. Copyright © Kurt Vonnegut, published by Gollancz, an imprint of Orion Books, is used by permission of Donald C. Faber, Trustee of the Kurt Vonnegut Trust.

First Emily Bestler Books/Atria Books hardcover edition September 2015

EMILY BESTLER BOOKS / ATRIA BOOKS and colophons are trademarks of Simon & Schuster, Inc.

For information about special discounts for bulk purchases, please contact Simon & Schuster Special Sales at 1-866-506-1949 or business@simonandschuster.com.

The Simon & Schuster Speakers Bureau can bring authors to your live event. For more information or to book an event, contact the Simon & Schuster Speakers Bureau at 1-866-248-3049 or visit our website at www.simonspeakers.com.

Manufactured in the United States of America

10 9 8 7 6 5 4 3 2 1

Library of Congress Cataloging-in-Publication Data
Connolly, John.
  A song of shadows : a Charlie Parker thriller / John Connolly.—First Emily Bestler Books/ Atria Books hardcover edition.
    pages ; cm.—(Charlie Parker ; 13)
  Summary: "Still recovering from his life-threatening wounds, private detective Charlie Parker investigates a case that has its origins in a Nazi concentration camp during the Second World War. Parker has retreated to the small Maine town of Boreas to regain his strength. There he befriends a widow named Ruth Winter and her young daughter, Amanda. But Ruth has her secrets. Old atrocities are about to be unearthed, and old sinners will kill to hide their sins. Now Parker is about to risk his life to defend a woman he barely knows, one who fears him almost as much as she fears those who are coming for her. His enemies believe him to be vulnerable. Fearful. Solitary. But they are wrong. Parker is far from afraid, and far from alone. For something is emerging from the shadows"—Provided by publisher.
  1. Parker, Charlie "Bird" (Fictitious character)—Fiction. 2. Private investigators—Maine_ Fiction. 3. Widows_Fiction. I. Title.
  PR6053.O48645S66 2015
  823'.914—dc23
              2015009509

ISBN 978-1-5011-1828-9
ISBN 978-1-5011-1831-9 (ebook)

For Ellen Clair Lamb

What would your good do if evil didn't exist, and what would the earth look like if all the shadows disappeared?

—Mikhail Bulgakov, *The Master and Margarita*

Winter dead, spring dying, and summer waiting in the wings.
Slowly, the town of Boreas was changing: seasonal rentals were being opened and cleaned, the ice-cream parlor was ordering supplies, and the stores and restaurants were gearing up for the advent of the tourists. Just six months earlier, their proprietors had been counting the takings to figure out how close they'd have to cut their cloth to survive. Each year seemed to leave them with a little less in their pockets, and brought the same debate at the end of the season: do we go on or do we sell up? Now those who remained standing were returning to the fray, but even the cautious optimism of previous years was not yet palpable, and there were those who whispered that it was gone forever. The economy might be improving, but Boreas was mired in steady decline: a slow, labored mortality, half-life upon half-life. This was a dying town, a failing ecosystem, but still so many stayed, for where else was there to go?

Out on Burgess Road, the Sailmaker Inn remained closed, the first time in over seventy years that the grand old dame of Boreas hotels would not be opening its doors to welcome the summer visitors. The decision to put the Sailmaker on the market had been made only the previous week. The owners—the third generation of the Tabor family to operate the inn—had returned from their Carolina winter refuge to prepare the Sailmaker for guests, and some of their seasonal staff were already occupying the residences at the back of the property. The lawn was being mowed, the dust covers taken off the furniture, and then, just like that, the Tabors had looked at their business, decided that they couldn't take the strain any longer, and announced they wouldn't be reopening after all. Frank Tabor, a good Catholic, said that making the decision had been akin to going to confession and unburdening himself of his sins. He could now go in peace, and not fret anymore.

The decision to close the Sailmaker sounded another death knell for the town, a further concrete symbol of its dwindling. The tourists had grown fewer and fewer over the years—and older and older, because there was little here to amuse the young—and more summer homes were being put up for sale, their prices pegged optimistically high at first before time and necessity slowly whittled them down to a more realistic level. Even then Bobby Soames, the local Realtor, could name off the top of his head five houses that had been on the market for two years or more. By now their owners had largely given up on them, and they functioned neither as summer retreats nor actual residences. They were kept alive by a slow trickle of heat in winter, and in summer by the flitting and scuttling of bugs.

The town was founded by a family of Greeks back at the start of the nineteenth century, although they were long gone by the beginning of the twentieth. Indeed, nobody was entirely sure how they had ended up in this part of Maine to begin with—and the only remaining clue to its origins lay in its name: Boreas, a northern outpost named after the Greek god of winter and the north wind. Was it any wonder, Soames sometimes thought, that its survival as a vacation destination had always been tenuous? They should have just named it Arctic South and had done with it.

Soames was driving slowly through Boreas on this fine April morning. Everyone drove slowly through Boreas. Its thoroughfares were narrow: even Bay Street, the main drag, was a bitch to negotiate if cars were parked on both curbs, and anyone who'd been in town longer than a wet afternoon learned to push in his side mirrors if he wanted them to be intact when he returned. Meanwhile, the local police liked nothing better than to meet their ticket quotas by pulling over motorists who were even fractionally above the speed limit.

It might also have been something to do with the area's later Germanic heritage, which encouraged a certain sense of order and adherence to the tenets of the law. German Lutherans had first come to Maine in the middle of the eighteenth century, settling in what was now Waldoboro, but was then known as Broad Bay. They had been promised houses, a church, and supplies, none of which materialized, and instead found themselves marooned in a hostile landscape. They resorted to building temporary shelters and hunting local game, and the weakest among them didn't survive that first winter. Later they fought the French and the Indians, and communities were split during the Revolutionary War between those who sided with the Americans in the cause of liberty and those who were reluctant to break their oath of allegiance to the English Crown.

By then, the Germans were firmly established in Maine. Sometime in the late nineteenth century, a bunch of them made their way to Boreas, usurped the Greeks, and had been there ever since. The town's register of voters boasted Ackermanns, Baumgartners, Huebers, Kusters, Vogels, and Wexlers. Farther down the coast, in the town of Pirna—named after the town in Saxony from which its homesick founders hailed—were more Germans, and even a small number of German Jews: a scattering of Arnsteins, Bingens, Lewens, Rossmans, and Wachsmanns. Soames, who was English on his great-grandfather's side and Welsh on his great-grandmother's (although for some reason nobody in his family liked to talk about the Welsh side), regarded them all in the same light—everyone was a potential client—although he could recall his grandfather's strong opinions on the Germans, a consequence of his great-grandfather's experiences during World War I, and his grandfather's own memories of World War II. Being shot at for years by men of a particular nationality will tend to impact negatively upon one's view of them.

Soames left Bay Street behind and turned onto Burgess Road. He paused outside the Sailmaker. The doors were closed, and he could see no signs of life. He had already made his pitch to the Tabors to act as Realtor for the property, and Frank had promised to call him later that day. Soames would miss the Sailmaker. It had boasted a pretty good bar, and he enjoyed shooting the breeze with Donna Burton, who bartended there on Tuesdays, Wednesdays, and weekends. She was the kind of flirtatious divorcée who kept customers returning, or male customers anyway, female customers being less susceptible to her charms, and also strangely reluctant to let their husbands or boyfriends spend significant amounts of unsupervised time in her presence.

Soames didn't know what Donna would do now that the Sailmaker was closing. She lived down in Pirna, where she worked as a secretary, and her part-time summer hours at the Sailmaker had made the difference between a comfortable winter and one in which the thermostat was kept a couple of degrees lower than ideal. Maybe Fred Amsel at the Blackbird Bar & Grill would give her a few hours, if his wife, Erika, allowed him. Donna would bring her Sailmaker customers with her, and Fred would be competing with the Brickhouse for their business. Maybe Soames would have a word with Fred about it, and Fred could then broach the subject with Erika. Mrs. Amsel might have looked like someone who had repeatedly had a door slammed shut on her face, with the temperament to match, but she was no fool when it came to money.

Who knows, thought Soames, but when Donna heard about his efforts on her behalf, she might even be willing to reward him with some carnal delights. Soames had given a great deal of thought to just how carnally delightful a night with Donna Burton might be. Those fantasies had sustained him through the dying years of his marriage.

Now that he was single again, he had laid siege to her over two summers with a stubbornness that would have shamed the Greek army at Troy. He hadn't yet managed to breach her defenses, but Fred Amsel might just be the man to boost him over the parapet. If that didn't work, Soames would have to figure out how to hide himself inside a wooden horse and pay someone to leave him on her doorstep.

Soames drove on until the houses started to thin out, and the line began to blur between Boreas's town limits and those of tiny, neighboring Gratton to the north. The two towns shared resources, including a police force, mainly because Gratton made Boreas look like Vegas, so any lines on a map were for informational purposes only. The Boreas PD also had contracts for Pirna to the south, and Hamble and Tuniss to the west, the latter two being townships that consisted of little more than scattered houses and dilapidated barns. Most everyone from the surrounding area went to Boreas or Pirna to do business, and the five towns had come together to form a single council, on which Soames sat. The bimonthly meetings, held every first and third Wednesday, tended to be fractious affairs: property taxes were higher in Boreas than elsewhere, and those in the town who resented seeing their dollars going to service sewers in Hamble, or road maintenance in Tuniss, whispered darkly of socialism.

Soames turned right off Burgess Road onto Toland's Lane, which wound its way down to Green Heron Bay, the most obscure of the inlets on the peninsula. It was long, and sheltered by high dunes, and something about its orientation made it particularly susceptible to winds from the sea, so that facing into even a comparatively mild breeze from a house along the shore felt like standing on the prow of a ship during a storm. It was always a couple of degrees cooler in its environs than elsewhere around Boreas, as though winter had chosen this place to leave a reminder of its eventual return. Tourists generally didn't bother using it, the occasional bird-watchers excepted, and they were usually disappointed by the absence of any herons, green or otherwise.

Only two houses stood on the bay, both of which were former summer homes, one bought in haste and repented at leisure, and the other a family bequest that had remained unloved and unused following the reading of the will. In truth, Soames had despaired of ever selling, or even renting, either of them, and it had come as a surprise and a relief when both attracted occupants within weeks of each other, even if the pleasure in finally securing some income for his clients—and a monthly percentage for himself—was tempered slightly by the identity of one of the renters.

Soames had read about the private detective named Charlie Parker, of course, even before the shooting and convalescence that had brought him at last to Boreas. Soames had some friends and former clients in both the Bangor PD and the Maine State Police, and was privy to barroom details of the man's life that had never made it into any newspaper. If Parker wasn't quite trouble, he was closely related to it.

Initially, though, the approach about renting the house came from a lawyer named Aimee Price down in South Freeport, who told Soames that she had a client who needed privacy and quiet, in order to recover from a recent trauma. She came up to Boreas to view the house, decided that it met her client's needs, and signed a lease, all in the space of a single morning. Yet negotiations over the rent made the meetings of the town council seem somnolent by comparison, and Soames had come out of the whole business bruised, battered, and checking to make sure that Price hadn't stolen his watch as well. Only when the lease agreement was signed did Price mention the name of her client: Charlie Parker.

"The private detective?" said Soames, as he watched the ink dry on the lease. "The one who got shot up?"

"Yes. Is that a problem?"

Soames thought about the question. It would only be a problem if the people who had tried to kill Parker came back for another attempt. The house had been hard enough to rent as things stood. The owners would be better off burning it to the ground if it became the scene of a massacre. It would also be likely to cost him his seat on the council. He wouldn't be popular if his lax standards led to Boreas becoming famous for something other than Forrest's Ice Cream Parlor and the shrimp étouffée at Crawley's Cajun Citchen. ("The Best Cajun Food in These Parts," which, all things considered, wasn't a slogan to set the heart alight, even if Crawley's did serve damned fine food, although that cutesy misspelling of "kitchen" caused Soames to twitch involuntarily every time he saw it in print.)

He decided that honesty might be the best policy.

"Look, a man like that has enemies," he said, "and nobody has ever been shot in Boreas. I mean, *ever.*"

"Maybe you could put it on your sign," said Price. "You know: 'Boreas: 75,000 days without a shooting,' like building sites do for workplace accidents."

Soames tried to figure out if she was being facetious, and decided that she probably was. It had seemed like a good idea, too, if only for a moment.

"Unhelpful suggestions about signage aside," said Soames, "his reputation might be a matter of concern."

"There's no risk of a repeat of the incident that led to his injuries."

"You seem very certain of that."

"I am."

She stared at him, as if inviting him to ask the question that danced on his lips and tongue. Soames swallowed. His office suddenly felt very warm. He thought about the rental income.

"Given the unusual circumstances, perhaps we could—"

"No."

"—look again at—"

"I don't think so."

"—the amount to be—"

"You're wasting your breath."

"Right."

"That house hasn't had a tenant in almost two years."

"We've had offers."

"No, you haven't."

"You don't know that."

"Yes, I do."

"Okay."

"Any further questions?"

"Will he be armed?"

"I don't know. You can ask him when you see him, if you like."

Soames thought about what he knew of the detective.

"I guess he'll be armed," he said, as much to himself as to Price. "If he isn't, he probably should be."

"That's the spirit," said Price. "And the fewer people who know about this for now, the better. Even when he gets here, it'll be up to him how he deals with folks. Some may recognize his name or face, some may not."

"We mind our own business in Boreas," said Soames. "As far as I'm concerned, you're the one renting the house, and if I'm asked who's going to be living in it I'll just say that I have no idea."

Price stood and extended her hand. Soames shook it.

"It's been a pleasure," she said.

"Uh, likewise. I think."

He walked her to her car.

"One last thing," she said, and Soames felt his heart sink. He hated "one last things."

"Some men from New York will be coming to look at the house. They're, well, kind of security consultants. They may want to make some slight alterations, just to ensure that the house is up and running in every way. They won't damage it. In fact, I imagine that any changes they make will only enhance its value."

The promise of enhanced value made Soames feel better about everything.

"I don't think that will be a problem."

"Good. They don't like problems."

Something in her tone made him want to reach for a stiff drink, which, when she was gone, was exactly what he did. His secretary saw him sipping from the glass.

"Are you celebrating?" she asked.

"You know," he replied, "I'm really not sure."

II

Soames participated in two further meetings before Parker's arrival in Boreas. The first involved a Maine State Police detective named Gordon Walsh, who appeared in Soames's office with Cory Bloom, Boreas's chief of police, in tow. Bloom was a good-looking woman in her late thirties, and had she not been happily married, Soames might have considered putting the moves on her. Of course, the small matter of Bloom's friendship with his ex-wife also had to be taken into account, which meant that Cory Bloom would be more likely to date a piece of gum that she'd peeled off the sole of her shoe than Bobby Soames, but a man could dream. So far, nobody had figured out a way to police fantasies.

Walsh hadn't exactly set Soames's fears to rest. He'd made it clear that Parker remained vulnerable, and stressed, like Aimee Price before him, how important it was that the detective's presence in Boreas remained as unpublicized as possible. But Bloom assured Walsh that one of the advantages of Boreas—at least until tourist season began in earnest, which wouldn't be for another month to six weeks—was the virtual impossibility of anyone being able to stop in town for longer than five minutes without being noticed. If strangers demonstrated unusual curiosity about any of its residents, someone would pick up on it. Bobby Soames could have confirmed the perspicacity of the town's residents from personal experience, had he chosen to do so, given that his marriage had come to an end precisely because Eve Moorer from the florist's shop had spotted him coming out of a motel on Route 1, accompanied by a woman twenty years his junior, a gamine who might even have been mistaken for his daughter, if he had had a daughter. But Walsh didn't need to know that story, and Cory Bloom already did.

Bloom suggested that, while it might seem counterintuitive to do so, it would be best if a handful of the town's more prominent and sensible citizens were quietly informed of the detective's impending residence. She named a number of bar owners; the town's Lutheran pastor, Axel Werner; and Kris Beck, who owned Boreas's only gas station, along with a few others. Walsh didn't object, and left it in her hands. A couple of other minor details were batted around, but otherwise Walsh's visit to Boreas boiled down to the kind of warnings dotted around train stations and airports: if you see something, say something.

"What I don't understand," said Soames at last, "is why he picked here." It had been bothering him ever since Aimee Price signed the lease on the detective's behalf.

"You know the Brook House Clinic?" said Walsh.

Soames did. It was an upscale private medical center about ten miles west of town, and more like a resort than a hospital. A couple of Hollywood actors, and at least one ex-president, had been treated there, although their presence at Brook House had never made it into the newspapers.

"Well, he spent time there as part of his rehabilitation, and they'll be taking care of his physiotherapy."

"He must have money, but he won't have much of it left once that place is done wringing him out," said Soames. He wasn't sure that he could even afford to have his temperature taken at Brook House.

"My understanding is that they struck a rate," said Walsh.

"Brook House? I heard they billed you just for breathing the air."

"You, maybe. Not him. You mind if we take a look at the house?"

Soames didn't mind at all. Bloom drove them out in her Explorer, and Soames found himself instinctively dropping into Realtor mode, pointing out interesting features of the landscape, and the proximity of stores and bars, until Walsh informed him that he was only here for an hour, and wasn't actually planning on relocating, which caused Soames to clam up and sulk the rest of the way to Green Heron Bay. Walsh made a single slow circuit of the house before entering. He then examined the interior thoroughly, opening and closing doors and windows, and testing locks and bolts.

"What about the other house?" he asked Soames, as all three of them stood on the porch, watching the waves break and the sands spiral.

"It's empty," said Soames. "Has been for a while, just like this place."

"Anyone makes any inquiries about it, you let the chief here know, okay?"

"Absolutely."

Walsh took in the dunes and the ocean, his hands on his hips, like he'd just conquered the bay and was considering where to plant his flag.

Soames coughed. He always coughed when he was nervous or uncertain about something. It was his only flaw as a Realtor, like a gambler's "tell."

"Um, the lawyer, Ms. Price, mentioned that some security consultants from New York would be coming by."

Walsh's mustache lifted on one side in what was almost a smile.

"Right, 'security consultants.' Is that what she called them?"

"I believe those were her words."

"Well, you'll know them when you see them."

Soames had visions of black-clad operatives, bristling with weaponry, rappelling from helicopters. Even though it wasn't a warm day, he took a handkerchief from his jacket pocket and used it to mop his brow. This was like preparing for a presidential visit.

"I guess there's not much more that we can do for now," said Walsh.

He started to walk back toward Bloom's car, where the chief was already waiting. Soames trotted along beside him, trying to keep up. Walsh's strides would have made Paul Bunyan's seem dainty by comparison.

"You got any idea when he's supposed to get here?" asked Soames.

"A week, I think."

"Will that be enough time for the, ah, 'security consultants' to do their work?"

"If it isn't, then he won't arrive until they're done. But I expect so. They're professionals." Walsh's mustache lifted again. "Are you concerned about them?"

"A little," Soames admitted.

"Good. You should be."

Soames tried to focus on his commission.

Back at his office, he poured himself a drink after Walsh and Bloom had left. He resisted having a second, because that way lay a slippery slope, but he was pretty certain that, before the detective's time in town was out, he'd be buying another bottle to keep in his desk drawer.

Maybe even more than one.

———

SOAMES WAS ALMOST RELIEVED when the consultants finally arrived, even though he'd been having disturbing dreams in which they appeared as versions of his father and complained about his alcohol consumption. He was starting to feel like Ebenezer Scrooge anticipating the visit of the third specter whose coming he feared the most, when a terse call from Aimee Price informed him that the consultants would meet him at the house first thing on Friday morning.

The men were already waiting when Soames arrived: one tall and black, the other shorter and whiter, although Soames thought that he might have been Latino, or part Latino, or part lots of things, most of them problematical. Soames knew better than to ask. All he knew for sure was that they made him nervous, the black one most of all. He introduced himself as Louis, but didn't shake hands. He was wearing a nicely cut dark suit. His head was shaved, and a hint of gray-flecked goatee adorned his face like moonlight reflected on a lake at midnight. The other man, who did shake hands, said his name was Angel, which was another reason for Soames to believe that he might be Latino. Or part Latino.

Or something.

Anyway, he couldn't say precisely why the men were unnerving. It might simply have been the pent-up concern inspired by the earlier references made to them. Then again, it might also have been to do with the fact that, when he began showing them the house, he got the distinct impression they were already intimately familiar with its layout. Okay, so it was possible that they could have looked up the description and dimensions on his website, but the website didn't detail which doors stuck, or which floorboards squeaked, and the men pointed out these flaws to Soames *before* they reached the doors or boards in question.

They were also interested in the panel for the old alarm system.

"How long has it been out of commission?" asked Angel.

"I can't say for sure. The house hasn't been lived in for two years, so at least that long. Why?"

"Just curious. We'll be replacing it anyway. There are signs of rot in the frames of the doors, front and back. They'll have to go. The windows look okay for now. We'll be changing the locks, obviously."

"Er, sure. Just as long as you leave a set of keys with me."

"Sorry, we won't be doing that."

"Excuse me?"

"Only one person is going to have keys to this house, and that's the tenant."

"I can't agree to that. Suppose something were to happen?"

"Like what?"

"A fire."

"You got insurance?"

"Yes."

"Then you're insured."

"What about a flood, or—I don't know—an accident of some kind?"

The one named Louis turned his head slowly in Soames's direction. He stared at the Realtor in a manner that made him feel like a tick on the end of a pair of tweezers, waiting to be squeezed.

"You just mentioned fires, floods, and accidents," said Louis. "What kind of death trap you trying to rent here?"

"That wasn't what I meant," said Soames.

"Better not be."

"You have to understand," said Angel, "that there are unusual security considerations. That's why we're here."

"I really do need a set of keys," said Soames, surprising himself with the determination in his tone.

"Okay, then."

"Really?"

"Yeah, we'll give you a set of keys."

"Good."

"What sort of keys would you like?"

"What do you mean?"

"I mean you can have any keys that you want, just not the keys to this house."

Soames felt his anger growing. He wasn't used to being treated like this. He didn't care who was coming to live in the house.

"Now listen here—" he said, before a heavy hand landed on his left shoulder. He looked up at Louis's face.

"We could go look for another rental—" said Louis.

"I'm starting to think that might be a good idea."

"—but that would inconvenience everyone involved," Louis continued, as though Soames had not spoken, "which would be bad."

He smiled at Soames. Soames wished that he hadn't. It was that kind of smile.

"How much is the lawyer paying you for this place?" asked Angel.

Soames gave them the figure.

"How much were you asking?"

Soames gave him another figure that was about 30 percent higher.

"You're a tough negotiator," said Angel. "It's amazing that you're not paying her."

Soames acknowledged that he had, at one point in his discussions with Price, believed this to be a distinct possibility.

"Let me make a call," said Angel.

He stepped into the empty living room and took out his cell phone. Soames heard him speaking in soft tones. When he returned, he named a figure closer to the original rent, along with an additional sum of $100 per month to Soames himself for what he termed "caretaking expenses."

"Caretaking?" asked Soames.

"Caretaking," said Angel.

"What does that mean?"

"It means that we want you to take care of yourself, and in return we'll take care of your house."

"Maybe I don't need the keys after all," said Soames.

"They'd just be one more thing for you to worry about," said Angel. "A revised rental agreement should be at your office when you get back."

He began guiding Soames gently but firmly out of the house.

"It'll take a few days to make the alterations required," said Angel. "It'll be done discreetly. You don't mind if we hold on to these keys for now?"

He waved the keys that Soames had brought with him. Soames patted his jacket. He was almost certain that he'd put the keys in his inside pocket after he opened the door, but he supposed that he could have been mistaken.

"You have my number," said Soames, "just in case there are any difficulties."

"There won't be, but thank you."

"Right. Well, I'll leave you to it."

"We appreciate it."

Soames got in his car. The two men had arrived in a new black Lexus LS 600h L, which Soames figured to be about $120,000 worth of machine. Clearly, being a security consultant paid well. He just wished that he understood exactly what that meant.

As Angel had promised, a revised rental agreement was waiting for him when he got back to the office. It wasn't until he was emailing a countersigned copy back to Aimee Price that he noticed the agreement had been sent at 8:15 a.m., when he was still on his way to meet the men called Angel and Louis.

Bobby Soames had just been railroaded.

Four days later, Charlie Parker arrived in Boreas.

III

Soames parked his car at the turnoff for Green Heron Road, which ran behind the two houses on the bay. A pair of dirt drives connected the homes to the road: Parker's first and then, about a quarter of a mile along, the second house, which had always been known as the Gillette House, even though no Gillettes had lived there since the 1960s.

It was now being rented by a woman named Ruth Winter and her nine-year-old daughter, Amanda. Soames had taken care of the paperwork, but only after running it by Walsh and the chief first. The Winters were given a clean bill of health. Their family was from Pirna, where Ruth Winter's mother still lived. Soames hadn't gone poking into Ruth Winter's affairs, or her reasons for moving to Boreas. It seemed to him that she simply wanted a little breathing space for her and her daughter. Residing in Boreas would allow Amanda Winter to continue her schooling in Pirna, as it was the same school district and the school bus would pick her up and drop her off near the house.

Soames had paid a couple of visits to the Winters since they had taken up residence in Boreas—more, if he were being honest, than might be considered entirely necessary under the circumstances, not least because Ruth was not unattractive. She was in her mid to late forties, with fair hair and blue eyes. Her daughter took after her, and was already tall for her age. It was only on the third visit that Ruth Winter inquired if Soames was always so attentive to his clients. She posed the question with a degree of good humor, but underpinning it was the clear message that Bobby Soames had delighted her long enough with his presence, which was why, on this particular morning, he had driven no farther than the road. His attention was instead fixed on the house occupied by the detective. Soames liked to think that he was taking a personal interest in Parker's continued good health, while also remaining concerned about the house itself. He didn't like not having access to it, and he was still worried by the possibility that Parker's presence in Boreas might bring trouble down on the town and, by extension, on Bobby Soames.

He had made only one previous visit to the detective, and that was on the day after Parker's arrival. Something odd occurred as Soames turned into the lane. He was listening to WALZ out of Machias when the signal was interrupted by a low buzzing noise. It passed quickly, and Soames thought nothing more of it, but Parker had been waiting outside for him when he reached the house, and Soames was certain that, under the detective's loose windbreaker, he had caught a glimpse of a gun.

Soames's first thought was that Parker did not look well. He moved slowly, and was clearly in some pain. His hair was streaked with strange markings, and it took Soames a couple of minutes to realize that his hair had grown back white where the pellets had torn his scalp. Two attackers, armed with pistols and a shotgun, had ambushed him as he entered his home. They'd have killed him, too, if he hadn't somehow found the strength to fire back at them. Even then, what really saved him was that he hadn't been given time to deactivate his alarm before they fired, and his alarm company was under strict instructions to notify the Scarborough cops if it went off. The police figured they must have missed cornering his attackers only by seconds. As for those assailants, the official story was that they had not been identified or found, but barroom scuttlebutt suggested they were dead.

Soames recalled those two "security consultants," and felt slightly ill at the memory of raising his voice to them.

In many ways—in his movements, his breathing, even the texture of his skin—Parker resembled someone older than his years, except for his eyes, which were unusually bright and piercing. Soames had never met the man before, so he couldn't say if they had always been that way, but they had an extraordinary clarity and—for want of a better word—insight. They were how Soames imagined the eyes of one of Christ's apostles might have looked as he came to understand the true nature of the being to whom he had devoted his life. They were the eyes of one who has suffered, and out of that suffering had come knowledge. Soames figured that being shot and almost killed might do that to a man.

Soames did not speak with Parker for long. He simply confirmed that the house was in order, and supplied him with an information file about the town containing a list of bars, stores, and restaurants; details of houses of worship and the times of services; and the names of various carpenters, plumbers, mechanics, and other tradesmen who could be relied upon in the event of a mishap. Soames had also underlined the contact numbers for the doctors in the area, and moved them from the rear of the file to the front, just in case.

"My card is in a pocket at the back," said Soames. "Call me anytime, if I can be of assistance."

"Thank you," said Parker.

The wind blowing in from the sea had only the slightest edge of cold to it. The tide had recently gone out, and gulls swooped down for stranded shellfish. Farther out, Soames could see the graceful ellipse of a cormorant's neck, just before the bird submerged itself beneath the waves.

"I hope you'll be happy here," said Soames. He didn't know where the words came from. They weren't just a Realtor's niceties; he meant them sincerely. Perhaps it was the sight of the cormorant that brought them out. "It's a beautiful spot."

"It is."

They appeared to be running out of conversation. Soames wanted to ask Parker how long he might be staying, although the rent had been paid three months in advance. Aside from any worries he might have had about reprisals against the detective, the additional income— "caretaking" bonus included—was welcome, and it would be nice to have a couple hundred extra dollars in his pocket. He decided not to pursue the subject until a month or more had gone by, and instead halfheartedly occupied Parker with small talk.

"Well," said Soames, "I just wanted to make sure everything was okay. I'll be on my way now. Any questions, just give me a call."

They shook hands. Parker might have looked frail, but his grip was strong.

"Thank you for your help," said the detective.

"I'm sure I'll see you around town."

"Probably."

Soames had returned to his vehicle and driven away. His radio came on, and the transmission was briefly interrupted at exactly the same point in the driveway. Soames paused, glanced to his left, and saw something flashing in the sunlight as he passed: a metal object, small and circular. Discreetly, he reached over as though to fiddle with the glove compartment. Yes, there it was: another little device set in the ground directly across from the first. Soames had continued on his way and said nothing about what he had seen, not even to the chief of police.

Now, three weeks since the detective's arrival in Boreas, Soames shielded his eyes with his right hand as he looked down on the beach and the sea beyond. The weather was growing warmer and warmer with each day, but out here at Green Heron Bay Soames was still glad that he was wearing a jacket. Farther along the strand, two figures walked—one tall, one smaller, their backs to him, their fair hair blown behind them by the breeze: the Winters, mother and daughter, out for a stroll by the high dunes.

Movement came from the house below, and the detective appeared on his porch. He was carrying a stick, and took the steps down to the beach carefully, and at an angle, using his free hand to support himself on the railing. It was only when he was already on the sand that he saw the woman and the girl walking north along the beach. Soames saw him stop and turn to go back to the house. He paused as he glimpsed the car on the road above. Soames raised a hand uncertainly in greeting. After a couple of seconds the gesture was returned, and then the detective was gone.

"They're nice people," said Soames to himself. "Wouldn't have hurt you to say hi."

But who was he to judge?

He got back in his car and left the detective to his solitude.

IV

A manda Winter did not fully understand why she had been forced to move to this house by the sea. She was aware only of an argument between her mother and grandmother, although she was not privy to the cause. She had simply learned to judge her mother's moods, for the two of them were close in the way that only a mother and daughter could be who had grown up without a man in their lives, and she understood that questions about the fight would not be welcomed.

Amanda's father had died while she was as yet unborn, and her mother rarely spoke of him. Amanda knew only his name—Alex Goyer—and that he had been a mechanic. Her grandmother had once used a funny word to describe him: "feckless." Amanda had looked it up online and found that it meant irresponsible, or worthless. There were other words too, but those were the ones that she understood. She didn't like to think of her father as having no worth, for if she was part of him then it meant that something of her lacked worth too. Her mother had tried to reassure her on that front. She insisted that her father wasn't worthless, no matter what Grandma Isha said.

Now that Amanda was older and growing accustomed to the nuances of adult speech and behavior, she had learned—mostly through Grandma Isha—more about the relationship between her father and her mother. She knew that Grandma Isha had been angry because Amanda's mother had become pregnant outside marriage, and her father hadn't wanted to marry her when he found out, instead cutting off all contact. The fact that her father had abandoned her mother while Amanda was still in the womb made Amanda sad, and seemed to confirm Grandma Isha's view of him.

Someone had murdered her father—shot him at the auto shop where he worked. The revelation was recent, and came from Grandma Isha. Amanda wondered if that might be one of the reasons for the big fight. She wasn't sure how she felt about her father's murder. Grandma Isha had mentioned drugs. Did that make her father a bad man? Amanda hoped not. Being bad was worse than being feckless. Her father didn't seem to have much family of his own: his mother was dead, and his father, again according to Grandma Isha, wasn't much better than the son. Her father's father—she couldn't really think of him as her grandfather—had died when Amanda was still a baby. His liver didn't work right, and then it stopped working altogether. Her mother went to his funeral, although, like so much else concerning the Goyers, Amanda didn't find that out until years later.

So Grandma Isha was Amanda's only grandparent, because Grandpa Dave, Isha's husband, was dead too. Amanda could barely remember him. He had gray hair, and wore thick glasses. Her mother said that Grandpa Dave used to call Amanda "Manna," like the bread from heaven. Sometimes her mother would call her that too, which made Amanda happy.

Grandma Isha loved Amanda. She doted on her, spoiled her, inhabited every facet of her life. Amanda and her mother had even lived in a house not far from Grandma Isha's, on land owned by her. Amanda missed living there. She missed Grandma Isha. There had been no word from her since they had moved to Boreas. She wanted to ask her mother about it, but her mother was lost in concerns of her own, and whenever Amanda tried to broach the subject, her mother would grow angry, or sad, and Amanda didn't like to see her mother that way.

So, when Amanda was not at school—which was often, because she had a sickness, and the doctors didn't seem to know what to do about it—she whiled away the days dozing, or reading, or watching TV until her head and eyes hurt. She had hated it in Boreas at first, hated being separated from her friends in Pirna, and from Grandma Isha. But slowly and surely the sea was beginning to lull her with its rhythms and sounds, for it was the same sea that broke near their old house, even if the view was different. She could not imagine being able to fall asleep without the shushing of waves, or waking without the scent of salt in the air and the tang of it on her skin.

The man who lived in the only other house on the bay had drawn her attention almost immediately. She had seen him walking on the beach that first day, as she sat on her new bed and stared out at the ocean. He stepped slowly and carefully, as though fearful of falling, even though the sand wouldn't have hurt him much if he had. He stayed close to the soft areas near the large dunes, and he used a stick. He wasn't old, though, which surprised her. In her limited experience, only old people like Grandma Isha used sticks, so she deduced that this man must be hurt, or disabled.

Because of the relative absence of males in her life, Amanda was curious about men. Not boys—she already understood them well enough to disregard them almost entirely, finding them temporarily amusing at best and irritating for the most part—but grown men: adults, like her mother. She could not quite conceive of the reality of them, and their thought processes and actions were alien to her. They seemed like another species from the boys in school, and she could not imagine how someone as dumb and useless in every way as Greg Sykes—who sat behind her in class, and had once spat in her hair—could possibly grow up to become capable of, say, driving a car, or holding down a job. Greg Sykes smelled like pee, and would walk around with his hand down his pants when he thought that no one was looking. She could only picture a grown-up Greg Sykes as a larger version of his current self: still spitting, still smelling like pee, and still juggling his junk because he couldn't tell the difference between "in private" and "in public."

So, on that first day, confused about this sudden upheaval in her life, she watched the man walk slowly along the strand, one hand on his stick, his head down, his lips—she thought—moving ever so slightly, so that he appeared to be talking to himself or, perhaps, counting his steps. He had paused for a moment to take in their house, noting the car parked outside, and the boxes and suitcases on the porch. His gaze moved up, and for a moment Amanda was certain that he was looking at her, even though she already knew that the angle made it hard to see her if she was lying on her bed. She'd checked when they first arrived, moving between her bedroom and the sand, gauging the room's suitability as an observation post. No, he almost certainly couldn't see her, and yet she felt the force of his gaze, and for a moment he might have been in the room with her, so aware was she of his presence.

Then he walked on, and she shifted position so that she could continue watching him. She wasn't the kind of girl who spied on people. Grandma Isha had once caught her rummaging in her closet, Amanda's infant eyes drawn by the old dresses that her grandmother kept but never wore, the boxes of shoes that remained new and unsullied, and other unknown treasures that might be concealed inside. Grandma Isha had been really annoyed, and gave Amanda a long lecture on the right to privacy. Since then Amanda had always been careful not to pry, but the man was walking on a beach, in full view of anyone who happened to be around, so it wasn't like she was doing something wrong by watching him. Even so, her attention might have drifted elsewhere, leaving him to become an object of ever decreasing interest until she finally failed to notice him at all, were it not for what he did next.

He stopped, reached down to the sand, and picked up something black and red before continuing on for another while. Finally, he stepped to his left, onto the clean white sand beyond the reach of the incoming tide, and dropped the item. He then turned and walked back to his own house, moving even more slowly and carefully than before. The expression on his face was one of tiredness and, she believed, pain.

She waited until he was out of sight, and, when she was certain that he had returned to his home, left her bedroom and wandered onto the beach. It didn't take her long to find the small bundle, for the breeze grabbed at the strip of red fabric that marked its position.

The man had discarded a cloth bag of what felt like stones, its mouth tied shut with the red material. The knot wasn't very tight, so it didn't take her long to open it. The contents, when revealed, didn't appear to be terribly interesting. They were just plain old pebbles, with no pretty patterns, no unusual striations. She examined them all, just in case there might be a gem hidden among them, but she found none. When she was done, she returned the stones to the bag, retied the knot, and replaced it in the little depression in the sand from which she had lifted it.

Later, the rain came. They listened to it beat upon the roof of their new home while they ate take-out pizza at the kitchen table, surrounded by possessions both boxed and unpacked, and Amanda asked her mother if she knew anything about the man who lived in the other house.

"No," her mother replied, but she was only half listening. She was always only half listening, half speaking, half noticing. She had been that way ever since she'd announced that they were leaving Pirna for Boreas. "I think his name is Mr. Parker, but that's all. Why?"

"Nothing. I just saw him walking on the beach, and I was wondering."

"Maybe we'll introduce ourselves, once we've settled in. Until then, you know about talking to strangers, right?"

"Yes, Mom."

"Good."

Her mother's attention wandered again. She'd been nibbling at the same slice of pizza for so long that it must have grown cold in her hand. Amanda had eaten two slices already, and was now on her third. She was ravenous. She finished that final slice and asked if she could be excused.

"Sure, honey," said her mother. "We'll be okay here, you know?"

But she didn't really look at Amanda when she spoke, and Amanda thought that she was trying to convince herself as much as her daughter.

———

THAT NIGHT AMANDA HAD a strange dream. She was standing on the beach in her pajamas, and in the distance the strip of red material flapped like a flag above the sand. A figure knelt over it, but it was not Mr. Parker. This one was smaller, and as Amanda drew closer she saw that it was a little girl, younger than she. The girl wore a nightgown, although she didn't appear to feel the cold. Her long blond hair obscured her face. Her right hand toyed with the red fabric.

Amanda stopped. In her dream, she sensed that it would be best not to approach this girl. She wasn't frightening. She was simply *other*.

"Hello, Amanda," said the girl.

"Hello. How do you know my name?"

"Because I've been watching you. You had pizza for dinner. I saw you eating. Later you went up to your room, and I saw you there too."

"How?"

"Through the window."

"But it's high up."

"Yes. You have a lovely view."

And even in her dream, Amanda shivered.

"What's your name?" she asked.

"My name is Jennifer."

"Do you live around here?"

"I suppose I do now."

A part of Amanda wished that she could see Jennifer's face. Another part was glad that she could not.

"You saw him drop the bag, didn't you?" said Jennifer.

"Yes."

"And you picked it up."

"Yes. Did I do something bad? I didn't mean to."

"No. You put it back where you found it, and that's the important thing. Do you understand what it is?"

"No, I don't think so." Amanda paused and reconsidered. "Maybe."

"Go on."

"It's a marker, but I don't know what it's supposed to be marking."

"Progress," said Jennifer, and Amanda thought that although she looked like a little girl, she spoke like someone much older. "Each day he tries to walk a little farther. Often it's only a few steps. And he marks the spot, so he will remember to take at least one step more the next day."

"Why does he do that?"

"He's been hurt. He's still hurting. But he's getting stronger."

"Is he—?"

But Jennifer stood and turned her back on Amanda. Their conversation was over.

"Why can't I see your face?" shouted Amanda, and she was sorry for asking as soon as the words left her mouth.

Jennifer stopped walking.

"Do you want to see it?" she said. "Do you really?"

Slowly she turned, her right hand lifting, pushing the hair away from her face.

And Amanda woke up screaming to find sand in her bed.

CHAPTER

V

Cory Bloom had been Boreas's chief of police for two years, and remained the youngest person ever to have occupied that position. By contrast, her predecessor, one Erik Lange, had been the longest-serving chief in the state when he retired, and even then the town pretty much had to force him out at gunpoint. Lange died soon after retiring, a fact that Bloom didn't particularly regret, although she kept such thoughts to herself. It was said by Lange's admirers—of whom, by the end, there were few—that the old chief's heart couldn't bear a life of relative indolence, although Bloom would have been surprised if his autopsy had revealed a heart larger than an acorn.

Lange was of sound German stock—incredibly, the old coot's father was still alive, knocking on the door of his centennial—and ran Boreas as his personal fiefdom. He was a chauvinist and a homophobe, and the best that could be said about him was that he kept the crime rate down, although it hadn't increased noticeably since his departure, which suggested that Boreas hadn't exactly been Detroit or New Orleans to begin with. By the end of his reign it was clear that the townsfolk wanted a change, and Bloom was appointed chief with relatively little fuss. It helped that she was married to a man who hailed originally from Pirna, and—although nothing was ever said to this effect—that she had no children.

For the most part, the transition to Boreas from Bangor, where Bloom had served before applying for the chief's job, had been painless, aided by the unanticipated bonus of Lange's sudden demise, as otherwise he would have been unable to resist sticking his nose in her business, and would have carried himself as the chief-in-exile. Yes, there were some who muttered about the public face of law enforcement being relatively young and, more to the point, female, but Bloom had the right touch, and even those who would happily have erected a statue to Erik Lange in the center of town had gradually warmed to her. A handful of holdouts remained, though, including Lange's deputy chief, Carl Foster, who threw his toys out of his playpen and left the force when the town passed him over in favor of Bloom. Good riddance to him. It had saved her the trouble of forcing him out.

She parked her Explorer at the edge of the beach at Mason Point, slipped out of her sneakers, and replaced them with the pair of black waterproof boots that she always kept in the trunk. She was supposed to be off duty, but had learned quickly that no chief of police in a small community is ever really off duty. Anyway, this was different. It wasn't every day that a body washed up on the shores of her town.

Two uniformed officers were already waiting for her by the water's edge, along with Dan Rainey, who lived close to the beach and had first seen the body floating in the surf. The officers were both women, and had been hired on Bloom's watch. Their employment had led, not coincidentally, to a couple of further male retirements and resignations from the department to go along with those of Lange and Foster, as their aging cronies negotiated settlements with the town and headed off into the sunset. The blatancy of it had irritated Bloom, but she shared her feelings only with her husband. He was an architect with a sideline in designing boats, and exuded the calm of a Buddha, helped by the occasional toke. Sometimes she threatened to arrest him for it, which he found mildly amusing. Still, the resulting purge of the department's deadwood had allowed her to redress the previous gender imbalance (female: 0 percent, male: 100 percent) while still holding on to a couple of senior male officers who were secretly glad to see the back of Lange, if only because it would enable them to work out their twenty away from his martinet gaze.

Mary Preston was the younger of the two officers on the beach. She was a big woman in her late twenties, and Bloom wasn't sure that she would have passed the physical fitness test over in Bangor, which required female recruits of her age to be able to do fifteen push-ups without stopping, thirty-two sit-ups in one minute, and run one-and-a-half miles in fifteen minutes. On the other hand, she was smart, intimidating, loyal, and very, very funny. When Bloom had gently raised the issue of her weight during the interview process, Preston informed her that she had no intention of letting a "perp"—and that was the word she used—get so far away from her that fifteen minutes of jogging would be required to capture him. If speed over distance did become an issue, she said, she'd run him down in her car. If she didn't have a car, she'd throw her flashlight at him.

If that failed, she'd just shoot him.

Bloom hired her on the spot.

The second officer was Caroline Stynes, who had twelve years under her belt as a sergeant up in Presque Isle. She was a decade older than Preston, and Bloom was grooming her to become deputy chief, just as soon as she could convince the town's human resources department to come up with an appropriate salary. For now, Stynes had brought her rank with her to Boreas, and was Bloom's de facto second in command.

"What have we got?" Bloom asked.

"Male," said Stynes. "Could be in his forties, but it's hard to say."

The body lay facedown on the sand, the retreating tide still lapping at its feet. He looked like he hadn't been in the sea for too long, although immersion in the cold, deep salt water of the North Atlantic would have inhibited putrefaction for a time. His body also wouldn't have started to rise until the gases inside decreased its specific gravity, creating enough buoyancy for it to reach the surface and float. In addition, the man was wearing a heavy jacket and a sweater, which would have kept him under the water longer, even allowing for the action of the gases.

Bloom pulled on a pair of blue latex gloves and gently pushed his hair away from his face. Fish and crustaceans had already been nibbling on the soft tissue, and one eye was gone. She could see some damage to his skull, although it would take an autopsy to determine if it was ante- or postmortem. Corpses in water always float facedown, and the buffeting of the waves, combined with any damage that the body might have sustained upon sinking initially, could well have resulted in abrasions to the head. The lividity to the visible parts of his upper torso was dusky and blotchy from his movement in the water. His right foot was shoeless, although he still wore a striped sock. The remains of his big toe poked from a hole. Something had eaten most of it down to the bone. His left foot had retained its shoe, and the right shoe was attached to it by the laces. So before he'd gone into the water, his shoelaces had been tied together.

Carefully, Bloom patted the pockets of his garments, looking for some form of ID. She discovered none.

"You thinking a suicide?" said Stynes.

Bloom leaned back on her heels. She'd heard of cases in which people had tied their shoelaces together, or bound their legs, before dropping, or shuffling, into the water, just so they could be sure that they wouldn't start kicking once the panic set in. She had even seen photographs of drowning victims with wire tied around their wrists, leading to an initial assumption that the bodies were put in the water by a third party, only for the autopsy to reveal marks in their mouth where they'd pulled the wire taut with their teeth.

She examined the man's fingers. The skin of the pads and the backs of the hands was macerated from his time in the water, but none of the fingernails were missing. As putrefaction developed, the epidermis and nails tended to peel off, but his were still intact.

"I'll inform the ME and the state police," said Bloom. "We'll see if there are any reports of abandoned vehicles, or somebody finding a discarded wallet or ID. In the meantime, we need to get him bagged and off this beach."

Now that he was out of the water, decay would start to set in rapidly. It was essential that they secure him in a cooler drawer as soon as possible, in order to facilitate an accurate autopsy. In addition, the discovery of a body inevitably attracted rubberneckers, especially in a small town. Kramer & Sons, the local funeral home, had the contract for dealing with floaters and similar unfortunates in this part of the county. They'd be glad of the work. Despite Boreas's relatively elderly population, nobody had died in town for a couple of weeks.

"Mary," she said, "I want you to go up to the road and establish a cordon. No unauthorized vehicles, no unauthorized personnel, and no excuses. Caroline, you stay with the body for now, and take Mr. Rainey's statement. I'm going to call in Mark and Terry to help us do a sweep of the beach while the tide is going out, just in case we can find anything to help us make an identification. All clear?"

They nodded, then Preston looked past her.

"Pastor's here," she said. "And Father Knowles."

Bloom turned to see the two men waiting at a polite distance. She could see only one car, though. They must have decided to travel together. Martin Luther would have had an embolism.

"Is it okay to come down?" Pastor Werner called.

Bloom waved them over. Both men were wearing clerical collars. She wondered if they'd put them on specially. Bloom wasn't religious, but she maintained good relations with both Werner and Father Knowles, the parish priest of Holy Mother. He was a tiny, energetic man, whose enthusiasm for everything sometimes wearied Bloom. She got on better with the Lutheran Werner, who was more laid-back and laconic. He probably had six inches on Knowles, and the smaller cleric usually deferred to Werner in community matters, for Werner's father had been pastor before him while Knowles was only in his second year at Holy Mother.

"We heard about it in town," said Father Knowles. "It's no one local, is it?"

"I don't believe so," said Bloom.

The two men looked past her at the face of the dead man, and winced at the sight of him.

"I don't recognize him," said Knowles, "but then, he's been in the water. Do you, Axel?"

Werner shook his head. "No, he's not familiar."

"Do you mind if I say a prayer for him?" Knowles asked Bloom.

Bloom told him that she didn't mind at all. It wasn't like it would hurt the dead man. "Just don't touch the body, okay?"

Knowles produced a rosary from his pocket and knelt by the corpse. Werner bowed his head, but said nothing. Bloom recalled that there was something in Lutheranism about not praying for the dead. Preston, who was Catholic, joined her hands, and crossed herself when Knowles was finished.

———

BLOOM WALKED WITH KNOWLES and Werner back to the parking lot, and watched them leave. She made calls to the Office of the Medical Examiner in Augusta, and the state police in Bangor, as well as to the Washington County Sheriff's Department in Machias. Finally she spoke with Lloyd Kramer and arranged to have the body bagged and put on ice until the ME determined how it should be handled.

She then decided to return home and change into her uniform. It always paid to look official in these situations. She turned the Explorer and headed for the main road. The gradient upward from the beach was comparatively gentle, and the entire strand was visible to passing traffic. As she prepared to make the turn, only one car was approaching, heading north to town: a Mustang that slowed almost to a stop as

it passed her. She caught a glimpse of the driver as he glanced first at
her, then at the figures on the sand: Rainey and Stynes by the body, and
Preston trudging back to her vehicle. He was wearing sunglasses, but
Bloom knew him by his car.

The detective, Parker.

She had spoken with him only once, when she spotted him at Hay-
man's General Store buying bread and milk. She'd introduced herself,
and asked how he was settling in, as much to be neighborly as anything else. He'd seemed pleasant, if distant. She knew that he sometimes liked reading the newspaper in the Moosebreath Coffee House,
although Bobby Soames had told her that he preferred the little seating
area at the back of Olesens Books & Cards. Soames fretted a lot about
Parker. He appeared to be under the impression that a gunfight could
break out at any moment up in Green Heron Bay. Parker also ate at
the Brickhouse a couple of evenings a week, although he usually didn't
drink anything stronger than a soda. Mostly, from what she heard, he
just walked on the beach by his house, and traveled twice weekly to the
Brook House Clinic for physiotherapy.

Now she nodded at him, and he nodded back. He took one more
look at the activity on the beach, and drove on. She stayed behind
him through town until he pulled up outside Olesens. In her rearview
mirror, she watched him take a copy of the *New York Times* from the
rack by the door and head inside. Guess it's true then, she thought. She
was curious about him. His presence in Boreas was incongruous given
his reputation. It was like having a grenade rolling around, one you had
been assured was defused but hadn't had time to check out for yourself.

But she had other concerns today. She thought that she could smell
the dead man on the plastic gloves she had discarded on the floor of her
vehicle, or maybe she was just imagining it. When she pulled into her
driveway, she took a pickup bag from the supply that she kept on hand
for the needs of her black Lab, Jodie, used it to dispose of the gloves,
and tied the bag. Ron, her husband, wasn't home. He was working

on a kitchen redesign in Eastport, and would be gone for most of the day. She let Jodie run in the backyard while she changed, then called her back inside and returned to the Explorer. Jodie's nose was pressed against the glass above the front door as she pulled away, a vision of abandonment. Bloom tried not to look.

Sometimes, she was grateful that she'd never had children. She wasn't sure that she'd ever have been able to leave the house.

VI

Olesens—which Larraine Olesen always felt should more correctly have read OLESEN'S, or even OLESENS' on the sign, since she and her brother, Greg, were joint owners—had been a fixture in Boreas since the midfifties, when Larraine and Greg's parents opened the store while still in their twenties. They'd continued to run it until the turn of the century, at which point they decided that enough was enough, and it was time for younger blood to take over. Neither of their children was married. Greg was briefly engaged to a local woman, but the relationship had never really taken, while Larraine—well, deep down Larraine probably preferred the company of women, but was too shy and too Lutheran to do anything about it. She wasn't bitter or unhappy, just a little lonely, but she loved her brother, and she loved books, and thus had found a measure of contentment in life.

Like independent bookstores everywhere, Olesens had struggled to adapt to the new age of bookselling. A family argument had erupted between the generations when Larraine and Greg began selling "gently used" books alongside new stock, which their parents regarded as a dangerous step down the slope toward not selling any books at all, but Greg had a good eye not just for a bargain but for rare first editions, and the store's Internet presence, along with a nice sideline in greeting cards, wrapping paper, and other materials that generated the kind of markup that books could only dream of, was keeping the store not only in business, but in profit. It had been Larraine's decision to add the little coffee bar at the back of the store. It faced out over Clark's Stream, which ran through the town, and the somewhat unimaginatively named Clark's Bridge, a pretty thing of stone and moss that looked as though it came from many centuries past, but was not much older than the store itself. The coffee bar sold mostly pastries and cookies baked by Mrs. Olesen, and decent coffee. It turned out that no small number of folk, both tourists and local, enjoyed the ambience of the Nook, as it was called, and the markup on coffee put even greeting cards to shame. There had been some tension initially between the Olesens and Rob Hallinan, owner of the Moosebreath Coffee House farther north on Bay, but it turned out that Boreas had just about enough customers for both of them, and more than enough in summer.

Charlie Parker had started coming in shortly after his arrival in town, because Olesens prided itself on carrying enough copies of the New York and Boston papers to satisfy demand year-round. The Olesens knew who he was almost as soon as he arrived, of course. Most everybody in town who was worth a damn had an early inkling of the detective's presence out on Green Heron Bay, and without exception they had become strangely protective of him. Even Chief Bloom had expressed surprise at how little muttering there had been, given that people in Boreas complained if the Brickhouse changed one of its draft beer taps, even if they never drank beer, and had debated for weeks about repainting the town's welcome sign in a softer shade of white. Perhaps it was something to do with his past: he was a man who had lost a wife and child, and had suffered grievous injury just for doing his job which, as far as anyone could tell, largely involved putting his mark on the kind of men and women without whom the world was a much better place. The shooting made him one of theirs, and the town had quietly closed ranks around him.

In the beginning Larraine and Greg kept their distance, allowing him his space to drink and read newspapers, books, and magazines, all of them bought at Olesens, with none of the books ever returned for a 30 percent trade-in, even though a big sign at the counter invited customers to do just that. But slowly they had tested the waters with him and found him to be gently, slyly funny, and aware of the strangeness of his situation in the town. Greg, in particular, got along well with him, and Greg was the archetypal dysfunctional independent bookseller. He gave the impression that he disapproved of most of his customers' book choices—which he did—and resented selling copies of books that he loved—also true—either because he wasn't sure that the buyer was worthy of the book or, in the case of the rarer editions, because he hated seeing them leave the store. The locals had become used to his ways, while Larraine tended to deal with the tourists. Just as there were broadcasters with faces made for radio, so too there were booksellers with attitudes designed for the Internet age, which limited the possible misunderstandings that might arise from any personal contact.

Now, while Parker sipped his Americano, and flipped through the Arts section of the *New York Times*, Greg approached him, carrying in the crook of his arm three hefty matching volumes—a psychiatric analysis of marital and sexual humor, which he felt certain he could sell at a considerable profit to some visiting shrink during the summer, assuming he could even bring himself to part with them when the time came.

Parker continued to read his paper. He did not look up.

"You ignoring me?" said Greg.

"Is it working?"

"No. You ever hear of a British band called the Smiths?"

"Yes, but you're too old for them."

"Anyway," continued Greg, now doing his best to ignore Parker's contribution to the conversation in turn, "their lead singer, Morrison—"

"Morrissey."

"—*Morrissey*, has a song called 'The More You Ignore Me, the Closer I Get.' I'm considering adopting it as a motto."

"Does that mean if I talk to you, you'll go away?"

"No, that'll just encourage me too."

He shifted the books to his other arm.

"You hear they found a body out at Mason Point?"

"Yeah, I drove by the beach on my way back into town." Parker looked up at Greg for the first time. "It seemed like Chief Bloom had only just got out there. News travels fast."

"In this place? Fast doesn't cover it. There are people here who probably knew the guy was dead before he did."

Greg thought about what he'd just said.

"I didn't mean that to sound, you know, like it sounded," he said. "Unless someone here killed him, but that doesn't seem likely."

"Why is that?"

"Tides. I'd say he went into the water farther south."

Parker returned to his paper.

"Well, it looks like Bloom has it all in hand."

"She's good. We're lucky to have her."

Greg remained hovering, his shadow falling slightly over the table.

"Can I ask you something?" he said.

"Sure."

"Do you miss it? You know, what you used to do. What you still do, I guess, assuming you'll go back to it. If you do."

"No."

Sometimes.

Yes.

"Just curious."

"I understand."

"I'll get back to work."

"Okay."

"Offer you a refill?"

"No, thanks. I'm good."

Greg returned to the office that lay between the Nook and the store itself. Larraine left the register to step inside and kick him forcefully in the shin.

"Can't you leave the man in peace for five minutes?"

Greg rubbed his shin to ease the pain. Sometimes, when it came to his older sister, he still felt like he was eight years old.

"It just came out," he said. "Ouch. I think you broke the skin."

"I'll break your skull next time."

"You almost made me drop the books."

"You're an idiot. You have waffles for brains. Go make yourself useful and sell something."

Greg sat down at his desk, still muttering about his injury. Larraine watched the detective. He had put down his newspaper and was staring out the window at the stream. She could see the reflection of his face in the glass. She thought that, if she were ever to be attracted to a man, it might be one like him. He wasn't handsome, not exactly, but he had depths. What swam through them, though, she could not tell.

VII

L ater that afternoon, out at Green Heron Bay, Amanda Winter opened the front door of their house to find an envelope lying on the step. Her mother had announced that she was keeping her out of school for the rest of the week. Amanda suffered from severe asthma, on top of her other problems. Her breathing had been especially bad the previous night, and she still hadn't been quite right that morning. She also seemed to be coming down with a cold, so it made sense to err on the side of caution.

Although the sea air was good for her, she was bored of the house. She had wrapped herself up warmly before going out for a walk along the strand. Now the envelope stopped her in her tracks. It was addressed to her mother in black block capitals, and felt heavy. It didn't have a stamp on it, which meant that someone must have dropped it off in person.

"Mom," she called. "There's mail for you."

Ruth Winter emerged from the dining room, where she had set up a small office area for herself. She worked as an independent financial planner and adviser, helping people with everything from cash flow and budgeting to investments and house purchases. Being self-employed had made the move to Boreas easier, even if her daughter still didn't understand the reasons for it. With luck, she never would.

Ruth took the envelope. There was something small but bulky inside. "Thanks, honey," she said. "Don't go too far."

"Yes, Mom."

"And keep your coat buttoned."

"I know."

"Do you have your inhaler, just in case?"

Amanda reached into her pocket and waved the device.

"Good girl."

She watched her daughter head out to the stones and sand, her hands buried in her pockets, her head up to smell the air, her chest expanding to take in almost comically exaggerated breaths, or as deep as her blocked airways would allow.

Ruth opened the envelope. Inside was a man's wallet. She removed the driver's license from it and read the name: Bruno Perlman. A yellow Post-it note, folded in half, was stuck to the interior of the wallet. She opened it up. In the same block capitals as the name on the envelope, it read

KEEP QUIET

She walked quickly to the bathroom and was violently ill.

———

FOR THE REST OF the day, the talk in Boreas was only of the body on the beach. Preliminary arrangements were made to transport it to Augusta for autopsy, although the Maine Medical Examiner's office had indicated that it might be some days before they could get to it, and hence there was no particular urgency, so the body stayed at Kramer & Sons. A description was given to the newspapers and the TV news shows, just in case anyone could come forward to help with identification.

And the one who knew the truth watched it all, and realized that he would have to act.

VIII

The house stood on the southern shore of Seven Stones Lake, a body of water southwest of Machias. It was an unspectacular family dwelling with a view of the water partially obscured by pine trees, and a two-car garage, half-filled with the accumulated junk of a family with three teenage children, and otherwise occupied by a battered Mitsubishi Lancer station wagon. Dream catchers, made by a Penobscot craftsman using twigs and natural feathers, were visible in two of the upper windows.

Through the yard, its grass recently mown, its borders trimmed. Past the rosebushes, past the herb garden. Up the porch steps, taking in the paintwork that remained just about presentable for another year. Into the living room.

Four bodies lay side by side on the floor: a father, a mother, and two daughters aged thirteen and fifteen. The radio played, and the table was laid for breakfast. A newspaper lay open, and had anyone been left alive to read it, they might eventually have come to an article below the fold about a body washed ashore at Boreas.

The parents had been shot first—their blood was on the kitchen tiles—and then moved into place on the carpet. The two girls had been killed next, one on the stairs, the other in the bathroom, and then carried down to the living room to lie beside their parents.

One child remained missing. He was outside, watching the house. His name was Oran Wilde, and his parents and teachers sometimes despaired of him. He was seventeen, and among his high school peers had not-so-secretly been voted "Person Most Likely to Die a Virgin." He had few friends, but he wasn't a bad kid. He was just angry and confused and solitary. He listened to music no one else had heard of, read thousand-page fantasy novels, and liked most kinds of clothing as long as it was black. His bedroom window, unlike those of his younger sisters, did not contain a dream catcher.

Oran should already have been at school along with his sisters, even if they always tried their best in public to pretend that they were not related to him. His father should have been behind his desk at the plumbing and bath supply company that he owned. His mother should have been doing whatever it was his mother did when her husband and children were not around. Oran sometimes wondered what that might be, but never asked. His job in life was to show as little interest as possible in his parents and their movements, in the hope that his lack of curiosity about them might be reciprocated, although it never was. They persisted in caring, which frustrated Oran greatly.

Somewhere in the house, a telephone rang. The sound stopped, only to be replaced by his mother's cell phone trilling. That was followed by the cavalry charge ringtone of his father's phone. It was probably the school, Oran figured. Mrs. Prescott, the school secretary, was responsible for tracking down students suspected of truancy. Not that Oran had ever skipped school: it wasn't in his nature. By doing so he would have drawn attention to himself, and Oran, as has already been established, preferred to fly under the radar. He just kept his head down, and tried to avoid getting the shit kicked out of him. He hated high school. He couldn't countenance the possibility that there were people in the world who looked back on their schooldays only with fondness; as the best time of their lives. How bad could your life be, Oran wondered, if your days in high school represented the best of it? He had always imagined that the happiest moment of his life would involve leaving his school behind, and perhaps blowing it up immediately after.

Would Mrs. Prescott call the police if she got no answer? Maybe. Clare and Briony, Oran's sisters, were the stars of their respective years. Everyone liked them, aside from a handful of bitches. The sisters wore their popularity easily, and did their best not to look down on anyone, their brother excepted. Even Oran liked them, and he thought that they secretly liked him too. They just put a lot of effort into not showing it. Their parents, Michael and Ella, turned up for school concerts, and basketball and field hockey games. They were a pretty regular family, Oran apart—and, truth be told, Oran was pretty regular too, despite appearances to the contrary. In a bigger high school he would probably have blended in better, or found more young people like himself. Tecopee Fields High was simply too small to allow the Oran Wildes of this world to grow and prosper, or even just to hide.

The first of the flames flickered in the hallway then, with startling rapidity, spread to the living room and raced up the stairs. In less than a minute, Oran thought that he could smell his family burning. He was shocked at how quickly the house ignited. He saw birds flying away in panic. The wind shifted, blowing some of the smoke back at him. His eyes watered. He tried not to breathe in the fumes, and the odor of roasting flesh that underpinned them. He was crying now, sobbing and retching, speaking the names of his mother and father and sisters in a language that could not be understood, the words emerging only as muffled sounds, as though in dying their identities had been lost and their names could no longer be spoken clearly, the flames stealing them away letter by letter along with their skin and flesh, turning them to black spirals that rose in the late-morning sky and dissipated against the clear blue of a fall day. He was sorry, so sorry. He wanted to tell them that. He wanted them to know that he loved them, and had always loved them. He just couldn't say it, but he would have done so, eventually. He would have made something of himself too. He was writing a book. It wasn't bad, and it would get better. He had planned to show it to them, once he'd gotten a little more done. He'd already won an essay competition—it was a religious essay competition, which was embarrassing, but it had still earned him $100 for first prize, which wasn't chump change—and he'd seen how happy it had made his mom and dad, even if he'd been too stubborn and tied up in his own world to acknowledge their pride in his achievement. He'd wanted to make them prouder still, but now that would never happen.

His home was a fiery specter of itself, its shape visible only as yellows and oranges and, here and there, spikes of angry red. He heard an explosion deep inside, and the frame seemed to shudder in shock.

And then the trunk of the car closed upon him, and there was only darkness.

IX

Amanda was playing by the shoreline. She was trying to master the art of skipping stones, but any that she threw simply sank. Her mother couldn't skip stones either, so there was no point in asking her for advice. It was at times like this that Amanda wished her father were around. Actually, she often wished for her father's presence, if only so that she could see him in the flesh, and ask him why he had rejected her mother and herself, and if he was bad, and, if not, what he had done to get himself killed. (But she felt that it would also be useful to consult him briefly about the art of skipping stones, and a couple of other small matters on which it might be productive to have a male perspective.)

Her mother had shown Amanda a picture of the two of them together. Amanda thought that her father looked very handsome, but also kind of rough, like some of the older high school boys. Beside him, her mother held on tight to his waist, smiling prettily. Seeing them in the same photo was like glimpsing her standing with a ghost.

She didn't spot Mr. Parker until he had passed behind her. The sight of him brought back the memory of her dream, and the girl's face that she had almost glimpsed, traces of red about to be further exposed before Amanda awoke. It was just a dream, of course: of that she was reasonably certain. She couldn't properly explain the sand in her bed, though. She supposed that it might have lodged between her toes unnoticed that day, but it hardly seemed likely. Her toes weren't webbed, so there was a limit to the amount of sand that could be stored between them. The other possibility was that she had somehow walked in her sleep, which worried her a lot. She didn't like to think of her sleeping self wandering down to the sea and into the waves to be lost forever, or at least until the tide found a way to wash her body back to shore again. The thought of her final footsteps frozen in the sand, of her mother crying at the realization of what had befallen her daughter, made her sad, but in an interesting way, like a tragic heroine in a book or movie.

Perhaps that image had come to her because of the body on the beach at Mason Point. The day before, she and her mother had headed out for a late breakfast at Muriel's, the big old diner that lay halfway between Boreas and Pirna. Amanda liked Muriel's because the pancakes were great, and the little jukeboxes at the tables still worked. On the way there, they had witnessed the activity down at Mason Point, and her mother had stopped to ask one of the officers on duty if there had been some kind of accident. That was when they found out about the body, and although Amanda still ate her pancakes later, they didn't taste quite as good as usual. Drowning sounded to her like a terrible way to die. Drowning, or burning: both of those were very bad. Then, later, she'd brought her mother the envelope that she'd found on the doorstep, and her mother had been very quiet for the rest of the evening, and the toilet had smelled of vomit.

Now here was Mr. Parker, walking more slowly than he had the last time, when she had watched him from her window. His face looked gray, and Amanda thought that she could see beads of sweat blistering on his skin even though a breeze was blowing, and it wasn't hot. She called out a greeting, but he didn't hear. He just stared fixedly ahead, placing one foot slowly and deliberately in front of the other. He didn't have his stick with him today. Either he had forgotten it, which didn't seem likely, or he was trying to make do without it. She saw the ribbon on the bag of stones fluttering in the wind, and Mr. Parker altered his direction to move toward it. He was almost within touching distance of it when he stopped and swayed, then slowly collapsed to the sand, his knees folding beneath him, so that he came to rest like a man saying his bedtime prayers.

Amanda ran to him. For a moment it looked as though he would fall flat on his face, but he managed to stay upright and instead slumped back, the backs of his thighs against his calf muscles, his hands by his sides, the palms raised upward. Amanda reached him, but did not touch him. She wasn't sure what to do. Should she run back to her mother to get help? But that would mean leaving Mr. Parker alone. Should she try to assist him? Yes, it was probably the best thing, although she figured that it would possibly break her mother's rule about having anything to do with strangers. But what else could she do? Still, she held back, uncertain.

"Are you okay?" she asked, even though it was clear that he wasn't.

He turned his head in her direction, only noticing her now that she had spoken.

"I just need . . . to catch my breath."

He was breathing shallowly, and she could see the pain in his face.

"Do you want me to get my mom?"

"No. I'll be fine in a moment."

She knelt by him. She didn't know what else to do, so she put her right hand on his shoulder and rubbed gently. She had seen adults do this to each other when one of them was sad or in pain, although when she was sad or in pain, she preferred a hug. She didn't think it would be appropriate to hug Mr. Parker. That would *certainly* have broken her mother's rule.

"I'm going to get up now," he said at last.

"I'll help you."

She wasn't sure that she could, but it was only right to offer. She held his right arm as he used his left to lever himself up. His right hand came to rest on her right shoulder, and she took some of his weight as he stood. He swayed again when he was upright, but he didn't fall. She saw him looking at the red ribbon in the sand, and she knew what he was thinking.

"I'll walk to it with you, if you like," she said.

"What?"

"I've seen you walking on the beach before. I saw you pick up the bag and move it along some. It's a marker, isn't it, so that you'll know how far you've gone, so you'll know that you walked a little more than last time?"

He smiled at her. He had a nice smile, and she felt sure that, although she had now resolutely broken *all* of her mother's rules about dealing with strangers, this man would never hurt her.

"That's very perceptive of you," he said, and Amanda wanted to tell him about the dream, but decided not to in case it made her sound weird.

"Well," she said, "do you want me to walk with you?"

"Yes," he said. "If you wouldn't mind."

So they walked together, and it made her feel grown-up to think that he found some reassurance in her presence. And although it wasn't far to the bag of stones, she understood the effort that it took for him to reach it. She saw it in the grimace on his face. When they got to it, she offered to reach down and pick it up for him, and he thanked her. They walked a little farther together, and after half a dozen steps he asked her to drop the bag, and she did.

"Does it still count if you helped me?" he asked, as they stood together.

"I just walked with you," she said. "I didn't carry you."

"You know," he said, "you kind of did. And we haven't even been properly introduced."

"My name's Amanda."

"I'm Charlie Parker."

"Winter. That's my second name. Amanda Winter."

"Thank you, Amanda Winter. You just moved here, right?"

He turned back in the direction from which they'd come, and she turned with him.

"Yes, me and my mom."

"What do you think of it?"

"It's pretty, but I miss my friends, and my grandma."

"And you're not in school?"

"I've been sick."

"Ah. I know what that's like."

"What happened to you?"

"You first."

"The doctors aren't sure. I get real tired, and then I get sick, and it's hard for me to move."

"I'm sorry to hear that."

"It's not so bad. I just miss a lot of school. What about you? Why are you sick?"

"I had an accident."

"In a car?'

"No. At home."

"In that house?"

She pointed to his roof in the distance, just visible over her own because the road ascended slightly to the south.

"No, at another one. I'm just staying here while I get better. My real home is down in Scarborough. You know where that is?"

He was walking more confidently now. Maybe moving the bag of stones along, even just a little, had energized him.

"Near Portland," said Amanda. "I've been there. To Portland, I mean. Not Scarborough."

"Did you like Portland?"

"It was okay. We had ice cream."

"Beal's?"

"Maybe. It was down near the water, on a corner."

"Yeah, that's Beal's. They make good ice cream. I take my daughter there sometimes."

"You have a daughter?"

Again, Amanda returned to her dream. There was something about the girl she'd seen, something familiar . . .

"Yes. She lives in Vermont with her mom."

"What's her name?"

"Samantha, but I just call her Sam. I think her mom calls her Samantha when she's in trouble."

"My mom calls me Amanda Jane when she's mad at me."

"You should treat it as a warning, like a siren going off, then run and hide."

Amanda giggled.

"How old is your daughter?"

"Younger than you. Six now."

"Has she got blond hair?" asked Amanda.

Parker stopped walking. He looked at her in a funny way.

"Why would you ask that?"

She knew that she'd been careless, that she'd overstepped some line, so she lied, even though lying was wrong.

"I just like blond hair, that's all."

She continued walking, and so did he.

"No, she doesn't have blond hair."

"Does she visit you?"

"Like you, I've only just moved here, but she'll be coming to stay very soon. I'll introduce you, if you like."

"Sure."

They kept pace with each other, talking about the sea, and birds, and the town, when Amanda's mother appeared on the sand, walking quickly toward them.

"Uh-oh," said Amanda. "I'm not supposed to talk to strangers."

"I bet she calls you Amanda Jane," he said, and even though her mother was trailing storm clouds, Amanda couldn't help but laugh.

Her mother stopped when she was about five feet away from them, her arms wrapped around herself against the breeze.

"Where have you been?" she said. "I was worried."

Not just worried, thought Amanda. You're angry.

"I was just walking," said Amanda. "And—"

"I fell," said Mr. Parker. "I fell on the sand, and I couldn't get back up. Amanda helped me. I'm sorry if I caused you any concern. You have a great daughter. Not every young woman would have stopped to help a man in trouble."

Amanda glowed at being referred to as a "young woman," but she still feared her mother's wrath. By walking and talking with Mr. Parker, she'd done the wrong thing for the right reasons—or was it the right thing for the wrong reasons? No, it was definitely the first. She wanted to explain it to her mom, but this was between adults now.

Something softened in her mother—only a little, but it was there.

"It's just that—well, I've warned her about talking to, you know—"

"Strange men," he finished for her, and she smiled slightly.

"Yes, strange men."

He reached out a hand to her.

"My name is Charlie Parker. We're neighbors."

His hand hung in the air for a couple of seconds before she took it.

"Ruth Winter," she said. "And I believe you've met my daughter."

"Yes. Like I said, a good kid."

Amanda tried not to scowl now that she was back to being a kid again, but at least Mr. Parker was doing his best to get her mother on their side.

"Sometimes," said her mother. "Go on, Amanda Jane. Inside. I don't want you catching a chill."

Amanda did as she was told, but looked back over her shoulder and gave Mr. Parker a smile. *Amanda Jane.* He'd been right, and he knew it.

He couldn't help smiling back. Her mother caught it, and turned to find out its cause, but by then Amanda was already running for the house.

"Again," said Parker, "I'm sorry. I really did fall, and she really did help me. If she hadn't, I might still be down there on the sand."

"You know how it is," said Ruth. "You can't be too careful."

"I have a daughter of my own, younger than Amanda. I know."

They stood awkwardly, facing each other, then Ruth Winter began to head back to her house.

"Thanks for bringing her home," she said.

"I think it was the other way around."

"Either way. Good-bye."

He watched her head back into the house, and noticed in passing the little mezuzah on the right side of the door, sealed in a pewter case. So she was Jewish. He hadn't asked her about Amanda's illness, and it struck him that any such questions wouldn't have been welcomed. She didn't appear to want anything to do with him, and she certainly didn't give the impression that she wanted her daughter having anything to do with him either. That was fine. He wasn't in a very sociable place, or he thought he wasn't. He had enjoyed talking with Amanda, though. She reminded him of Sam, in some ways. He wondered again why she had asked him if Sam had blond hair. He was still mulling it over as he entered his house and slipped off the laceless sneakers that he wore for walking. He sat down in an armchair facing the kitchen. On the table before him lay his pills, but he didn't have the strength to get up again and take them. He was on what was known as the "analgesic ladder"—Tylenol, tramadol, MS Contin, gabapentin—which, apart from constipating him like crazy, caused him to worry about becoming a prescription drug addict. So he took the hard-core pills less often than he should have, and generally relied on the Tylenol.

Just before he fell asleep, he discerned a flash of movement in the shadows, and the blond hair of his dead daughter caught the fading afternoon light as she watched her father's eyes close.

———

AMANDA WASN'T SURE WHAT she was expecting from her mother, but it wasn't to be wrapped in a huge hug, and kissed over and over again on the forehead and cheeks.

"I'm okay, Mom," she said. "Honest. Mr. Parker is nice."

Her mother released her, and ruffled her hair. Behind her, the television was on low, and Amanda saw images of a burned house, and policemen, and a photograph of a family.

"Did something bad happen?" Amanda asked.

"Yes, honey," said her mother. "Something real bad."

Amanda Winter often dreamed: strange, fevered visions, filled with confusion and dislocation. It was why the dream of the girl on the sand hadn't disturbed her more, for she'd had worse. Had she been older, she might have understood it as a function of the headaches and muscle pains that she experienced. Sometimes her mother would give her half a sleeping pill to help her drift off, especially if her condition had been particularly bad for a couple of nights.

Her illness had a name—chronic fatigue syndrome, or more commonly myalgic encephalomyelitis, ME—but one of the pupils in her old school, a girl named Laurie Bryden, had claimed that ME wasn't really an illness at all. She'd heard her father say so. Her father said it was just something that lazy people used as an excuse not to get off their asses and work or, in the case of someone like Amanda, as a means of getting away with low grades because she was really kind of dumb. It had taken all of Amanda's willpower not to sock Laurie Bryden in the jaw and knock her flat on her back, but what good would have come of it anyway?

Amanda hated being sick. She hated being tired. She hated waking up and wondering if today was going to be a good day or a bad day. On good days, she would sometimes try to do too much, with the result that the bad days to follow were so much worse. She hated the low-level headache that always seemed to throb in her skull, and how long it took her to recover from colds and infections. She hated the night sweats and the weird pains and the tenderness in her armpits. She hated the way some perfumes brought on her illness, and not being able to swim in heated pools because the chlorine made her head woozy. She hated knowing the answer to a question but not being able to find it in the muddle of her brain. She hated that, even among her friends, she was an outsider, because her stupid sickness meant that she kept on missing stuff: parties, movies, even just the day-to-day business of interacting at school. She wanted to be normal. She hadn't chosen to be this way. She just was.

The doctors said her condition might last a couple of years, and then gradually start to disappear, but she had already endured it for two years and could see no sign of any improvement. Sometimes she got so depressed that she'd just lock herself in her room and cry, but that made her feel even more pathetic.

The girl with the blond hair returned to her in a dream that night, except Amanda wasn't sure that she *was* dreaming. The pains in her limbs felt too real, as did the thumping headache and the discomfort in her right ear where she had sweated onto the pillow and somehow irritated her skin. She could hear the sea and smell its salt, yet all was kept at arm's length, for she was running a temperature, and so dream and reality were not so easily discernible from each other.

But through that night landscape walked the girl, and although Amanda could still not quite see her face, she understood the sign that the girl was making, for she could just about discern the index finger of her right hand pressed against her lips. It was the universally understood gesture for silence. Slowly, Amanda turned her head on the pillow. She tried to make it look as much as possible as though she were simply shifting in her sleep. She kept her eyes almost—but not entirely—closed.

A wooden staircase led up the back of the house to a door at the rear of Amanda's room. The view from the doorway wasn't as good as the one from her bedroom window because it faced away from the sea. Nevertheless, Amanda sometimes liked to put on her coat and sit there with a book, and she'd watched one good sunset from it. Her mother insisted that she keep the door locked at all times, not that Amanda needed to be told: even somewhere as apparently safe and peaceful as Green Heron Bay might not be immune to lunatics and child-stealers. The door was slightly recessed, but if Amanda lay on the very edge of her bed, she could just about see it. The top half was mostly glass, with a shade that could be pulled down, but Amanda rarely bothered with that.

Now, through barely open eyes, she could see that a man was standing on the topmost step, peering in at her through the glass. His upper body was exposed, and Amanda had a gut feeling that he was naked from the waist down too. His face was cast in shadow, just like the dream girl's, but Amanda could see that his skin was very pale, yet only as far as the base of his neck. From there it was curiously mottled all over—the torso, the upper arms, even extending over his stomach to where she knew his thing was hanging loose below—although there was a regularity to the pattern. It was, she thought, almost as though someone had pieced together a jigsaw puzzle of a man and placed it by her door, except that this one was moving. As she watched, the figure raised his left hand.

And waved.

In the dream that wasn't quite a dream, Amanda understood that he *wanted* to be seen. He wished to get a reaction from her—why, she did not know—and it took all of her willpower not to rise up and scream for her mother. Instead she nuzzled into her pillow, still keeping one barely open eye on the man on the step, and she saw his hand flinch, then form a fist. For a moment she thought that he was about to thrust it through the glass, shattering it so that he could get at the bolt inside, but he merely lowered his head and moved away, and she felt rather than heard his footfalls on the wood of the steps. Even then she did not move, not until she was certain that he wasn't playing some kind of trick on her. Then, and only then, did she climb from her bed and crawl carefully to the window. She shifted the drapes where they met, exposing the slightest triangle of sand and surf beyond the window.

The man was walking into the sea. His back, his buttocks, and his legs, all were covered with the same patterning that she had seen on his torso and upper arms. Even though the water must have been very cold, he moved steadily into the darkness of it, step-by-step, the waves breaking against him, yet barely seeming to jostle his body. He was like a statue slowly sinking, a figure mired in the sand as the tide came in around him. The water reached his waist, then his chest, then his neck, but he did not try to swim into it. Instead, he was eventually immersed entirely, and then he was gone.

This was no dream. The presence of the girl had confused her. She was not of this world. She belonged in another, but she drifted between both. The man, though, was part of this one.

Only then did Amanda start to cry, and she did not stop until her mother appeared and took her in her arms.

"I saw someone," said Amanda, turning away from the black sea, weeping into her mother's breast. "I saw a Jigsaw Man."

XI

Cory Bloom got the call just as she was heading home for the evening. It came from the dispatcher at the station house, Karen Heller, who was also just about to leave. Bloom kind of wished that Karen had just let Stynes or Corbin take care of it. In fact, Bloom couldn't understand why Karen was bothering her with this in the first place.

"You say there's a man standing on the beach, near where the body was washed up?" she said.

"Uh, that's right, Cory. Dan Rainey just called."

Dan had taken a proprietary interest in the whole matter of the drowned man. From what Bloom heard, he'd held court at the Brickhouse after the body was discovered, and hadn't once needed to put his hand in his pocket to pay for a drink.

"With respect, Karen, it's still a free country. Also, the beach isn't sealed off, and even if it was, we couldn't do a whole lot to stop the tide from washing away any more evidence."

"I know that," said Karen, and Bloom detected the note of annoyance in her voice. Clearly there was something here that Bloom wasn't fully understanding, but it would sure help her a whole lot if Karen would just get around to telling her what it was, which Karen duly did.

"It's the private detective," she said. "It's Charlie Parker who's standing out at Mason Point."

———

BLOOM PARKED AT THE edge of the strand. She knew better than to drive down onto the beach, even with the Explorer. That damn sand was treacherous, and not a week went by in the summer without some dumb tourist ignoring the signs about not parking on the strand, and being forced to call Smalley's Towing Service to get a vehicle back on terra firma.

If Parker heard her pull up, he gave no sign. He simply continued to stare out to sea, and she might have thought it nothing more than a man seeking a slight change of surroundings on a cool evening in late spring were it not for the fact that he was standing almost exactly on the spot where the body had washed up. He was wearing a dark overcoat that hung just below his knees, the collar raised to cover his neck. The wind created sand specters, and Bloom felt fine grains sting her cheek.

Only when she was almost within touching distance of him did he turn slightly to acknowledge her approach, speaking her name at the same time. She wondered how he had known. In all the time she had been watching him, his gaze had not left the sea.

"Chief Bloom," he said, and she experienced a kind of nervousness, a sense that the world had shifted slightly off-kilter. He had about him a conflicted air, a fusion of contradictions: pain, yet peace; rage, yet equanimity. She caught the white patterns in his hair, the suffering etched in his face.

And his eyes . . . Had she been on more friendly terms with Bobby Soames, they might well have found common ground in their impression of Parker. She had only ever seen pictures of him before he arrived, but she wondered if his eyes had always been so haunted, and so haunting. They were the eyes of someone who had witnessed events beyond the comprehension of others, and perhaps even beyond his own. She knew that his heart had stopped three times after the shooting, and he had been resuscitated on each occasion. Perhaps the victim of such traumas lost a little of himself every time, and left part of his being behind in the darkness. Or perhaps he brought something of the darkness back with him. Yes, that was it. These were not the eyes of a man who was less than he once was. No, they were the eyes of one who was much more.

"Mr. Parker," she said. "You mind if I ask what you're doing out here?"

"Did I miss an ordinance about not enjoying the view?"

He didn't speak testily. He sounded only amused.

"We haven't passed that one yet, although there are some folks in town who'd like to find a way to charge for it, if they could. No, I'm simply wondering if it's a coincidence that you're filling your lungs steps from where, as I'm sure you know, a body was recently washed up."

"Do you have a name yet?"

She noticed that he hadn't answered her question, although in a way, he just had.

"We haven't made an official identification, but we've found what we believe to be his vehicle."

He waited. She sighed. This wasn't the way that it was supposed to go, but, damn, the man had a way about him.

"Bruno Perlman, forty-five. Resident of Duval County, Florida."

"Long way from home. Rental?"

"No, it's his own."

"He drove all the way up here from northeast Florida?"

"It seems so."

"Just to throw himself in the ocean?"

"We haven't yet made any determination on that."

"You sound like you're already practicing your lines for the press."

"Maybe I am. We'll be releasing the name once his family has been informed. It's just that—"

Again, he simply waited.

"Well," Bloom continued, "he doesn't seem to have any close family that we can find. He appears to have been pretty much on his own."

"What about the state police?"

"They have their hands full looking for that Oran Wilde kid. Same with the ME's office: she's got four charred corpses on her hands. They'll all get to us when they can. They've been in touch, but . . ."

She trailed off. He finished for her.

"It's a car by a beach, and a body on another beach—a body, what's more, that nobody is rushing to claim or mourn. Did you find a note?"

"No."

"There's a lot of water to throw yourself into between Florida and here, most of it a lot warmer than this."

He gestured at the ocean with a pale hand. Bloom half expected to see an albatross appear as though summoned before them.

"Is there a logic to taking your own life?" she asked.

He considered the question.

"You know, I expect that there probably is," he said. "Would you mind if I took a look at his car?"

"Why would you want to do that? And why are you so interested?"

"It used to be my job," he said.

"And now?"

He looked at her, and she felt the full force of his gaze.

"Call it my vocation," he said. "I'm out of practice. Indulge me, Chief Bloom. After all, what harm can it do?"

But those last five words came back to Cory Bloom later, as it all blew up, as she felt her life draining away, and she knew that she would take them to her grave.

———

THE CAR, STORED IN the police garage at the back of the town office, was a 1989 Chevy Caprice in a dull silver-gray. It had 91,000 miles on it, according to the odometer, but Bloom told Parker that it had probably turned over at least once, given that the car seemed to be held together with goodwill and Bondo, and the a/c was shot. She'd draped the vehicle with a tarp to protect it from getting any more fingerprints and marks on the paint job than it had already.

She handed Parker a pair of latex gloves.

"You can open the door and take a look inside, but try not to touch anything, even with the gloves on, okay?"

She felt ridiculous giving him the warning. After all, he'd once carried a detective's shield. He might have been a renegade, but, if so, he was one who knew the drill. He'd also made her uneasy with his questions on the beach, and his wish to examine the vehicle. Bloom knew better than to make assumptions, or so she told herself, but she had to admit that she'd mentally filed the corpse away as a probable suicide. Perhaps it was, in part, the reaction of the state police. Yes, the minds of its detectives were elsewhere—on four bodies, and the missing, possibly troubled youth who might well be responsible for their deaths—but, even so, they didn't seem particularly interested in the body that she currently had on ice. Right or wrong, these attitudes were contagious. Now, though, Parker's reactions reminded her of the importance of taking nothing for granted, and she didn't want the chain of evidence interfered with, if it turned out that Bruno Perlman had not entered the sea of his own volition.

But Parker didn't seem interested in searching the interior, not yet. He walked around the car under the bright fluorescents of the garage, his brow furrowed in the slightest of frowns. Only when he had done that did he open first the driver's door, then the front passenger door. He took in the mess on the floor—soda bottles, chip bags, candy wrappers, a copy of the *Boston Globe* dated a couple of days before the body washed ashore—then leaned in and searched the glove compartment without coming upon anything that caught his attention. He checked the newspaper, and the copy of *The Yiddish Policemen's Union* that lay on the backseat, flicking through the pages but finding nothing. So much for not touching stuff, thought Bloom. He used the release handle in the car to open the trunk. Inside was a single traveling bag.

"Did you take a look in here?" he asked.

"Yes," she said. "It's just clothes and toiletries."

"You mind?"

"Sure," she said resignedly. "Go ahead."

He unzipped the bag carefully, and went through its contents piece by piece, searching inside T-shirts, underwear, and jeans. He even examined the cans of deodorant and shaving cream. Finally, he zipped the bag, closed the trunk and the two doors, and stepped away from the car. He removed the gloves and handed them back to her.

"Thanks," she said. "I'll treasure them always. Are you done?"

"Sure," he said. "For now. Was I keeping you from something?"

"A husband. A dog. A bath. Dinner."

"Nothing urgent, then."

"Seriously, do you have any friends?"

"Enough. I'm not recruiting more."

"I wasn't offering. Anything you want to share with me from your examination of the vehicle?"

"Suppose I sleep on it and we talk in the morning," he said. "After all, you have a husband at home, and a dog, and a bath, and dinner. There's nothing here that can't hold, and Bruno Perlman won't be any more dead tomorrow. He's long beyond waiting on us to figure out his final moments."

They stepped out of the garage into the cool evening air.

"I have one last request," he said.

Bloom sighed. Ron was cooking lasagna tonight. She'd told him that she'd be home well before six, and he would have aimed to have food on the table by seven. It was long past that now. She had a vision of a blackened meal and a sulking husband.

"Go on," she said.

"Did somebody compile a list of what was found on the body and in the car?"

"You think we're complete rubes? Yes, I had Stynes type it up and include it in the report."

"Could I have a copy?"

"No," she said, and realized as soon as she said it that she sounded snippier than she would have liked. "But I'll let you look," she relented, "just as long as you don't spend all night with it."

He followed her into the town office, and waited at her door. The report-in-progress on Bruno Perlman lay on her desk. She found the item list and handed it to him.

"You know," she said, "if it turns out to be murder, I may just have handed that list to a suspect."

"If I'd killed him, I'd have made sure to check the tides before I put him in the water."

She tried to figure out if he was kidding, but couldn't. He worked his way quickly through the list, then returned it to her.

"Are you free for a cup of coffee tomorrow?"

"Only if you're buying."

"How about Olesens, around ten?"

"Do you have shares in that place?"

Now he raised an eyebrow at her, but said nothing. Hey, she thought, what did you expect: that I wouldn't be keeping tabs on you?

"Ten is fine," she told him.

They walked out together.

"Thank you," he said.

"For what? For letting you look at a dead man's car?"

"For not telling me to mind my own business."

"If you do turn out to have killed him, I'm going to be real upset with you."

"If you pin it on me, I'm going to be real upset too."

Suddenly she wanted to go back to the office and look at that list again. She wanted to reexamine the car, just as he had done. She had the sense that she was missing something, something that he had spotted.

But she had a husband waiting, and a dog, and dinner. And maybe that bath too. Yes, almost certainly a bath. She did some of her best thinking in the tub. She watched him walk away and thought:

What have we allowed into our town?

XII

The Hurricane Hatch stood at the end of a strip of land midway between Jacksonville and St. Augustine on the Florida coast, far enough away from the real tourist traps to ensure that it retained a degree of local custom while still attracting enough business of any stripe to sustain it. A man named Skettle owned 90 percent of the Hurricane Hatch, but he rarely frequented it, preferring to leave the running of the place to its chief bartender and 10 percent shareholder, Lenny Tedesco. Skettle liked to keep quiet about the fact that he had a big piece of the Hurricane Hatch. His family, from what Lenny knew of them, contained a high percentage of Holy Rollers, the kind who visited the Holy Land Experience down in Orlando a couple of times a year, and regarded the Goliath Burger at the theme park's Oasis Palms Café as damn fine dining, although Lenny doubted if they would have used that precise term to describe it. Lenny Tedesco had never been to the Holy Land Experience, and had zero intention of ever visiting it. He reckoned that a Christian theme park wasn't really the place for a Jew, not even a nonobservant Jew like himself, and he didn't care if it did boast a re-creation of a Jerusalem street market.

Then again, the Hurricane Hatch was about as authentic in Florida bar terms as the Holy Land Experience was as an accurate reflection of the spiritual makeup of Jerusalem in the first century AD.

It looked like what a classic Florida beach bum's bar was supposed to look like—wood, stuffed fish, a picture of Hemingway—but had only been built at the start of the nineties, in anticipation of a housing development named Ocean Breeze Condos that never got further than a series of architect's plans, a hole in the ground, and a tax write-off. The Hurricane Hatch remained, though, and had somehow managed to prosper, in large part because of Lenny and his wife, Pegi, who was a good fry cook of the old school. She prepared fried oysters that could make a man weep, the secret ingredients being creole seasoning, fine yellow cornmeal, and Diamond Crystal—*kosher*—salt. Neither did Skettle evince too much concern about making a large profit, just as long as the Hatch didn't lose money. Lenny figured that Skettle, who didn't drink alcohol and appeared to subsist primarily on chicken tenders and chocolate milk, just enjoyed secretly giving the finger to his holier-than-thou, pew-polishing relatives by owning a bar. Lenny's wife, however, claimed that Skettle's sister Lesley, a Praise Jesus type of the worst stripe, was not above polishing other things too, and could give a pretty accurate description of half the motel ceilings between Jacksonville and Miami, giving rise to her nickname of Screw-Anything-Skettle.

Lenny was alone in the bar. Entirely alone. This was one of Pegi's nights off, and Lenny had sent the replacement cook, Fran, home early, because he knew she'd have better luck selling fried oysters in an abandoned cemetery than in the Hurricane Hatch on this particular evening. Midweeks were always quiet, but lately they had been quieter than usual, and even weekend business was down from previous years. There just wasn't as much money around as before, but the Hatch was surviving.

Lenny glanced at his watch. It was nine thirty. He'd give it until ten, maybe ten thirty, then call it a night. Anyway, he was in no hurry to go home—not that he didn't love his wife, because he did, but sometimes he thought that he loved the Hatch more. He was at peace there, regardless of whether it was empty or full. In fact, on evenings like this, with the wind blowing gently outside, and the boards creaking and rattling, and the sound of the waves in the distance, visible as the faintest of phosphorescent glows, and the TV on, and a soda water and lime on the bar before him, he felt that he would be quite content just to stay this way forever. The only blot on his happiness—if blot was a sufficient word for it, which he doubted—was the subject of the TV news report currently playing in front of him. He watched the footage of the two old men being transported by US Marshals into the holding facility somewhere in New York City: Engel and Fuhrmann, with almost two centuries of life clocked up between them, Engel barely able to walk unaided, Fuhrmann stronger, his gaze fixed somewhere in the distance, not even deigning to notice the men and women who surrounded him, the cameras and the lights, the protestors with their signs, as if all of this was a show being put on for another man, and the accusations leveled against him were somehow beneath his regard. The men disappeared from the screen, to be replaced by an attorney from the Human Rights and Special Prosecutions Section, the arm of the Justice Department entrusted with investigating assorted human rights violations and, particularly, Nazi war criminals. The attorney was a pretty young woman, and Lenny was surprised by the passion with which she spoke. She didn't have a Jewish name, or Demers didn't sound like one. Not that this was a requirement for justice under the circumstances. Perhaps she was just an idealist, and God knew the world needed as many of those as it could find.

Engel and Fuhrmann, she said, had been fighting the US government's decision to rescind their citizenship, but that process had now been exhausted. The delivery of the arrest warrant for Fuhrmann from the Bavarian state public prosecutor's office in Munich a week earlier meant that his extradition could now proceed immediately, and Engel's deportation would follow shortly after for breaches of immigration law, regardless of whether or not charges were filed against him in his native land. Soon, she said, Engel and Fuhrmann would be banished from American soil forever.

Deportation didn't sound like much of a punishment to Lenny, whose family had lost an entire branch at Dachau. He hadn't understood why they couldn't be put on trial here in the United States until Bruno Perlman explained to him that the US Federal law precluded criminal prosecutions for crimes committed abroad before and during World War II, and the best that the United States could do was send war criminals back to countries that did have jurisdiction, in the hope that proceedings might be taken against them there. Not that Perlman was happy about the situation either. He would tell Lenny admiringly about the activities of the TTG, the Tilhas Tizig Gesheften, a secret group within the Jewish Brigade Group of the British Army who, after the German surrender, took it upon themselves to hunt down and assassinate *Wehrmacht* and SS officers believed to have committed atrocities against Jews; and of the Mossad killers who trapped the Latvian Nazi collaborator Herberts Cukurs, "the Butcher of Riga," in a house in Montevideo in 1965, beating him with a hammer before shooting him twice in the head and leaving his body to rot in a trunk until the Uruguayan police found him, drawn by the smell. The gleam in Perlman's eye as he spoke of such matters disturbed Lenny, but he supposed that the end met by such foul men was no more than they deserved. Lately, though, that light in Perlman's eyes had grown brighter, and his talk of vengeance had taken a personal turn. Lenny worried about him. Perlman had few friends. Obsessives rarely did.

"How do they even know it's really them?" said a voice. "Old men like that, they could be anyone."

A man was seated at the far end of the bar, close to the door. Lenny had not heard him enter. Neither had he heard a car pull into the lot. The visitor's face was turned slightly away from the television, as though he could not bear to watch it. He wore a straw fedora with a red band. The hat was too large for his head, so that it sat just above his eyes. His suit jacket was brown, worn over a yellow polo shirt. The shirt was missing two buttons, exposing a network of thin white scars across the man's chest, like a web spun by a spider upon his skin.

"Sorry, I didn't hear you come in," said Lenny, ignoring the question. "What can I get you?"

The man didn't respond. He seemed to be having trouble breathing. Lenny looked past him to the parking lot outside. He could see no vehicle.

"You got milk?" the man rasped.

"Sure."

"Brandy and milk." He rubbed his stomach. "I got a problem with my guts."

Lenny prepared the mix. The milk was cold enough to create beads of condensation on the glass, so he wrapped it in a napkin before placing it on the bar. The man exuded a sour, curdled odor, the rankness of untold brandy-and-milk combinations. He raised the glass and drank it half-empty.

"Hurts," he said. "Hurts like a motherfucker."

He lowered the glass, raised his left hand, and removed the hat from his head. Lenny tried not to stare before deciding that it was easier just to look away entirely, but the image of the man's visage remained branded on Lenny's vision like a sudden flare of bright, distorted light in the dimness of the bar.

His bare skull was misshapen, as pitted with concave indentations as the surface of the moon. His brow was massively overdeveloped, so that his eyes—tiny dark things, like drops of oil in snow—were lost in its shadow, and his profile was suggestive of one who had slammed his forehead into a horizontal girder as a child, with the soft skull retaining the impression of the blow as it hardened. His nose was very thin, his mouth the barest slash of color against the pallor of his skin. He breathed in and out through his lips with a faint, wet whistle.

"What's your name?" he asked.

"Lenny."

"Lenny what?"

"Lenny Tedesco."

"This your place?"

"I got a share in it. Skettle owns the rest."

"I don't know any Skettle. You're a bitch to find. You ought to put up a sign."

"There is a sign."

"I didn't see none."

"Which way did you come?"

The man waved a hand vaguely over his shoulder—north, south, east, west: what did any of it matter? The only issue of consequence was that he was here at last.

"Tedesco," he said. "That's a Sephardic name. Some might mistake it for Italian, but it's not. It means 'German,' but you most likely had Ashkenazi forbears. Am I right?"

Lenny wished that the bar had remained empty. He didn't want to engage in this discussion. He wanted this vile man with his pungent emanations to be gone.

"I don't know," he said.

"Sure you do. I read once that the word 'Nazi' comes from 'Ashkenazi.' What do you think of that?"

Lenny worked on polishing a glass that didn't need a cloth taken to it. He rubbed so hard that the glass cracked under the pressure. He tossed it in the trash and moved on to another.

"I've never heard that before," he replied, and hated himself for responding. "My understanding is that it refers to National Socialism."

"Ah, you're probably right. Anything else is just the frothings of ignorant men. Holocaust deniers. Fools. I don't give no credit to it. As though so much slaughter could be ascribed to Jew-on-Jew violence."

Lenny felt the muscles in his neck cramp. He clenched his teeth so hard that he felt something come loose at the back of his mouth. It was the way the man spoke the word "Jew."

On the television screen, the news report had moved on to a panel discussion about Engel and Fuhrmann, and the background to their cases. The volume was just low enough for the content to remain intelligible. Lenny moved to change the channel, but that same voice told him to leave it be. Lenny glanced at the glass of brandy and milk. A curl of red lay upon the surface of the remaining liquid. The man saw it at the same time as Lenny did. He dipped a finger and swirled the blood away, then drained the glass dry.

"Like I said, I got a problem with my guts. Got problems all over. I shit nails and piss broken glass."

"Sorry to hear that."

"Hasn't killed me yet. I just don't care to think about what my insides might look like."

Couldn't be any worse than what's outside, Lenny thought, and those dark eyes flicked toward him, as though that unspoken wisecrack had found form above Lenny's head.

"You got another of these?"

"I'm closing up."

"Won't take you much longer to make than it'll take me to drink."

"Nah, we're done."

The glass slid across the bar.

"Just the milk then. You wouldn't deny a man a glass of milk, would you?"

Oh, but Lenny wanted to. He wanted to so badly, yet still he poured three fingers of milk into the glass. He was grateful that there was no more left in the carton.

"Thank you."

Lenny said nothing, just tossed the empty container in the trash.

"I don't want you to get me wrong," said the man. "I got no problem with Jews. When I was a boy, I had a friend who was a Jew. Jesus, it's been a long time since I thought about him. I can hardly remember his name now."

He put the thumb and forefinger of his right hand to the bridge of his nose and squeezed hard, his eyes closed as he tried to pull the name from the pit of his memory.

"Asher," he said at last. "Asher Cherney. That was his name. Damn, that was hard. I called him Ash. I don't know what anyone else called him, because no one else palled around with him much. Anyway, I'd hang out with Ash when none of the other boys were there to see. You had to be careful. The people I grew up with, they didn't care much for Jews. Niggers neither. Fuck, we didn't even like Catholics. We stuck with our own, and it wasn't good to be seen making friends outside your own circle. And Ash, you see, he had a deformity, which made it worse for him. You listen to Kiss?"

Lenny, who had somehow been drawn into the tale despite himself, was puzzled. Following the man's thought processes was like trying to keep track of a ricochet in a steel room.

"What, the band?"

"Yeah, the band. They're shit, but you got to have heard of them."

"I know them," said Lenny.

"Right. Well, their singer has the same thing that Ash had. They call it microtia. It's a deformity of the ear. The cartilage doesn't grow right, so you have a kind of stump. Makes you deaf too. They say it usually occurs in the right ear, but Ash, he had it in his left, so he was strange even among other people like him. Now they can do all kinds of grafts or implants, but back then you just had to live with it. Ash would grow his hair long to try to hide it, but everybody knew. If his life didn't suck already, being a Jew in a town that didn't care much for anyone who wasn't in some white-bread church, he had to deal with the ignorance and bile of kids who spent their lives just looking for some physical defect to hone in on.

"So I felt sorry for Ash, though I couldn't show it, not in public. But if I was alone, and I saw Ash, and *he* was alone, then I'd talk to him, or walk with him, maybe skip stones by the river if the mood took us. He was okay, Ash. You never would have known he was a Jew, unless he told you his name. That microtia, you think it's a Jew thing?"

Lenny said that he didn't know. He felt as though he were watching some terrible accident unfold, a catastrophic collision of bodies that could only result in injury and death, yet was unable to tear his eyes away from it. He was hypnotized by this man's awfulness, the depth of his corruption only slowly revealing itself by word and intonation.

"Because," the man went on, "there are diseases that Jews are more likely to carry than other races. You, being Ashkenazi from way back, are more likely to get cystic fibrosis. I mean, there are others, but that's the one that sticks in my mind. Cystic fibrosis is a bitch. You don't want to get that. Anyhow, I don't know if this microtia thing is like it. Could be. Doesn't matter, I suppose. Unless you have it, and don't want to pass it on to your kids. You got kids?"

"No."

"Well, if you're thinking about having them, you ought to get checked out. You don't want to be transmitting shit to your kids. Where was I? Oh yeah: Ash. Ash and his fucked-up ear. So, me and Ash would do stuff together, and we'd talk, and I got to like him. Then, one day, this kid, a degenerate named Eddie Tyson, he saw us together, and next thing you know they were saying I was queer for Ash, and me and Ash were doing things under bridges and in his mom's car, and Eddie Tyson and a bunch of his buddies caught me alone on my way home and beat the living shit out of me, all on account of how Ash Cherney was my friend.

"So you know what I did?"

Lenny could barely speak, but he found the strength to say the word "No."

"I went around to Ash's house, and I asked if he wanted to go down to the river with me. I told him what had happened, because I looked like hell after what they'd done to me. So me and Ash went down to the

river, and I got a stone, and I hit Ash with it. I hit him so hard in the
face that I was sure I'd knocked his nose into his brain. I thought I'd
killed him, but somehow he stayed conscious. Then I threw the stone
away and used my fists and feet on him, and I left him by the river in a
pool of his own blood, spitting teeth, and I never heard from him again,
because he never came back to school, and his parents moved away not
long after."

He sipped his milk.

"I guess me and Ash weren't such good friends after all, huh?"

The television was showing black-and-white footage of emaciated
men and women standing behind wire fences, and holes filled with
bones.

"You ever wonder what would make men do such things?"

He wasn't looking at the screen, so Lenny didn't know if he was still
speaking of what he had done to Ash Cherney, or about the evidence
of atrocities committed decades before. Lenny was cold. His fingertips and toes hurt. He figured that it didn't matter what the man was
referring to. It was all part of one great mass of viciousness, a cesspit of
black, human evil.

"No," said Lenny.

"Course you do. We all do. Wouldn't be human if we didn't. There are
those who say that all crimes can be ascribed to one of two motives—
love or money—but I don't believe that. In my experience, everything
we do is predicated on one of two other things: greed or fear. Oh, sometimes they get mixed up, just like my brandy and milk, but mostly you
can keep them separated. We feel greed for what we don't have, and
fear because of what we might lose. A man desires a woman who isn't
his wife, and takes her—that's greed. But, deep down, he doesn't want
his own wife to find out because he wants to keep what he has with her,
because it's different, and safe. That's fear. You play the markets?"

"No."

"You're wise. It's a racket. Buying and selling, they're just other names for greed and fear. I tell you, you understand that, and you understand all there is to know about human beings and the way the world works."

He sipped his milk.

"Except, of course, that isn't all. Look at those pictures from the camps. You can see fear, and not just in the faces of the dying and the dead. Take a look at the men in uniform, the ones they say were responsible for what happened, and you'll see fear there too. Not so much fear of what might happen if they didn't follow orders. I don't hold with that as an excuse, and from what I've read the Germans understood that killing naked Jews and queers and Gypsies wasn't for every man, and if you couldn't do it then they'd find someone who would, and send you off to shoot at someone who could shoot back.

"But there's still fear in those faces, no matter how well they try to hide it: fear of what will happen to them when the Russians or the Americans arrive and find out what they've done; fear of looking inside themselves to see what they've become; maybe even fear for their immortal souls. There will also be those who feel no fear of that at all, of course, because sometimes men and women do terrible things just because they gain pleasure from the act, but those ones are the exceptions, and exceptions make bad law. The rest, they just did what they did because they were told to do it and they couldn't see much reason not to, or because there was money in gold teeth and rendered human fat. I guess some of them did it out of ideology, but I don't have much time for ideologies either. They're just flags of convenience."

The man's voice was very soft, and slightly sibilant, and held a note of regret that most of the world could not see itself as clearly as he did, and this was his cross to bear.

"You hear that woman on the TV?" he continued. "She's talking about evil, but throwing around the word 'evil' like it means something don't help anyone. Evil is the avoidance of responsibility. It doesn't explain. You might even say that it excuses. To see the real terror, the real darkness, you have to look at the actions of men, however awful they may appear, and call them human. When you can do that, then you'll understand."

He coughed hard, spattering the milk with droplets of blood.

"You didn't answer my question from earlier," he said.

"What question was that?" said Lenny.

"I just can't figure out how they know that those two old men are the ones they were looking for. I seen the pictures of the ones they say did all those things, the photographs from way back, and then I see those two old farts and I couldn't swear that it's the same men sixty, seventy years later. Jesus, you could show me a picture of my own father as a young man, and I wouldn't know him from the scarecrow he was when he died."

"I think there was a paper trail of some kind," said Lenny. To be honest, he didn't know how Engel and Fuhrmann had been traced. He didn't much care either. They had been found at last, and that was all that mattered. He just wanted this conversation to reach its end, but that was in the hands of the man at the bar. There was a purpose to his presence here, and all Lenny could do was wait for it to be revealed to him, and hope that he survived the adumbration.

"I can't even say that I've heard of the camps that they're supposed to have done all that killing in," said the man. "I mean, I heard of Auschwitz, and Dachau, and Bergen-Belsen. I suppose I could name some others, if I put my mind to it, but what's the place that Fuhrmann was at, or the one they claim is Fuhrmann. Ball Sack? Is that even a place?"

"Belsec," said Lenny softly. "It's called Belsec."

"And the other?"

"Lubsko."

"Well, you have been paying attention, I'll give you that. You had people there?"

"No, not there."

"So it's not personal, then."

Lenny had had enough. He killed the TV.

"I don't want you to mistake me," said the man, not even commenting upon the sudden absence of light and sound from the screen. "I got no problem with any race or creed: Jews, niggers, spics, white folks, they're all the same to me. I do believe, though, that each race and creed ought to keep to itself. I don't think any one is better than the other, but only trouble comes when they mix. The South Africans, they had it right with apartheid, except they didn't have the common sense, the basic human fucking decency, to give every man the same privileges, the same rights. They thought white was superior to black, and that's not the case. God made all of us, and he didn't put one above another, no matter what some might say. Even your own folk, you're no more chosen than anyone else."

Lenny made one final effort to save himself, to force this thing away. It was futile, but he had to try.

"I'd like you to leave now," he said. "I'm all done for the night. Have the drinks on me."

But the man did not move. All this was only the prelude. The worst was yet to come. Lenny felt it. This creature had brought with him a miasma of darkness, of horror. Maybe a small chance still remained, a chink in the wall that was closing in around him through which he might escape. He could not show weakness, though. The drama would play out, and each would accept the role that had been given to him.

"I haven't finished my milk yet."

"You can take it with you."

"Nah, I think I'll drink it here. Wouldn't want it to spill."

"I'm going to be closing up around you," said Lenny. "You'll have to excuse me."

He moved to take the drawer from the register. Usually he counted the takings before he left, but on this occasion he'd leave that until the morning. He didn't want to give this man any cause to linger.

"I'm no charity case," said the visitor. "I'll pay my own way, just as I always have."

He reached into his jacket pocket.

"Well, what do you think this is?"

Lenny couldn't help but look to see what had drawn the other's attention. He glimpsed something small and white, apparently drawn from the man's own pocket.

"Jesus, it's a tooth." The man pronounced it "toot." He held the item in question up to the light, like a jeweler appraising a gemstone. "Now where do you suppose that came from? It sure ain't one of mine."

As if to put the issue beyond doubt, he manipulated his upper row of teeth with his tongue, and his dentures popped out into his left palm. The action caused his mouth to collapse in upon itself, rendering his appearance stranger still. He smiled, nodded at Lenny, and replaced his appliance. He then laid the single tooth on the surface of the bar. A length of reddish flesh adhered to the root.

"That's certainly something, isn't it?" he said.

Lenny backed off. He wondered if he could get away for long enough to call the cops. There was no gun on the premises, but the back office had a strong door and a good lock. He could seal himself inside and wait for the police to come. Even if he could make it to a phone, what would he tell the operator—that a man had produced a tooth for his inspection? Last he heard, that wasn't a crime.

Except, except . . .

Like a conjuror, the customer reached into his pocket again and produced a second tooth, then a third. Finally, he seemed to tire of the whole business, rummaged for a final time, and scattered a full mouth's worth of teeth on the bar. Some were without roots. At least one appeared to have broken during extraction. A lot of them were still stained with blood, or trailed tails of tissue.

"Who are you?" asked Lenny. "What do you want from me?"

The gun appeared in the man's hand. Lenny didn't know from guns, but this one looked big and kind of old.

"You stay where you are now," said the man. "You hear me?"

Lenny nodded. He found his voice.

"We got next to nothing in the register," he said. "It's been quiet all day."

"I look like a thief to you?"

He sounded genuinely offended.

"I don't know what you look like," said Lenny, and he regretted the words as soon as they left his mouth.

"You got no manners," said the man. "You know that, you fucking kike?"

"I'm sorry," said Lenny. He had no pride now, only fear.

"I accept your apology. You recognize this?"

He gave the weapon a little jerk.

"No. I don't know much about guns."

"There's your first error. It's not a gun, it's a *pistol*: a Mauser C96 military pistol, made in long nine millimeter, which is rare. Some people call it a Broomhandle Mauser on account of the shape of the grip, or a Red 9 after the number carved into it. Consider that an education. Now move away from the door. You pay attention to me and what I say, and maybe this won't go as bad for you as it might."

Lenny knew that wasn't true—men who planned to let other men live didn't point guns at them without first concealing their faces—yet he found himself obeying. The man reached into his pocket again. This time his hand emerged holding a pair of cuffs. He tossed them to Lenny and instructed him to attach one to his right wrist, then put his hands close together behind his back and place them on the bar. If he tried to run away, or pull a fast one, he was assured that he would be shot in the back. Once more, Lenny did as he was told. When he turned his back and put his hands on the bar, the second cuff was quickly cinched tight around his left wrist.

"All done," said the man. "Now come around here and sit on the floor."

Lenny moved from behind the bar. He thought about running for the door, but knew that he wouldn't get more than a few feet without being shot. He gazed out into the night, willing a car to appear, but none came. He walked to the spot indicated by the man, and sat down. The TV came on again, blazing into life at the gunman's touch on the remote. It continued to show images of the camps, of men and women climbing from trains, some of them still wearing ordinary clothing, others already dressed in the garb of prisoners. There were so many of them, and they outnumbered their captors. As a boy, Lenny would wonder why they didn't try to overcome the Germans, why they didn't fight to save themselves. Now he thought that he knew.

The man leaned against the bar, the pistol leveled at Lenny.

"You asked me who I am," he said. "You can call me Steiger. It doesn't matter much. It's just a name. Might as well have plucked it from the air. I can give you another, if you don't like that one."

And again Lenny felt a glimmer of hope warm the coldness of his insides. Perhaps, just perhaps, this night might not end in his death. Could it be that, if he was withholding his true name, this freakish individual planned to return to the hole from which he had emerged and leave Lenny alive? Or was all this a ruse, just one more way to torment a doomed man before the inevitable bullet brought all to an end?

"You know where these teeth came from?"

"No."

"Your wife. They came from her mouth."

Steiger grabbed a handful of the teeth from the bar and threw them on the floor before Lenny. One landed in his lap.

For a moment Lenny was unable to move. His vomit reflex activated, and he tasted sourness in his throat. Then he was moving, trying to rise to his feet, but a bullet struck the floor inches from the soles of his shoes, and the noise as much as the sight of the splintered mark upon the floor stilled him.

"Don't do that again," said Steiger. "If you try, the next one will take out a kneecap, or maybe your balls."

Lenny froze. He stared at the tooth stuck to his jeans. He didn't want to believe that it had once been his wife's.

"I'll tell you something," said Steiger. "Working on your wife's teeth gave me a renewed admiration for the skill of dentists. I used to believe that they were just like failed doctors, because, I mean, how difficult can it be to work on teeth, all the nerves and stuff apart. I hated going to the dentist as a kid. Still do.

"Anyway, I always thought extractions would be the easy part. You get a grip, and you yank. But it's harder to get a good grip on a tooth than you might think, and then you have to twist, and sometimes—if there's a weakness—the tooth just breaks. You'll see that some of your wife's teeth didn't emerge intact. I like to think that it was a learning experience for both of us.

"If you doubt me, and are trying to convince yourself that they're not your wife's teeth," said Steiger, "I can tell you that she was wearing jeans and a yellow blouse, with green—no, blue—flowers. It was hard to tell in the dark. She also has a mark here, on her left forearm, like a big freckle. That would bother me, I have to say. She's a nice-looking woman, but I'd always have been aware of that mark, like a reminder of all that's wrong inside, because we all have things wrong with us inside. That sound like your wife? Pegi, right? Spelled with an *i*. Short for Margaret. That's what she said, while she could still speak.

"No, no, don't go getting all upset now. You'll move, or you'll try to lash out, and this will all get a whole lot worse for you both. Yeah, that's right: she's still alive, I swear to you. And—listen to me, now, just listen—there are worse things than losing your teeth. They can do all kinds of miracles with implants now. She could have teeth that are better than her old ones. And if that's too expensive, or just doesn't work out because of the damage—like I said, I'm no professional—then there's always dentures. My mother wore dentures, just like I do, and I thought that they made her look younger, because they were always clean and even. You ever see old people with their own teeth? They look like shit. Nothing you can do about old age. It's pitiless. It ravages us all."

He squatted before Lenny, still careful to remain just beyond his reach should Lenny's anger overcome his fear, but he needn't have worried. Lenny was weeping.

"Here's how it will go," said Steiger. "If you're straight with me, and answer my questions, I'll let her live. She's all dosed up on painkillers, so she's not feeling much of anything right now. Before I leave, I'll call an ambulance for her, and she'll be looked after. I promise you that.

"As for you, well, I can't promise anything other than, if you're honest, you won't be aware of your own dying, and you'll have saved your wife in the process. Are we clear?"

Lenny was now sobbing loudly. Steiger reached out and slapped him hard across the side of the head.

"I said, are we clear?"

"Yes," said Lenny. "We're clear."

"Good. I have only two questions for you. What did the Jew named Perlman tell you, and who else knows?"

———

WHEN THE QUESTIONS WERE answered at last, and Lenny Tedesco was dead, Steiger removed from the dishwasher the glasses that he had used and placed them in a bag. He also emptied the register for appearances' sake. He had been careful to touch as few surfaces as possible, but he went over them once again with some bleach that he found behind the bar. Some traces of his presence would still remain, but they would be useless without a suspect, or a record against which to check them, and Steiger was a ghost. He traced the hard drive for the bar's security camera, and removed it. He turned off the lights in the Hurricane Hatch before he left, and closed the door behind him. Lenny's car was parked behind the bar, and would not be noticed unless someone came looking for it.

Steiger walked for five minutes to where his car was parked, out of sight of both the bar and the road, then drove to the Tedescos' small, neat home. He opened the door with Pegi Tedesco's key, and went upstairs to the main bedroom, where he had left her tied to the bed. Beside her were the tools with which he had removed all of her teeth, along with some others for which he had not yet found a use. The pain-killers were wearing off, and Pegi was moaning softly against the gag.

Steiger sat down beside her on the bed, and brushed the hair from her face.

"Now," he said, "where were we?"

CHAPTER

XIII

A ngel and Louis sat at the window of Gritty's brewpub on Fore
Street in Portland, two cask ales before them, the world beyond.
They were watching a man arguing with a woman on the street
outside. Both were probably in their thirties, at most, but with a lot of
city miles on their clocks. The man was wearing sneakers, but in his
right hand he held a single tan Timberland boot. He was waving it in
the face of the woman until she, tiring of having a boot hanging inches
from her nose, wrenched it from his hand and proceeded to beat him
across the head with it, yelling something in time to the blows.

"You know," said Angel, "there are a lot of fucked-up people in this
town."

Louis couldn't disagree. It said something when one could travel
north from New York City—a place that, to be straight, was not entirely
lacking in fucked-up people of its own—and take the view that, well,
yes, given its size and population, Portland, Maine, was more than
holding its own in the fucked-up stakes.

"More to the point," said Angel, "there are some fucked-up tattoos
in this town. Did you see that woman's leg? It looked like she'd been
burned in a fire."

"I think it was supposed to be a face," said Louis.

"Whose face?"

"Could be anyone's. Could be mine and I wouldn't know it."

Louis considered the matter, and decided that it was less a reflection on Portland's tattoo artists than on the people who came to them, possibly hoping to have something done about their fucked-up tattoos.

The couple moved on—or, more correctly, the man moved on quickly, the woman hot on his trail, still yelling, still hitting him with the boot.

"Lot of fucked-up people," said Angel, again.

"Interesting, though."

"It has its charms."

They had rented an apartment in Portland's East End, once again in order to be near Charlie Parker. When first they'd done so, he had seemingly been dying in a hospital bed. Now he was recovering in Boreas. They had considered finding somewhere closer to him, maybe even in Boreas itself, but he'd made it clear that he didn't want them hovering over him like a pair of demented Florence Nightingales. He didn't mind them coming up to see him, but even then he wasn't prepared to have them stay under his roof. Two lesser men might have been hurt by this, but Angel and Louis were familiar with pain and suffering, and the various ways in which individuals coped with it. Whatever Parker was enduring as he worked his way back to health, he did not want others to witness it. He would present a face to the world, but he would do so on his own terms.

So Angel and Louis stayed more and more in Portland, and they missed Manhattan less than either of them would admit to the other. Portland was curious and colorful. All right, so an attempt by the American Planning Association to categorize Congress Street as one of the ten greatest streets in the nation took a little time to digest. They had also decided that Portland was growing hotels like mushrooms without much thought of who might fill those rooms come winter, seeing as how even most of the city's residents didn't want to be there come December and January. Anytime they raised this question, someone would mention cruise liners, although any cruise liner hoping to dock in Portland in the depths of winter might need to hire an icebreaker first, and the last time they checked, the whole point of cruise liners was that you got to sleep on the boat. It wasn't like the liner dumped you on dry land and then floated away, like some Robinson Crusoe outfit, with all the crew laughing their asses off as you signaled for help from the dock. Portland was also playing host to a couple of restaurants that, even in New York, would cause a man to shake the check at the end of the night, just in case a zero might drop off the end.

But all these were objects of bemusement, and no more. Each understood, too, that their fates were now tied up with this place, and with the detective to whom both were bound by bonds of loyalty, affection, and—whisper it, but do not speak it aloud, and certainly not to each other—the inevitability of their own deaths.

They had been out to check on Parker's house in Scarborough. Its doors remained secured, the alarm system had been upgraded, and they had arranged for his more valuable possessions to be placed in secure storage. His computers and his files had been carefully boxed by Louis's people, then removed to a warehouse in Queens, and locked away under the name Gray Nemesis, Inc. Louis had the utmost confidence in the security of the warehouse, since he owned it (although any lawyer would have trouble proving as much) and stored most of his weapons there (and here, once again, the question of ownership remained nebulous, to say the least).

They had not yet broached the subject with Parker, but they doubted that he would be returning to the house that overlooked the Scarborough marshes. In their opinion, it would be hard for him to resume his life in a home in which he might no longer feel secure. Parker's defenses had been breached not only physically, but psychologically too. He could never have the same faith as he once had in his home's capacity to withstand intrusion, perhaps not even in his own ability to defend himself, or so they believed.

On a practical level, the house had appeared on news bulletins and in newspaper reports. The address and location were familiar to many people now. Angel and Louis were under no illusion that the detective's enemies had not previously known where to find him, should they have wanted to act against him. Even the fact that some of them had, at last, succeeded in wounding him so severely was not, to these men, entirely a surprise. No, what mattered was that the site of his home was now general knowledge. News reports linked to it via Google Maps. If he went back there, what peace would he have, even if he somehow managed to overcome the psychological and emotional difficulties of living in a dwelling in which he had almost met his death—in which he had, in fact, technically died before being resuscitated for the first of three times.

Then there was also the question of what kind of man he would be. He had nerve damage to his left hand. One kidney had been removed. They had dug so many shotgun pellets out of his skull and his back that the surgeons had filled two glass dishes with them. Sometimes, when speaking, he would forget a name, or misidentify an object. Once, over coffee in Boreas, he asked Angel to pass him a "bell."

"A bell?" asked Angel.

"Yes, a bell. A little bell. To add to my coffee."

And as Angel had grown more confused, so Parker had grown more frustrated, until at last he stood up, walked behind Angel, and grabbed a creamer of skim milk for himself.

"See?" he said. "Bell!"

Then, moments later, as he read the words on the side of the creamer, he seemed to realize what he had done, and began to apologize, but his voice broke, and all they could do was watch as he tried to hold back tears of rage and shame.

Was this the end of them, Angel wondered. Was this to be the final, undignified conclusion, the grand anticlimax? A broken Parker, living on whatever he could make by selling his house and its surrounding land and moving into a small apartment somewhere, supported—when required, and only if it could be discreetly done—by his friends? Dave Evans, of course, would give him a bartending job at the Great Lost Bear, but what if, like confusing the words—if not the concepts—of milk and bell, he proved unable to function?

And there were moments when Angel and Louis found it hard even to conceive of Parker doing what he once did, hunting the worst of men. They had trusted in his strength, in his knowledge, in his ability to understand situations that seemed only smoke and shadows to them. How could they stand with him if he could not be relied upon to watch their backs, to come to their aid if they were in trouble?

But at other times Angel would look at Parker, and see fires coldly burning behind his eyes, and in that instant he could make himself believe that all was not lost.

"What will we do about him?" said Angel, as soft rain began to fall, and Louis did not need to ask to whom he was referring.

"We'll wait," he replied, "and we'll see."

CHAPTER

XIV

ory Bloom arrived at Olesens—and the absence of that damned apostrophe bothered her too—shortly after ten to find Parker already seated at a table by the window at the back of the store. He hadn't heard her enter, and she saw that he was holding an object in his left hand. It looked like a red rubber ball, the kind office workers used for stress relief, but as she drew closer she saw it had dark loops that hooked around the fingers. She thought that she'd seen something resembling it in a sporting goods store at the Bangor Mall, when she'd gone to look for new sneakers. It was in the climbing section alongside the ropes and crampons and carabiners: a grip strengthener. The effort of squeezing it showed on his face. He winced with each compression, but did not stop until he saw her reflected in the glass, at which point he slipped the strengthener into his pocket.

"Is it working?" she asked.

"It hurts, so I have to hope so."

She took a seat across from him. He already had coffee, alongside a copy of the *New York Times*, although he didn't yet appear to have opened the newspaper.

"Is it to do with what happened?"

"Shotgun pellets," he said. "I sustained nerve damage to the hand, and some fracturing of the bones. I've had surgery, but it's about maintaining range of motion and muscle tone. The physio is helping. Massage works too."

"Are you asking?"

"Are you offering?"

"People might talk."

"Not least your husband."

"I'm sure he'd understand, if it was for medical reasons."

"I'm sure he wouldn't."

"You're probably right."

Were they flirting? Bloom couldn't recall the last time she had flirted with anyone. She didn't even flirt with her husband. There didn't seem to be much point.

Larraine Olesen came over and took her coffee order. Bloom thought that Larraine might inadvertently have overheard them. She just about managed to keep herself from grinning, but it was a hard-fought battle. Bloom was relieved when she left to make the coffee.

"Do you mind if I ask how you are otherwise?" said Bloom.

He looked away.

"Aches and pains, mostly," he said. "I had some . . . *discomfort* after they removed the kidney, but it went away after a week or two. I get headaches. A lot of headaches. I sustained muscle damage to my back, some shattered ribs, a broken clavicle, a couple of holes where there shouldn't have been any. I'm weaker than I was. That's the worst of it. I get tired quickly. Nauseous too. I lost my balance on the beach a couple of days ago, and if it wasn't for the Winter kid coming along I might still have been there when the tide came in. And it's the strangest thing, but sometimes I have trouble with words. I'll look at something, and I'll know what it is—a table, a chair, a book—but when I try to describe it, another word entirely comes out. It happened a lot at the start, less often now, but it's frustrating. And embarrassing."

He faced her once again.

"More than you needed to know?"

"No—and I did ask. You shoot with your right hand?"

"Yes, but I haven't held a gun much since that night."

"Are you planning to again?"

"I haven't given it much thought."

She saw something then—a flicker—and knew that he was lying. What would it do to a man's confidence to find himself on the verge of being butchered in his own home, lying in his own blood, his body torn by fragments of metal? His recovery would not only have to be physical, but psychological and emotional too. Heading out to Mason Point, and examining Bruno Perlman's car, might be considered a version of that grip improver: a means to test, strengthen. . . .

Her cappuccino arrived. Larraine had attempted some kind of art with the foam, but it hadn't worked out. It might have been a heart, or a smiley face. It might have been nothing at all. Larraine moved quickly away, well out of earshot. She knew better than to try and eavesdrop on the chief. Actually, she wasn't really the kind to eavesdrop at all, which made her unusual in Boreas. When she died, they could have her stuffed and mounted as a behavioral model for others.

"So," began Bloom, as she tried her coffee.

"There were no maps in the car," said Parker.

"No, there weren't."

"Does that trouble you?"

"Not really. Does anyone even use paper maps anymore?"

"I do."

"Seriously?"

"I like knowing where I've been, and where I'm going, not just where I am. Also, there are times when it's better not to leave a record of your travels."

"Are you admitting to the commission of a crime?"

"How long have you got?"

"Pretend that I never asked."

"You ever hear of a guy named Boris Cale?"

"It rings a bell, but I can't say why."

"He killed his ex's new boyfriend down in Providence, Rhode Island, a year or two ago. He didn't know the city so he put the guy's address into his GPS. He was found so fast that the blood hadn't dried on the floor when the cops arrested him."

"A salutary lesson. Back to Perlman: in theory someone could follow 95 all the way from Florida to Maine."

"Only as far as Houlton."

"And this isn't Houlton."

"It's prettier than Houlton."

"Not difficult."

"No, not really," said Parker. "Anything on a phone?"

"I've asked the sheriff's department down in Duval County to take a look at Perlman's apartment, see if they can find any records, or any sign of a laptop or desktop computer. If we confirm his phone details, we can see about contacting the phone company to find out who he might have called recently, especially anyone up here. They'll probably ask for a court order, but we'll cross that bridge when we come to it."

"It's still odd that he didn't have an atlas, or even just a cheap map, the kind they give away at the information centers when you cross the state line."

"He could have been using a GPS app on his phone," said Bloom.

"Assuming he had one."

"He was a male in his forties. He might have been an exception, but it's probably a safe guess that he owned a phone."

"Which, if he walked into that water, he took with him?"

"It's possible."

"Who needs a phone if he's going to commit suicide by drowning?" said Parker. "And I noticed something on his windshield. It was a circular mark on the glass, the kind left by the sucker attachment on one of those grips for a phone or a GPS. I only spotted it because it was cleaner than the rest of the windshield. Did you find anything like that in the car?"

"If we did, then it would have been on the list. No, there was nothing like it."

"Again," said Parker, "what kind of suicide takes the holder for his phone or GPS with him when he steps into the sea? He wasn't going to need GPS to find where he was going."

Bloom shifted in her seat. It wasn't that she'd exactly wanted Perlman's death to be a suicide, but if it wasn't, it was going to make life in Boreas very complicated. And there was the other thing, the one she hadn't yet mentioned to this man . . .

"Perlman had a series of numbers tattooed on his left forearm," said Bloom. "Lloyd Kramer found them when he was bagging his clothing. I didn't mention it to you before. I mean, I . . ."

She didn't know why she felt the need to apologize. She just did.

"It's okay," said Parker. "It wasn't any of my business until I chose to try and make it so. When you say numbers, what do you mean?"

"They're not uniform. One is four digits long, the next six, then there are two more four-digit sequences, but beginning with the letter *A*. They look professional—I mean, they weren't done in a jailhouse. I took a photograph."

She removed her phone from her pocket, pulled up the picture, and handed it to him. The numbers ran horizontally along the arm, one beneath the next. He gave the phone back to her.

"They're clearly not gang tattoos," she said. "Unless accountants have gangs."

"They could be concentration camp numbers," said Parker. "With a name like Perlman, he was probably Jewish."

"My married name is Bloom and my husband and I aren't Jewish," she argued.

"If your name was Perlman, I think you would be."

She conceded the point.

"But Perlman was far too young to have been in a camp during World War II," she said. "And why four sequences?"

"I don't know," said Parker. "A reminder? A memorial of some kind?"

Bloom admitted that it made a kind of sense, although she remained open to other possibilities too.

"I suppose I could ask around," she said. "I think there's an orthodox synagogue in Bangor, and there's got to be at least one down in Portland. And there's always Google."

She performed a quick search with her phone.

"God, there's a lot of stuff on concentration camp numbers. They were used to identify prisoners at Auschwitz, and only there. Hey, I didn't know that. Just from glancing over this material, they could be camp identifiers, I guess."

"Can I see those numbers again?"

She returned the phone to him, and he wrote them in a Moleskine notebook that he took from his jacket pocket.

"I could just have sent them to your phone," she said.

"I like writing things down."

She let it pass.

"I know someone in New York—a rabbi—who might be able to help with this," he told her. "If these are numbers from Auschwitz, then there must be a way to link them to the original prisoners."

"They may have nothing to do with why Perlman ended up in the sea."

"It won't hurt to ask."

"Okay, but I also think we need to inform a local synagogue that we have Perlman's remains up here. I don't know much about Jewish burial traditions, but I remember that they prefer the dead to be buried within twenty-four hours, and we're past that now."

"I'll get an answer for you on that as well. Not much you can do about it, though, until the autopsy has been performed."

They talked on while Bloom's coffee grew cold. She thought about ordering another, then decided against it. She had business to attend to, including naming Perlman officially to the press, and she didn't think it was advisable to spend longer than necessary in public with Parker. Other people had come and gone since she'd arrived, and would have noticed them talking.

"I could be wrong," she said, as she stood to leave, "but it strikes me that you don't seem anxious for me to talk to anyone local, or even semilocal, who might be Jewish, or know about Jewish history and traditions."

Parker signaled to Larraine for a refill.

"What if Perlman's death wasn't suicide?" he said. "The fact that he's Jewish might be entirely incidental. Then again, it might not be. If he was killed, he was put in the water in the hope that he'd stay there, but the tides betrayed his killer. I don't know what percentage of the population of this state is Jewish, but it can't be much more than 1 percent, if that, and only a few of them are this far north. If his death is linked to his faith, then we should be careful about letting a small community of people know that we're curious about the circumstances. Not yet, anyway. Not until we find out more about those tattoos, and from a neutral source."

"You don't believe that he killed himself, do you?" said Bloom.

"You know, I've seen a couple of cases where what looked like suicide turned out to be something else. One of them led to my almost being killed. It could be that I've just been unlucky, but it's made me suspicious. This feels wrong, and looks wrong."

"And if it feels and looks wrong . . ."

"Exactly."

"If you're correct, and this turns out to be some kind of hate crime, we won't just have the state police up here, but the FBI too."

"If you think about it," said Parker, "every murder is some kind of hate crime."

"That's very philosophical," said Bloom. "Are you paying for the coffee?"

"Sure."

"Thanks."

"My pleasure."

He didn't watch her leave. She could see him reflected in the mirror on the wall as she walked away, and he was already reading his paper.

She felt a twinge of disappointment.

———

LATER THAT DAY, JUST as the sun was beginning to descend, Parker walked up the beach to the house occupied by Ruth and Amanda Winter. He carried a bag from Olesens containing a selection of young adult books, most of which had been chosen by Larraine Olesen, including an illustrated edition of *The Girl Who Loved Tom Gordon* by Stephen King that he thought Amanda might enjoy. He had no concern that it might be too frightening for her. Amanda Winter didn't strike him as a girl who scared easily. In the bag was also the only bottle of kosher wine from Chandler's General Store, bought as a housewarming gift for Ruth Winter—assuming she even drank wine, kosher or otherwise—and as a kind of apology for causing her concern when her daughter helped him.

Ruth's car, a '99 Neon, sat at the back of the house, but he got no reply when he rang the doorbell, and the place was quiet. He returned to the beach and thought that he saw two figures walking at the far end of the strand. He considered leaving the bag of books and wine at the door, but he didn't have a pen to add a note, and didn't want to return to his own house just to get one. He decided instead to take a seat on the porch rocker and wait for them to return. He had nothing better to do. He'd left a message for Rabbi Epstein in New York, telling him about Perlman and the tattoos. He knew that the call would be returned as soon as Epstein had some answers.

Epstein brought back memories of Liat, the mute woman who protected the rabbi. Parker felt mild stirrings of desire at the thought of her, the first in what seemed like a very long time. Liat was the last woman with whom he had slept, and Angel told him that, while he was unconscious in the hospital, she remained nearby, and nobody—not the state police, nor the Portland PD, nor even the occasional Fed—had seen fit to deter her from watching over him. By the time he came out of the coma, she was gone. Not that he believed she would ever sleep with him again. By taking him into her bed, and then only once, she was trying to discover some truth about him. It was a test, and he had passed, but only barely. Had he not, he was convinced that she would have killed him.

Maybe, he thought, he should be more careful in his choice of lovers.

He took one of the books from the bag: E. L. Konigsburg's *From the Mixed-up Files of Mrs. Basil E. Frankweiler,* which he recalled reading as a child, although it was one of Larraine Olesen's picks. He was already halfway through the first chapter when he paused and looked over at the doorframe.

The little mezuzah in its pewter box was gone.

XV

Steiger hadn't washed since finishing with Pegi Tedesco. He had, though, kept his promise to her husband and called an ambulance when he was done with her. She was probably still warm by the time it arrived. Blood-sated, and blood-dazed, he drove back to his motel in a kind of stupor, not considering the possible consequences if the police stopped him, or if someone saw him as he returned to his room. But he passed no one, drew no attention, and as his room was on the first floor, he was able to park right outside and enter without being seen. He was fortunate, he supposed, but he had always been so. He removed his heavily stained clothes and placed them in a plastic bag, then licked at the blood on his fingers and face. It was dry now, but he could still smell it. He lay on his bed, turned on the TV, and hit the mute button. He stayed like that for an entire day, the DO NOT DISTURB sign hanging outside his door, the chain and security lock in place. He heard nothing and saw nothing, the television screen a series of unconnected images without meaning: static with colors and shapes. He simply relived his time with Pegi Tedesco.

His guts no longer even hurt.

———

IT WAS THE CALL that brought him back. The particular ringtone, used to denote that caller, and that caller alone, roused him.

"What have you done?" said the voice.

"What I was supposed to do," he replied. "I silenced."

"You were meant to be discreet."

"I got carried away."

"There will be repercussions. You drew attention."

"There was always going to be attention drawn."

He looked at his left index finger. There was blood beneath the nail. He worked at it with his tongue.

"Had Perlman spoken to Tedesco?"

"Yes."

"And to anyone else?"

"Tedesco didn't think so. Perlman didn't have many friends. Tedesco was it."

"Leave," said the voice. "Move north. Watch Ruth Winter."

"Has she done anything more?"

"No. She's been warned."

"But will she listen?"

"She will, for the sake of her child."

"What about you?"

"I have other things to do. But understand this: you make no move without checking with me first. Are we clear?"

Steiger had progressed to digging out the blood with one of his canines. He thought that he could still taste it.

"We're clear."

There was silence for a time.

"Did you hurt the Tedesco woman very badly?" said the voice.

"What does it matter to you?"

"I disapprove of sadism."

"I was out of practice," said Steiger. "And I'd forgotten how much I enjoyed it all."

The connection was broken. Steiger put the phone down. The caller had made him feel slightly ashamed of his behavior, but only slightly. Steiger supposed that, from the outside, what he had done to the Tedesco woman must have appeared strange, but at least he had derived some pleasure from it. The other, though, had killed only once before—well, until recent events spurred him into further action—and then without pleasure, although neither made him feel any particular regret. Then again, he wasn't a professional, not like Steiger. He was simply a fanatic. It was odd how these things came around: Steiger's accomplice had killed Ruth Winter's lover, the father of her child. Now, if no other option presented itself, he might have to kill Ruth as well.

Steiger showered, using bleach to sanitize the shower floor when he was done, then dressed and checked out of the motel. He double-bagged the bloodstained clothes, bought a container of lighter fluid in a smoke shop, and burned the bag in a trash can behind a disused strip mall just north of Jacksonville. He drove for twenty-four hours, barely resting, stopping only for coffee and two naps, conscious that he was traveling the same route as the late Bruno Perlman. He wondered what it was like to drown. He tried to imagine it, but his capacities were ill-suited to inhabiting the consciousness of others. Empathy was not in his nature.

Tiredness eventually overcame him shortly after he left Boston. He took a room in a cheap motel on Route 1, and ate cold hamburgers that he'd picked up along the way. He slept for only a few hours, the drapes closed against the light, before the pain in his stomach woke him. Still, it was enough.

He got back in his car and drove on to Boreas.

CHAPTER

XVI

Ruth and Amanda Winter returned home to find the detective waiting on the porch, a book balanced on his right thigh. Ruth didn't know how long he might have been there, but he didn't seem to have read more than a couple of pages. He watched her thoughtfully as she approached, and although he smiled at her, there was a feral element to it, and she felt horribly exposed beneath his gaze. She didn't want him here. She knew who he was. Just that morning, she'd heard someone mention him in Chandler's General Store. He'd been in earlier, buying wine, and a woman unknown to Ruth had commented on how odd it was that a body should have washed up shortly after "that man" had moved to Boreas. Edwyn Weeks, who worked behind the counter at the store most days, told her to hush up with that kind of foolishness, and everyone had laughed, even Ruth, but they did so in the manner of people denying some truth that they had no wish to hear spoken aloud.

Here, Ruth sensed, was a man who smelled out secrets the way hogs sniffed for truffles.

Amanda, by contrast, was pleased to see him. She asked him how he was, and he said that he was fine. He told her that he'd brought some books along as a thank-you for her kindness, and apologized for starting one of them while he was waiting for her and her mother to return.

Then he gave Ruth the wine as a token of apology for any worry he might have caused her, and after that she couldn't very well not invite him in, because she felt that it would not only be rude but might set those senses of his jangling. She was fairly certain that he had come only for the reasons stated: to thank Amanda, and to apologize to her, but she couldn't be sure. For the other thing she had heard while shopping was that Parker and Chief Bloom had been noticed talking together at Olesens, and someone said that Dan Rainey was sure he saw Parker down on the beach where the body had washed ashore.

So she and Parker sat at her kitchen table while she made coffee. She had brought her Nespresso machine with her to Boreas. She found that she couldn't live without it now.

"I can open the wine," she said. "If you'd prefer."

"No, it's yours. Anyway, I'm trying to be careful when it comes to alcohol."

She brought two cups of coffee to the table. Amanda opted for milk. She took it to the couch in the living room and was soon lost in one of the books, the adults in the next room apparently forgotten.

"You're very fortunate," said Parker, indicating Amanda.

Even as she tiptoed carefully around this man, Ruth couldn't help but be pleased at the compliment.

"I know," said Ruth. "She's rarely been any trouble, her illness aside."

"She mentioned that she was sometimes sick."

"She has chronic fatigue syndrome. The doctors keep telling us it'll get better, and we keep waiting, but so far, nothing. There are days when I have to fight the urge to wrap her in blankets and keep her from leaving the house in case some harm befalls her." She winced, and the blue pools of her eyes clouded, as though something had stirred up the mud at the bottom. "Sometimes I think we're only put here to watch over our children until they're ready to take care of themselves."

"We all have those thoughts," he said, and Ruth instinctively flashed on what she had read and heard about him, of the child that he had lost and the wife who had died alongside her. What do we say at such times?

Nothing, she decided. We say nothing.

"And how are you?" she asked.

"Recovering," he said.

"They talk about you in town."

"They talk about everybody."

"Not the way they do about you."

"We all trail our histories behind us," he said.

Ruth glanced at him, but he did seem to be talking only about himself. Still, she wanted to get him off that track.

"I'm sorry, I'm so rude!" she said. "I should have offered you something to go with your coffee. We have cookies."

"Really, it's okay. The coffee's great. I wouldn't want to spoil it by adding the taste of anything else."

"As long as you're sure . . ."

They tiptoed around the details of each other's lives. She was conscious of his not prying—no questions about Amanda's father, for one thing—until at last they came to their respective reasons for being in Boreas.

"A change of scenery," said Ruth, walking the tightrope of the lie. "I felt cooped up where I was."

"Amanda told me that you used to live near her grandmother."

Ruth looked at her coffee as she answered.

"That's right."

"It can be hard. My daughter lives with her mother in some converted buildings on her parents' property in Vermont. Even though Rachel likes her parents a lot, there are times when she still wants to run away to Bermuda. Or maybe even Siberia."

"How old is your daughter?"

"Six, going on twenty-six. Her name's Sam. She's coming up here the day after tomorrow. Well, I'll pick her up in Bangor and she'll stay with me for a couple of nights. Maybe Amanda might like to meet her."

Before Ruth could say anything, Amanda had chipped in with a "Yes, please!" That child, Ruth thought: she gave the impression of being lost in her book, but either she had an internal radar that picked up anything of interest or she had secretly been listening to everything that was said from the start. Ruth suspected the latter. It was why she was always so careful about what she said on the phone when Amanda was around.

"I guess it's settled, then," said Ruth.

"It seems so."

"Well, give me a call or just drop by. We won't be doing very much. If we take it easy then, with luck, Amanda will be well enough to go back to school next week."

A long sigh from the living room greeted that expression of hope.

"You know that you're bored," Ruth told her. "It'll do you good to be in school."

"I'm not *that* bored." Another sigh.

Ruth raised her eyes to heaven, and walked Parker to the door.

"Thanks again for the wine and the books. It wasn't necessary, but it was still very kind of you."

He acknowledged her thanks with a nod, his right hand against the frame of the door. He tapped the place where the mezuzah had once been. A pair of nail holes marked the spot.

"Didn't you have an ornament or something here?" he asked.

He watched her search for an answer.

"Oh, yes. That. I just didn't care much for it. I'll find something else to replace it."

"Something else Jewish?"

Their eyes met. She folded her arms across her chest.

"I haven't decided."

He nodded.

"Good-bye, Ruth."

"Good-bye," she said, then added: "We'll see you and your daughter over the weekend."

"I look forward to it," he replied, and she waited until he was on the sand before she closed the door.

Somehow, she even managed a farewell wave.

CHAPTER

XVII

From the dunes, Steiger watched in the fading light as the visitor departed from the Winter house. He'd been in there for a long time. Steiger wondered if he was fucking the Winter woman. It didn't matter to Steiger that her child appeared to be with them in the house. Steiger had spent so long among those to whom morality was an alien concept that he simply assumed all of humanity resembled himself in the baseness of its appetites.

Whether or not this man was screwing Ruth Winter didn't concern Steiger per se. Steiger would probably have screwed her himself, given the opportunity, but it wasn't that kind of job, not yet. What worried Steiger was pillow talk. The Winter woman had a lot of hurt and confusion bottled up inside her right now, and a stranger's touch might be just the catalyst required to pop the cap. If she started talking, then who knew where it might lead? Well, Bruno Perlman knew, as did Lenny Tedesco and his wife, but now none of them was in a position to explain the possible consequences of loose talk to anyone.

The first step, thought Steiger, was to establish this man's identity.

The second, if necessary, was to wipe him off the map.

———

ON NOVEMBER 19, 1900, a woman named Mildred Elizabeth Sisk was born in Portland, Maine. Her name changed to Gillars after her mother remarried in 1911, and when Mildred was sixteen the family migrated to Ohio, where she studied dramatic arts at Ohio Wesleyan University. Eventually she drifted east to New York in search of work, then on to Paris for a time, and Algiers, before finally moving to Germany, where she found employment with the Reichs-Rundfunk-Gesellschaft, the Reich Broadcasting Company.

When her German-born fiancé was killed on the Eastern Front, she fell under the spell of Max Koischwitz, the program director in the USA Zone for RRG, who broadcast anti-Semitic and anti-British propaganda under the name Doctor Anders. Gillars and the married Koischwitz became lovers, and worked together on a show called *Home Sweet Home*, designed primarily to arouse feelings of homesickness in American troops fighting the Germans in North Africa. Thus Gillars became the original Axis Sally. Broadcasting as "Midge," and through judicious use of music, she played on the soldiers' concerns about their mission, their officers, the women they had left behind, and what awaited them after the war. The propaganda was heavy-handed, and largely ineffective, but the GIs liked the music choices. If nothing else, Gillars had good taste in tunes, with a particular fondness for swing.

Gillars continued to broadcast from Berlin until the German surrender, after which she vanished in the postwar chaos, but the United States attorney general was determined to track her down. The alias Barbara Mome was linked to her, and the net began to close when an antiques dealer sold a table for a woman of the same name, leading soldiers to an address in the British sector of Berlin in March 1946. Gillars was arrested, taking with her only a photo of her now deceased lover, and returned to the United States for trial. She served twelve years for treason in the Federal Reformatory for Women in Alderson, West Virginia, before being paroled in 1961, after which she became a teacher at the Sisters of the Poor Child Catholic Convent

School near Columbus, Ohio. She died, largely unknown, in 1988.

In the quiet of his home, the Jigsaw Man listened to a re-creation of one of Axis Sally's broadcasts. He had put it together himself, interspersing recordings of her slightly German-accented voice with tunes from the era of which he was fond.

"As one American to another," Sally purred, *"do you love the British? Well, of course the answer is no. Do the British love us? Well, I should say not. . . ."*

Her voice faded away as Count Basie emerged from the mix with "Lullaby of Birdland." Only when Earl Steiger tapped on the window glass did the Jigsaw Man reluctantly pull himself from his reverie to admit him.

XVIII

arker didn't wake gradually, but shot up straight in bed, his head exploding, his vision pinpricked by white-hot explosions of light, like phosphorous flares in the night. He felt the shotgun pellets ripping through his scalp, embedding themselves in his skull. He tried to hide from them and tumbled to the floor, his head in his hands, as bullets tore through his torso, one of them breaking a rib, a second nicking the upper part of his pelvis and sending shards of bone tearing into his intestines. A third came, bursting a kidney, and now every pain receptor in his body was alight.

He curled in upon himself on the bare boards, his mouth wide in agony both real and remembered, no longer capable of separating one from the other. This headache was the worst yet: in its intensity it reactivated the hurt of half-healed wounds, and returned him to that night in Scarborough when he had crawled through his home, trailing blood, wishing for them to come, willing them to end it all.

The pain, incredibly, grew more ferocious. The scar left by his laparotomy—the vertical abdominal incision used to open him up after the shooting—started to burn, and he thought he could feel the holes left by the chest drains stretching and opening. He tried gritting his teeth against it, and tears were forced from the corners of his eyes, but he was brought no release. He was certain that tonight, after all he had endured, he must surely die.

A cool hand was laid on his forehead, the skin so chill as to be spangled with frost. Through his tears he saw it gleaming in the moonlight, sparkling like the light of dead stars. A voice spoke

daddy

and he felt the coldness of her breath, and smelled the scent of a world beyond this one. He began to tremble, for her touch was icy, but the agony slowly subsided, and his wounds ceased their singing, and her lips touched his cheek and left a mark that he would see in the mirror for days to come.

hush daddy hush

And he lay on the floor in a fever dream as his dead daughter comforted him.

CHAPTER

XIX

The next day, the Maine State Police got their first break in the search for Oran Wilde.

Oran owned a smartphone, but it had only been used once since the morning of the killings, when Oran had sent his closest friend, Clyde Marshal, a link to an article on Reddit relating to the weaponry used in the movie *Lone Survivor*, which Oran had seen on cable the night before. This link, relatively innocuous in itself—Oran was simply identifying weaponry that he had used in various PS3 games—was taken by police as further evidence of his disturbed nature, and its discovery resulted in Clyde Marshal being questioned for twenty-four hours about any possible foreknowledge he might have had of the events at the Wilde house. Marshal was eventually released without being charged, but his phone, too, was being monitored, and when Oran Wilde's phone eventually pinged back into action, it was to Marshal that he sent the following message:

> I'm okay, Cly. Just need to figure shit out. This is all a big mistake. I didn't mean for it to happen. I'll explain when I can. Oran.

While the phone was immediately switched off after the message was sent, the battery was not removed, allowing the MSP to begin the process of triangulation. The trace was almost complete when Oran apparently realized that he had forgotten about the battery, whereupon the signal was lost, but not before the MSP had narrowed the source down to a square mile of ground that took in the Veterans Cemetery outside Augusta.

And it was there that the body of the homeless man was found.

His name was Richie Benoit, and he was a veteran of the first Iraq war, a drug addict, and the father of three children by two different women, neither of whom he had ever gotten round to marrying. He had been roughing it, on and off, for about five years, and died from three stab wounds to the chest from a short-bladed knife, which was discovered near his body. Although he carried no identification, Benoit was well known locally, mainly because there was hardly a convenience store in Augusta from which he hadn't at some point been ejected for attempted theft. Fingerprints on the knife were matched to prints taken from Oran Wilde's bedroom, and further forensic examination found traces of Oran's blood on the fingers of Benoit's right hand, indicating that a struggle might have taken place during which Benoit had scratched or otherwise injured the boy. In the narrative under construction, it appeared that Oran might have killed Benoit in order to rob him of what little money he had, although it was also suggested that some altercation might have occurred between them, possibly when Oran came upon Benoit sleeping on the streets, or vice versa.

Roadblocks were put in place on all major and minor roads in and out of Augusta, and police began canvassing the area around the cemetery, searching garages, basements, empty lots, Dumpsters—anywhere a teenage boy might try to hide from his pursuers.

But no trace of Oran Wilde was found.

II

She had confronted Barbie during the pretrial proceedings—
what the French call *l'instruction*—and when he was asked if
he recognized her, he said, "When you have been in prison
for seven months it's always agreeable to see a desirable
woman." When Simone Lagrange said that his remark insulted
her, he said, "The trouble with you is you can't take a joke."

—Klaus Barbie, the "Butcher of Lyon," in exchanges with Simone Lagrange,
who, at the age of thirteen, was beaten and interrogated by him at Gestapo
headquarters in Lyon before being sent to Auschwitz (from "Voices from the
Barbie Trial" by Ted Morgan, *New York Times*, August 2, 1987)

CHAPTER

XX

While police swarmed Augusta, a TV news crew traced one of the mothers of Richie Benoit's children, a woman named Muriel Landler, who lived in the smallest apartment the reporter had ever seen, made even more cramped by the presence of two children and three cats. Landler appeared genuinely upset to hear of Benoit's death, but still managed to negotiate a cash payment of $500 before speaking to the camera, in order to pay off her auto loan lender, which had disabled her car using the starter interrupt device in the dashboard, even though she was only four days late with her payment.

"Who said," as she told the reporter while pocketing the cash, "that fucking technology makes our lives easier? Ten years ago they'd have had to send some fat fuck to find me."

The reporter blanched slightly and asked her not to swear on camera.

"Who's swearing?" asked Muriel.

"You just did."

"Did I? Fuck."

In the end, they only had to bleep her once, which was considered a minor miracle under the circumstances.

THE CALL FROM EPSTEIN came as Parker was throwing back his second painkiller. It helped the thumping in his head, but didn't do much for the nausea.

"Where are you?" asked Epstein.

"In Boreas. It's—"

"I know where it is. I thought that I might come visit you."

"When?"

"In a couple of hours, I should think."

"Are you serious?"

"When am I not? Liat is driving me. You remember Liat, don't you?"

Oh yes, thought Parker. Yes, I do.

"I have a favor to ask of you, too," said Epstein. "It relates to the late Bruno Perlman. . . ."

———

EPSTEIN AND LIAT ARRIVED in Boreas shortly after one p.m. Parker was waiting for them at Kramer & Sons Funeral Home, along with Cory Bloom. The rabbi hugged Parker, and introduced himself and the woman with him to Bloom. The woman, Liat, said nothing, which caused Bloom to bristle slightly until Epstein explained that Liat could neither speak nor hear. It was the interaction between Liat and Parker that particularly interested Bloom, though. There was a tenderness to the way the woman looked at him, and when she held him her lips brushed his cheek, and she closed her eyes for a moment. When she parted from him, he placed his right hand to his mouth, the fingers close to the lips, then moved it forward and down in her direction, so that he appeared almost to be blowing her a kiss. Liat's face lit up at the gesture, and Bloom found herself gasping at the woman's true beauty, which had been concealed until then by her sternness.

It emerged that Epstein had been in Boston for a meeting, and had already been considering a detour north to visit Parker and see how he was. He informed Bloom that he considered the subsequent call about Bruno Perlman "a nudge from the Most High."

Erik Kramer, one of the "& Sons," brought them to a room in the basement of the funeral home, and Perlman's body was briefly removed from the refrigerated unit in which it was being kept. This was the favor that Epstein had asked of Parker, and Cory Bloom had seen no reason to object. As Epstein had explained to Parker, it was not just the bereaved who were troubled by death, but the dead themselves. According to the Talmud and Kabbalah, the soul did not completely leave the world until after burial. Until then it was in a state of transition, of disconnection, which was why the deceased should not be left alone between death and burial. Out of this had come the Jewish tradition of *shemira*, or watching over the body.

But, as Erik Kramer explained to Epstein, Kramer & Sons was a very old-style funeral business, and his father and mother continued to live on the top two floors of the home, for they were not troubled by the presence of the dead. In this way, although they were not Jewish, he suggested that they were performing a kind of *shemira*. Epstein thanked him for this kindness, but said that he knew of a Chevra Kadisha, a Jewish burial society, who would be able to find volunteers to act as *shomrim* until the time came for Perlman's burial.

The rabbi then said a prayer over the body before it was returned to the cold and the dark. After that, Epstein remained silent until they arrived at the Brickhouse, where he ordered salad and spoke to them of numbers.

TATTOOED NUMBERS, AS BLOOM had already established, were used to identify prisoners at just one concentration camp—the Auschwitz complex in Upper Silesia—and then just from 1941 onward. Only prisoners selected for work received a serial number, Epstein explained. Those who were sent directly to the gas chambers—including the elderly, the weak, and children—were not tattooed, although in the early days of the camp those who were in the infirmary or marked for execution were also tattooed on the chest using a metal stamp made up of interchangeable centimeter-long needles that allowed the tattoo to be created using a single blow, after which ink was rubbed into the wound.

The digits were generally tattooed on the outer side of the left forearm, although some prisoners from transports in 1943 received tattoos on the inner forearm. The numbering sequences used varied over time, according to intake and the nature of the prisoners involved. An AU series denoted a Soviet prisoner, a Z series a Gypsy. A and B sequences up to 20,000 were used to identify male and female prisoners arriving at the camp after 1944, although an administrative error resulted in the B series exceeding 20,000. The Nazis' original intention was to get as far as the final letter of the alphabet if required.

"So," said Epstein, "your initial surmise was right: these *are* Auschwitz identity numbers. Perlman lost four family members—the Nemiroffs— in the camps: a great-uncle, a great-aunt, and their son and daughter. But the curious thing is that they didn't die at Auschwitz. They were killed at another camp entirely. They perished at Lubsko."

———

EPSTEIN HAD NEVER MET Bruno Perlman while he was still alive—his first sight of him had come that day at Kramer & Sons—but he knew of him. Perlman had been a troubled youth. He was involved in minor criminality, and was a heroin addict for a number of years. Eventually he rediscovered his faith with a vengeance, which led him to begin researching his family. In the actions of those who had killed the Nemiroffs, he found an outlet for his rage at himself, and grew obsessed with the Holocaust. He also became involved with a number of organizations targeting neo-Nazi groups, although Perlman was by nature and inclination more of a loner, and was regarded by most as a dabbler who could not be relied upon. He was also essentially self-absorbed, seeing everything through the prism of Lubsko.

Parker had heard the name used recently. It came to him.

"Engel," he said. "The war criminal they're trying to deport from New York. He was a guard at Lubsko."

"Indeed," said Epstein. "He's the first of the Lubsko staff that the US government has been able to lay hands on. Lubsko was a nasty, sordid little footnote to the Holocaust, as if such a thing could even be required.

"To understand Lubkso, you have to recognize something: Nazism was, at heart, a criminal enterprise, a product of which was the Holocaust. The Nazis were gangsters and thugs. As much as they were ideologically driven, they were also greedy. Pure idealogues don't pull gold teeth from the mouths of the dead.

"And lest you should be mistaken, we are speaking here of sums of money almost beyond comprehension, of quantities of looted assets that defy the imagination. Take one man, just one: Ernst Kaltenbrunner, who in 1943 became the head of the Reichssicherheitshauptamt, or RSHA, the Reich Main Office for Security, which was responsible for the implementation of the Final Solution. Kaltenbrunner had a house at Altaussee called the Villa Kerry, and when he was forced to flee from the American advance, he decided to bury his wealth in his garden. He had at his disposal fifty kilograms of gold; fifty cases of gold coins, plate, and jewelry; two million US dollars; two million Swiss francs; five boxes of gemstones; and a stamp collection valued at five million marks. It was too much to bury, so he hid what he could and had to be talked out of putting the rest in a cave and dynamiting it. This is *one man*—just one. Do you understand?"

Epstein banged a thin finger on the table before him. Parker had never seen the old rabbi so animated, so enraged.

"This was not simply about gassing and shooting and burning millions of innocent men, women, and children, about turning Europe into one vast funeral pyre: it was about robbing these people along the way, about taking everything they had from them down to their spectacles, their hair, even the clothes that they wore so they were forced to go to their deaths naked."

Epstein regained his usual composure. His point had been made.

"But the Nazis were worried about wealth slipping through their fingers, for they wanted nothing to get past them. So a unit was formed within the RSHA to identify Jews and other prisoners who might have managed to hide significant transportable assets—gold, jewelry, art—before being sent to the camps, and put pressure on them to reveal their location. It drew on staff from Amter II, the Administration, Law and Finance Section, along with Adolf Eichmann's Referat IV B4, but it was secretive about its work, to the extent that those who were involved in Lubsko did not even have it listed on their service record. It took years for the Allies just to figure out that 'Special Adminstration (Amter II-L)' was a reference to Lubsko.

"Now there were some who advocated torture and the threat of immediate execution as a stimulus, but given that most of the prisoners in the camps were already brutalized and facing death, further threats struck those involved in Amter II-L as redundant. Instead a more refined approach was decided upon, and Lubsko was created.

"The idea for the deception came from the death camp at Treblinka, of all places. I don't know if any of you have ever visited a slaughterhouse, but the trick is to hide from the cattle the imminence of their death. It makes them easier to handle. So you don't want them to smell blood and panic until the end, and you don't want them to hear the sounds the animals inside make when they sense what is about to happen. Most of those who ended up in Treblinka survived only minutes before being herded to the gas chambers, but in order for the operation to be conducted with the minimum of fuss and panic, the prisoner transports arrived at what looked like a village train station, with timetables and flowers, and the path to the chambers led through a grove of trees. You see, the best slaughterhouse is one that doesn't look like a slaughterhouse at all.

"So Lubsko was a death camp disguised to resemble a work farm, with small chalet-type huts and a minimal guard presence. It had a proper infirmary for prisoners, with no more than four to six prisoners to a hut, although the preference at Lubsko was to give each family its own dwelling. Prisoners would be expected to work, but compared to Auschwitz the labor was minimal, even pleasant. They would be required to farm, plant vegetables, feed chickens, and do some light maintenance—painting, cleaning—to keep the camp looking fresh. An *Obersturmbannführer* named Lothar Probst was given command of the camp, along with his wife, Magda. She was twenty years younger than him, and very pretty, by all accounts. She was almost the perfect wife for an SS officer; her only flaw was that she could not give him the children he wanted, but whose fault that was, I do not know. She was the local leader in the League of German Girls before she joined the party, and trained as a nurse at Grafeneck Castle near Stuttgart.

"You have heard of Grafeneck? No? It was the headquarters of the Nazi euthanasia program. Before they began slaughtering us, they practiced on their own: the mentally ill, the physically disabled, the weak, the deformed, the ones who did not match the Aryan ideal. In 1940 alone, they killed almost ten thousand people at Grafeneck: first, an injection of morphine to calm them, then the gas, although by the time they got to the Jews, they had dispensed with the morphine. After Grafeneck, Magda moved around hospitals as part of Operation Brandt, the expansion of the euthanasia program to geriatrics and the war-wounded, before being posted to the Ukraine in the *Ostrausch*, the 'Eastern Rush,' the great colonization, and there she met Lothar Probst. As a regional commander, Probst was responsible for *Aktions* on the Ukrainian-Polish border: he worked alongside a man named Wilhelm Westerheide, and together they reduced the Jewish population from twenty thousand to five hundred in the space of fourteen months. One of their tricks was to force Jews in the local ghetto to hand over their money and valuables in return for guarantees of protection—which, of course, never came. That was why Probst was chosen for Lubsko: he had experience in deception.

"The first intake arrived in the spring of 1944: seventeen individuals, most of them Jews, including three children. They came from Belsen and Auschwitz, and perhaps could not quite believe what was happening to them. They were given the opportunity to shower, and offered clean clothes and decent food. They found one couple, the Dreschers, from near Koblenz, already in residence. They were not Jews, they said, but had been incarcerated for sheltering them. They claimed to have been at Lubsko for a month, and had helped to get the camp fit and ready for the first intake. They had been treated well, but before they could say any more, Lothar Probst and his wife arrived to explain the arrangements to the new arrivals. It was very simple: they could choose to return to their original camps, where they would immediately be executed, or they could find a way to pay for the relative privileges and comforts that Lubsko offered. They would be given one week to decide.

"By this time, of course, there were whisperings, both among the Germans and the prisoners, that the war could not last forever, and it was only a matter of time before the Allies invaded. It was a question of surviving to see the end. Also, who would choose to go back to the gas chambers and the death pits if there was another option? The RSHA researchers had done their job well: all those who had been picked gave up assets of some type. This information was sent back to Amter II-L, and trusted officers were sent to secure the items in question.

"But this was a kind of blackmail, so two weeks later Probst came back to the prisoners again, seeking further assets. Those who could not pay were publicly threatened with being returned to their camps, but those who could pay stepped up and offered to save not just themselves, but the others too, for the Nazis understood that goodness can be exploited just as much as evil. And even if the prisoners at Lubsko

quickly began to realize that they were the victims of a terrible duplic-
ity, they had no choice but to go along with it. To borrow a gambling
analogy, if they folded now, they lost everything.

"Four weeks after the first intake arrived, they were all murdered.
The adults were shot in the woods and buried in a mass grave. The children were separated from them, taken to the infirmary by Frau Probst,
and killed by injection. Only the Dreschers were spared, because they
were part of the deception, and were in reality a pair of loyal party
members, the Kuesters. They were the Judas goats, leading the cattle to
the slaughter.

"One week later, the next intake arrived, and the Dreschers were now
from Zwickau instead, for a pair of Jews from Koblenz were among
the new prisoners. And so it went on—Bruno Perlman's family being
among the final prisoner drafts, incidentally—until it became clear that
the Allies would soon be at the gates, at which point Probst and his wife
died in what appears to have been a murder-suicide pact, after which
some of the guards must have turned on one another, possibly over the
division of spoils. It's clear from surviving documentation that concerns were being raised in Berlin about possible inconsistencies in the
level of assets being reported to the RSHA from Lubsko. Some skimming was probably to be expected, but it seems likely that the Probsts
were engaged in holding back information about the location of significant quantities of hidden wealth. Had the Reich not collapsed, there's
a good chance that the Probsts could have found themselves facing
the same fate as their prisoners. Instead, with the Russians advancing
from the east, and the British and Americans from the west, the Probsts
chose death.

"The Americans found all of the bodies when they arrived—the Dreschers and the Probsts among them—along with one survivor, a Jewish
woman named Isha Górski, who escaped from the camp and hid in the
last death pit when the shooting began. It was from her that we learned
the details of Lubsko. The rest is based on research, and admittedly

some speculation, especially concerning those final days. I have to confess, though, that I am no expert, and I had to make some calls to find out what I've told you. Such information I don't keep at my fingertips."

"And what happened to Isha Górski?" Bloom asked.

"I don't know. I didn't ask. If she is still alive, then she is a very old woman by now."

"The question remains," said Parker. "What was Bruno Perlman doing up here in the first place?"

"You can say, with some assurance, that it was linked either to Lubsko or to neo-Nazism," said Epstein. "From what I hear, he had little interest in anything else."

"Was he—?" Bloom started to ask, then tried to find another way to phrase the question before deciding to follow her original path. "Was he suicidal?"

"The Jewish view on suicide is very severe," said Epstein. "It's a serious sin. That's not to say that Jews do not commit suicide, but Perlman, with his newfound religious fervor, would not have been unaware of the consequences of it for his soul. But who is to say what goes through a man's mind at such moments? Not the torments of the next life, I think, but an end to the pain of this one, and Bruno Perlman was, I believe, a man in a great deal of pain."

It was time for Epstein and Liat to leave if they were to make their flight to New York. Epstein fell back as they walked to his car, and Parker joined him.

"You are recovering," said Epstein. It came out as a statement, not a question.

"I hope so," Parker replied.

"No, I can see it in you."

"I think that's partly thanks to you."

"Why would you say that?"

"The Brook House Clinic. I noticed that two members of its board share your surname."

"Oh, that," said Epstein, as though it were nothing, when Parker's time and treatment there had made months of difference to his progress. "Distant relatives. It's a commandment: every Jew has to have a doctor in the family. It was on the third tablet that Moses couldn't carry down from the mountain, then left up there when he realized his people would have enough trouble keeping up with the ten commandments he already had."

"Nevertheless, I'm grateful."

"You know, you never cease to surprise me. I think you may outlive us all. Liat, she worries about you. I think that, if you were a Jew, she might even consider marrying you, if only to keep an eye on you. Have you ever considered converting?"

"You're kidding."

"A little, yes. But she does care about you, as do I. Get well. Return to doing what you do best. Perhaps investigating Bruno Perlman may be a step on the way."

They reached the car. Epstein hugged Parker again, and whispered, "Don't leave Perlman in that place for much longer. Make some calls. Let him be buried so that his soul can rest at last."

"I'll try."

"I'm grateful to you."

Liat opened the door for Epstein, and when he was safely inside she returned to Parker. She mouthed the words clearly so that he could understand her.

Earlier you signed "Thank you."

"Yes."

For what?

"For everything."

For sleeping with you?

"I didn't want you to think I was ungrateful."

She smiled.

"And for watching over me in the hospital."

The smile faded, to be replaced by something unknowable.

You died.

"I know."

So I was your shomeret, *for a time. I don't want to do it again.*

"I'll try my best to make sure you don't have to."

This time, it was Liat who signed "Thank you." She kissed him once more before leaving, this time brushing the corner of his lips with her own.

Bloom and Parker watched them go. She considered asking Parker about Liat, then thought better of it. Some things, she knew, should remain unexplored and unremarked.

CHAPTER

XXI

The next day, Parker arrived in Bangor more than an hour before he was due to meet Rachel and Sam, and just in time to pick up a message from Rachel to say that they had been late in leaving Vermont, and wouldn't get to town until early afternoon, which left him with even more time to kill. He was a little relieved. The headache from two nights before—when he'd woken to find himself on the rug by his bed, a pillow beneath his head—lingered as a dull throb, and he'd been nauseous again on the drive to Bangor. He had no idea how he had come to be lying on his floor, and retained only a vague memory of a dream in which his dead child whispered words of comfort to him. He still wasn't sure how he'd managed to spend all that time with Epstein and Liat the day before without vomiting, which might have been taken amiss. Viewing Bruno Perlman's body and listening to the story of the camp at Lubsko hadn't helped.

He parked in the lot by the Bangor Public Library, picked up some books for Sam at the Briar Patch on Central—he was becoming something of an expert on books for younger readers—and then, on the off chance that he might be free, called Gordon Walsh. He figured that, if things worked out, he might be able to do everyone a favor, Perlman included, and scratch the itch that had been bothering him ever since he had first spoken with Bloom about the body.

The MSP investigator picked up on the second ring.

"Long time," were Walsh's first words, after Parker had identified himself.

"I got the flowers you sent," said Parker.

"I didn't send any flowers."

"I know."

"I did come to visit you in the hospital, but you were sleeping."

"So you just stood there and looked at me? You'll forgive me if that makes me uneasy."

"I didn't touch you under the sheet, if that's what you're asking. Where are you?"

"Bangor."

"And you just figured I'd be in Bangor too. Sorry if that makes *me* uneasy."

"Oran Wilde," said Parker.

Although the state police's Major Crimes Unit North operated out of Augusta, Bangor was the de facto forward base for the Wilde case. While now based in Gray, which put him in the south of the state, Walsh was one of the MSP's senior investigators. Leaving him out of the Wilde case would be like leaving Santa Claus out of Christmas.

"Right. Me and just about every other cop in the state who can string two words together and walk in a straight line. I'll see you at Java Joe's. Order me a java mocha."

———

WALSH ARRIVED ABOUT TWO minutes after Parker, just as Parker was putting the coffees on the table. Walsh took a sip of his beverage through the plastic lid, and scowled.

"This isn't a mocha," he said. "This is just regular coffee."

"I was too embarrassed to ask for a java mocha," said Parker, "and I didn't think they'd believe me if I told them it was for someone else.

They'd suspect I was trying to hide something. Anyway, that's probably better for you."

"At least you added milk."

"Skim."

"Jesus, I already got one mother. And a wife."

Walsh removed the lid, went back to the counter, added half-and-half to his coffee, then sprinkled chocolate on the top. He tasted the result, looked a little happier, and came back to the table.

"That's the most disgusting thing I've seen in a while," said Parker.

"Well, that's because you were out of circulation. You look okay for someone who's been dead, by the way. Not great, but okay. For anyone who doesn't like you, it must be a source of great frustration that you seem to be immortal. You die, but you don't stay that way."

"You want to know what's on the other side?"

Walsh eyed the detective carefully, as if gauging the seriousness of the question.

"Is it seventy-two virgins, like the Muslims believe?"

"That's the good news. The bad news is that they're all guys. It's like being at boarding school."

"I knew there had to be a catch."

Walsh tasted his coffee again, and discovered more cause for dissatisfaction. He returned to the dispensers and added enough regular sugar to kill a diabetic at ten paces. At last he was content.

"Not even sweetener this time?" Parker said, when he resumed his seat.

"That stuff'll kill you. It's not natural."

Walsh sat back and scratched his chest. The movement exposed the dried sweat stains under his arms. He was on at least his second day with that shirt, Parker guessed, and although he'd shaved, he had razor burns on his neck, and the dark blotches beneath his eyes made him look as though he'd been in a fight, and lost.

"I hear you're up in Boreas," he said.

"That's right."

"The hell are you doing there?"

"Recuperating. Taking the sea air."

"It's full of Germans."

"You don't like Germans?"

"My grandfather fought in World War II. Took a bullet in the head at Arnhem."

"Yeah? I didn't know that."

"It didn't kill him. Didn't even slow him down, as far as I could tell. He lived to be eighty. My grandmother used to say it was because the bullet didn't encounter any resistance on the way through. But he used to talk about some of those people up in Boreas, the ones who came over from Europe in the fifties, when we let in just about anyone who claimed to be in danger of persecution from the Communists. My grandfather believed there was a pretty good chance that somewhere in Boreas was a German who, if he didn't fire the bullet that hit him, probably knew the guy that did."

"If it's any consolation, I haven't seen a single swastika since I arrived."

"That's because they keep them in the basement, and only dust them off for Hitler's birthday."

"I'll bear it in mind."

"On that subject, how long are you planning to stay in Boreas?"

"I haven't decided."

"You keeping the place in Scarborough?"

"So far."

"I saw it. They did a fine job of shooting it up."

"They did a fine job of shooting me up as well."

"Like I said earlier, that depends on the degree of affection in which you're held." He twisted his cup. "You planning on heading back south when you're fit and well?"

"Again, I haven't decided. Probably. I don't know about the house, though."

"Have you been back there since, you know . . . ?"

"Just to collect some things. I didn't linger."

"These crime-scene cleaning companies, they can make it like it never happened."

"Really? Can they get rid of the holes in me as well?" Parker couldn't quite manage to keep the sarcasm from his voice.

"You know what I mean."

"I guess I do."

"Maybe it's not what you want to hear—I'm not even sure it's what *I* want to hear, and I can guarantee you it's not what some folk in law enforcement want to hear—but if you're tiring of being a hired gun, we have room for a good investigator."

"You're kidding, right?"

"State police not good enough for you?"

"That's not it, as well you know. I've been out for too long, that's all. And nobody in this state will give me a shield anyway, not even with you playing cheerleader."

"You're wrong about that. You've been protected for a long time, and don't even try to fucking pretend that you haven't. You should have lost your license ten times over, and not just once like you did. Hell, you should be in jail. How do you think you're still on the streets? You think a fairy godmother waved a wand and made the bodies go away? You have a lot of people here on your side."

Walsh's voice had risen in anger, and heads were turning in their direction. Parker raised a hand to placate him.

"Even if you're right," he said softly, "and you may be, I don't think I could work within those constraints again, and that assumes I could even nail the medical. You see my hand?" He raised his left hand. "Take it."

"What? Are we dating now?"

"You know, you're a homophobe. If you want me to sign something before you touch me, I will."

"If anyone I know sees me, I'll tell them it was assault," said Walsh, but he reached over and took Parker's hand loosely in his.

"You feel that?" asked Parker.

"This gets weirder."

"Just answer the question."

"Yeah, I feel it, but barely. You're squeezing."

"That's all the strength I have in that hand, but compared to what it was, it's like being able to bench two-fifty with it. Without pills, I get maybe two or three hours of interrupted sleep a night. I have pains in my gut, my back, and my head, and I can't tell which of them are real and which are phantoms, but all I know for sure is that they hurt the same."

He released his grip on Walsh, who seemed relieved to get his hand back.

"The offer still stands," said Walsh.

"And it's appreciated," said Parker. And it was, even if he felt, rightly or wrongly, that there was an undertow of charity, maybe pity, to it. He forced the feeling away. He had no intention of taking up Walsh's offer, but deep inside him, at the edge of his awareness, the first of a series of connections had been made that would ultimately lead him to New York, and a conversation with the FBI.

An abandoned copy of the *Bangor Daily News* lay on the next table. The search for Oran Wilde still dominated the front page, just as it did the news cycles on TV.

"What do you think?" asked Walsh.

"I only know what I've read in the papers."

Walsh gave him chapter and verse, but it wasn't much more than Parker had already gleaned from the news reports, apart from one recent development: Oran's friend Clyde Marshal had received another message from Oran's phone, letting him know that he was okay and everything was not the way it was being painted in the news. Oran also claimed in the message that Richie Benoit had tried to assault him, which was why he'd been forced to hurt him, but he hadn't meant to kill him. Other than that, Oran had remained under the radar, avoiding a massive police search operation.

"Oran Wilde appears to be smarter than any seventeen-year-old boy has a right to be," said Parker.

"That's what we're starting to think too."

"An accomplice? Someone who's protecting him?"

"Maybe, but I don't see how it fits with Wilde stabbing Richie Benoit. Well, I can, but it involves this other party standing back and watching him do it. And if someone is helping him, then why has Wilde been reduced to rolling and killing homeless junkies? That kind of help is kin to no help at all."

"It's odd that he stayed in the state," said Parker. "Accomplice or no accomplice, it would make sense to put some serious miles between him and Maine."

"Could be a question of resources. He is still a kid, smarter than average or not."

Walsh scratched himself again, and gazed out the window, seemingly lost to the world. The detective watched him.

"You don't think Oran Wilde did it," said Parker.

Walsh barely reacted. He didn't even turn his gaze back to Parker.

"Why would you say that?"

"I can see it in your face."

"You're wrong, or just half-right," he said. "I'll buy the accomplice: if Oran Wilde did it, then he didn't act alone. And all of this bullshit about him being a disturbed child? It's just smoke. He's no more disturbed than I was at his age, and the thought of shooting my family never crossed my mind, even though my old man was a bastard. But I'm starting to wonder if Oran didn't fall under someone's influence, if he wasn't groomed to do what he did, like that shooter down in DC, curled up in the trunk of a car with an older man. The more I find out about Oran Wilde, the less I see him having it in him to kill anyone, and yet here we are, tearing up the Northeast looking for him."

"Anything on Facebook or social media?"

"Nothing so far. If he met someone, it wasn't online."

They knocked it back and forth for a while longer, but Parker couldn't help. He was outside looking in, and even allowing for what Walsh had shared with him, he was still removed from all of the fragments of the investigation. A conversation in a coffee shop wasn't worth a murder book.

"I have a favor to ask," he said, as Walsh looked set to leave.

"And here I was thinking that it was just because you wanted to hold my hand over coffee."

"You hear about the body that washed up in Boreas?"

"I saw the bulletin. What of it?"

"The weight is toward suicide or accidental drowning."

"Let me guess: you don't buy it. Your viewpoint has been tainted by experience."

"I think the chief up there, Cory Bloom, is starting to agree with me."

"That place is small, and she's trapped in close quarters with you. You could probably convince her that day is night, given time."

"Come on, man . . ."

Walsh relented. "Give it to me. One minute."

And Parker did. Spoken aloud, it didn't sound like much: the absence of maps or GPS; no computer or phone; and the distance Perlman had traveled from Florida to Maine only to end up washed ashore on a remote beach. He also mentioned Epstein's visit, and Lubsko.

"Lubsko," said Walsh. "That fucking Engel, they should drown him in a tub. Odd that the name Lubsko should come up again so soon, but then we could be looking at cause and effect: Engel was in Maine, so Perlman the amateur Nazi hunter decides to poke a stick into the hole to see what else he might scare out."

"And if he did succeed in scaring someone?"

"Seriously? Perlman's shoelaces were tied together, but his hands were free, and even your friend the rabbi says he was shaky. And have you seen Engel? He's, like, a hundred years old. If any of his buddies are living up here, then they're ancient too. They'd have trouble getting themselves in and out of the tub, never mind dumping a middle-aged man in the ocean."

"His car was found parked at an overlook south of Boreas. At high tide, it's a straight drop into the sea. Wouldn't have taken more than a push to put him in."

"So what do you want?" asked Walsh.

"An autopsy. Bloom has been told to keep him on ice until the Wilde thing comes to an end, but that could be weeks at the current rate of progress, even assuming that Perlman is fast-tracked."

"The ME's office has been told to hold off on all nonessential cases. You know how hard it is to conduct an autopsy on burn victims?"

"Almost as hard as it is to do one on a body that's spent days in the sea, and more days on ice."

"The Wilde case has already sent the ME's office over budget, and it's only April."

"There's more to Perlman than a simple drowning. The Lubsko angle alone raises a flag."

"Has Bloom asked?"

"She got the party line."

"Shit, I'll see what I can do. The best—and I mean the *best*—case scenario might be to grab an assistant ME, but I can't guarantee that they'll be able to give you much on a floater, not without a battery of lab tests, and you won't get those."

"Anything would be a help."

Walsh extended his hand, and Parker shook it.

"Good seeing you," Walsh lied.

"And you."

"For somebody who's all shot up, and recuperating, and reconsidering his role in life, you do seem very curious about a body that washed up on a beach."

"Old habits."

"Yeah. Well, don't give up on them all, not yet."

He said good-bye, and Parker watched him cross the street, chased by the shadows of clouds.

XXII

Marcus Baulman stood at his front door as the visitors walked back to their car, the woman dressed in the kind of fitted dark blue suit that gave the impression of curves where there were none. He had recognized her the instant he opened the door, from closely following the news reports about Engel and Fuhrmann. She was Marie Demers, the attorney with the Human Rights and Special Prosecutions Section of the Justice Department responsible for prosecuting the two old men. He tried to think of the appropriate description for her. He rarely spoke German anymore, not even among other German Americans. He had made that decision many years before, and had worked hard to remove the rough Teutonic edges from his accent. *Eine dünne Frau*: was that it? No, not quite. It didn't capture her sharpness, her angularity, the danger that she posed. The man with her didn't worry him quite so much, although he was not entirely without threat. She had introduced him as Toller, a historian and researcher with her section, and maybe that was what he was, but he was a researcher who could have punched a hole in a wall, if he chose. Nevertheless, it was clear that it was Demers who was in charge.

Baulman had denied it all, of course. That was the first rule, the one they had learned in the immediate aftermath of the war. Deny, deny, deny. No, I am not this man, this Kraus. I am Marcus Baulman. This is my family history. I can trace it back for generations. Yes, I have some records, some documents, although they are, regrettably, incomplete. So much was lost in the confusion after the war. You could not understand, for you are young. Our cities were bombed to rubble. Papers were burned, reduced to ash. Yes, I fought. I was proud to fight. I believed what I was told, at the start. Later, though, this changed. But I fought in the *Wehrmacht*. I never went anywhere near this camp you speak of, this Lubsko. Look, here is my *Wehrpass*. I kept it safe, along with my identity disk. No, I do not know why there is a discrepancy between my *Wehrpass* and the copies of the *Soldbuch* that you are showing to me. A mistake must have been made. As I told you, so much was lost, so much burned. . . .

He could tell that they did not believe him. They would not have traveled from Washington on a whim. Perhaps they expected him to break down, to confess, but he did not. In a sense, he had been preparing for many decades for just such a moment. He would practice answering questions just like the ones they had posed, watching himself in a mirror, composing his features into the appropriate expressions: surprise, shock, righteous indignation, even a little fear, because an honest man would be afraid.

The car started up. The woman put on her sunglasses. He could not tell if she was watching him or not. He raised his hand, although it was a hesitant gesture. He thought that this, too, was what an honest man would do.

Extradition was a complicated business. First of all, the German government would have to be convinced of its obligation to accept him, for, as of now, there was no German warrant for his arrest. The Germans were notoriously reluctant to allow former Nazis back into Germany. If they accepted a suspected war criminal from the United States, and then failed to follow through with their own investigation and an effort at prosecution, they risked being branded a safe haven. But Baulman believed that a deeper psychological malaise, a national illness, underpinned the Germans' reluctance to act. It wasn't stated publicly, and it was possible that even those involved in such matters were either unaware of it or chose not to acknowledge it, but they were all simply waiting for the last of the old Nazis to die so that their crimes could safely be consigned to history. As long as they lived, they remained a marker for old evils waiting to be called in, an embarrassment to the new Germany. Nobody wanted to be reminded of their continued existence.

But set against this was the acknowledgment that time was running out for prosecutions. With every week, every month, that passed, the possibility of bringing old men and women to justice grew slimmer and slimmer, and so the pressure on the authorities to act when evidence of wrongdoing was discovered grew commensurately greater. The Americans, perhaps in part because of the power of the Jewish lobby, were particularly diligent in their efforts, although such things were relative. In a little over three decades the Americans had managed to file legal proceedings against no more than 140 or 150 former Nazis, resulting in the expulsion of fewer than half of those involved through extradition, deportation, or voluntary departure. Over twenty more had died while their cases were still pending, and it was decided not to continue proceedings in the cases of that many again because of ill health.

Yet even the Americans were compromised. After all, their counterintelligence services had recruited former Gestapo officers, SS veterans, and confirmed collaborators in an effort to bolster their own anticommunist efforts. They helped Klaus Barbie, the "Butcher of Lyon," flee to Argentina in return for his cooperation. They permitted Mykola Lebed, the Ukrainian sadist and Nazi collaborator believed to be responsible for the murders of an unknown number of Jews and Poles, to work for American intelligence in Europe and America until the 1980s. And that was without mentioning the former Nazis who were given safe haven on the grounds that they were fleeing Communist persecution in Europe. No, the Americans were in no position to point a finger at anyone.

Baulman wondered if the young woman from the Human Rights and

Special Prosecutions Section knew any of this, or cared about it if she did. When he watched her on the news, he saw in her the fanaticism of the true zealot. Her actions might have been linked to personal ambition, but she was also convinced of the justice of her cause: these were evil people, and they deserved to face the full force of the law for their crimes. Baulman knew that this was part of the fascination that the young had with the Second World War. It appeared to have no nuances, no gray areas. There were only good guys and bad guys. The bad guys even wore black, and decorated their uniforms with skulls. How much easier could they have made it for others to brand them as evil?

When he had first heard mention of the Human Rights and Special Prosecutions Section, Baulman had not been aware of what it was. He was familiar with the old Office of Special Investigations, which had spent so long hunting his kind, until natural mortality caused it to seek other targets—war criminals from the former Yugoslavia, from Rwanda—to salve its collective conscience. He knew that the hunters had not gone away, although he had somehow missed the fact that, in 2010, the OSI had been merged with the Domestic Security Section to form a new unit within the Justice Department's Criminal Division. It just showed, he supposed, how lax he had become, how certain he was that he had escaped their notice and would see out his last days in peace.

Baulman made himself a cup of hot chocolate and stood at his kitchen window. The birds were picking at the feeder. He could usually spend a contented half hour watching them, but not now, not today. He turned and leaned against the counter. An open connecting door led into the living room. He could see the couch on which the woman and the man had sat, their file of papers on the old chest that he used as a coffee table, copies of documents sliding across it as they probed his story. Should he have called a lawyer? He was not being charged with any crime. The woman had stressed this. They simply had questions for him. No, he did the right thing in not insisting upon counsel. An honest man would defend himself. An honest man would have nothing to hide.

Where had this come from? he wondered. Why now?

The answer came in the news report later that evening. Fuhrmann had left the United States for Germany, but Engel had not traveled with him, said the reporter, "due to poor health."

Baulman did not believe it.

Engel had talked.

XXIII

Toller was driving. Demers was on the telephone to her superiors in Washington.

"What do you think?" said the voice of a deputy director.

"It's him," said Demers. "But I think he was waiting for us to come. I think he's always been waiting."

———

IT IS AN UNPOPULAR point to make in some circles, but both the best and worst thing to happen to Nazi hunting was Simon Wiesenthal. Wiesenthal was, in many ways, a kind of fantasist: his various memoirs contradict one another, and it is likely that he lied about some of the details of his early life, including his professional qualifications as an architect, and his many brushes with near death during the Holocaust. One of his most famous sketches—the murder of three Jewish prisoners by a firing squad at Mauthausen concentration camp, their bodies slumping against the stakes to which they had been tied—was plagiarized from a *Life* photograph of the execution of three Germans by American forces. He exaggerated his role in the capture of Adolf Eichmann, the architect of the Final Solution, to the extent that he told stories about wrestling Eichmann into a ditch during his capture in Buenos Aires in 1960. In actuality, Wiesenthal had been in Europe at the time, and was convinced that Eichmann was in hiding in Cairo. Although he did nothing to deny credit for helping to capture more than 3,000 former Nazis, his actual achievements in that field can be counted on one hand—two, if one were being generous. His exaggerations and inconsistencies provided valuable ammunition to his enemies, including neo-Nazis and Holocaust deniers.

And yet . . .

Wiesenthal was a driven man, and the justice of his cause is beyond any criticism. He was also ahead of his time in recognizing that, if interest in Nazi war crimes was to be sustained, the news media required not just a story but a legend in all the senses of the word: a figure somehow real yet beyond history, a human being of extraordinary achievement, and, in the language of the intelligence field, a legend in the sense of an identity that is not entirely one's own. By regularly conjuring up the specters of Josef Mengele and Martin Bormann, the bogeymen of Nazism, Wiesenthal was able to keep the crimes of the Third Reich in the limelight, and allow a little of it to shine upon himself in the process. He was the Man Who Would Not Forget, the Detective with Six Million Clients, the lone hunter with a mission to bring to justice a regime of unquestionable evil. Such an image, such a story, was irresistible to the media, and in helping to perpetuate it—even through the occasional use of tall tales—Wiesenthal performed a valuable service to the world.

But the reality of hunting Nazis is far more mundane, and its history is largely shameful. In 1942 the United Nations War Crimes Commission was formed by the Allies to create a list of "ringleaders" to be tried for mass murder when the war was over. It took the Commission two years to complete its work, by which point it had come up with a grand total of only 189 names. As if this wasn't embarrassing enough, it had to be pointed out to the list's compilers that they had forgotten to include Adolf Hitler.

· But the Allies showed little interest in devoting valuable resources to tracking down war criminals in the aftermath of World War II, and even less as the distance from the conflict grew greater. There was no one reason for their absence of drive, although laziness and inefficiency loom large, and later sheer political expediency, for in the fight against Communism, my enemy's enemy became my friend. German operations on the Eastern Front provided the West with a valuable information bank upon which to draw, and it is common knowledge that German scientists were recruited for the rocket program in the United States.

Eventually, though, the United States was spurred—perhaps even shamed—into acting. The result of pressure from both inside and outside the United States was the establishment in 1979 of the Office of Special Investigations, tasked with investigating Nazi and Imperial Japanese crimes of persecution, and removing the perpetrators of such crimes to countries with criminal jurisdiction over their alleged offenses. But the individuals they were pursuing were already beginning to die by 1979, and the OSI—and later the HRSP—was instructed to work "as fast as you responsibly can" to bring its quarry to justice before mortality intervened, a task that was compared to running a mile in four minutes one year, then in three fifty-five the next, then three fifty . . .

It is a curious fact, but war crimes cases are generally a direct inversion of most standard criminal investigations. The latter begin with a crime and end with a suspect, but war crimes inquiries usually begin with a suspect and end with proof of an atrocity. Names of wanted individuals would be checked against the records of the immigration services by birth date and variations in spelling, since the Cyrillic alphabet offered many possibilities for error or deliberate obfuscation. When hits, or potential hits, came back, the OSI would determine whether the suspect in question was still alive and then, usually through a non-identifying phone call, check on the health of the person. Once it was confirmed that he or she was still living, and reasonably compos mentis, an OSI investigation number would be assigned, and a team of attorneys and historians would commence pulling apart the details of his or her life. Record checks would be requested from Berlin or the ZS, the Central Office of the State Justice Adminstrations for the Investigation of National Socialist Crimes in Ludwigsburg. These would include, where available—since the Nazis did their best to burn most of their paperwork in the final months of the war—the records of the actions of units of the German military; while individual soldiers and officers might not be named, it was possible to connect a soldier to the crimes of his unit through its presence at a particular location, and its actions while it was there.

After the justification for a full OSI investigation was established, a file would be opened, and at that point the office would begin to engage personally with the suspect. Originally a letter would be sent, requesting attendance for an interview, which was noncompulsory. But after a couple of years, the question was raised of why the OSI was effectively warning suspects in advance, and from then on "knock and talk" interviews became the standard approach. At first most of those interviewed were surprised to find Justice Department officials—sometimes accompanied by a discreetly armed investigator—on their doorsteps, for the unheralded establishment of the OSI had passed them by. But very quickly the OSI's existence became common knowledge, and the section was attacked on a regular basis in the newspapers of the Baltic-American and Ukrainian communities for allegedly collaborating with the Soviets, to the extent that one Ukrainian-American newspaper even published a list of investigators' names.

Over the thirty-five years of its existence, the OSI succeeded in winning more cases against suspected Nazi war criminals than all other governments in the West combined. It was, as Marie Demers recognized, still not enough. She had joined the OSI as an intern, and now, despite her relatively youthful looks, had been working with it for more than fifteen years, transitioning to the so-called legacy Nazi team after the formation of the HRSP. That team now numbered only four attorneys, two historians—Toller was one, despite any appearance to the contrary—and a handful of paralegals, but could draw on additional personnel when necessary.

Those instances, though, were becoming increasingly rare. The old Nazis were slipping through their fingers one by one, like the last grains of sand held in a fist. The apprehension of Engel and Fuhrmann had been the result of two years of meticulous investigation. In the entire history of the OSI and the HRSP, only one prosecution had ever resulted from a tip-off: that of Jacob Tannenbaum, a *kapo* at the Görlitz concentration camp who had brutalized his fellow Jews, and was recognized by a former inmate. The reality of their work would have made poor drama.

It was also hugely frustrating. She had been warned about that on her first day. "You'll require a high frustration threshold," she was told, but she really had no idea of what was meant by it, not then. So many had evaded them, and at the lowest points it sometimes seemed that Europeans were engaged in a form of collective denial of responsibility, demonstrating an unwillingness to step up and do their duty that bordered on the shameful.

And now they had Engel and Fuhrmann, both discovered living about a two-hour drive from each other, Engel in Augusta and Fuhrmann farther south in Durham, New Hampshire. Fuhrmann, who had served as a guard at Sachsenhausen, gave his interrogators nothing. He was a name, rank, and serial number type. He also had few family ties in the States. Two wives had predeceased him, and one son. He was entirely estranged from his other children, all daughters. The evidence against him was solid, and the Germans were confident of a successful prosecution. Fuhrmann fought the extradition proceedings against him more as a matter of course than anything else, accepting the role that he was required to play without complaint. He lost his appeal with little more than a shrug.

Engel was different. His wife was still alive, and he had a large family. He was active in various local organizations, and was an advocate for the rights of seniors. His prosecution sent fissures running through his community and even his own family, creating complex, angry divisions among those who believed him guilty, those who blindly declared him innocent, and a strange, gray collective of those who could not make the connection between the lively, jovial old man they knew and the SS guard alleged to have marched naked men and women to a pit at Lubsko before shooting them in the back of the neck. Somehow they managed to accept the guilt of the younger man while regarding the older as a different being entirely.

So Engel had battled them all the way. While denaturalization and deportation prosecutions were civil, not criminal, they required prosecutors to reach an evidentiary standard that had been ruled by the Supreme Court as "substantially identical" to the criminal standard of beyond reasonable doubt. With each battle won against Engel, the opposing forces simply moved on to the next field, from district to circuit court, from the Board of Immigration Appeals to the federal appellate system, until finally only the Supreme Court remained, at which point Engel appeared to concede, possibly because he had exhausted his finances. But then came the call from his lawyer, and the offer to name names. Engel would sell out other war criminals in order to remain in the United States.

The first name he had given them was that of Marcus Baulman. Baulman was not who he claimed to be, according to Engel. No, Baulman was really Reynard Kraus, who had learned his trade with a one-month assistantship to Mengele at Auschwitz before moving to Lubsko. Under Mengele's careful tuition, Kraus had learned how to euthanize children: an intravenous injection of the barbiturate Evipal into the right arm to put the child to sleep, followed by 10 cc of chloroform injected directly into the left ventricle of the heart. The children barely twitched before they died. Now the HRSP wanted Marcus Baulman. They wanted him very badly indeed.

And Demers was determined to be the one to bring him in.

CHAPTER

XXIV

Rachel and Sam arrived shortly after Parker finished talking with Walsh. He had spent the intervening time walking, trying to balance the pain that it caused him with his desire to spur his body toward a full recovery. He despised how slow he had become almost as much as he despised the biweekly physical therapy sessions—treadmill, stretching, water baths—designed to help him, not so much for the discomfort they caused but because he hated being surrounded by those like himself. He did not want to see his own weakness reflected in others. He hated the headaches, and the medication, and the scars, and the wounds, and he transferred some of this rage to the streets he now walked.

He had always struggled with Bangor as a city. Attempts were being made to breathe life back into downtown, but the Bangor Mall had sucked it dry years before, and the damage would always be hard to undo. It was better now than it had ever been before, but it lacked the students and artists who had sustained Portland's center when the Maine Mall had similarly annihilated the business district along Congress Street.

Eventually he came to St. John's Church on York Street, built in the mid-nineteenth century to accommodate the hordes of Irish immigrants who had come to the city. He had not set foot in a church since the shooting. He could not say why. He had been raised Catholic, and still occasionally attended Mass, but mostly he just dropped by a church if he felt the need to offer a prayer for Rachel and Sam, or simply to think in silence. Now he felt himself drawn to the old redbrick building with its great spire and its ornate Tyrolean stainedglass windows, perhaps because it reminded him of St. Dominic's in Portland, one of the oldest and most beautiful churches in the state, until it was closed by the diocese in 1997. His grandfather had taken him to worship there at Christmas and Easter, when he felt the occasion justified something grander than St. Maximilian's in Scarborough, and so, in Parker's mind, redbrick churches were associated with his grandfather, and his memories of the old man were entirely fond.

He stepped inside St. John's, blessed himself, and took a seat halfway up the aisle. It was empty, and he was alone. St. John's was not an austere environment, not with its onyx, bronze, and marble, its ornately decorated walls and ceilings, its sculpted Stations of the Cross. No, this was an architectural hymn to God.

He asked himself what he was expecting: to feel the immanence of the Divine, to be bathed in His radiance? He had no answer, and no one to whom he could turn to speak aloud his thoughts. He had no father, no mother. Behind him stretched only a column of the dead.

Parker closed his eyes, and in his mind he was once again seated by a lake, but this time his dead daughter was not with him, and from the distant hills a wolf howled, registering his presence once again in that place. While he sat in St. John's, his mind re-created a world beyond this one, and he tried to connect the two environments. He was not mad, and neither were his memories the products of trauma, anesthetic, or postoperative medication. He believed that he had, however briefly, and while either dead or dying, found himself stranded between realms. He knew this because of what he kept in a pocket of his jacket. He reached for it now, his eyes still closed, and felt it between his fingers.

He removed it and held it in the palm of his right hand, his thumb following its textures and striations.

It was a single black stone, damaged on one side. He had held just such a stone when he sat on the bench by the lake in that in-between world, trying to choose whether to embrace physical dissolution or return to the agony of existence, and when he finally threw the stone, that fragile world had shattered. It had been there with him when his dead daughter held his hand, the warmth of her like a brand against the chill of his own skin, for in that place she was restored to light, and he was the faded one. And he was clutching it in his fist when he returned to consciousness in the hospital in Portland, and no one could tell him how it had come to be there.

It was his proof, and his alone.

He opened his eyes. The church remained empty. He still had questions, but no doubts. His thumb continued to brush the stone as he prayed for Sam and Rachel, and for those whom he loved. Finally, he offered up a prayer for Amanda Winter and her mother, although he could not have said why, beyond his knowledge of the daughter's illness, and a feeling of disquiet about the mother. When he was done, he placed the stone back in his pocket, knelt, blessed himself once again, and left.

His pain had dulled. The brief respite had done him some good.

———

THE HANDOVER OF SAM was brusque, like the delivery of a hostage, although he could see that Rachel was worried about him, and she found a moment to ask if he was sure that he would be okay with Sam (and unspoken, and more to the point, that Sam would be okay with him). He assured her they'd both be fine. He even managed to ask after Jeff, Rachel's boyfriend, without retching. Rachel spotted the effort that it required.

"You almost sounded sincere there," she said.

"I am sincere," he replied. "I think."

He didn't wish Jeff ill. Jeff was an asshole, but there was a lot of that around, and if he condemned everyone who was sometimes an asshole then the prisons would be full and the streets empty. In fact, Parker was pretty certain that, in such a brave new world, he'd have a cell all to himself.

He and Sam waited for Rachel to drive away, then Sam got in the front seat of the Mustang beside her father.

"You know your mom likes you to ride in back," said Parker.

"I know. You're going to let me ride up front, though. With you."

"Really?"

"Yes."

And, figuring that the issue had been dealt with, he pulled away from the curb.

———

THE DETECTIVE'S RELATIONSHIP WITH his daughter was a construct of great complexity, of nuance and shadow. He could never see as much of her as he might have wished, and yet curiously he did not miss her as deeply as he might have under other circumstances, for she was always with him. In that, he thought, she was like his first daughter, his dead daughter. He carried Sam in his heart, and when he conversed with her in her absence—alone at night, or when driving along I-95 with the music down low—he heard her responses as assuredly as if she were seated next to him.

And while there was much about Sam that he did not know—and this was both a consequence of the physical distance between them and the natural gap in comprehension between a father and a growing daughter—he also felt that he understood her in ways that her mother did not. The workings of Sam's mind sometimes baffled Rachel, but not Parker. Sam was a child of the unsaid, and perhaps because they were away from each other for such long stretches, he had learned to read the spaces, the gaps, and the silences; to listen to what was unspoken as much as to what was offered aloud. She said nothing without thinking about it first, which meant trying to trace the thought processes that had led to whatever pronouncement finally emerged. He regarded her as strangely fearless, and even her concerns for his health were tempered by an apparent conviction that all would be well, in part because she willed it to be so.

She was older than her years—Rachel, too, saw that—but this did not manifest itself as a self-aggrandizing precociousness. She simply came across as unusually self-possessed, gifted with stillness, quiet, and the ability to watch and absorb without involving herself. But, when she chose, she could inhabit the role of a child, even if Parker always felt that she was often playing to the gallery when she did so. On the drive back to Boreas, though, she was unself-consciously herself—or herself as a six-year-old—entertaining him with a stream of observations, questions, and non sequiturs that took in everything from the height of fencing in relation to cows to how badly everyone must have smelled at the end of the first installment of *The Hunger Games*, which she had watched on Netflix with a babysitter, and of which she had subsequently denied all knowledge to her mother in order to protect the guilty.

They stopped along the way to buy supplies, and it was dark by the time they reached the house. Sam liked preparing pizza, so they made and rolled their own dough, divided each pizza into four sections, and experimented with toppings. They ate outside, wrapped up warm against the sea breeze, the whiteness of the breaking waves like hope made manifest in darkness, the sound and movement of them like that of living creatures. Later Sam fell asleep on the couch while her father read and listened to music. He carried her up to the room that he had set aside for her use and carefully undressed her, although she remained lost to the world throughout. He left a light on by the door, and another in the hall, in case she needed to use the bathroom during the night.

Then he went to his own bed, and slept more soundly than he had in months.

XXV

The wind died. The night was still. The breaking of the waves was a distant thing now, and in their retreat they sounded a whisper of warning.

In the darkness, Sam awoke. The dead daughter stood at the end of her bed.

Sam rose on her elbows. She looked at the being in the shadows and yawned. She had been dreaming. It was a good dream.

"You don't have to stay," she told the dead daughter. "I'm here now. I'll keep him safe."

She fell back on her pillow and was instantly asleep again.

The dead daughter turned away, and was gone.

XXVI

S teiger had lunch in a secluded corner booth of an all-you-can-eat buffet. He liked buffet restaurants because their clientele allowed him to blend in easily, especially at lunch and dinner when there was a high turnover on the tables. With his straw hat pressed low on his forehead he could almost pass for normal, and few other customers ever gave him a second look in these places, so focused were they on the plates before them. As for the food, well, Steiger didn't really care. He suffered from a number of ailments and impairments, including both hyposmia and hypogeusia—decreased abilities to smell and taste. Only very rich and spicy dishes impacted on his senses, but he couldn't eat them due to his delicate guts. Food for Steiger was purely functional. It was necessary fuel, and he consumed it without either joy or displeasure.

Now he sat with his back to the wall, a cup of lousy coffee growing cold before him. The check had been brought to his table, but he wasn't ready to leave yet. The noise of the restaurant and the ugliness of its décor allowed him to retreat into himself. It gave him space to think.

The identity of the man living next to Ruth Winter was now known to him, and Steiger was troubled by his presence there. His instructions were to observe and not to intervene, not yet, but this man Parker was potentially dangerous. Who knew what the Winter woman might be sharing with him? Nevertheless, Steiger's attempts to convince the one Amanda Winter knew as the Jigsaw Man of the risks involved in leaving Parker alive had proved fruitless. He was too busy playing his games with the police. Dead families, burning houses: Steiger would have counseled against all of it, had he been asked, but the Jigsaw Man was both client and accomplice, which made Steiger a compromised employee. Steiger also knew that the Jigsaw Man was deliberately freezing him out, making abundantly clear his continued unhappiness with what had been done to the Tedesco woman down in Florida.

Someone nudged Steiger's table in passing, causing his coffee to slop into his saucer and splash on the Formica. Steiger reacted with a jerk of his head, and briefly stared into the face of a middle-aged man carrying a plate of salad. Their eyes met, and the other man quickly looked away. Gazing into Steiger's eyes was like peering into a pair of sump ponds. Still, Steiger was more amused than annoyed. Who came into a buffet restaurant and ate the salad? Any nutritional value had probably been scoured from the leaves and raw vegetables anyway. They had the artificial regularity of decorative plastic.

Steiger returned to the problem of Parker. The private detective was recovering from grievous injuries, but he remained the kind of individual who was driven to act on behalf of others. If Ruth Winter revealed to him the truth behind her retreat to Boreas, then Steiger was certain that Parker would take action. To do otherwise would make him complicit in a greater evil. So if Winter talked, Parker would become a threat.

But would she talk? The appearance of the body on the beach had been both fortunate and unfortunate: unfortunate in that it would have been better had Perlman not surfaced at all, but fortunate in that it had provided an opportunity for the Jigsaw Man to warn Ruth Winter of the importance of remaining silent, for her daughter's sake as much as her own. Winter was now well and truly frightened, of that Steiger had no doubt, yet the current situation could not persist. The central issue—Winter's daughter, Amanda—had not been resolved, which meant that, ultimately, either the mother would act, which would present enormous difficulties, or someone would be forced to move against her before that happened.

Thus Steiger's personal view was that it would be best for all concerned if Ruth Winter ceased to exist. The detective was another matter. If the opportunity presented itself, and it could be achieved without further complication, then Steiger would kill him too, regardless of what the Jigsaw Man wanted. It would be easiest, though, if Ruth Winter died before she had the opportunity to share anything significant with Parker. But this was not a move that Steiger could make without the consent of others.

He called from a phone booth by the men's room. He was going over the Jigsaw Man's head, but in his way the Jigsaw Man, too, was beholden to another. Steiger detected hardly a moment's hesitation before the voice on the other end of the line told him to do whatever he deemed necessary. But Ruth Winter was not to suffer. That was made clear to him. There was to be no repeat of the business in Florida.

On his way through the restaurant he passed the man who had jostled his table. Either he had piled high another plate with salad, or had not made much progress on the original portion, because it was largely untouched.

Steiger stopped at the table. The man looked up, his fork poised midway between his mouth and the plate. Steiger decided to spare him the effort of consuming any more of the salad. He leaned over, and spat heavily on the lettuce, tomatoes, and onions. His sputum, he noticed, bore worm-twists of blood.

"You ought to have apologized for spilling my coffee," he said.

He didn't wait for the man's reaction. He knew what it would be: none at all. He could see it in his face. Steiger was aware that he exuded an essence potent and vile from his pores, like the poisons secreted by certain amphibians to discourage predators, except that he had yet to encounter any threat worse than himself.

He walked to his car. The sun shone with growing warmth on the parking lot. Steiger's guts hurt. They always hurt after food. Steiger knew that he was dying. He didn't need a doctor to tell him, and he wasn't about to submit his body to more suffering through needles and therapies. When the pain became too much to bear, he would end it all himself. For now, he could go on.

He opened the glove compartment, removed a fresh bottle of Mylanta, and drank half of it down. He still had a couple of Vicodin and Percocet in there as well, but he wanted to keep a clear head. The Mylanta helped some, although he suspected that the effects might be placeboic as much as actual. He thought back to the man who had struck his table. He should simply have let him be. There was no percentage in threatening him that way, just as there had been no point in making the Tedesco woman suffer so much. Perhaps, thought Steiger, he was simply growing ornery in his old age, or maybe a way to dull one's pain was to inflict it on another. Whatever. Like the Mylanta, it seemed to work, and that was enough for him.

He started the car and headed back to Boreas.

XXVII

Parker took Sam to Olesens for a late brunch, where Larraine made a fuss over her and Greg produced a pile of used children's books from some box in the basement, only a few of which Sam had read and all of which she was happy to accept as gifts, once it became clear that Greg didn't want money for them. Another thing Parker had noticed about his daughter, and which amused him, was that she was careful with money. She wasn't stingy—she would happily insist on buying ice cream or treats, and liked the sense of perceived authority that came with paying for other people's pleasures—but she was acutely conscious of value. She wouldn't have bought the books for herself, and was too young to feel obligated to pay for something that she didn't want, but free was free.

He watched her as she examined the books carefully, separating them into two piles: those to be read as soon as possible, and those that could wait—perhaps indefinitely in a couple of cases, judging by the expression of disapproval that crossed her face.

"Are the lady and the man married?" she asked, when she was certain that they were out of earshot.

"No, they're brother and sister."

"Oh. They *act* like they're married."

"But they're not."

"Because they're brother and sister."

"Yes."

"If they weren't brother and sister, would they get married?"

"I don't know. I have to say, it's kind of a strange question."

"I don't think it's strange," she said.

"Maybe not, then."

She seemed satisfied that her father had conceded a point to her.

"What do you want to do today?" he asked.

"Can we go and meet Amanda?"

He had told her about Amanda when he and Rachel were working out the details of where and when they'd meet in Bangor. He didn't think that Sam would have minded coming to Boreas for a few days even without the promise of another child's presence, but it certainly added some extra appeal to the visit.

"I'll call her mom, just in case," he said. "But I'm sure you'd be welcome whenever you'd like to go over."

"Good." She picked a collection of old *Peanuts* cartoons from the "to be read" pile. "I'm going to give Amanda this one."

"I think she'll like it."

"It's Snoopy. Everyone likes Snoopy. Do you have a pen?"

He took one from his pocket and handed it to her. Inside the cover of the book, she inscribed the words "To Amanda, From Sam," and added an *X*.

"But I'll tell her that Greg gave it to me for free," she concluded, when she was done.

"You don't have to do that."

"Yes, I do."

"If you think honesty is the best policy, then fine. You all finished?"

She picked up her books, the most urgent piled on top of the less so. Larraine gave her a cloth bag decorated with literary characters, thanked her for coming, and hoped that she'd come back before she left. Like royalty, or General MacArthur, Sam assured her that she would return, and she and her father stepped out into the sunlight. They were heading across the street to where he'd parked the Mustang when a car pulled away from the curb and passed slowly before them, preventing them from crossing. It was a brown Cadillac Sedan de Ville with white-wall tires, its windows slightly tinted. Parker caught a glimpse of the driver, a hat pressed low on his forehead. The car wasn't traveling fast, so he had no reason to complain about the driver's behavior. It simply struck him that he could easily have stopped to let them cross. It was what most people in town would have done. This car, though, bore Pennsylvania plates. Parker recalled an incident when he'd been wait-ing for a flight at the Philadelphia airport, and a man had cut the line at the newsstand to pay for a paper and gum. When the guy at the head of the line objected, the jumper responded with the immortal words "Hey, welcome to Philly!"

Beside him, Sam tightened her grip on his hand. He looked down to see her face wrinkled in distaste.

"Did you smell it?" she said.

"Smell what?"

"I don't know. Something icky."

He sniffed the air, but detected nothing.

"It was the car," said Sam.

"Really?"

The Cadillac hadn't been emitting any more fumes than might have been expected from a vehicle of its vintage. Actually, it had appeared to him to be well maintained.

"Daddy, it smelled bad."

He watched the Cadillac turn the corner, the silhouette of its driver just about visible as it headed north along Burgess Road, his head a darker patch behind the colored glass.

"If you say so. Anyway, it's gone now."

He checked twice before crossing, but the road was clear. They reached the far sidewalk, and headed for the municipal parking lot where he'd left his car. As the lot came into sight, Sam let go of his hand.

"I feel sick," she said, and with that she released a stream of milk and French toast onto the sidewalk. All that Parker could do was hold back her hair and let it come. When she was done, he found a tissue in his pocket and used it to wipe her mouth. Her face was very pale. Even her lips seemed more bloodless than before.

"You want to sit down?" he asked.

She shook her head.

"I'm okay."

"Where did that come from? Did you feel bad earlier?"

"No."

"You think it was the French toast?"

"No."

He looked down at the mess on the pavement. They weren't far from the Blackbird Bar & Grill, and the door was open. He brought her inside and sat her down at one of the booths in the bar, which was otherwise empty. Fred Amsel appeared from a back room, and Parker told him what had happened and asked for a bucket of water to clean off the sidewalk. Fred told him that he'd take care of it. He poured a Sprite for Sam, but did not add ice.

"The sugar will help," he said. "She's probably feeling light-headed."

Sam sipped the soda. Fred filled a bucket, sluiced down the sidewalk, then used a brush to wash any residue into the gutter. The color returned to Sam's face, and she assured her father that she was happy to get in the car so they could return to the house. Parker thanked Fred for his kindness, and offered to pay for the soda, but he knew that no cash would be accepted. They got back to the car without any further incident, but he kept the windows rolled down on the ride back to Green Heron Bay.

Parker suggested that perhaps they should leave the visit to Amanda until the next day, but Sam would hear none of it.

"I'm fine, Daddy," she said. "It was the smell that made me sick. That man in the car, he smelled bad. He smelled *real* bad. . . ."

CHAPTER

XXVIII

Sam seemed fully recovered by the time they returned to the house at Green Heron Bay, but Parker insisted that she take it easy for an hour before he brought her to meet Amanda Winter. She did so reluctantly; her mood improved only slightly by being given relatively unlimited access to Netflix on her father's laptop.

While she lay on the couch watching an episode of *Cow and Chicken*, Parker went outside and thought about the brown Cadillac, and his daughter's reaction to it. Her vomiting could have been a consequence of travel and excitement, he supposed, although Sam generally boasted the constitution of a young horse. He himself hadn't felt any unease at the sight of the car, and he was sensitive to such things—acutely so. But he acknowledged that he had been left weakened by recent events, and none of his responses were as sure as before.

He called Gordon Walsh, but the call went straight to voice mail. He left a message with details of the car and its license plate number, and asked Walsh, as a favor, to run the vehicle through the system. He was curious, and nothing more, not yet. He checked on Sam once again, then went to his room. He worked on strengthening his grip for awhile before reading the *New York Times*. He must have dozed off, for when he woke there was a message on his phone from Cory Bloom requesting that he call her, and Sam was standing at his bedroom door.

"I'm ready," she said.

He didn't bother asking her again how she was feeling. He knew that it would only annoy her. In that way, she was like her mother. As for Cory Bloom, he would return her call as soon as Sam was safely with Ruth Winter and her daughter.

"Then let's go," he said.

————

PARKER STOOD WITH RUTH and watched their respective daughters make their way across the sand toward the rock pools that now lay exposed by the outgoing tide. The girls wore loose windbreakers and brightly colored waterproof boots. The sky was clear, and the sun gave some warmth despite the seemingly ever-present breeze. Fearless little purple sandpipers hopped among the rocks at their farthest point, where the waves still broke upon them, the winter yellow of the birds' legs now almost entirely gone.

"You say she was ill?" asked Ruth.

"French toast."

"That'll do it, you eat enough of it. I'll keep an eye on her, though—both eyes. They won't be out of my sight. Speaking of which . . ."

She buttoned her coat to go and join Sam and Amanda.

"Call me if there's a problem," said Parker. "I won't be far away."

"You going back to your house?"

"No, I have some errands to run in town. Shouldn't take too long."

"Well, maybe you'd like to join us for dinner later? Sixish?"

"That would be great. I'll pick up dessert."

"Don't worry about it. We have enough ice cream here to start a business."

He had a sudden impulse to kiss her cheek in farewell, although it quickly passed. It was not a manifestation of desire. She was a good-looking woman, but he felt no particular attraction to her, and saw no evidence that she felt any differently toward him. No, it would have been a gesture almost of reassurance, or an invitation to her to share with him whatever it was that was troubling her. He watched her walk after the children, and his eyes moved on to the place on her right doorpost where the mezuzah had been. Green Heron Bay and Mason Point were similar in size and geographic features. He followed the shoreline with his gaze. If he squinted, he could almost picture a body stretched upon it, like an offering from the sea.

There was no evidence that Boreas had been Bruno Perlman's ultimate destination. Neither had Parker any reason to believe that, if Perlman had been on his way to the town, Ruth Winter was someone with whom he might have wished to speak. All he knew was that she cared enough about her faith to affix the mezuzah to her door, and if it was important to her to put it up in the first place, then she wouldn't have taken it down again lightly.

He went to her front door to check if the mezuzah had been restored, but it had not. The holes left by the nails were still there. He lifted his right index finger and touched the space where the little vessel had been. Epstein had once recited to him the blessing required upon fixing a mezuzah, when he was explaining to Parker the importance of such matters. His brief Internet search, after he noticed Ruth Winter had taken the mezuzah down, had reminded him of it: "Blessed are You, Lord Our God, King of the Universe, Who sanctified us with His *mitzvot*, and commanded us to affix a mezuzah."

Why would someone consciously choose to disobey something that she appeared to regard as a mitzvah, a commandment? It was possible, even likely, that some prosaic explanation might offer itself. The mezuzah could have fallen off or become damaged, in which case a scribe would have been required to make the necessary repairs. He could almost hear Ruth Winter's previous hollow excuse for its absence: *"I didn't much care for it. . . ."*

He felt that she would lie to him again if confronted about it, and he realized that he had already convinced himself she was hiding knowledge. No, not hiding, but lying by omission, by silence. And she was frightened. He had a sense for it. It was this fear that made him want to reach out to her, as much for her daughter's sake as for her own.

Parker left the porch and descended to the sand. Ruth had joined Sam and Amanda over at the rocks, sending the sandpipers fleeing. They stood out darkly against the sky, and he had the urge to go to them, to take his daughter by the hand and lead her away from this woman and her child.

But he did not. Instead he headed for his car. He had decided not to call Cory Bloom, but to visit her in person since he was going to be in town anyway. He had not yet made up his mind whether to mention his concerns about Ruth Winter. By the time he reached his car, he had decided to hold his peace for now. Perhaps he would talk to Ruth after dinner.

Perhaps.

―――――

DESPITE HER MESSAGE, CORY Bloom didn't seem particularly pleased to see Parker appear at the door of her office. He supposed that he ought to have kept a lower profile with her, but then he was used to a certain kind of reaction to his presence. It came with the territory, and if he started worrying about it, then he'd never have left the house. Officer Preston came out of a small kitchen carrying a cup and a muffin. She didn't look pleased to see him either, but then her default expression was one of pained displeasure, as though someone had recently forced her to lick a succession of batteries.

"Can I come in?" he asked Bloom. "Or should I just loiter outside with intent?"

Bloom relented. Preston didn't. He didn't much care either way.

"Take a seat," said Bloom, indicating a chair in front of her desk. "I'll be right with you."

He took the chair, but was conscious that Preston hadn't moved from her position by the kitchen door. Bloom noticed her too, and shot a "Yeah, what?" look over Parker's shoulder, combined with spread arms. Just to amuse himself, Parker turned to Preston and mimicked the gesture and the expression. He saw himself burning in Preston's eyes, and made a mental note not to go over thirty within the town limits for the duration of his time there. When he faced Bloom again, she was staring exasperatedly at him.

"I can see why someone tried to shoot you," she said.

"They didn't just try. They *did* shoot me."

"Well, if you've got names, I think Officer Preston would like to shake their hand."

She returned to the paperwork on her desk, signing her name at the bottom of a series of forms and requisition orders.

"I hope she doesn't mind digging first," said Parker, and the pen froze for a moment before resuming its movements. He didn't interrupt her, but kept his left hand down by his side, slowly clenching and unclenching his fist. He'd noticed some improvement that afternoon: he'd been able to hold the grip strengthener at full tension for longer than he'd yet managed since the shooting.

She finished writing, put the papers to one side, then leaned forward and clasped her hands on the desk before her.

"Do you want coffee?"

"Will Officer Preston be making it?"

"Probably."

"Then I'll pass."

Parker waited.

"It looks like whatever favors you called in worked," said Bloom. "The chief medical examiner and her deputy are still tied up with the Oran Wilde business, but Bruno Perlman's body was transferred yesterday evening to the ME's office in Augusta, and an autopsy was performed this morning by Dr. Robert Drummond, who is first on call when the ME or her deputy is tied up or on leave. I spoke to him on Skype. He looks about twelve years old, but he's good."

"How good?"

"Very, if his lectures are anything to go by. I got one on drowning. Apparently determining if someone has died by drowning is more complicated than I'd really like it to be, and he gave me ten minutes on the tests that should be done in order to establish, and I quote, 'with any degree of medicolegal confidence,' that drowning was involved. Then he lost me at 'intravascular fat globules,' to be honest. But it's enough to know that, under normal circumstances, we'd be waiting on the results of a full toxicological screening, histologic analyses of all organs, and something called a diatom test before any pronouncement could be made."

"Algae," said Parker.

"What?"

"Diatoms are algae. Little unicellular plants. They're found in water, and their concentrations vary according to, I guess, temperature, mineral content, acidity, and whatever else affects water. So you can tie a body to a particular area of water, and a particular time, through analysis of the diatom concentrations in tissue."

Bloom was staring at him. He shrugged.

"Call it gene memory."

"*So . . .*" she continued, after a suitable pause, "we would have been waiting for those results if it wasn't for this."

She pulled a sheet of paper from a file, and passed it to Parker. It was a pretty-good-quality print of a skull X-ray. He'd have spotted the mark even if it hadn't been circled. It stood out as a small dark vertical against the pallor of the skull, just above the socket of the right eye.

"That's the supraorbital foramen," said Bloom. "See, I know stuff too."

"Did Dr. Drummond tell you that?"

"Yes, but at least I was listening."

"What does he think it is?"

"I got another lecture when I asked," said Bloom. "Did I mention that Dr. Drummond, in addition to being good, is also cautious?"

"I took it as a given. Let me guess: after he'd prevaricated for a while, he told you that it could have been made by a blade. But you'd probably already established that yourself."

"I didn't want to show off. He found other marks inside the orbital fissure—not as pronounced as that one, but still visible. They don't show up as well on the copies."

Parker returned the print to her. He didn't need to be given any more photos, and he didn't need Bloom, Drummond, or anyone else to tell him what had happened to Bruno Perlman, probably before he died.

"What kind of blade was it?" he asked.

"Drummond thinks it was surgical: a scalpel of some kind."

"Did it kill him?"

"No. Drummond believes Perlman was still alive when he went into the water, but there probably wouldn't have been much left of his eye. Drummond's report has gone to the state police. I'm expecting them here within the hour. I just thought you'd like to hear it from me first."

He thanked her, and stood to leave. Bloom returned the print of the skull to her file.

"I appreciate your advice and your help," she said. "It was—"

But when she looked up again, Parker was already gone.

CHAPTER

XXIX

Parker drove to Green Heron Bay, walked to his bedroom, and reached behind the big closet that faced his bed. His fingers found the butt of the gun taped to the wood, and wrenched it free. The weapon was already loaded, although without a bullet in the chamber. He had hidden the gun away when he first arrived at the house, although he could not say why. It was a licensed firearm, and he had more cause than most to feel that a gun might be necessary for his protection. Those who had shot him were themselves dead, as were the ones who had sent them to dispatch him, but such acts of vengeance left trailing tendrils, and their stings could hold their potency for lifetimes, generations.

Yet still he had not wanted to look upon the gun, and had rarely touched it since coming to Boreas. Now he held it in his right hand, and the grip and weight were instantly familiar. He went back downstairs, unearthed the cleaning kit from the storage area beneath the stairs, disassembled the weapon, cleaned and oiled its component parts, then reassembled it. And in putting it together again it felt to him that he was also piecing back something deep inside himself, an element of his being that had been mislaid but not lost. When he was finished, he tucked the gun into the waistband of his trousers. They fitted him more loosely than before, and he had gone down two notches on his belt.

Two was comfortable, if slightly less snug than he might have wished, while three was too tight. With the gun in place, his trousers now sat perfectly. He wondered if he should take it as a sign.

He changed into a clean shirt. Like his trousers, his shirts didn't fit as well, but in this case the looseness served to hide the gun. He walked outside, closed the front door behind him, and looked upon the waves. The tide was coming in again, and while the sky remained clear, the sea appeared to have taken on a darker tone. He had always loved the sea, had loved it ever since his first memory of his mother and father taking him north to Scarborough to meet his grandfather. He recalled walking on Ferry Beach with the old man—for his grandfather had always appeared old to him but not, strangely, as old as his wife, a strange, near-silent woman who simmered with disappointment and regret. Parker had never spoken his feelings about her aloud, but he remembered being secretly, shamefully glad when she died and, as he grew older, he believed that his grandfather, although bereaved, might have felt her passing as a kind of blessing, an easing of the burden on both of them.

Parker felt the sand beneath his feet, and for a moment he was a boy again, his grandfather beside him. And so convinced was he of the old man's presence that he closed his eyes, and his right hand reached out and tested the air, and he experienced a twinge of disappointment when it made no contact with his shade. Yet still he walked with him in his memory, and heard his grandfather's voice telling tales of Scarborough, and of the violence of its origins. Parker had been fascinated as a boy by tales of cowboys and the Old West, and it delighted him that he could walk in places where natives and settlers had fought and died, their blood leaching into the ground so that the memory of it was retained in the very atoms of the earth. Scarborough even boasted a Massacre Pond, where Richard Hunnewell and eighteen other men were slaughtered in 1703, and a Garrison Lane, after the fortress built at Prout's Neck at the start of the eighteenth century. Curiously, these seemed

more real to Parker than Old Fort Western in Augusta, the oldest surviving wooden fort in New England. Oh, he had been entranced by it,
and had loved to visit—the fort was a compulsory stop during their
family vacations in Maine—yet the images he had re-created in his
head of the Scarborough settlements were more visceral, more immediate. Old Fort Western had to be shared with others, but the shadow-
Scarborough was his alone. It lived in him and he, when he walked
through the physicality of its present incarnation, lived in it.

He opened his eyes again. To his left was the Winter house. Lights
burned in its downstairs windows. He began walking toward it. Already
he had ceased to notice the gun at his back.

XXX

The two detectives from the Major Crimes Unit of the Maine State Police arrived in Boreas shortly after Charlie Parker left Cory Bloom's office. The detectives were named Tyler and Welbecke, and were based out of Belfast. Both were female, and only slightly younger than Bloom herself. Tyler was the chattier of the two, Welbecke the more reserved, but Bloom didn't pick up bad vibes from either of them. As was now obligatory whenever two or more cops were gathered together, talk turned to Oran Wilde. Tyler and Welbecke were about the only detectives in the MCU who hadn't been dragged into the investigation and search. Initially, said Tyler, they'd been kind of pissed at being out on the periphery, but now the media was starting to ask how one teenager suspected of five killings could continue to evade the combined might of Maine's finest, and consequently Tyler and Welbecke were among the few currently out of range of that particular shitstorm.

Together the three women went over the paperwork accumulated so far, which wasn't a whole lot, and then Cory Bloom accompanied them as they looked at the parking lot where Bruno Perlman's vehicle had been found, and the beach at Mason Point. By now the light was fading. The sea was dark, darker than Cory Bloom could remember seeing it in many months, so that it seemed slowly to be contaminating the sky. Beside her, Tyler shivered.

"Grim place to wash up," she said.

Bloom took in the strand, trying to look at it through fresh eyes. She supposed that Mason Point wasn't the prettiest stretch of beach in Maine, but in summer it was okay. It was just one of those places that needed people to bring it alive—living people, that is. A corpse was never going to do much for it.

"It's not so bad," she said. "Anyway, I don't think it mattered to Bruno Perlman."

"No, I suppose not."

Welbecke spoke up. She had said very little since arriving in Boreas, preferring to let Tyler do most of the talking, and interjecting only to clarify points. She was more attractive than Tyler, but in a hard way, and she exuded tension. Bloom guessed that she probably didn't have many friends. She was equally threatening to both sexes.

"When did Charlie Parker get involved in all this?" she asked.

Bloom tried to detect the nuance behind the question. Dislike? No, that wasn't exactly it. There was a tone, though.

"A day or two after the body was found."

"What did he say?"

"He just raised some questions, that's all."

"Such as?"

Welbecke was persistent, Bloom would give her that. Bloom had nothing to hide, so she went through her dealings with Parker as thoroughly as she could.

"You let him examine the vehicle?" said Welbecke, and this time Bloom *really* didn't like her tone. "You let him potentially contaminate a crime scene?"

"If I hadn't," said Bloom, "then Perlman's body would still be in the undertakers' refrigerator. Nobody from MCU was in a hurry to come calling until Parker took an interest."

"You need a private investigator to tell you how to do your job?" said Welbecke.

"No, but you clearly do."

Welbecke made a movement with her neck, loosening it up in preparation for a fight. Bloom had only ever seen men do that before, and then largely the kind of oversized assholes who were looking for trouble but were too dumb to understand that telegraphing the fact gave their opponents time to react and take them out. It made Bloom respect Welbecke less, which gave her no pleasure. She didn't like seeing women behave as badly as men, and especially not cops. Law enforcement remained a profoundly sexist environment, and women would always be held to a higher standard than men under all circumstances, while simultaneously being expected to fail to reach it. She was just glad that her predecessor was no longer around to witness this pissing match. It would simply have confirmed all that Erik Lange and his cronies believed about women.

Tyler, who had been looking on in something like amusement, chose that moment to act as peacemaker.

"Whoa, whoa!" she said. "Nobody's pointing fingers here, okay?" She addressed herself to Bloom. "You'll just appreciate that there are certain ways of doing things, and this is all maybe a little unorthodox, you know? But I don't think any harm has been done, right, Stacey?"

Welbecke gave the impression that she thought harm might have been done in spades, but contented herself with looking away and offering a "Like I could give a shit" shrug to the world in general. Meow, thought Bloom: saucer of fucking milk for Detective Welbecke, please.

Tyler turned her back on her partner and walked toward the outcrop of land that gave Mason Point its name. Bloom followed, not caring to remain alone in Welbecke's company for longer than necessary. Tyler was watching the movement of the incoming tide. Even from where she stood, it was possible to detect the vicious crosscurrents.

"Do people swim here?" she asked.

"There are signs in the parking lot warning about the tides," said

Bloom. "We usually have a couple on the sand too, but they're being repainted at the moment, before the season kicks in."

Tyler took a deep breath of sea air.

"How long have you and Welbecke been partners?" asked Bloom.

"Couple of months. My turn: did you tell Parker about the marks on Perlman's skull?"

Bloom felt her face redden. She still didn't believe that she'd done anything wrong by keeping him informed, but strictly speaking she shouldn't have shared any of it with him. That was true of all that had occurred, which brought them right back to square one: a body frozen in a locker while the best part of thirty detectives in Maine, and more cops in adjacent states, chased a teenage ghost.

"Yes," she said. "I did."

"Welbecke is a by-the-numbers kind of person, you understand? And, technically, all that she said was right. Do you know Gordon Walsh over at MCU?"

"No."

"I guess you'd call him my mentor. He's good police. He's also the one Parker spoke to about Perlman. If Welbecke has a problem with anything that's occurred here, she'll have to bring it to Walsh, and he has a lot of respect for Parker. But she won't complain. She's just blowing off steam. Like I told you, she's by-the-numbers, but that's not always a bad thing, especially now that we may be opening a murder book on this."

"I understand."

And she did. Tyler was letting Bloom know that she'd take care of Welbecke, and in return Bloom needed to close down the channel of communication between Parker and herself.

"Does he live far from here?" asked Tyler.

"Just a couple of miles away, on the other side of town. He has one of two houses on Green Heron Bay."

"Who has the other?"

"A woman named Ruth Winter and her daughter."

"Local?"

"Almost: she's from Pirna. She moved here not long ago. Why do you ask?"

"Just curious."

"If you want to go out and talk to Parker, I can give you directions. It's easy to miss the turn for the bay, especially when it's getting dark."

"Tomorrow will be fine," said Tyler. "Right now, I'd like copies of all your paperwork, and then I'm going to check into my motel, take a shower, and go get dinner somewhere. Any suggestions would be welcome."

Bloom recommended a couple of places as they marched over to where Welbecke stood, then together the three women headed to their respective vehicles. Bloom led the way back to her office. She had made the required copies before the detectives arrived, in anticipation of the request, and all other relevant information was already in the system, so the handover didn't take long. Welbecke thanked Bloom as she left, and seemed to mean it. Bloom watched them drive away through the slats in her blinds. Preston joined her.

"How were they?" she asked.

"They were okay."

"Both of them?" said Preston. "The tall one looked like a bit of a bitch."

"No, she was okay too."

"Huh," said Preston, in a way that suggested the ways of the world never failed to surprise her.

"By the way," said Bloom, "if Mr. Parker calls again, either by phone or in person, you take a message, but tell him I'm not available."

"Understood. Is he in some kind of trouble?"

Bloom saw her own reflection in the window, and caught herself smiling.

"Mary, I think with him, trouble's a perpetual state of being."

XXXI

Ruth Winter looked surprised and flustered to see Parker at her door so soon. She was wearing an apron, and had flour on her hands.

"Sorry, I must be running a little late," she said. "The girls are watching TV, and I've just started making the pasta. You're welcome to come in, but dinner will be awhile. . . ."

She managed a smile, but it was clear that she didn't particularly relish the prospect of having to entertain him and prepare dinner at the same time. He didn't smile back.

"Can I talk to you for a moment?" he said. "In private."

He could hear the sound of the TV coming from the living room. A woman's voice was singing, but he couldn't identify the song. It sounded saccharine, and he thought it might be from a later Disney movie, one of those that had largely passed him by.

Winter nodded and stepped outside, closing the door behind her. She was wearing a sweater and jeans beneath her apron, but she shivered as the wind from the sea struck her.

"Is something wrong?" she asked.

His eyes went to the little holes on the doorframe.

"Why did you take down your mezuzah?" he said.

"What?"

"Your mezuzah. It was on the doorframe when I first met you, and then it was gone. I was wondering where it went?"

She bristled, but tried to retain her composure.

"There was a crack in the case, and I was worried about water getting in."

It was a different explanation from the last, a new lie, and he was a man who had been lied to so often that he could almost ascribe to untruths a color and a shape, the way certain synesthesic musicians gave form and hue to notes.

"Did you know Bruno Perlman?" he asked.

"Who?"

"Bruno. Perlman." He repeated the name slowly and distinctly. "He was the man whose body washed up at Mason Point."

"Why would I know him?"

The wrong answer, he thought, or the answer to a different question, but not the one that had actually been asked.

"Do you know who I am, Ms. Winter? Do you know what I did for a living?"

"Look, I'm sorry, but I don't have time for this."

She made a move for the door, but he blocked her way with his arm.

"What do you think you're doing?" she said.

"Helping you, if you'll let me."

"I don't need your help. I don't even know why you think that I might."

"I've been a private investigator for more than a decade," he said. "Before that, I was a police officer, and a detective."

"And?"

She wouldn't meet his eyes. She looked through the glass of the door to her kitchen. She just wanted to get back inside, and away from this man.

"I can tell when people are in trouble, when they're frightened, when they're hiding something. And when they're lying."

"Get your hand down," she said. Her voice trembled a little. "You're scaring me. I want you to leave now. If you need to take your daughter with you, then I understand, but I want you to go."

She reached under his arm to take the handle of the door. He didn't try to stop her.

"Bruno Perlman was murdered," he said. "Before he went into the sea, someone put a blade through his right eye. It didn't kill him—it seems that he died in the water—but it must have hurt like hell itself. It was an act of torture, probably designed to elicit whatever he knew. It takes a very particular individual to inflict that kind of pain on another."

Her hand froze on the door handle. She still refused to look at him. He didn't know where her gaze lay, only that it was elsewhere, directed within more than without.

He spoke softly. He was not trying to bully her, and he regretted that he had been forced to block her way into her home, but he needed her to listen, and he wanted to watch her as she listened. He wanted to be sure.

"This is what I think," he said. "Bruno Perlman was coming up here to see you. Maybe he'd been in contact by phone or e-mail. Perhaps he even sent you a letter—I hear people still do that sometimes. Someone intercepted him, brutalized him, and then left him to drown, but his body wasn't expected to wash ashore so soon, if ever. When you heard about the discovery of a man's body at Mason Point, you may have suspected that it was Perlman, or you may not, but you weren't about to take any chances. There was only the slightest possibility that a connection could be made to you through your shared faith, but it was enough to make you remove the mezuzah."

"I don't know what you're talking about," she said, but her words had all the weight of gossamer, and the wind threw them to the sand and the sky.

"If that's the case," Parker continued, ignoring her, "—and, as I've told you, it's what I think—then you probably already had reason to believe that Perlman was murdered before anyone else, and certainly before the mark of the blade was discovered during the autopsy. There is another possibility, of course."

She waited. Her eyes briefly fluttered closed.

"Go on," she said. "The sooner you finish, the sooner I can get back to my child."

"The other possibility is that you killed Perlman yourself. You arranged to meet him at the parking lot, stabbed him in the eye, then dragged him to the edge of the bluff and threw him into the sea. He wasn't a big man, and he might not have been expecting an attack from a woman, or you might have had an accomplice who did the hard work while you baited the trap. But that doesn't ring so true to me, and it's not what I sense from you. You're frightened—I'm certain of that—but not of your involvement in a crime being revealed. I think you're scared that whoever killed Perlman may come after you next, and your daughter too."

Now she turned to face him for the first time since he had begun speaking.

"Are you done?" she asked. She tried for boredom and contempt, and almost conjured up a good imitation of both, but failed at the last.

"Just about," he said. "If it's all right with you, I will take Sam home with me, because I believe that she's at risk in your company. You can have tonight to consider what I've said, because tomorrow I'm going to talk with Chief Bloom and tell her what I've just told you. It could be that I'm completely wrong about everything, but I'll let her decide after I've spoken to her."

He lowered his arm.

"If you'll bring Sam to me, I'll be on my way."

She opened the door, but paused before reentering her house.

"Why can't you just leave us in peace?" she asked.

"You're not at peace," he replied. "And you won't be until you tell the truth."

"Go fuck yourself," she said, "you and your sanctimonious bullshit."

"My daughter. Please."

She went inside, closing the door in his face. She reappeared after a minute or two, helping Sam into her coat, Amanda following behind them looking upset. Sam simply appeared puzzled. When she emerged, she took her father's hand and said good-bye to Amanda and her mother. Only Amanda replied, and then the door closed again and the light in the hallway was extinguished, leaving the porch bulb shining upon them. Parker and Sam broke its cocoon and headed down the steps to the beach.

"Why aren't we staying for dinner?" Sam asked. "Did you and Amanda's mommy have a fight?"

"We had a discussion."

"*Like* a fight?"

"A disagreement."

"It was a fight," said Sam, with conviction.

"What was the movie?"

"*Mulan*."

"Sorry you missed the end."

"It's okay, I've seen it before."

They walked on.

"Did Amanda's mommy do something bad?" asked Sam.

"Why would you say that?"

"Because you only fight with people who do bad things."

"No, she didn't do anything bad. I think she may be in trouble, but she's too scared to ask for help."

"Are you going to help her?"

"I'm going to try."

"Good."

Sam stumbled on the sand, and when he stopped to make sure that she was all right, he saw that she was looking at the small of his back, where the gun lay. He thought that his shirt was concealing it, but he figured that the wind might have revealed its shape beneath the material. His daughter did not remark upon it, but she remained silent for the rest of their walk home.

Once again Steiger stood on the dunes above the house, and watched Parker and the little girl depart. He had been feeling apprehensive all day, but could not pinpoint the source. He put it down to the fact that he was not yet in possession of all the information required to make a decision on how to act. Yes, he had been given permission to kill the Winter woman, but the problem of the detective still remained, and now he had a child with him. Steiger was not above killing children—Steiger was not above killing anything—but this whole business had already grown too fancy. Others had made it so. Steiger would have dealt with it differently from the start: kill Perlman, kill Tedesco, kill Winter, and vanish. He would not even have left bodies to be found.

But then Perlman's remains were washed ashore, and Oran Wilde became a pawn in the game. Steiger would not have chosen to go down that route, to take an already complicated situation and add further layers of complexity. It was, he thought, to do with degrees of intelligence. Steiger did not consider himself a stupid man, but neither did he believe himself to be brighter than he was. He had come to realize that there were those in the world who were so clever that they regarded simplicity as beneath them. If they had to connect two points, they invariably chose to do so by adding a third, making a triangle. The Jigsaw Man was just such an individual. As a consequence, Steiger had decided not to work with him again. Once this job was done, he would inform Cambion, who always acted as his intermediary in such business.

He could no longer see Parker and his daughter—he assumed that was who the girl was. They were lost in the gathering dimness between the two houses, and the farther away they got from him, so too did his agitation begin slowly to dispel. Parker, Steiger believed, was the cause of his disquiet. The man was uncommon, strange. He should have been dead. The detective was like a broken insect that continued to crawl across the floor, waiting for the second blow that would put it out of its misery. Steiger had shadowed him throughout the day, even following him to the police department in town. Steiger had dearly wanted to know what was being spoken of inside, and it was only good fortune— and, perhaps, instinct—that caused him to linger after the detective departed, so that he was nearby when the car carrying the two women arrived. Even without the telltale motor pool vehicle, he smelled them as detectives, and his concerns only increased as they followed the chief of police out to Mason Point.

Steiger didn't hang around. He made a call to the local undertaker, claiming to be a friend of Perlman's, and was informed that the body had been removed to Augusta for autopsy. After that, it was easy for him to make the final connection and surmise that something about Perlman's body had aroused the suspicions of the state police.

Steiger's shoes were almost submerged in the soft sand of the dunes. He shook them free, and sought firmer ground. He did not enjoy the proximity of the sea. He could not swim, and so the ocean had always been a threatening presence, a dark mass that called to him, inviting him to test himself against it, immersing himself inch by inch until finally he would no longer be able to feel the sand and stones beneath his feet, and he would drown.

Sometimes in his dreams, he would find himself floating in an infinity of black water—oddly safe, as long as he did not struggle—and slowly become aware that a presence was emerging from the depths below, ascending toward the surface, coming to consume him, and he would wake just before he saw it, before he felt its jaws close upon him, and he knew that neither did its form matter nor any physicality he might project upon it because it would always be the same in essence: it would be his own death.

The dunes, too, were a part of this threat: formed by the sea, and so to him neither land nor water, and composed of organic and inorganic matter, of that which had once lived and that which had no life at all. Seen from a distance, the dunes took the form of hidden vertebrae, as though they concealed beneath them a creature lost to time and memory, but one that, if woken, would want only what all such beasts want: to bite, to tear, to feed.

Steiger was, of course, insane.

Now this being of violence and hate, of envy and loneliness and loss, stood on the dunes and watched as Ruth Winter passed before the kitchen window below. He saw her put plates on the table and serve the food. He noticed that she did not eat much, and he wondered why she had not invited the detective and his daughter to stay for dinner. Some disagreement could have occurred between them, or it might simply have been that Amanda Winter had not gotten along with the detective's daughter, and it was decided by mutual consent that the playdate should be brought to an end.

He saw Amanda return to the living room while her mother remained at the kitchen table with a glass of red wine before her. She did not read, and no music carried to him from the room in which she sat, although he could hear the faint sounds of the television.

And so Ruth Winter stayed where she was, and Steiger watched her, unmoving, even as minutes became hours. He was capable of great stillness, of complete silence: it was the only way that a man such as he, one so blighted and benighted, could negotiate the world.

Finally, Ruth rose. She cleaned the glass. The noise of the television ceased, and the lamp in the living room went out. A bathroom light came on on the floor above. Ruth returned to the kitchen. She walked to the window and looked out at the dunes, and for a moment she might have been locking eyes with the man who had come to kill her, some primitive part of her acknowledging his presence while her conscious mind took no notice of it. Then she was gone, and the light was extinguished.

Steiger waited until all was quiet, until all was dark.

And then he descended.

CHAPTER

XXXIII

S am had gone to her room shortly after she and her father had eaten toasted sandwiches for dinner. He'd looked in to find her reading one of her new books. If she was unhappy with him for taking her prematurely from Amanda Winter's company, then she did not show it. When he checked on her a second time, she was already asleep beneath her sheets.

Parker read distractedly for a while. He was not tired. His mind kept returning to Ruth Winter. He knew that he could have handled their last confrontation better. He was out of practice. He checked his messages, but Walsh hadn't returned his call about the brown Caddy. When he turned out his light to go to sleep, he thought that he could hear voices calling to him through the white noise of the sea.

———

ALTHOUGH SAM WAS IN her bed, and the hours and minutes were ticking by on her bedside clock, she did not feel as though she had slept. It seemed to her that she simply tossed and turned, unable to find a comfortable position in which to rest, her body alternately too warm—which caused her to kick off her sheets—and then too cold. Her stomach hurt as well, and when she burped she could still taste stale French toast in her mouth despite what she had eaten and drunk since she had thrown up.

She supposed that she must have dozed off at some point, though, for the texture of the darkness had changed when she opened her eyes. It felt physically oppressive to her, almost tangible. She thought that she might even be able to reach out and grasp a handful of it, and feel it ooze through her fingers.

The dead daughter had returned, standing at the end of Sam's bed, her head bowed so that her hair might conceal the ruin of her face. Sam felt sorry for her, the way she felt sorry for anyone who was forced to endure a form of disability or physical disfigurement. She also understood that it had to be this way for the girl. When she crossed over to this world, she took the last form in which she had inhabited it when she was alive. Her beauty was for another place.

But Sam was also irritated. She had told the girl to go away, that she would look after their father, but now she had returned. Sam could order her to leave, of course, but she knew that the dead daughter wouldn't like it.

None of them ever did.

"I said—" Sam began, and then the dead daughter was gone. It took a moment for Sam to realize that she had moved to one of the windows, and was looking north. She had shifted position in less than the blink of an eye, but Sam was used to their ways. Now she saw that the dead girl was trembling, a shivering that commenced at her head and moved all the way to her toes, like a tightly coiled spring set in motion. Without shifting her gaze, she stretched out her left hand and crooked a finger at Sam.

come

The word was not spoken. There was no sound. It simply fell into Sam's head, like a pebble dropped into a pool.

Sam left her bed and joined the dead girl. She was careful not to touch her, or even brush against her. The dead burned coldly, and contact with them left marks on her that sometimes hurt for days. They also acted as emotional transmitters, broadcasting with an intensity that was painful to pick up, and Sam was a receiver beyond compare, for no one like her had walked the earth in a very long time. These bursts of feeling—anger, sorrow, fear, confusion—were enough to bring on headaches and nausea, not unlike what she had felt this morning when the nasty brown car drove past. Just before the French toast came back up, she wondered if she had unwittingly come in contact with the dead, as the experience was not dissimilar. But the car had been real, and her father had also seen it.

Her father saw other things too, oh yes, things that were both there and not there. He didn't understand why, not yet. Sam could have told him, but she knew the importance of remaining quiet, and not drawing attention to herself. . . .

Now Sam stood by the dead daughter. She could smell her. She didn't smell bad, just smoky. Sam knew her name—Jennifer—but she never thought of her by that name. The dead girl was both more and less than her father's first daughter, her own half sister. You couldn't pass over and not be transformed, not be changed utterly. She might have looked like a little girl, but she was much older inside. Clever. Dangerous, even, although not to Sam.

The drapes were drawn across the window. They were no obstacle to the dead daughter, but Sam had to move them. She did so carefully. The dead daughter was still shaking, and Sam took it as a warning. Through the gap she had created, she could barely discern the outline of the Winter house.

look

"I don't see anything."

look harder

Sam concentrated, and her eyes grew used to the dark. She picked out the south-facing front door of the house, the window of the living room, the second window halfway up the stairs—

There: a shape against the glass, pausing for an instant as though compelled to do so by forces unknown, framing himself for her. Her stomach gave a little lurch, and she tasted vomit again. The image of the brown car once again flashed across her mind, and the memory of the man's stink was so strong that she caught it as surely as if he were standing next to her, and not on the stairs of the Winter house.

"Daddy," she whispered, then again, louder: "Daddy!"

The dead daughter gripped her arm. The pain of her touch was so intense that it was all Sam could do not to yelp, and her head was filled with the unspoken words of her non-voice:

careful careful
he'll hear
the bad man will hear

CHAPTER

XXXIV

Steiger padded up the stairs, placing his feet as close as he could to the edges in the hope of minimizing any creaks. The wind had picked up in the last hour, buffeting the house, so noises already masked his progress, but there was a difference between the slight tapping of doors on frames, or the rattling of windows, and the purposeful tread of a foot upon a stair. People had died for not recognizing the distinction.

He wore lightweight blue plastic overalls to protect his clothing, and disposable gloves. A surgical mask covered the lower half of his face. He wasn't worried about being seen. He just wanted to ensure that he got as little blood as possible on his skin. His shoes were soft-soled, and he moved with a grace that belied his frame and appearance. His guts ached, though, and he'd finished the last of the Mylanta that afternoon. Once this final act was done, he would allow himself a couple of Vicodin and embrace the peace that it brought. For now, though, the pain spurred him on. The sooner the woman was dead, the sooner he could take the pills.

The walls, painted cream throughout, were largely bare, except for some pictures of flowers and sunsets that he thought had probably come with the house, and a handful of smaller photographs of Ruth Winter and her daughter, some of them housed in frames made from

Popsicle sticks and decorated by a child's hand. The carpet on the stairs was pale nylon—cheap, but durable.

He paused as he neared the topmost step. Amanda Winter's door was slightly open, and a night-light burned in an outlet. It cast the shapes of stars upon the wall above her bed. He could see one of her feet poking out from beneath the comforter. She shifted position as he watched, her breathing momentarily disturbed, and he wondered if he had intruded upon her dream, if her subconscious might have picked up on his presence and manifested it for her. Steiger had not lived for so long in such a dark trade as his without recognizing the importance of the atavistic.

But the girl did not wake. He heard her breathing return to normal. Three more doors stood before him. He had taken the trouble to research the layout of the house, for it was still listed on the Realtor's website. He knew that the mother's room was probably the largest: it lay kitty-corner from her daughter's. Beside it was the main bathroom. Opposite it was a spare room, just big enough to accommodate a small double bed.

Steiger had a gun beneath his arm: not the Mauser with which he had killed Lenny Tedesco—a forgivable piece of theater under the circumstances—but a lightweight Ruger .38 with the hammer concealed within the frame. It was for backup only. He was not worried about noise. If he found himself in a situation where he was forced to use it, then the sound of shots would be the least of his problems, but the only such scenario he could envisage involved Parker, for he was the sole threat. If, for some reason, he did come, Steiger would have to kill him too, and any warnings against doing so aside, he wasn't being paid to kill him. Then again, he hadn't been paid to torture Lenny Tedesco's wife either. He'd simply taken her as a bonus.

So the Ruger remained where it was, and in his right hand he held a short-bladed knife. He wanted Ruth Winter's death to be as quick and painless as possible, and not only because those were his instructions. A struggle or a scream risked waking her daughter, and the first inkling Steiger wanted her to have was when she found her mother dead the next morning.

As he had anticipated, Ruth's door was slightly ajar, just like her daughter's. A single mother would want to be able to hear if anything was wrong. The sound of light snoring came to him. The door creaked slightly as he entered, but not enough to wake her. He stepped into the room and approached the bed. She was lying on her back, which made it easier for him. He shifted his grip so that the bladed edge was turned away from him, and at that moment her eyes opened—slowly, drowsily at first, then wider. But by then his left hand was over her mouth, and his right was swinging in a fast slashing motion across her throat. He held her down as the blood came, holding his face away to protect him from the worst of it. He felt her bucking against him, and the headboard thudded—once, twice—against the wall, before she began to weaken. The pumping of the blood slowed and then ceased entirely. He looked down at her. Her eyes were still half-open, as though she were about to slip back into sleep again. He closed them with the fingers of his left hand. It was odd, but he didn't want the daughter looking into her mother's dead, clouded eyes when she found her. There was blood on the wall, on the sheets. He could even feel some dripping from his forehead, but that was a minor concern. Not for the first time, he was glad that he'd taken precautions to protect himself. The overalls and the mask would burn easily, and he would dispose of the knife by throwing it into the sea farther down the coast. It was a good knife, but replaceable, and no one had yet established a foolproof way of removing all DNA traces from a blade. Even soaking in bleach wasn't entirely reliable, and why go to such trouble when the stores were unlikely to run out of knives anytime soon?

Ruth Winter was already receding from his memory as he turned away from her body and found himself facing her daughter.

Parker woke at the sound of Sam's footsteps entering his room.

"What's up, honey?" he asked.

"Daddy, there's a man in Amanda's house."

He sat up. He was wearing shorts, and he saw Sam's eyes drift to the new scars on his upper body that had been added to the old, which were more obvious now that he had lost so much weight.

"What? How do you know?"

She had considered how to answer this question on the way to her father's room. She didn't like lying, but sometimes you had to.

"I couldn't sleep," she said, "so I got up to look out at the sea and I saw him. He's in there now. Daddy, you have to hurry. You have to call the police."

He was already moving as she handed his cell phone to him, but he did not dial 911, not yet. Ruth Winter's number was in his contacts list, so he tried that first, cradling the phone between his chin and shoulder as he pulled on a pair of jeans and slipped into his sneakers. The number rang without an answer.

"Shit," he said. Sam, who was not above admonishing her father when he used bad language, remained silent.

Parker zipped up a hooded fleece, and reached for the gun that was now taped to the frame of his bed. He dropped it into the pocket of the fleece before gripping Sam by the shoulders.

"You stay here, you understand? You lock the door after me and you don't come for anyone, not unless I'm with them. Are we clear, Sam?"

"I don't want you to leave," she said. "Please."

"I'm going to call the police on my way, but I don't know how long they'll take to get here. Now I have to go. Come on, follow me."

She trailed after him, down the stairs and across the hall to the door. He opened it, went outside, and waited until she had closed it behind him, and he heard the dead bolt slot into place. He nodded at her once through the glass, and then the night took him.

CHAPTER

XXXVI

Amanda Winter stared at the man before her, then past him to where her mother lay. Even in the dim light she could see the spray of arterial blood against the cream wall, the great stain on the white sheets, and the terrible gash at her mother's throat, the darkness of each contrasting with the pallor of the backdrop. She opened her mouth but no sound came. She wanted to call her mother's name, to scream, but she could not. Terror and grief rendered her silent and immobile. But for the first tears that began to creep from her eyes, she might have been a doll.

Steiger took only a second to overcome his surprise at the sight of the child. He clasped the knife closed and shifted it to his left hand as he advanced upon her. The sight of his approach broke the spell holding Amanda in place, and she turned to run, crying out as she did so, but he was too fast for her. He caught her by the left arm and pulled her back. She struggled against him, and he dropped the knife. Her bare foot hit it, causing it to skid away into the gloom of the hall. She tried to shout again, but Steiger's hand closed around her throat, constricting the airway. Amanda clawed at him through the glove, ripping the plastic and drawing blood, but the pressure remained. Steiger held her against the door until she lost consciousness, then gently eased her to the floor so that she did not hurt her head. He checked her pulse, even though he was certain that he had used just the right amount of force on her. It was not an exact science, though, and one could never be entirely sure. He felt the beating against his fingers, and was satisfied.

He looked at the torn glove, and the cuts to his skin. There would be DNA beneath her fingernails, but he did not have time to remove it. Under other circumstances he might have taken the girl with him, or even cut off her fingers, but his instructions were clear: Amanda Winter was not to be hurt. He had already overstepped the mark by rendering her unconscious.

He found his knife near the bathroom. The door was open, and a bottle of Clorox stood by the toilet. As with cleaning a blade, it was an unsatisfactory compromise, but at least it would leave the girl with her fingers and her life. He took the bottle, unscrewed the cap, and poured it over Amanda's right hand, rubbing it beneath her fingernails as best he could. It would burn, but it was still a mercy.

He had only been in the house for a matter of minutes, but it felt to him as though hours had gone by. It was always the way, just as he invariably experienced a sense of deflation after the act of killing. It was not sorrow at the deed but a kind of disappointment that there was not more to it, that the taking of a life could be so easy, and the extinguishing of it could pass unnoticed by the universe.

He did not give Amanda Winter or her dead mother another thought as he left the house.

XXXVII

Parker had not tried to run in many months, not since before the shooting, and the action sent waves of pain coursing down his back and through his abdomen. He was conscious that lives were at stake, and he tried to keep up a steady pace, but his body resisted the effort. He thought that he felt old wounds opening, the parts of his internal organs that had been ruptured and sewn together again ripping along the scar tissue. He tasted blood in his mouth. Some of it had sprayed on his cell phone when he called the police.

And still he stumbled on.

The door to the Winter house was wide open when he reached it. He entered with his gun in his hand but held close to his body. His vision was blurred, and he was perspiring heavily. He checked the downstairs rooms first, and when he was sure that they were clear he tackled the stairs. The climb brought more pain, and each time he lifted a foot a shock coursed through his being. He reached the first floor and saw Amanda Winter lying against a wall, but he did not approach her immediately. Instead he looked into the room at his back, which turned out to be her bedroom, and empty. Only then did he move toward her. He found her pulse, and even in the dim light he could detect the bruises that were rising on her skin. He could also smell bleach, and it transferred itself to his own hand after he touched her.

Then, beyond Amanda, he saw her mother, and he knew that there was nothing he could do for her, nothing beyond ensuring that her daughter remained alive. Still, he took the time to clear Ruth's room—where he lifted a glass of water carefully from her bedside table and used it to dilute the bleach on her daughter's fingers—and then the bathroom and spare room. In the latter, through the open drapes, he saw a figure on the dunes, watching the house. It was a man silhouetted against the pale moon like a stain on creation, his coat billowing behind him as the wind caught it, and Parker knew that he was willing him, daring him, to approach, to seek vengeance for a dead woman and, by doing so, to bring his own destruction down upon himself.

And all of Parker's rage, all of the agonies that he had endured, found an outlet in the invitation. He was blind to the unconscious girl, blind to the body of her mother, blind to the possibility of his own demise. He wanted only to lash out, to visit pain on another, as though by doing so he could rid himself of some of his own, and watch it soak like oil into the dead sand, and in this he bound himself unknowingly to the man on the beach. Distant sirens sounded, but by the time he heard them he was already outside, the surf pounding in time with the blood in his head, the moon, cold and massive, silvering the strand and forming a great halo behind the one who waited for him, the one who offered a blood respite. Even as the man disappeared, retreating farther into the dunes, luring him on, a warning sounded in Parker's ear: not of injury or further pain, not of death or dying, but of the loss of self, of all the changes his sufferings had wrought upon him that might become twisted and fixed, like the branches of a dead tree. He was acting now not out of a sense of justice, nor of a need to bring a great wrong to an end, but out of a desire to destroy, to burn.

He staggered up the first dune, the soft sand moving beneath his feet, swallowing his shoes, and the gun was a living thing in his hand, a creature that demanded to be fed, the bullet like the tip of a tongue waiting to shoot from the mouth of the barrel. He was once again the man who, years before, had stared down at the ruined bodies of his wife and daughter, and set aside his humanity in his determination to find the one who had taken them from him. His empathy was slipping away as surely as the white grains through which he advanced, the hissing of their fall like a snake at his back. He was the killer, the avenger. He was the dark angel, the true angel, linked by blood and wrath to those who slaughtered the firstborn of Egypt, and he shut himself off from the child's voice that cried

no no

at all that now must surely come to pass.

Parker reached the top of the dune, but could find no sign of the one he sought. He released a breath of exhaustion, and a fine mist of blood flew from his mouth. The sirens were louder now. He glanced south, and saw the lights of emergency vehicles moving toward the beach.

Suddenly he was aware of movement. He reacted, but too slowly. The punch was hard and well aimed. His injured left side exploded and for an instant he was blind, the moon and stars above replaced by a red veil that collapsed upon him with the force of a wave, smashing him to the ground and buffeting him with its wake. When his sight returned he had somehow managed to crawl to his knees, but his gun was gone. The pain that he had experienced earlier was a distant memory, its insignificance made clear by the damage that had been inflicted on his internal organs, on wounds that were still healing and now would never heal, for death would deny the possiblity of it.

Before him stood the man who had taken the life of Ruth Winter, his right foot aimed for a kick. Somehow Parker managed to block it with his arm, protecting himself from the blow that would open him up inside, but his arm went numb with shock, and the man was already poised to strike again. Parker waited for the second kick to come, his upper body swaying slightly, the red veil parting, the stars a blur, frozen in the act of shooting across the night sky.

The man lowered his foot. Parker forced himself to focus, but the face of his tormentor remained distorted, and Parker saw the profound baseness of him, and smelled the poison that seeped from his pores. Beyond lay the sea, and then the sea became a lake, and he knew that he would return there, and his first daughter would be waiting for him. A car would come, and from it the hand of a woman would reach for his, and he would take his seat for the Long Ride.

His eyes turned south once again. The lights of the vehicles were closer now, but the one who stood above him did not seem troubled by their approach. Parker found his voice.

"Who are you?"

"What does it matter?"

"I want to know."

"Here, and now, I'm Steiger. Tomorrow I'll be someone else. Does that satisfy you?"

"Yes."

"And I know who you are."

Steiger removed his right hand from his pocket. It held a gun.

"Look at you," he said. "A fractured man, a broken thing. I asked for money to kill you, but none would give it. Now I understand why. There is no value to you. You're nothing, and therefore nothing is what your life is worth. But I will kill you anyway, out of pity. I'll make it fast, if you tell me what the woman shared with you. If not, I'll shoot you in the guts and leave you to bleed out in shit and pain. Which will it be?"

"Nothing. She told me nothing."

"Then the guts it is. Good-bye, Mr. Parker."

He raised the gun. Parker did not look away. It would make no difference.

He heard the shot, and instinctively closed his eyes, but felt no impact. A cry of hurt and surprise came instead from behind him. It was a woman's voice. Despite his own pain, he moved his head enough so that he could turn and look.

Cory Bloom was standing in a patch of marram grass, one hand braced against a half-toppled fence post from which a length of wire curled down to earth itself belowground. She was wearing a blue wind-breaker with a white sweatshirt under it. Across the white, a bloody cloud spread from within her. She stared directly at Parker for a moment, then toppled backward and was lost from sight.

The ground shook, as though the beast buried deep beneath the sands had been disturbed in its sleep. Steiger's mouth opened. He looked to his feet as the dune began to collapse, and then it was gone and he with it, the edge now barely inches from where Parker knelt. Parker looked down, but no trace of Steiger remained below, only a hill of white. Grains flowed from the slope in rivulets, but when they reached the beach they grew still, and remained undisturbed by the final struggles of the man suffocating beneath them.

The last thing that Parker saw before unconsciousness came was a small figure standing by Steiger's still-forming grave.

"Sam," he said, but she did not hear him, and did not look at him. Her eyes were fixed solely on the funeral mound before her, and her gaze was as pitiless as an ancient god's.

CHAPTER

XXXVIII

As with Bruno Perlman's remains, the requirement for an autopsy meant that Ruth Winter's body could not be buried before nightfall, as directed by the Talmud, and her burial only took place days later. Once her body was released, the corpse was purified and dressed in shrouds, and placed in a simple wooden casket for the funeral service at Sinai Memorial Chapel in Bangor. Amanda Winter was present, a black ribbon attached to the left lapel of her new over-coat, bought for her by her grandmother, Isha. Amanda did not cry until the casket was lowered into the ground, and the kaddish prayer was recited, and after that she could not stop, so that her head stayed bowed as she passed through the mourners and on to the waiting funeral car.

Amanda Winter's grandmother was very old, but she carried herself like a much younger woman. Her hair was gray, but her face bore only the finest tracery of lines, like ancient porcelain. Gordon Walsh was present, observing all that had taken place. So too was Marie Demers. The police now had a reason for Bruno Perlman's presence in Maine, for Ruth Winter's mother was Isha Winter. Almost seventy years earlier, as Isha Górski, she had been the sole survivor of the camp at Lubsko.

As Isha saw her granddaughter safely into her seat, Walsh approached the old woman and offered his condolences. She nodded at him, and said, "They will never leave us in peace. Never. Always they will hunt and persecute us."

She climbed into the car, and it pulled away.

———

THE BASEMENT DOOR OPENED, and Oran Wilde tried to shield himself from the sudden shaft of light. His hands were cuffed in front of him, and a length of chain led from a manacle around his left leg to a D ring on the wall. He had lost some weight, and was even paler than before. Other than the single occasion when his captor had drawn blood from Oran's arm using a disposable syringe fresh from the wrapper, he had not been harmed in any way. Oran had a bucket in which to urinate and defecate, which the man slopped out twice daily, making sure to clean it with some bleach so that it didn't smell. Every morning he would also bring Oran a second bucket filled with hot water so that he could wash, each time accompanied by a fresh towel and a little bar of wrapped soap like those left in motel bathrooms. For the first couple of days, Oran had limited himself to washing only his face and hands, because he thought that the man might be watching him and he didn't want to be naked in front of him. A subsequent search of the basement revealed no cameras as far as Oran could tell, although he wasn't an expert and there was really no way of knowing just what might be concealed in the brickwork. Eventually Oran had stopped caring about such things. He just preferred not to be able to smell himself.

A TV hung from a bracket in a corner, slightly too high for Oran to reach. It was basic cable, but better than nothing, and he had a remote with which to change channels. He had also been supplied with books, magazines, and a couple of graphic novels. He had an armchair on which to sit and a sofa bed on which to sleep. The basement was windowless, but adequately ventilated through a series of grilles. Heat came from a radiator, and the room was lit by a pair of lamps. Oran had tried to figure out where he was being held, but no sound penetrated the basement, either from the floors above or the world outside. The car had been driven into a garage when they'd arrived, so Oran's first sight of the man's world was shelves lined with paint cans and jars of screws and nails, and a series of boards on which his tools hung. The sight of all those implements had frightened Oran at first, for he feared being cut by them. But his captor had merely helped Oran from the trunk of the car and guided him down to the basement, and Oran had been there ever since.

The man had spoken little to Oran since taking him, beyond asking if there was anything that he needed, and warning him to keep still when the blood was being drawn. He did not raise his voice, did not threaten to harm Oran in any way, but the boy remained terrified of him. He could still recall waking up at home to find the masked man looming over him, his hand closing on Oran's mouth, and the appearance of the gun. It all happened quickly after that: the cuffs, the gag, the heavy-duty tape around Oran's legs.

Then the shooting began.

Oran had no idea why his family had been targeted. He had no idea why he was being held in the basement. He had asked the man, but received no reply. Oran knew only that he was still alive, and so far his captor had continued to keep his face concealed behind a ski mask. That was good, as far as Oran was concerned. It gave him hope. If the man didn't want Oran to see his face, it was because he didn't wish to be identified, which meant that, at some point, he intended to release him.

But Oran—quiet, clever Oran—thought that he might have some inkling of who his captor was. The voice, although rarely used, was familiar. He had heard it before. The competition, the essay . . .

Now he came down the staircase and stood before Oran, his hands on his hips. He was wearing a big L.L.Bean olive field coat, the kind that Oran's father used to wear when he went hiking. Oran wondered if it might not even be the same coat, taken from their house before the flames consumed it. He forced the thought away. He tried not to think of his parents and his sisters. He regretted all the times that he'd fought with them, all the occasions on which he'd called his sisters bitches, or spurned his mother's demonstrations of affection and his father's awkward attempts at bonding. He would have given anything to be able to rewind time, to spend just one more day with them.

"You've been a good boy, Oran," said the man. The ski mask muffled his words slightly because the mouth hole was too small.

Oran didn't reply. He was too afraid.

"I'm sorry for what happened to your parents, to your sisters," the man continued. "I know that it's caused you a lot of pain. It's going to come to an end now."

He reached up and yanked off the ski mask.

And Oran began to cry.

III

There is no reason why good cannot triumph over evil.
The triumph of anything is a matter of organization.
If there are such things as angels, I hope that they
are organized along the lines of the Mafia.

—Kurt Vonnegut, *The Sirens of Titan*

CHAPTER

XXXIX

The Office of the Chief Medical Examiner of the State of Maine was located in a nondescript building on Hospital Street in Augusta, conveniently situated behind the State Police Crime Laboratory. It had always operated under some degree of financial constraint, in large part because the state legislature, like most elected bodies of its kind, had generally been reluctant to approve significant budget increases for it because the dead do not vote. Thus, while the national standard for determining a cause of death was sixty days for uncomplicated cases, and ninety days for homicides, the determination of a cause of death in Maine could take up to six months. There was a backlog of cases, and the office had been forced to become increasingly selective about those that it felt obliged to investigate.

None of this was the fault of the appointees to the post of ME over the years, who had done their utmost to squeeze every nickel while pleading for additional resources from the state, usually to little avail. It was fortunate for Maine, therefore, that the various holders of the office were not only conscientious in their duty, but clever in the bargain, and were therefore capable of taking the kind of imaginative leaps that enable important institutions to keep functioning even when no money is left in the cookie jar. To the untrained eye, some of those leaps might have been perceived as somewhat unorthodox. For example, it is a requirement of medical examiners that they should retain samples of internal organs—typically the liver, lungs, heart, and kidneys—from autopsied bodies, in case any questions or queries should arise at some future date. These are generally preserved in formalin, and stored in glass sample jars. (It is considered inadvisable to keep tissue samples in a chocolate box, as one Tennessee medical examiner was alleged to have done, a lapse which, perhaps unsurprisingly, contributed to the loss of his license.) Nevertheless, specialized sample jars are expensive, when all that is really required for the task is a simple glass container with an airtight seal. Thus it was that one former Maine medical examiner, perhaps lost in contemplation of a bottle of mayonnaise or jelly, noticed that such comestibles came in resealable glass jars of a kind not entirely dissimilar to those for which his office was paying top dollar. And so—assiduously collected, carefully cleaned, and scrupulously delabeled to avoid any embarrassing, and possibly traumatic, confusion—jelly jars became sterile storage containers, and the money saved was put toward providing answers to more pressing problems, namely the manner in which someone might have died, and how, in cases of homicide, that knowledge could be used to apprehend the person or persons responsible.

Maine, though, was not alone in struggling with poor funding and inadequate facilities, and it was a further credit to all those involved in the ME's office that it had not been forced to endure scandals such as that in neighboring Massachusetts, where bodies had lain unclaimed and corpses were mislaid, or, as in Oklahoma, to cease autopsying apparent suicides due to staffing problems. But the investigation into the death of Oran Wilde's family, the associated homicide of a homeless man, and the Perlman autopsy had stretched the resources of the office to its limits. Now two more bodies had been added to the office's roster of corpses awaiting examination, although there was, at least, no question of how either of them had died. Ruth Winter's body had already been handed over for burial, but one corpse still remained.

The three men who arrived at the medical examiner's office shortly after dark were concerned only with this second body: the remains of the man who had suffocated to death beneath the sands of Green Heron Bay. They entered from the rear of the building, and the staff member who was on duty at the main desk didn't even turn his head to watch as they approached the room into which, for their convenience, the body had been moved. He had already been advised that he could not speak about what he did not know, and so no names were logged, and no faces seen. He breathed out only when he heard the door to the autopsy room close, after which he carefully checked the lock on the front entrance and retreated to a secluded office, where he remained until the three men left and he was, once again, alone with the dead.

———

THE FLUORESCENT LIGHTS REFLECTED on glass, metal, and tile, and illuminated the body that lay beneath a sheet on a gurney. Gordon Walsh pulled on plastic examination gloves, and handed clean pairs to the two men who stood behind him, before drawing back the sheet and revealing the face of the dead man. The top of the Y-shaped incision on his chest was just visible, raw against the blue-gray pallor of his skin.

"Hey, it's your mom," said Angel.

"How the fuck old are you?" said Walsh. "Jesus."

Louis stepped forward.

"Can I touch him?"

"Be my guest."

Louis moved the man's head gently, examining the deformation of his face and head, and the lobeless ears. He pulled back the man's lips and looked at his white, even teeth.

"Partial dentures," said Walsh.

"Maybe he thought they'd improve his dating chances," said Angel.

"Yeah," said Walsh. "I figure he needed any help he could get."

"They pump all the sand out of him?" asked Louis.

"You kidding me? He must have swallowed half the beach."

"Bad way to die."

"If you want to pray for him, now's the time. So, does he remind you of anyone you may have met?"

"Your mom," said Angel. Again.

"Shut the fuck up. I was warned about you."

"Any identifying marks on the rest of his body?" asked Louis.

"Nothing," said Walsh. "He's entirely hairless, though. Alopecia universalis: I just learned that today, and I like saying it. Oh, and his bowels were riddled with tumors. The ME thinks he must have been in constant pain. He probably had less than a year to live."

Louis stepped back and removed the gloves, careful to ensure that his bare hands did not touch any part of the material that had been in contact with the dead man's skin.

"What did you say his name was?"

"We found a Georgia driver's license in the name of Earl Steiger when we pulled him out of the sand. It was the only ID he was carrying, but it wasn't the only one that he had."

"Earl Steiger," said Louis. "No, I don't recall it."

"He had to be staying somewhere local," Walsh continued, "so we canvassed the area and found a motel outside Belfast called the Come Awn Inn. He'd been staying there for a couple of days, cash on the nail."

"The Come Awn Inn?" said Angel. "You're kidding."

"No, for real. You don't want to stay there. We hit the room with UV light. Let me tell you, it looked like you could come on anything in the Come Awn Inn, and a lot of folks started with the sheets and the comforter. I wanted to burn my shoes by the time we were done."

"And?" said Louis.

"We picked up four other licenses, none of them in the name of Earl Steiger. All were from southern states, and all were legit, at least in the sense that they weren't forgeries. So far, we've traced three of them back to dead children, including Earl Steiger. He was killed aged fifteen in an automobile accident with the rest of his family in 1975 in Wilkinson County, Georgia."

For the first time, Louis evinced some kind of real interest.

"Dead children?"

"Ghosting," said Angel. "Old-school."

Ghosting was the product of a different time, one before computers and the routine exchange of information—whether in theory or actual practice—by government agencies. Before the advent of the income tax in 1913, and later the introduction of the Social Security system in 1935, it was possible for a man or woman in the United States to live openly without any formal documentation from the government. Even after 1935, it was difficult to check if an individual's claimed identity was his or her own. Only the invention of databases, and the increasingly long reach of the government, rendered such imposture harder to achieve—although, ironically, the Internet, with its proliferation of intimate personal details, now made identity theft easier than ever before.

The practice of ghosting involved finding a dead person whose age roughly matched one's own, discovering the person's date of birth— often from the gravestone itself—and then using the information to obtain a birth certificate in that name. Once the birth certificate was in hand, it was a relatively simple process to begin obtaining government-issued identification, thereby cementing the assumed identity.

"What about the other children?" asked Louis.

Walsh consulted his notebook.

"Noble C. Griffis, Eureka Springs, Arkansas. Drowned in 1962 at the age of three while in the care of a Methodist benevolent institution. And William H. Pruett, Tarboro, South Carolina: nine years old when he died in a fire with his mother, two sisters, and three brothers in 1971. Father predeceased them."

Louis didn't speak for a time. He was assimilating the information from Walsh, sifting it in his mind. The dead man—Earl Steiger, for want of a better name—or someone acting on his behalf, had been clever in his choice of assumed identities. First of all, poorer areas in the South were targeted, possibly on the grounds that records might be more haphazard, and the spelling of names open to more than one interpretation: "Griffis," for example, sounded like a bastardization of "Griffin" or "Griffiths." Some risks were attached to this approach due to the close interrelationships between families in small rural communities, and the long memories of those responsible for guarding their records, but they were outweighed by the benefits.

Secondly, the names assumed were from boys who were either orphans or whose immediate relatives had died alongside them, which decreased the likelihood of anyone poking around in their family history and discovering that little Earl or Noble or William appeared to be enjoying an existence beyond the grave. Finally, all of the children had been born within one three-year period between 1959 and 1962, which probably roughly corresponded to the age of the man lying on the gurney before them.

"I take it you're trying to find out when copies of the birth certificates were issued," said Louis.

"Old men and women are trawling through records as we speak," said Walsh.

"Concentrate on Earl Steiger."

"Why?"

"It was the one he was using when he came here, but I'll also bet you a dollar that he relied on the Steiger identity more than any other. No matter how many false identities a man has, he'll be drawn to one in particular, because even a ghost needs some kind of anchor. Also, if you keep alternating identities you get confused, and you're likely to make a mistake. Finally, it leaves you with nothing to fall back on if you need to disappear."

"You strike me as worryingly well-informed," said Walsh.

"You didn't ask me here because I'm pretty."

"I didn't ask you here at all."

The suggestion that Angel and Louis should be contacted about Ruth Winter's killer had come from Special Agent Ross of the Federal Bureau of Investigation. Ross was a man who took a special interest in matters relating to Charlie Parker, for reasons that even Ross himself might not have been in a position to explain fully.

"You'll find that the replacement birth certificate for Earl Steiger was issued within a year of his death—two years at most."

"And why do you figure that?"

"Because Earl Steiger was the oldest when he died, which means that his was probably the first identity acquired for our friend here. His potential would have been spotted early, but not before he was fifteen or sixteen."

"You know who he really is," said Walsh.

"No, and by the time he died I don't think even he knew who he really was either," said Louis. "But the southern children, the ages—that is familiar to me."

He gripped the edge of the plastic sheet and pulled it over the face of the dead man.

"You need to call your friend Agent Ross," he said. "Tell him that it might be one of Cambion's people who died out here."

XL

The woman stank of cats and cookies, of piss and mothballs, but Cambion, whose sensory abilities had long been ruined by his disease, and who had grown used to the reek of his own decay, barely noticed it. It was enough that she cooked for him, and helped him to get in and out of chairs, and beds, and baths. Edmund could do all that too, of course, but he lacked her delicacy. He was compassionate, but not gentle, and as Cambion entered the last stages of his life he appreciated tenderness, even that which was offered out of instinct, not inclination.

Cambion was once a torturer and killer, a sadist and despoiler of flesh, until Hansen's disease took hold of him, and he became known as Cambion the Leper, Cambion the Outcast. As the illness destroyed his body, rendering him unable to function in his preferred role, he became a middleman, a point of contact between the most vicious of clients and those men and women base enough to do their bidding. It had made Cambion wealthy, but now most of that money was gone. He had squandered it in his early years—for his tastes were no less depraved than those of whom he represented, and such vices are expensive to maintain—and then, following his diagnosis, doled it out as carefully as he could in an effort to counter his disease. Cambion was a hunted man—one does not spend one's life arranging torments and tortures without question and not build up an impressive roster of enemies—and so conventional medical intervention was not open to him: he would not have survived for an hour once news of his presence in a hospital became known. He was also cursed early in the leprosy's progress by treatment with incorrect medicines, a consequence of his need to use backroom doctors. He spent years punishing the practitioner responsible by holding him captive and carving pieces from his body on a regular basis, but it provided small consolation.

Only a handful of Cambion's old associates had remained willing to work with him, and see that he got his share. The rest had abandoned him long ago, which was why Cambion, in turn, had fed their names to his hunters in the hope that, by betraying others, he might be allowed to die in peace. It had not worked; they still circled him. He was reduced to living in near squalor, tended by a woman who had once occupied his bed but was now little more than a walking corpse herself, but whose need for money was even greater than his own.

He rang the bell over his bed by tugging on a length of rope. The bedpan was out of reach, and he needed it. He could not feel the rope against his skin, for he no longer had sensation in his hands or feet. His muscles had grown weaker, even in the last few months, and the extent of his disfigurement caused him to shun all reflective surfaces. His kidney functions were also becoming impaired due to renal amyloidosis, for which hemodialysis was the standard recommended treatment, but Cambion could not show himself to receive it. It was possible that the treatment might be arranged privately, but it would require funds to pay for both the surgery and the silence after, funds he did not possess. His sight was failing: he could still see the television screen close by his bed, and read words as long as they were magnified for him on a screen, but everything at a distance was a blur. It was fortunate in the case of the room in which he lay. It meant that he could no longer see the filthy carpet, or the paper peeling from the walls, or the damp stains on the ceiling which, at his worst moments, had assumed the patterns of demonic faces, or seemed to spread like blood from a recent wound, the Rorschach blots of his own guilt.

The woman did not answer his summons, and instead Edmund appeared. The giant owned only two suits, both of them a vile yellow. While one was being cleaned at some cut-price laundry, he would wear the other. The color on both had faded over the years, although not enough to render their appearance any less painful to the eye, and they had accumulated soiling that even the most assiduous of attention could not remove, including food, wine, and various bodily fluids, Cambion's own among them.

"Where have you been?" asked Cambion, for the giant had been gone since early that afternoon, and night had since fallen.

Edmund handed Cambion a number of newspapers, all open at the same story. Cambion could only read the headlines, but they were enough to reveal to him the murder of Ruth Winter, and the death, in turn, of the man responsible for killing her. Cambion let out a small moan of grief. Cambion had found Steiger, nurtured him, molded him since boyhood. He was the last of them, and one of the few Cambion had not betrayed in an effort to save himself. At least, thought Cambion, recovering himself, they had banked a portion of the fee before Steiger died, and he had completed his assigned task before succumbing to the sands, so further funds would be forthcoming.

Edmund accessed the stories on a laptop so that the print could be magnified. While he worked, Cambion recalled his final conversation with Steiger, the one in which Steiger had notified him of the presence of the private investigator Charlie Parker near the Winter woman's house. How peculiar it was that Cambion's fate and Parker's should once again intersect. Steiger had wanted to know if there was a price on Parker's head, if there were those in the shadows who might be willing to pay to have it served to them on a platter, but Cambion had dissuaded him from moving against the detective. Those who had come closest to killing him barely months before were now all dead, and a town had been put to the torch as a further act of retribution. If the whispers were true, certain others who might have wanted Parker dead had chosen not to act against him for reasons to which Cambion was not privy, and they were the only ones he could think of who might reasonably have been expected to pay for his murder by another.

Yet it appeared from reading between the lines of the newspaper reports that some confrontation had occurred between Parker and Steiger in the moments before the latter's death. The result was that Steiger had been buried alive. An accident, the newspapers said. Dune collapses were not uncommon, although nobody could recall any previous such incident at Green Heron Bay. If Cambion had believed in God—which, for many years, he had not, although his position on that subject was modifying rapidly—he might have assumed that the deity was watching over Charlie Parker.

Cambion was a foul man, and a hateful one, but he was not entirely without humanity, even if it was tied up almost entirely with his own sufferings. As his death inexorably approached, he found himself persecuted by memories of his own wickedness. He wondered sometimes if God had punished him by visiting his disease upon him. If so, God was then partly to blame for its consequences, for Cambion's pain had only fed his natural sadism. God had created Cambion, just as Cambion had created Steiger. Each, it could be said, was an instrument of a superior being's will.

But now Cambion found himself turning to Pascal and his infamous wager: all humans bet with their lives that God either exists or does not. The wager is not a matter of choice. By the act of living, we place the bet. A rational person, according to Pascal, lives as though God exists, for if He does exist, then the rewards are infinite, and if He does not exist, then the sacrifices made in life based on erroneous belief are finite. While Cambion had read extensively of the arguments against Pascal, he had, as death cast its shadow upon him, become more and more convinced of the reality of a world beyond this one, and of a

Supreme Being beyond his understanding. He felt it as a corollary of his own evil and corruption, just as an awareness of cold might bring with it an acknowledgment of the existence of its opposite.

Yes, had Cambion inquired more deeply, there might possibly have been someone else willing to pay for Parker's death—although the private detective's surviving enemies were few—but what would the money have bought him? Just painful surgery, catheters, and a few extra months, or a year, added to an already cursed life. No, he had no need for any of it. He should have refused even to accept the contract on the Winter woman, but once the instruction had been given, and payment made, Steiger could not be recalled. That was the rule, and the money was welcome.

Perhaps, too, he was afraid: Steiger was only part of the equation, and there were others involved who were beyond Cambion's control, and for whom the death of Ruth Winter was of hugely personal concern. Cambion had provided Steiger for them in the past, and he had no illusions about the source of the cash that paid for his services. Even as a creator of monsters, Cambion was wary of those who had hired Steiger.

Cambion finished reading the reports in silence. He gestured for the bedpan, and Edmund assisted him by placing it in position. Cambion thought that the big man was more careful than usual, and appeared troubled by the obvious pain that the act of urination caused his employer. The bedpan was removed, the sheets rearranged, the pillows adjusted to make him comfortable.

"We are almost done," he told Edmund, but he did not know if he was understood or not.

Edmund departed, and in the darkness of his death room Cambion's lips moved in something like prayer.

CHAPTER

XLI

Angel and Louis followed Walsh's car to the Gin Mill on Water Street when they were done at the ME's office. While he drove, Walsh called Ross in New York and told him what Louis had said about Cambion.

"That guy just won't die," said Ross. "He's like some kind of virus."

"You know the name?"

"Oh yeah: Cambion the Leper. He's a middleman for murderers, now that he can't torture and kill for himself because of his ailment."

"You telling me he's a real leper?"

"Full-blown. He gives the disease a bad name. He didn't contract it— it contracted him. Are they still with you?"

"I'm taking them to dinner."

There was a noticeable pause.

"Are you that lonely?" said Ross.

"Hey, I figured I might learn something more."

"You'll learn not to do it again."

"Can I bill you for it?" asked Walsh.

Ross was still laughing as he hung up the phone.

————

BOTH ANGEL AND LOUIS went to the men's room to freshen up. For all of their experience in unpleasant matters—and Walsh was under no illusion about what these men were capable of—the smell of the autopsy room had gotten to them. It didn't bother Walsh, though, which worried him only slightly.

He was shown to a table, from which he ordered an Allagash Black. He leaned back against the cool brick wall and called his wife. Both she and his younger son were nursing colds, and she'd kept the boy home from school that morning. They seemed to be on the mend, though. His son was apparently curled up on the couch with hot chocolate, one of those god-awful Transformers movies on the TV, which Walsh thought was like watching someone moving around the contents of a silverware drawer. And his wife certainly sounded better than she had earlier. When he'd first heard her in the morning dark, he felt like he'd woken up next to that kid from *The Exorcist*. He listened to her bitch about the neighbors for a while, then said good night. He wasn't sure what time he'd be home, he told her. He just knew that he would be.

Walsh loved his wife a lot. He loved his kids. He was happy with his life. He wasn't particularly troubled or haunted by his work, not like those cops in movies or mystery novels. You couldn't do the job if you took it home with you the way they did. You couldn't have a family and a normal life. Walsh had learned that early on from Miro, his first sergeant. Get yourself a wife, Miro told him. Have kids. When you're done with your day, go home to them. There will be times when you'll want a drink after what you've gone through, but maybe those are the times, more than any other, when you should just head back to your family. If you need to, take a walk alone before dinner, or bring your dog along for company. It'll help. Then again, Miro didn't drink. He didn't begrudge anyone else a drink, and when he did go out he'd buy his round without complaint, but he still had a point. Walsh figured that if he couldn't talk about stuff with his wife, then with whom could he talk? He didn't tell her everything, but he told her enough. The rest he kept inside, because some sights and sounds just had to stay there.

Walsh did enjoy the occasional beer, though. It wasn't a way of escaping or drowning his pain. He just liked beer.

And with that, his beer came. He looked at the menu. Although, as has been established, he loved his wife, he also enjoyed dining without her sometimes, especially at places like the Gin Mill. If she'd been with him, she'd have given him the cool eye until he announced that he was skipping the appetizers and, hey, the house salad with grilled chicken looked real good! Now he was free to order smoked sausage, or Cajun fried shrimp or—Lord have mercy—the nachos, followed by a burger or the BBQ sandwich platter. He wouldn't lie if she asked him what he'd eaten, but he hoped she might give him a pass and acknowledge that, as in the case of the ME's assistant earlier that night, ignorance was some-times the best defense.

Angel and Louis emerged from the bathroom. Walsh saw women glance at Louis and do that thing where they adjusted their hair frac-tionally, or sipped from a straw in a manner somewhere between flirta-tious and downright lewd. For a gay man, he sure managed to stir the ladies. Women also gave Angel a look, but they usually followed it by checking that their purses were close by, and they hadn't left any money on the bar.

Man, thought Walsh, my life has taken some strange turns if this is where I've ended up: in a fine Augusta drinking establishment, accom-panied by one man who used to kill for a living—and, who knew, maybe still did when the price was right—and another who had been a pretty good thief by all accounts, but also wasn't above using a gun when circumstances required it. How the hell Parker had become involved with them, Walsh couldn't say, but there was a part of him that envied the detective the loyalty and friendship of these men. They might have been criminals, but they were the right kind of criminals.

They slipped into the booth across from him. He wondered if they were carrying guns. He assumed they were. He wondered if the guns were licensed. He assumed they weren't. Once again, better not to ask.

The waitress returned. She wasn't immune to Louis's charms either, stopping just short of rolling on her back and asking to have her tummy tickled. At least, thought Walsh, we'll get good service. Louis asked Walsh for advice on beer, and ended up trying an Andrew's English Ale out of Lincolnville, with a bottle of white wine to follow. Angel opted for a Bar Harbor Blueberry Ale.

"I don't approve of fruit in beer," said Walsh.

"Really?" said Angel. "You don't *approve* of it. What are you, some weird branch of the Women's Temperance League? I like it. Not pumpkin, though. Fuckin' pumpkin," he added, with venom.

The waitress brought their beers, and they ordered food. Angel and Louis stuck with fish, and Walsh went for the smoked sausage and, in a break from tradition, a full rack of St. Louis pork ribs.

"A full rack?" asked Angel. "You expecting someone else?"

"I hope not," said Walsh.

"Jesus, your arteries must be like the inside of the Holland Tunnel at rush hour."

Walsh let it pass. He was pretty sure that his arteries weren't like the inside of the Holland Tunnel, or not all of them anyway.

"So," he asked Louis, "any other thoughts on Steiger spring to mind on the way over here?"

"I got a question for you first," said Louis. "What are you to Ross?"

Louis didn't like the FBI man. He believed in keeping his distance from most federal agencies, especially ones that might have a file on him.

Walsh didn't even blink. He'd been expecting this, and he had nothing to hide. Ross had briefed him well. They needed these men, because no two people in the world were closer to Parker, his daughter and her mother possibly—only possibly—excepted.

And Ross wanted to know all there was to know about the detective.

"I work with him," said Walsh.

"Officially? Unofficially?"

"The distinction is moot in Ross's case. If there was ever a line between the two, it's disappeared over the years."

"And you watch Parker for him."

"Actually, 'watching' may be too strong a word for what I do. Mostly I just clean up the mess afterward, and help make sure that he keeps his license and stays out of jail. You might have noticed that Parker's actions occasionally exceed the bounds of legality by some considerable degree. Not that you'd condone such behavior."

"Heaven forbid," said Angel.

"And is it just Parker in whom you're interested," asked Louis, "or are there others?"

"Others like him?"

"There are no others like him," said Louis. "You don't need me to tell you that."

"No, there are no others—like him, or not."

"And you watch him to what end?"

"You know, you can talk real nice when you choose. I'd heard you were, like, monosyllabic."

"I tell him that all the time," said Angel. "The problem is, I can't figure out which way of speaking is really him."

"I guess he's just all hidden depths," said Walsh.

"I guess he is all that. By the way, you didn't answer his question: why watch Parker?"

Angel had a lazy smile on his face, and Walsh thought that it would be very easy to underestimate him.

"I'm afraid that's above my pay grade."

"Because you just work here, right?"

"Right." Walsh finished his beer and waved at the waitress for another. "I hear that you had a conversation with Ross not too different from this one, back when Parker was shot. He told you then what he thought it was all about."

"People who believe in buried gods," said Louis. "Do you believe in buried gods, Detective Walsh?"

"I'm Episcopalian. I believe in everything."

Walsh's second beer arrived, along with the appetizers, which were huge. Walsh tried to blot out his wife's disapproving face so that he could enjoy his food. He bit into a mouthful of sausage and continued talking through the meat.

"I suppose I accept what Ross does: there are individuals whose own belief systems cause harm to others, and they have to be stopped. That's as true of radical Muslim clerics who preach that it's okay to behead apostates as it is of the boards of selectmen of small Maine towns who aren't above killing to protect their privileged position."

If he was expecting a reaction from Angel and Louis, he was destined to go unrewarded.

"I know you tried to burn the town of Prosperous to the ground," Walsh added, just for clarification.

Louis dipped a piece of crab cake into habanero mayo. Angel tried some of Walsh's smoked sausage. Walsh had the sense that they were slightly disappointed in him for being so obvious. Walsh didn't give a damn. He objected to men—especially from New York, although Massachusetts would have been almost as bad—coming into his state and setting fire to towns. It was unmannerly, and caused unrest.

"Anyway," he went on, "it seems like Parker exerts a kind of gravitational pull on some of these individuals, which brings us closer to them. And Ross believes that an endgame may be in sight, and Parker has a role—maybe a significant one—to play in that too."

"And do a lot of folks share your analysis of the situation?" said Louis.

"We tend not to broadcast it too widely," said Walsh. "Makes us sound flaky."

"So Ross suggested that you should let us take a look at the body in the morgue—" Angel began, but Walsh interrupted.

"Because we were clearly looking at the body of a professional killer," Walsh finished for him.

"And how did you figure that?"

"Our pretty friend turned up on a piece of security footage in Florida not so long ago. A place called the Hurricane Hatch down near Jacksonville got ripped off, and the bartender, name of Lenny Tedesco, was killed, or that was what it looked like until Tedesco's wife was found dying in her bed. She went hard. Whoever killed her—and we're assuming it was Steiger—took the trouble to remove her teeth before leaving her for dead. Curiously, the Florida cops think that it was probably him who called the ambulance, although he must have known that she wouldn't survive another hour.

"The bar had surveillance cameras hooked up to a hard drive, but Tedesco's killer was smart enough to take it with him when he left. Now, the owner of the Hurricane Hatch is a guy named Skettle. Tedesco had a piece of the bar—just 10 percent—but Skettle was of the opinion that he was upping that to fifteen, maybe twenty, by skimming. To prove it, he'd installed a second pinhole camera behind a mirror over the register. It didn't take in much of the rest of the bar, just the register, but when the footage was examined it came up with a good shot of Earl Steiger in profile—and that's a very distinctive profile—cleaning out the night's takings.

"So now we have Steiger killing a bartender and his wife near Jacksonville—maybe for kicks, or maybe because he really needed the whole four hundred and change in the register, or a combination of both—then coming all the way up here to cut Ruth Winter's throat, except he doesn't rape or mutilate her, and he leaves her daughter alive. Again, that could have been an accident—he might have thought that he'd applied enough pressure to kill the child, and been mistaken—but I don't buy it. I think he knew exactly what he was doing every step of the way."

"Okay," said Louis. "So even before I took a look at his body, you made him for a pro. But are you assuming a connection between what happened in Florida and what took place up at Green Heron Bay? Could be two separate jobs."

"We considered that too, but you're forgetting something: Boreas has supplied us with three bodies in total. We have Ruth Winter, and Steiger, but we also have Bruno Perlman, who washed up at Mason Point with a mark on his eye socket that may or may not have been caused by a blade. Bruno Perlman happened to be a native of Duval County, Florida, with an address in Arlington, which is about a thirty-minute ride from the Hurricane Hatch. We think that there's a good chance Perlman might have known Lenny Tedesco, at least casually."

"Why?"

"He had a Hurricane Hatch T-shirt in his closet. And then there's the fact that Perlman, Tedesco, and Ruth Winter were all Jewish. Finally, and here's the clincher, last month Bruno Perlman visited Ruth and Isha Winter at their home in Pirna."

"Wait," said Angel. "How come you're only finding that out now? You'd think Ruth Winter might have mentioned that fact when Perlman's body appeared a couple of beaches away from her house. Maybe her mother might have brought it up too."

"Isha Winter doesn't read newspapers and doesn't own a TV," said Walsh. "She's also older than Mount Katahdin. As for Ruth Winter, she's not around to ask anymore."

"Doesn't fit, them both staying quiet," said Louis.

"No," said Walsh, "it doesn't. The mother I can buy, but not the daughter."

"And," said Angel, "Ruth never called her mother and said, 'Hey, remember that guy who came to visit a while back? Well, you'll never guess where he is now. . . .'"

"Isha Winter says she didn't. We spoke to some of Ruth's friends down in Pirna, too. She didn't have many—she was pretty solitary— and they say she didn't discuss Perlman with them at all, either before or after his body was found."

"So why would Ruth Winter keep quiet about it?"

"Either she was afraid or she was involved," said Louis.

"Or both," said Walsh.

"Why was Perlman visiting the Winters in the first place?" asked Angel.

"Because Isha Górski, later Isha Winter, was the sole survivor of a small Nazi concentration camp called Lubsko, and Perlman lost relatives there. Apparently he wanted to talk with her about her memories of the place. Isha says that her daughter arrived while she was speaking with Perlman, but the visit didn't last for long. She doesn't like recalling what happened to her during the war, and I can't blame her for that. I'd never even heard of Lubsko until this week."

Walsh shared what little he knew of the camp with Angel and Louis, but it was enough.

"Parker says he and Cory Bloom got the story of Lubsko from Epstein when he came to Boreas, but at that time nobody knew that Isha Winter was once Isha Górski."

"So now you have a link between Florida and Maine," said Louis. "You also have a cluster of Jewish victims, which could make it a hate crime."

"And brings in the FBI," said Angel.

"Hence Ross."

"Well, Ross would have been involved just because of Parker, but, yeah, the feds have expressed an interest," said Walsh. "We also have the Justice Department pulling up a chair because of Engel, the war criminal. He was on the staff at Lubsko, and two Lubsko hits in the same state have set lights flashing at the Human Rights and Special Prosecutions Section."

"And you already had enough to be getting along with," said Angel. "Like not finding this Oran Wilde kid."

"Yeah, thanks for reminding me."

"It's gone pretty quiet around him."

"Yeah."

"Clever for a teenager."

"Yeah."

"In fact, cleverest teenager I've ever heard of. Kid is practically a criminal mastermind."

"Yeah."

"Unless he isn't."

"Yeah. You done?"

"Yeah."

"Good."

"So you think Steiger killed Perlman as well?" asked Louis.

Walsh shifted in his seat.

"We're running Steiger's IDs through Homeland Security to see if anything pings on air travel, because that's the only way I can see him doing both. We know when Perlman arrived in Maine from the toll cameras on I-95, and a food receipt in his car from the Starbucks at the Kennebunk service plaza. Steiger could have put him in the water, then taken a flight back to Florida in time to kill the Tedescos before bouncing back up to murder Ruth Winter, but why not kill Winter along with Perlman and then head south to take care of the Tedescos? We also have Steiger's car driving all the way from Florida to Maine, just like Perlman did earlier, which is major miles on the clock. Perlman was afraid to fly. Steiger probably just chose not to, given how he looked. A man like him would be memorable for all the wrong reasons, and that's bad news in his line of work."

"But why kill them at all?" asked Angel.

Walsh was about to tell Angel what he thought of people who stated the fucking obvious when he caught that lazy smile again and held his tongue.

"Yeah, why?"

"And in that order?"

"Uh-huh." Walsh considered the question. "Perlman is tortured and killed, but before he dies he reveals something to Steiger about the

Tedescos, and before they die they give him something that brings him back to Ruth Winter?"

Walsh drummed his fingers on the table, then shook his head.

"No, it's still a lot of back-and-forth. Too much."

He assumed his best interrogator's pose. He'd started out determined not to get too comfortable with these men, knowing something of what they'd done in the past, and might do again in the future. It disturbed him that he'd fallen so easily into conversation with them. They were chatting like they'd all attended crime school together.

"So, now that we've cleared the air, and I've shared what I know while tacitly warning you against burning down any more towns in my state, why don't you add to my store of knowledge about Earl Steiger and his kind?"

Just then, the waitress arrived to clear away the appetizer plates.

"You barely touched your crab cakes," she admonished Louis. "Were they okay?"

"They were real good," said Louis. "I just need to watch my food intake, stay slim and handsome. My friend over there"—he indicated Walsh with an outstretched finger—"he's not so concerned."

Walsh raised his ring finger, displaying his wedding band.

"I'm married," he said. "Means I can eat anything I like. Woman's stuck with me."

"I'm sure you were quite the catch," said the waitress.

"The whole crew had to pull together to land him," said Angel.

Walsh scowled at him. The waitress patted Walsh on the shoulder.

"Don't pay them any attention, honey," she said. "I don't like seeing food wasted."

"Burn," said Angel, once she'd departed. "You're like a food disposal unit to her."

"Fuck you," said Walsh, and returned his attention to Louis. "Go on: Steiger."

"I can't tell you more than that he may—*may*—have worked through this man Cambion," said Louis, "and probably has for a long time, given the children's identities that he's assumed. Using dead kids for ghosts is one of Cambion's hallmarks."

"This Cambion—is he the kind to answer questions?"

"Only with half-truths. The problem is finding him. He'd gone underground for a decade, and only surfaced earlier this year before disappearing again. He's a hunted man. Even if Steiger was one of Cambion's, and you could track him down, he wouldn't give away the identity of the buyer on the job, or not for a price that you could afford."

Their main courses arrived. Walsh's plate was almost entirely hidden by dry-rub ribs. It looked like someone had killed and barbecued a dinosaur.

"If you finish those, I'll give you five bucks," said Angel. "Well, I'll send your widow five bucks."

"You're drinking a white wine called Queen Anne's Lace," said Walsh. "As a straight man, I'm ashamed to be seen with you."

"Since we're playing guess-the-reasoning," said Louis, "why did Steiger let Ruth Winter's child live? You saw his face: a man who looks like that doesn't stay hidden by leaving witnesses to his crimes."

Walsh used a stripped rib held in his right hand to count off the possibilities on the fingers of his left.

"One: he's softhearted."

"Unlikely."

"Two: he was only paid for one killing, and doesn't murder for free."

"I've known men like that. They'd make an exception for a witness, though."

"Three: he was told not to harm the girl."

"I'd go with three," said Louis.

"So would I."

Louis sipped his wine. It was good, as was his blackened haddock. The killings, and the motivations behind them, did not trouble him on an emotional level, beyond the fact that they had put Parker back in the hospital, if only for a couple of days. As a professional, though, they struck him as curious. He noticed that Walsh had gone quiet and was concentrating on his food. Perhaps it was the effort of eating all those ribs, or Walsh had decided that he had obtained all that might prove useful from his dinner companions for now. In truth, Louis had not given him very much, yet had certainly held nothing back.

Parker should have been with them. The private detective had a way of making the kind of imaginative leaps that were beyond so many of his peers in law enforcement, and were certainly beyond Louis. He would have found the flaw in their reasoning, the diverging paths at which they had gone astray. After all, it was Parker, from his hospital bed, who had told Walsh about the mezuzah on Ruth Winter's door, and how that had initially caused him to speculate on a connection between Perlman and herself. It was also Parker who had set in motion the chain of events that led to Perlman's body being autopsied in the first place, and all of this while he was supposed to be recuperating from gunshot wounds. As Walsh had noted, there were no others like Parker.

Louis and Angel missed Parker's company. They had grown so used to being part of the investigator's existence, and the investigator being part of their own, that the months since his shooting seemed strangely empty, as though they were being held in stasis, waiting for Parker to return to them. All Louis could say for certain was that when he looked into Parker's eyes he saw a man in the process of reformation, and he had an image of a sword melting in a forge, there to be molded into a new instrument, although if that was to be a weapon remained to be established.

Suddenly Louis didn't want his fish, or his wine. He looked at Angel, and Angel looked back at him. His partner smiled, and had they not been in the company of Walsh, Louis might well have touched his hand.

Outside the night pressed itself enviously against the glass, seeking to break through and smother them all.

XLII

At the Eastern Maine Medical Center in Bangor, Charlie Parker stared out at that same darkness and saw his reflection floating in its midst, as though he himself were lost in a void. Below him lay the city, and traffic, and people, but he took in none of it. In his mind he walked by the shore of a lake, a child holding his hand, his dead wife shadowing them, whispering warnings to him while she hid herself from her god.

A nurse entered his room, pulling him back to reality. He had moved from his bed and was lying semirecumbent on an adjustable armchair, his feet outstretched. Sitting upright was uncomfortable for him, but standing or lying caused him little trouble. The nurse adjusted his cushions—he hid the pain that it caused him behind a wince disguised as a smile—and inquired if he needed anything. He wanted nothing but to be left alone, yet asked if she could pour him some water from the pitcher on the bedside table. He didn't want to give her any cause to be concerned about him because of silence or withdrawal. He had been told that he might be able to leave in the morning once the surgeon had given him the all clear, and he planned to let nothing get in the way of that likelihood. (The smartest move he'd ever made was not allowing his health insurance to lapse, otherwise he'd have been living out of his car. His policy had even covered his therapy at Brook House, once they'd moderated their rate. That said, he still **made** sure that any doctor who even looked in his direction did so as part of his coverage.) The nurse gave him the water, and he sipped it for appearance's sake before she left.

He was no longer receiving fluids intravenously, but the needle remained inserted in the back of his hand. He disliked the feel and the sight of it. He wanted it gone. It bothered him more than the stitches in his side from the keyhole surgery, where they'd gone in to repair the damage caused by the blow he had received from the man who called himself Earl Steiger. He had been fortunate, the surgeon told him, once he'd come out of the anesthetic: had Steiger gone at him with a vengeance, and delivered some more punches or kicks, he might well have killed him. It hadn't seemed worth pointing out to the surgeon that Steiger had only stopped kicking him because a bullet required less effort, so the end result would have been the same. Anyway, the fact that Cory Bloom remained in the center's Intensive Care Unit following surgery to remove the bullet that had punctured one of her lungs said everything about Earl Steiger's ultimate intentions.

Parker had been thinking about Steiger a lot, but not in the way that the counseling psychologist might have wished. She had paid a brief visit earlier that day, offering her services. She was young and genuine, and so far out of her depth with him that, even had he felt the urge to open up to her, he would have stopped himself for fear of frightening her out of her chosen profession.

The fact that he had been under Steiger's gun didn't register with Parker. He had been under guns before, and learned that there were only two possible outcomes: either the gun did not fire, leaving all relatively well, or the gun fired, leading to death—in which case he would know nothing more—or injury. He had survived the latter, and he knew that he could take the pain. It was terrible, but it had not killed him.

No, what he kept coming back to was the look of surprise on Steiger's face as the dune collapsed beneath him: shock at the disappearance of the ground from under his feet, but also a kind of astonishment that Death could have found time in his busy schedule to come calling at last, and in such a form.

And then, beyond Steiger and his dying, there was Sam, and her demeanor as the man who had been threatening her father vanished in a flood of white sand: her implacable fury, and the depth of her concentration, evidence of the exertion of a great effort of will. In that moment she was both his daughter and something else, something beyond reckoning. He did not want to say it. He did not want to speak it aloud. But he still heard his own voice say the words as he stared into the dark, conversing with the ghost of himself that hung suspended in the blackness.

She did it. My daughter willed him dead, and he died.

My daughter. What is my daughter?

CHAPTER

XLIII

They were almost done. Louis tried to ignore the fact that Angel was having coffee with his wine, although the flicker of annoyance that crossed his face every time Angel followed a sip of one with the other gave him away. Walsh, having reached his limit on beer, was sticking to water.

As the meal concluded, the conversation moved on to other subjects: Parker, briefly; Cory Bloom's condition; and, once Walsh realized that they weren't trying to score points off either him or the Maine State Police, Oran Wilde.

"So you're looking for an accomplice?" asked Angel.

"Like you said earlier, he's damn bright for a teenager. Somebody has to be hiding him."

"Unless he didn't do it," said Louis, "and someone else killed his family."

"But then why spare Oran?"

"Maybe he didn't."

"'He'?"

"Does it look like the work of a woman to you?"

"Gunshots? Fire? No, it doesn't. We're keeping an open mind—mainly because we don't have a whole lot of choice—but Oran doing the killings still looks like the most obvious solution. It's like that

Occam's razor business: the simplest solution is usually the right one."

"Except Occam never wrote that," said Louis.

"Didn't he?" said Walsh. "Next you'll be telling me that he didn't even own a razor."

"He was a monk, and they had to shave their heads, so he probably did—or else he borrowed one," said Louis. "That's not the point. The point is that Occam didn't think that the simplest solution was usually right. What he wrote was that 'plurality must never be posited without necessity,' and only in a limited context. He wasn't thinking of homicide investigations, or not that anyone can tell. Neither was he suggesting that the simpler a solution, the better."

"Is he always like this?" Walsh asked Angel.

"Only with wine," said Angel. "Actually, strike that: yes, he is always like this. He does still surprise me with his knowledge, though, even after all these years."

Louis let them talk. He was gifted with considerable patience. He could not have remained with Angel otherwise. When they had finished amusing themselves, he continued speaking as though they were not present, and he was working out the solution to a problem aloud, but alone.

"Oran Wilde's family dies one day after the body of Bruno Perlman washes up at Boreas," he said. "There is a certain type of man—a certain type of *criminal*—who might take the view that the way to distract attention from one violent crime is to commit another, especially in an area, or a state, where violent crime is untypical. It won't work in Detroit or Oakland or Memphis, not in the same way. In those cities, it would be a question of hiding one body among others. In Maine, it would be a matter of stretching resources, a sleight of hand, forcing the authorities to concentrate on one action or the other, but not both at the same time."

"You're suggesting a connection between the Wilde family and what happened in Boreas? On what evidence?"

"None but my own impressions. If I were ruthless enough"—Louis let the conditional clause hang for a moment, as much to give himself time to consider its implications as his listeners—"and the stakes were sufficiently high, then I might consider it worth my while to kill many to draw attention from one. It would be like starting a fire in one corner of a room to disguise the fact that you'd lit a match in another."

"I don't buy it," said Walsh.

"Of course you don't," said Louis. "You just misquoted William of Occam. A man clever enough to do this would know that an over-worked police force, even with the help of outside agencies, would be inclined to follow the straightest path, the most obvious solution. He's adding variables in the knowledge that you'll dismiss them, or most of them. Ultimately, it's a smoke screen: the solution is simple, but not as simple as you've made it out to be. There is no connection between the Wildes and Boreas, but that's the connection."

"You'd never make a cop," said Walsh. "You're too creative."

"Damn," said Louis. "And I was banking on that thirty-five grand starting salary to buy my yacht."

"What about the message that Oran Wilde left?"

"From what I read, he didn't *leave* a message. The message was sent later. And what did it say: 'I hated my family and burned our house down, but I'm misunderstood' or some shit like that? What the fuck kind of kid kills his family, then takes the time to sit down a day or two later and write a message to his buddy that basically says nothing at all, that doesn't even ask for help?"

"That wasn't really the first message," said Walsh, "but I take the point. Yeah, the texts we've picked up are odd. Again, could be the accomplice. Suppose I accept the idea of complications and variables. The messages, the dead homeless guy, they're just muddying the waters. But I have no reason to buy your central thesis about a link between Oran Wilde and Boreas."

"True," said Louis. "I was just thinking aloud."

"And Earl Steiger couldn't have killed the Wildes, the Tedescos, Perlman, *and* Ruth Winter. That's just not possible."

"No, it's not. You're back to an accomplice, but maybe just not the kind you thought."

Walsh wanted to go home, in part because his wife would be in bed by the time he got back, and he liked slipping under the sheets when she was already there, to feel her move as she woke to his presence, to return her good-night kiss and hear her sigh contentedly as she returned to sleep, happy that her husband had come back to her safe and sound. Such small pleasures made life worth living. But he was also looking forward to the journey, because he did a lot of his best thinking when he was driving alone, and Louis had given him much to think about.

Walsh called for the check. When it eventually arrived, it remained in the center of the table, untouched and unwanted.

"Hey, man," Angel said to Walsh, "why don't you pick that up and see what it is?"

Walsh reluctantly reached for his wallet.

"I figured you'd stiff me."

"And after all we've done for you," said Angel.

"Yeah, yeah."

Walsh placed his credit card over the check, and the waitress whisked both away.

"One final question," said Walsh. "How does a man who looks like Steiger manage to stay under the radar for so long?"

"If you look strange or different, you get pretty good at hiding yourself," said Louis. "You could choose to remain in sight, if you're brave enough, but that wouldn't work for a killer like Steiger. He needed the shadows. And he had help."

"This Cambion."

"Cambion knows how to hide."

Walsh's credit card was returned. He added a good tip. He wasn't cheap.

"Either of you ever hear of a man named Francis Galton?" he asked, as he reached for his coat.

Both Louis and Angel took their time answering. With Louis in particular, it was a matter of flicking through the Rolodex in his head just to make sure that, at some point in the past, he hadn't killed someone called Francis Galton.

"Not that I can recall," he said at last. Angel concurred.

"He was a founder of the science of eugenics—you know, improving the human race through selective reproduction, that kind of thing."

"A Nazi?" said Angel.

"No, he was pre-Nazi: late nineteenth century, I think. He thought you could identify character types through their features, so he set about photographing all kinds of people, including criminals. I think he was mostly interested in murderers. He'd line up the portraits, and expose each one to a photographic plate for a fraction of the time usually required for a full exposure so that he had a kind of composite, an average, on a single frame—you know, faces superimposed over one another."

"Why?" asked Angel.

"He was trying to find a common feature in their appearance: the essence of their criminality—of their evil, if you like. He wanted to believe that he could isolate it, that men who had committed terrible crimes might show some evidence of it on their faces. That way, you'd be able to tell who was a criminal just by looking at him. All he ended up with, though, was a series of distortions, and a kind of generalized degradation. But the photographs are interesting. Unsettling. I've been trying to figure out all evening why, when I looked at Steiger, there was something familiar about him. I just now remembered what it was: his face reminds me of one of Galton's composites, as if what was wrong with him inside had seeped through his pores and caused his skull to mutate."

"Your job would be a whole lot easier if you could tell the bad folk by the way they looked," said Angel. "Or you could just end up putting behind bars a whole lot of ugly people who'd never done anyone any harm, and leave a bunch of beautiful people with dead souls free to walk the streets."

They stood to leave.

"Galton had it all wrong," said Walsh. "The worst of them, the really foul ones, they hide their badness deep inside. They look just like average Joes and Janes, but underneath they're rotten right down to the core, and we don't find out about them until it's too late."

They left the restaurant and walked together to their vehicles.

"You know, Walsh, you're all right," said Angel. "For a cop."

"Likewise," said Walsh. "For whatever it is you are."

Louis simply nodded. None of them shook hands.

"Don't forget what I said about burning down towns," said Walsh. "You keep that shit for south of the Mason-Dixon."

He watched them head back to Portland. Tomorrow, he knew, they would return to Bangor to pick up Parker. He wished them luck. He wished them all luck.

Walsh drove home, the car silent, casting the miles behind him like discarded paper, shifting pieces of information in his mind, trying to make connections. When he got back to his house he removed his shoes on the doorstep, used the downstairs bathroom, undressed in the hall, and slipped between the sheets beside his sleeping wife. He felt her stir. Half-awake, she reached for him. He accepted her kiss, and returned it. He listened for that sigh, heard it with satisfaction, and watched her curl up like a cat. He turned over and thought that he would not sleep, but when he opened his eyes his wife was gone, and he heard the sound of the radio from below, and the clattering of breakfast dishes, and the voices of his children.

Enough, he thought. This is enough, and more.

XLIV

Marcus Baulman attended the interrogation—they called it an "interview," but Baulman knew better—at the Office of the United States Attorney, District of Maine, on Harlow Street in Bangor, without a lawyer in attendance. The formal letter had been delivered the day after Marie Demers's visit to his house, informing him of possible irregularities relating to his admission to the United States under the Displaced Persons Act of 1948, and the Immigration and Nationality Act of 1952. The letter noted that he could bring legal counsel with him, should he choose to do so.

Baulman had thought hard about the approach he should take, and decided that an innocent man, an old German American who had lived a blameless life, would not arrive with a lawyer in tow. He dressed in his best suit, and took his funeral shoes from their box in his closet, dusting them lightly with a cloth before putting them on. He looked at himself in the mirror and saw, beneath the wrinkles and liver spots, and the white of his sparse beard and hair, the specter of the man he used to be.

Baulman was frightened, but no more than anyone who was forced unwillingly into contact with the institutions of law and justice. He was not about to panic. It was not in his nature. He wished that his wife were still with him, for he had never been ashamed to rely on her for comfort and reassurance. On another level, though, he was glad that she had predeceased him. Kathryn had, in her way, been a simple woman: she loved her husband, and trusted him. He looked after the bills, the bank accounts, the mortgage, the purchase of cars, the planning of vacations, and she was happy to let him do so. She, in turn, took care of him. It was an old-fashioned relationship, but what was bad about that? He had never been unfaithful to her, and was certain that she had never been unfaithful to him. They had enjoyed more than fifty years together before she passed away in her sleep, and the only shadow on their marriage was the absence of children. Perhaps that, too, might now be seen as a blessing, just like Kathryn's absence from his life at this juncture. The loss of her had caused him so much pain, and he still lived with it every day, but at least it had spared her the hurt and confusion of all this. He would have denied everything, of course, and she would have believed him because she wanted to, and because her love for him was predicated on her faith in his honesty, but some doubt would surely have taken seed and prospered like a weed in a disused corner of her mind.

Marie Demers was waiting for him in the conference room with the historian, Toller, along with a third man whose purpose and affiliation they did not explain, merely referring to him as a "colleague," an Agent Ross. Baulman took an instant dislike to Ross. He had the eyes of one who was never disappointed because his expectations of humanity were too low to allow for it. They thanked him for coming. Baulman asked if he was under arrest. They told him that he was not, that this was a civil matter. They emphasized that point. They simply wanted to talk, they said, but he knew that, just like in the movies, anything he said could be used as evidence against him. They didn't warn him of this because they didn't have to. He wondered how they could think him such an old fool. Then he remembered that what they believed they were seeing was not Marcus Baulman, a retired bus driver, but Reynard Kraus, a war criminal.

Yet he had become adept at playing Baulman, and was not about to falter now. He had been Baulman for longer than he had been Kraus. In that sense, the former was more real than the latter, and when he protested his innocence he spoke with conviction, for it was Marcus Baulman speaking.

They went over some of the same territory as before, and he gave them the same denials. Then they moved on to specific allegations, including claims that, as Reynard Kraus, he had trained at the SS-Junkerschule Bad Tölz; that he had spent time at the SS Race and Resettlement Main Office in Posen before moving to the RSHA; that he had served as a "medical attendant" for one month at Auschwitz, following which he had been sent to Lubsko *Experimentallkolonie*, where he remained until the Allied advance forced the closure and liquidation of the camp. He was, they told him, not Marcus Baulman, who they now believed had been executed by the SS for desertion near the Dukla Pass on the Slovak-Polish border in September 1944, his death quietly concealed on orders from Berlin, where contingency plans were already being put in place to assemble new identities in the likely event of the collapse of the Reich.

Baulman asked, as before, where they had received such false information, and they spoke only of sources and documentary irregularities, and as he listened he smelled smoke without the heat of fire. It could yet bloom into flame, but if they had solid evidence then surely they would have confronted him with it. This was *ein Angelausflug*—a fishing trip. Baulman supposed that, in the past, some of their targets had confessed quickly, admitting their guilt. He was not about to join their number.

Then, just as he was allowing himself to relax a little, they sprang the next question on him.

"Have you ever heard of a man named Bruno Perlman, Mr. Baulman?"

Perlman, Perlman. He thought. Should he deny it outright? No, there was another way.

"Yes," he said, "I think I have."

He watched them all lean forward slightly, even the one called Ross, and he had to fight back a smile. It was as though he had caught their mouths with hooks. They were not the only anglers here.

"I read that name in the newspaper," he said. "He was the man who was found drowned at Boreas."

"You have a good memory for names," said Toller.

Had he made a mistake? No. A little anger. Just enough.

"I'm an old man," he replied, "but I'm not senile. I still read newspapers and watch the news, and Boreas is not so far from where I live. A lot has been happening there lately. Perhaps you should read the newspapers too."

He sat back in his chair and let them see that he thought he had scored a point.

"And Ruth Winter?" said Demers. "You knew of her, didn't you?"

"Yes," he said. "She was murdered. I saw it on the news. This was a terrible thing."

"Did you ever meet her?"

"No."

"Are you sure?"

"Yes. Or I don't think I ever did."

"So you're sure that you never met her, or you think you never met her?"

"I don't know!" He raised his hands in helplessness. "Could I have passed her on the street? Yes. Could I have raised my hat to her? Yes. Do I remember these things? No."

"And her mother, Isha Winter?"

"Again, I may have passed her on the street, but I could not put a face to that name."

Demers made a note on her legal pad with a pencil. He watched her write, and wondered what he might have said that was important enough to set down in print when a device on the table before them was recording everything. Nothing, he decided. It was another move in the game.

"Bruno Perlman," she said, "whom you say you did not know—"

"I did not know him. I do not 'say' this. It is true!"

Demers continued as though he had not interrupted her "—had four numbers tattooed on his arm. They were Auschwitz identification numbers, and corresponded to the names of four members of his family, the Nemiroffs. Does that name mean anything to you?"

"No."

"They were transferred from Auschwitz to Lubsko at the end of 1944."

"I told you before, I knew nothing of this place until you came to me and began speaking of it."

"I thought that you kept up with the news," said Demers. "It's been mentioned a lot lately. Thomas Engel served as a guard there. You know who Thomas Engel is, don't you?"

"I think I remember now. I have seen him on TV. They say he may be a war criminal."

"He is a war criminal, Mr. Baulman. We have no doubt of that. Have you ever met Thomas Engel?"

"No."

"Are you certain?"

"Yes."

"He lived in Augusta. That's not too far from you, is it?"

"Lots of people live in Augusta," said Baulman. "I haven't met most of them either."

"So you know of him?"

"Yes, but only from what I have learned on TV."

"Which mentioned Lubsko."

"I suppose it must have."

"Just to bring you up to speed, then: Lubsko was a nasty piece of SS trickery, designed to make prisoners—wealthy prisoners—believe that an alternative to being worked or gassed to death might be available, and their families might also be saved. Small, clean huts, with gardens in which vegetables could be grown. No mistreatment. No brutality. No gas chambers. But you had to be willing and able to pay for it. Those who were sent there were very carefully selected. They were prisoners who were strongly believed to have squirreled away significant wealth, maybe in the hope that, even if they didn't survive the war, their children might, and they would be looked after. So these wealthy men and women would be brought from other concentration camps and shown an alternative way of seeing out the war—along with their families—if only they could afford it, the clear implication being that, if they chose not to reveal the whereabouts of their gold, or their paintings, or their gemstones, they, and their children, and anyone else related to them, would be dead within days.

"Most paid up, Mr. Baulman. They died anyway, of course, once they'd been bled of whatever they had managed to hide. Lubsko operated on a regular cycle, so every month a new set of families would be transferred once every trace of their predecessors had been scrubbed from the camp. To further strengthen the illusion of possible salvation, a pair of Judas steers was kept there: a German couple masquerading as liberal intelligentsia, victims of political rather than religious persecution, as it was deemed too difficult to have Aryans pretend to be Jews for fear their imposture would be discovered.

"Only one person survived the camp: a young woman named Isha Górski. The Russians were advancing, and the guards were ordered to get rid of all remaining prisoners and torch the camp. Isha survived by hiding among corpses. Later, when she came to this country, she married a Jew named Isaac Winter and—"

"Isha Winter," said Baulman softly, as though he had just made the connection.

"Mother of Ruth Winter. You're telling me that you did not know her history?"

"No, I was aware of none of this. How could I be? I was not friends with her. I do not think I ever met the woman."

"Were you avoiding her?"

"No! Why would I avoid her?"

"For fear that she might recognize you."

"But how could she? I told you: we did not know each other."

"You live—what, maybe ten miles from Pirna? Surely you must have visited the town."

Baulman didn't even have to pretend to sound weary. "I repeat to you: I rarely go into Pirna. It is a small town. Things are expensive there. When I shop, I shop at the big supermarket outside Boreas, or maybe go to Bangor."

"And you don't socialize?"

"Miss," said Baulman, "I am over ninety years old. My wife is dead. My friends are dead. With whom do you suggest I socialize?"

He thought that he caught the man named Ross smiling. Demers did not smile.

"I still do not understand what all of this has to do with me," Baulman continued. "I think someone has been telling lies."

"Reynard Kraus, the man whom you deny that you are, was sent to Lubsko as a general assistant with 'special duties' at the start of 1944. Those duties included murdering children by lethal injection. We have confirmation of that in a note from Josef Mengele to the RSHA inquiring after Kraus's progress, and confirming that Kraus had attended the killing by injection of groups of children at Auschwitz, following which he had been permitted to perform the procedure himself, under Mengele's expert gaze. Apparently Mengele was concerned that his pupil might embarrass him, but the RSHA's response was entirely positive: Kraus had given no cause for complaint at Lubsko, and his conduct reflected well on his tutor.

"You see, Mr. Baulman, the difficulty with Lubsko was that, in order for the illusion of possible salvation to be maintained, very particular types of guards had to be used to staff the camp. They couldn't be your usual brutes. They had to possess a degree of refinement, of sensitivity.

But that presented problems when it came to disposing of the prisoner intakes, because refined, sensitive individuals tend to be bad at executing terrified naked men, women, and children. That was where Engel came in. We think that he and a couple of other men were kept off camp, and were only brought in when the killing needed to be done. But children—the few of them who had survived the other camps—were dealt with separately: a quiet injection was deemed less damaging to morale, even that of a killer like Engel. That became Reynard Kraus's job."

"I am not Reynard Kraus. I have told you this before."

"We've struggled to find pictures of Kraus," said Demers, as though she had not heard him. She flipped through some papers before her, and came up with a single photocopied page.

"Is this your driver's license, Mr. Baulman?"

He peered at the document.

"Yes."

"It's from your most recent renewal, right?"

He looked at the date.

"Yes." The state required people over sixty-five to renew their license every four years. He had been pleased not to be deprived of it.

"Thank you."

She put the document back in the pile before her, like a magician hiding a card.

"And this?"

He accepted a photocopied picture from her. It was the photograph taken of him when he first immigrated to the United States in 1952.

"Again, this is me."

He'd had some work done after the war, just enough to blur his appearance in case anyone might remember Reynard Kraus: a thinning of the nose, a tightening of the eyes, a reduction in the size of his earlobes, which were conspicuously large, a family trait.

"And this one?"

He recognized his party membership photo immediately, even

though it was blurred and damaged. He peered at it. He took off his glasses, wiped them on his tie, and examined it again.

"It is a very bad photo," he said.

"It was part of a batch that someone tried to burn," said Demers. "Thankfully, the fire was put out before it could do too much damage."

"I cannot tell who this is," he said, "but I do not think that it is me."

"You don't think that it's you," asked Demers, "or you know it isn't?"

Baulman was conscious of walking on treacherous ground. He was tempted to deny entirely that this was his photo, but it still bore some resemblance, he supposed, to the man who had come to the United States in 1952. Already he was thinking forward to any possible attempts to deport or extradite him, just in case it came to that. A good lawyer might be able to use that photo in his favor.

"It looks a little like me, but it is not me," he concluded. "Is this where the mistake was made?"

"I don't think there is a mistake, Mr. Baulman. Is this your handwriting?"

He looked at the document before him. It was some of the paperwork from his Petition for Naturalization filed in 1958, after he had lived in the United States for long enough to apply.

"Yes."

"And this?"

Another document, this time in German. It was a requisition form, filed during his time at the RSHA and dated 1942. Again, there were superficial similarities between the handwriting on the American form and the German, but he had practiced hard at changing his handwriting in the intervening years.

"No."

"We've begun preliminary handwriting analysis, Mr. Baulman. Already we've picked up some points of similarity."

Baulman didn't think "points" would be enough. He was growing more confident. They had very little on him, and nothing that would stand up as evidence. He was increasingly convinced that all they really had was Engel's testimony against him, but Baulman knew what hearsay was worth in a court of law, especially coming from an old Nazi trying to save his skin.

Demers set the three photographs of Baulman side by side: young, older, old.

"We're thinking of showing these photos around to see if they jog anyone's memory." Only now did she smile at him. "We'll be in touch again once we're done. Thank you for your time, Mr. Baulman."

She stood, and the others stood with her.

"Wait!" said Baulman. "What do you mean by this 'showing around'? Showing them to what people? You cannot do this. This is not legal. You are spreading lies about me!"

But they did not reply as they trooped out, and then a uniformed officer appeared at the door to escort Baulman from the building. Still, Baulman knew what they planned to do.

They were going to show his picture to Isha Winter.

XLV

The surgeon gave Parker the all clear, along with more painkillers and some advice about taking it easy, not straining himself, and not chasing armed men over dunes, only some of which he intended to take. He made a call to Angel and Louis, and read a newspaper in his room while he waited for them to pick him up. Only once did he venture from his room, and that was to peer through a window at Cory Bloom. A man was sitting by her bed, his face in profile. He was holding Bloom's hand and speaking to her, even though she was unconscious. Parker did not disturb them.

Shortly after midday, a worried-looking female nurse appeared at the door, along with an orderly pushing a wheelchair. He looked worried too.

"I don't need a chair," said Parker. The hospital had given him a crutch, but he had no intention of using it. He had only just decided to rid himself of his stick—his fall on the beach conveniently dismissed as an aberration—before the encounter with Steiger, and he wasn't about to replace one support with another.

"We thought it might be, um, quicker this way," said the nurse. She had a detectable Scottish accent.

"You in that much of a hurry to get rid of me?" Parker asked, as he shifted from his seat to the chair.

"No, it's just that, well, the men who are here to collect you are"—she struggled to find the right word, and settled for "large."

Parker closed his eyes. The fucking Fulcis. Maybe I should just stay here, he thought. I could barricade the doors. Then he had a vision of the Fulci brothers breaking through like a pair of rampaging monsters, tossing aside fragments of wood and furniture like so much kindling.

"I'm sorry," he said, although he wasn't sure what he was apologizing for.

"They haven't done any harm," said the nurse, walking alongside him as he was being pushed. "They just look intimidating. Are they friends of yours?"

"Yes. Kind of."

He felt about nine years old, like he was being picked up from school by a pair of embarrassing uncles. The Fulci brothers had their hearts in the right place—well, most of the time, depending on the other parties involved, and the degree of offense that they'd caused. The trouble was that the same couldn't be said for their brains, which had a resistance to chemical intervention to rival the Ebola virus.

"They can't help how they look, I suppose," said the nurse, adding, slightly hopefully, "I imagine they're lovely men, really."

He was wheeled into an elevator.

"That depends," said Parker.

"On what?"

"On whether or not they like you."

"Oh, that's the same for most people, isn't it?"

Parker recalled the tale of the driver—an insurance salesman, if he remembered correctly—who had consistently parked in the disabled spot at the back of the Fulcis' mother's house. He'd received one warning, which he ignored. That in itself was surprising. People who were warned by the Fulcis usually stayed warned. The next time he offended, the Fulcis pushed his car into the sea with their truck. The salesman was lashed to the driver's seat when they did it, and as the water climbed slowly to the level of his chest, he tried to tell them that he intended to reconsider his parking habits, although the ball gag in his mouth muffled his words somewhat.

Subsequently, when he'd started to dry off, he might have made noise about pressing charges, until it was pointed out to him that the Fulcis knew where his house was and were not above, as Tony Fulci put it, "picking that up as well and putting it in the fucking ocean," a point they emphasized by returning the salesman to his car and pushing the car, once more, into the sea, this time until the water reached his chin. Since then, the Fulcis' mother had enjoyed problem-free parking—and her vehicle insurance bill had gone down in the bargain.

"Maybe they react more emotionally than most people," said Parker.

"I always think big men like that have very deep feelings," said the nurse.

"That must be it."

The elevator opened, and he was wheeled through the lobby and out the main door, where the Fulcis' monster truck stood waiting by the curb, although it was hard to see because the Fulcis themselves were standing in front of it. Had they stood in front of the hospital itself, then it would largely have disappeared too. They were dressed in matching Izod golf shirts and tan pants that could have been filled with air and used as barrage balloons. As they lumbered in Parker's direction, the security guard at the door uttered an involuntary "Fuck me."

"Don't run," said Parker. "It'll just set them off."

The guard glanced at Parker to see if he was joking. When he looked away again, he didn't appear reassured.

"How you doin', Mr. Parker?" said Paulie.

The Fulcis had a habit of calling him "Mr. Parker." He supposed that it was a token of respect, in the same way that Tony, the less well-adjusted of the two—although this, too, varied depending on circumstance, inclination, and possibly the cycles of the moon—had once told

Parker that if anyone ever pissed him off, *ever*, Tony would feed him to crabs "and wouldn't even ask why."

"I've been better," Parker replied.

"Sure, sure. You want us to push you?"

He looked ready to fight the orderly for control of the chair, which wouldn't have worked out well for anyone involved.

"No, this guy's got it. Just get the door open, please."

"I'm on it."

He hurried back to the truck while Tony stayed alongside the detective, ready to leap in and save him should a stone on the ground cause the chair to wobble. When they reached the truck, Parker had to stretch to get in the back. He couldn't help but give a small groan of pain, which led each of the Fulcis to lend a hand, almost propelling him headfirst into the bench seat.

"We got him now," Tony told the nurse.

He radiated reassurance, as if their possession of her patient could not possibly be a cause for concern. The strange development, Parker thought, was that the nurse now looked as though she might be falling in love with one or both of the Fulcis, or it could just have been shock. Whatever it was, she kept staring at them as they drove away. Parker wouldn't have been surprised if she had waved a white handkerchief in farewell.

He couldn't recall ever being in their truck before, and wasn't sure that he ever wanted to again. Paulie drove with a hunched intensity: not particularly quickly, and not unduly slowly, but with the single-minded implacability of a tank commander advancing on a retreating foe. Other vehicles didn't linger long in his way, preferring to take their chances in adjoining lanes, or even on the curb. Paulie did stop for red lights, but appeared to take them very personally, and glowered in their direction until they were terrorized into changing.

"We bought you grapes," said Tony.

He gestured to a Whole Foods bag on the floor beside Parker.

"That's kind."

Tony waited, grinning encouragingly.

"Right," said Parker. He could see where this was going. He dipped into the bag and popped one of the grapes into his mouth. He grimaced. He thought about spitting it out, but somehow managed to force it down.

"Guys, those are olives."

Paulie punched his brother in the arm.

"I fucking told you!" he said.

"You don't like olives?" Tony asked, rubbing his arm while hoping to salvage something from the situation.

"It was just that I was kind of expecting a grape."

"You see?" said Paulie to his brother. "You fucking idiot."

"I never been in Whole Foods before," said Tony. "I didn't recognize nothing there."

"It's okay," said Parker. "It's the thought that counts."

Tony wasn't to be comforted. He stared out the window and didn't speak. Paulie put on some music. It was a Carpenters' compilation. He patted his brother's shoulder.

"It's okay," he said. "I shouldn't have gotten angry with you."

"Only Yesterday" began playing. Tony cheered up some.

Parker vowed, someday, to kill Angel and Louis for this.

––––––

ANGEL AND LOUIS WERE waiting for them at Dysart's Truck Stop and Restaurant on the outskirts of Bangor. Dysart's had been around since the 1940s, and counted as a Maine institution. It also housed the city's Greyhound bus station, so the whole place was busy, although not so busy that the arrival of the Fulcis and their truck didn't attract attention. The world could have been ending and people would still have stopped screaming for long enough to pause and stare at them.

Angel and Louis were sitting across from each other in a booth at the back.

Parker was using his crutch as he advanced on them. Tony had insisted: "You know, just until you're sure you can walk again."

"I'm not crippled," Parker told him.

"Man, that's what all crips say," Tony replied. "And I don't think you're allowed to call them crips no more."

"I didn't call them crips. You did."

Tony shrugged and gave his brother the eye, as if to say that he wasn't about to argue with a sick man, but, well, you know . . .

"You mind moving to the other side?" Parker asked Angel as he reached the booth. "It's less uncomfortable if I can stretch out."

Tony and Paulie took the booth across from them and started studying the menu.

Angel moved. He gestured at the crutch on his way past.

"What's that?"

"It's called a crutch."

"I know what it's called. You need it?"

"Just to shove up your ass for having me collected by the Hardy Boys over there. If I'd known, I'd have asked for a second one to use on your friend too."

"They wanted to help," said Louis. He was keeping a straight face, but it was clearly a struggle.

Parker slid into the booth.

"They fed me an olive disguised as a grape."

"It's an easy mistake to make," said Angel.

"I hate olives."

"Man, you're touchy today."

Parker let out a long breath.

"Yeah, I am touchy. If only I had a reason."

A waitress came over. Parker ordered some dry toast and a decaf coffee. Angel and Louis asked for refills. The Fulcis opted for a pair of club sandwiches. Each.

"So what do you want to do now?" said Louis.

"I can't drive for a couple of days. I'd appreciate a ride to Vermont. I want to see Sam."

"Did you speak to Rachel?" asked Louis.

"From the hospital. She said Sam was okay—a bit shaken up, but that's all."

"You know," said Louis, "I'm sure Tony and Paulie would be glad to act as chauffeurs."

"Don't even joke about it. Seriously."

"In that case, we're happy to help," said Angel, acting as peacemaker. "What about where you're going to stay? You don't want to go back to Boreas, right?"

"Boreas is still in the cards," said Parker. "After that, I may go home."

"Back to Scarborough?"

"Yes."

"You sure?" said Angel. "There's an apartment for rent across the hall from the one we got in Portland."

"Why are you still holding on to that?"

"We're starting to like Portland. We might move permanently."

"I'll tell the city fathers. I'm sure they'll be pleased, once they've had a chance to sell their homes. Look, you don't have to stay in Portland for me. I'm okay. In fact, I'm better than okay."

And Angel thought that there might be some truth to what Parker said. The distance that he had maintained since the shooting, the sense of his being at arm's length from what was going on around him, had lessened. He looked tired and drawn, and he was grumpy as a dying wasp, but he exuded a sense of purpose.

"Scarborough is still a mess," said Angel.

"I know."

As he'd told Walsh, he had been back to pick up some things before moving to Brook House. A medical orderly had wheeled him inside, and Parker had been forced to point out what he needed, or shout instructions from the bottom of the stairs. Someone had come in—

probably at the instigation of Angel and Louis—to clean up the blood, but damage remained to the doors and walls in the kitchen, the hallway, and his office. He hadn't lingered. He wasn't prepared to spend longer in his home than necessary, not then: the sense of intrusion, of violation, was too strong.

But he was ready now.

"You know," said Louis, "Paulie and Tony, they're pretty good with their hands. Let them go in while we're in Vermont, see what they can do. They love you. You're like a god to them. You ask, and give them long enough, they'll turn it into your own palace."

Parker had to admit that it wasn't a bad idea—not the palace part, but the rest. When he put it to the Fulcis, they reacted as though he were doing them a huge favor, and their genuine delight made him feel bad. They even tried to refuse payment for any work they did on the house, but he wasn't about to be made to feel like a charity case, or more of a charity case than he already felt himself to be.

"That's a done deal, then," said Angel. "We go to Vermont, they head to Scarborough."

Parker's coffee and toast came, along with the Fulcis' food.

"So," said Parker, "tell me about your dinner with Walsh."

CHAPTER

XLVI

Marie Demers sat at the old mahogany dining table in Isha Winter's home. The wood was a deep brown, and polished to within an inch of its life. Demers couldn't see a mark on it, and she doubted if it was used more than once or twice a year. It would seat ten people comfortably, twelve at a squeeze, and she could picture it set for Thanksgiving or Hanukkah. She doubted if those holidays would be celebrated this year, not after what had happened to Ruth Winter. Demers already felt bad for intruding on Isha's grief.

Ruth's death had set in motion a complicated series of negotiations about Amanda Winter's future, although all involved, whether state or family, agreed on a number of important issues: that the girl's grandmother loved her very much, but was too old to take care of the child alone; nevertheless, it would be good for Amanda to be close to her grandmother, and to remain in the area where she had grown up and was attending school; and suitable foster parents should be found as a matter of urgency.

Those parents might already have presented themselves, it seemed, for Amanda was currently staying with the Frobergs, a couple in their early forties with two children of their own, a boy and a girl, respectively a year older and a year younger than Amanda. They lived only five minutes from Isha's house. It helped that Isha approved of them, and Amanda was already friendly with their kids from school. While the whole process was still in its early stages, signals from the Maine Department of Health and Human Services were favorable.

Isha Winter arrived from the kitchen, carrying a tray containing a pot of coffee, cups, cream, sugar, and three plates, the topmost of which was dominated by a massive cake. She had declined Demers's offer of help with her preparations. This was her domain, but it also struck Demers that the old woman might be anxious to show just how strong and independent she remained, as if to further enhance the case for her granddaughter's continued presence in the town—not that Demers would have any say in what was going to happen, although if anyone did ask, she would have no compunction about remarking on Isha's continued vitality, which was remarkable for a woman in her nineties.

They had met a number of times before, the first during the investigation into Thomas Engel, when Demers had visited Isha to ask if she recalled him. Isha didn't, but that was not surprising: from what the HRSP had been able to piece together from fragmentary evidence about Lubsko, Engel only came when there was killing to be done. When he came to Lubsko for the final time, chaos had already erupted, with guards turning on guards. Isha, initially alerted to what was happening by the sound of gunfire, and then confirmed in her fears by the sight of her parents lying dead outside their hut, was by then already trying to hide herself.

Their second meeting had occurred after Isha became aware of Bruno Perlman's death. She recalled him as an intense man who had wanted to record their conversation, and whose questioning bordered on the insensitive, particularly for an old woman who lived every day with the memory of what happened at Lubsko yet, like some who have been through great trauma, endure only by refusing to speak of it aloud, as if to do so would be to give it substance, and return them to the reality of it. But Isha felt some obligation to help this man who was clearly so haunted by his family's past. She could tell him little that he did not already know, though, for she had not been at the camp when his relatives died. Eventually her daughter had returned home and, seeing how upset her mother was being made by the interview, terminated it as gently, yet as forcefully, as she could.

Demers and Isha had then met briefly at Ruth's funeral, and now Demers was sitting in Isha's home, with what she hoped might be a sliver of connective tissue between Ruth's murder and the man who called himself Marcus Baulman.

Isha set the tray down on the table, and carefully placed cork mats on the mahogany before adding the cups and plates. She poured the coffee, and allowed Demers to add her own milk and sugar.

"You will have some babka?" she said, although Demers felt that it was more an order than a question.

"I'd love a piece," she said, and Isha cut her a slice as thick as her arm, and a smaller portion for herself.

Demers tried it. God, it was good—not that she knew babka from bupkis, but this really was fantastic. It was crumbly and chocolaty, with a hint of familiar essence to it.

"What do you think?" asked Isha.

She had not yet touched her own slice. Her attention was fixed entirely on her visitor. Had Demers expressed dissatisfaction, even just through an absence of enthusiasm, she was certain that Isha would have been unable to eat, and might never have prepared her babka again. But there was no cause for Demers to feign enthusiasm. She thought she might actually weep, the cake was so good.

"It's wonderful. Are those nuts I'm tasting?"

"Are you allergic?"

"No, not at all. I just can't figure out what nut it is."

Only then did Isha take a bite of her own cake.

"No nuts," she said.

"Seriously?"

"Mascarpone cheese. Others use cream cheese, but mascarpone is better. It gives the dough that flavor. Before you leave, I must write down the recipe for you."

Good luck with that, thought Demers. She wasn't a bad cook, but baking was too much like science—or alchemy—for her liking. It required the kind of precision that she instinctively applied to her work, but when she got home she preferred to be a little more relaxed in her culinary endeavors.

"How is Amanda doing?" she asked.

Isha finished her own mouthful before answering.

"Good and bad," she said. "She has nightmares, and her condition, her syndrome, has worsened again. They say that maybe she should talk to a therapist."

"It might help."

"But I am here for her. I will always listen to her."

"And that's good," said Demers. "She needs that stability. But the circumstances in which her mother died were particularly awful. Amanda saw her mother's body, and her killer, and was assaulted by him in turn. She's still just a child, and if she receives the help that she needs now, it'll ease the burden later."

"You're right, of course," said Isha. "Yes, a therapist. I will tell them."

She used her fork to cut away another piece of babka. They spoke of the ongoing investigation into her daughter's death. Just as the police had done, Demers asked if Isha could think of any reason why Bruno Perlman might have wished to contact her daughter, but she could not.

At last Isha placed her fork on the plate, leaving the rest of her cake untouched. There was silence as she waited for Demers to explain why she was here.

"Mrs. Winter," she began, "does the name Reynard Kraus mean anything to you?"

Isha reacted as though she had been stabbed with the point of a blade. She grimaced, and her right hand lifted slightly as though to ward off a second assault.

"Yes," she said. "I know that name."

"He was at Lubsko, right?"

"He was a killer of children. I saw him take them away, when the Russians were coming. He had a small room at the back of the medical clinic, but I didn't know what he was planning to do with them in there, not then, not until I saw the bodies being carried out. Then we heard the first shots, and my father told me to run, and I ran."

Demers let a few seconds pass before proceeding. She had met many former concentration camp prisoners in her time, and survivor guilt was a common trait. She could only begin to imagine the kind of guilt Isha Winter carried from being the only one to have gotten out of a camp alive.

"I'd like to show you a picture, if I may," said Demers.

"Certainly."

Isha wore her glasses on a chain around her neck. She put them on as Demers reached into her satchel and removed a blue plastic folder. From it she took the photograph of Baulman taken when he was first admitted to the United States. She placed it before Isha, who took it in her hands and examined it closely.

"I don't know this man," said Isha.

"Please, look at it again. Take your time."

Isha did as she was asked, but in the end she shook her head.

"No, I don't know him. Who is this?"

"Isn't it . . . Reynard Kraus?"

"No, this is not Kraus."

Demers couldn't believe it. She had been growing increasingly sure about Baulman, even if it was only circumstantial evidence—and the claims of Engel as he tried to wriggle his way off the hook of extradition—that pointed toward the possibility that he was Kraus. It took Demers a moment to find her voice, and she couldn't prevent it from betraying her disappointment.

"You're sure, absolutely sure?"

"You think I would not remember his face? No, this man is not Reynard Kraus. Who is he?"

Demers didn't know how to answer. She put the picture of Marcus Baulman on the table, and handed Isha instead Reynard Kraus's party membership photo.

"What about this one?"

Isha puffed out her cheeks. She held up the photo, adjusting it so that the light shone better upon it.

"It could be Kraus," she said at last. "Don't you have a better photograph?"

"This is all we have."

"I—I want to say yes. You know, it might be him, but I could not swear to it. Why are you asking me this? Do you think you've found him? Have you found Kraus?"

"I thought we had," said Demers. "Please, look again at that first photo. It's possible that Kraus may have had some work done on his face to alter his appearance."

"I don't need to look at it again," said Isha. "The eyes are wrong."

"The shape of them?"

"No, the spirit revealed through them. The soul. Can a man change this?"

"No," said Demers. "I suppose he can't."

But Isha's attention had been drawn to the final photo in Demers's file, the one from Baulman's driver's license. Isha's face reflected confusion, then a kind of recognition.

"I have seen this man."

She tapped the photograph. Demers could see her straining to remember where, or when, she had encountered Baulman. This was dangerous territory for Demers. By showing the picture to Isha Winter, she was letting her know that the shadow of suspicion had touched him. Who knew what impact that might have in a series of small, close-knit coastal communities? Baulman's reputation—even what was left of his life—could be tainted or ruined entirely if word got out that he was being investigated on suspicion of war crimes. Isha had already undermined Demers's case by failing to identify Kraus from his immigration photo, although the damage was not fatal. Despite what Isha had said, memories alone were unreliable, especially as people got older. The problem for Demers and her colleagues was that what they had on Baulman was flimsy: the word of Engel, some inconsistencies in Baulman's paperwork in Germany that could probably be explained away by a good lawyer, and the incomplete records from Lubsko indicating that Reynard Kraus had been responsible for the deaths of at least seventy children. Had Isha Winter, the sole survivor of Lubsko, confirmed that Baulman and Kraus were one and the same, it would have significantly strengthened their case against him.

"He lives not far from here," said Demers carefully.

"What is his name?"

"I can't tell you that for now. Could he perhaps be Kraus? Can you picture Kraus as an elderly man?"

And once more came the same answer.

"No. I'm sorry: it is again the eyes. This is not the man who killed those children."

"And you're absolutely certain of this? I apologize for persisting, but you of all people will understand how important it is."

Isha removed her glasses.

"I wish I could tell you it was him. More than anything, I want it to be so. But I cannot say what is not true."

A throbbing commenced in the left side of Demers's skull. Suddenly the light streaming through the window was too bright, and when Isha poured fresh coffee the noise of the pot striking against the cup resonated so painfully that Demers felt it in her teeth. The migraine would be on her within the hour.

Isha perceived her discomfort.

"Miss Demers, are you unwell?"

"Sorry," said Demers. "I feel a headache coming on, and I don't think I've brought any pills with me. Would you have some painkillers? Not aspirin, though: I'm allergic. Acetaminophen, maybe?"

"I'll see."

She left the room, and Demers heard her searching in the kitchen cupboards.

Demers put her head in her hands. She had wanted so badly to have Isha make a positive identification. They'd continue looking into Baulman, of course, but some of the momentum had now gone from the investigation, and the clock was always ticking. It was merciless, implacable. No matter what they did, or how hard they tried, it would continue to run down until there was no time left at all, and justice would be lost in that final silence.

Isha could only find some Alka-Seltzer cold medicine, the kind that caused drowsiness, but the pain in Demers's head was getting worse. She decided to take one of the soluble tablets instead of two. With luck, it would keep the migraine at bay while not impairing her ability to drive, or not too much, until she could check into her hotel and rest. She knocked the tablet back.

"Would you like to lie down?" asked Isha.

"No, thank you. I have to go."

Demers stood and gathered her things.

"I don't know what I can do," said Isha. She looked distraught, as though she had let Demers down by failing to give her the answer she was expecting.

"Nothing," said Demers. "It's not your fault. We'll keep looking. We'll keep trying. If I have any news, I'll be in touch."

Isha accompanied her to the door. Halfway down the hall, she stopped and took Demers's arm.

"The recipe," she said. "I meant to give you the babka recipe."

"Another time," said Demers. "It'll keep."

But Isha had something more to say, for she had not relaxed her grip.

"Please," she said, "I don't want you to take this the wrong way."

"Take what?" asked Demers, not understanding.

"I wonder sometimes why this matters so much to all of you."

Demers was taken aback. How could it not matter? How could Isha even ask such a question?

"Don't you want these people found and punished, Isha?" she replied. "They're criminals. What they did was monstrous, without equal in history."

"This, I know," said Isha. "But you must understand something, Miss Demers. I have thought long about this, and I believe that you and your superiors are acting out of guilt, because you failed all of us so long ago."

It hit Demers with the force of a blow.

"What do you mean?"

"You knew that the Jewish people were under threat. Your American government even convened a conference at Evian in 1938 to seek a solution to the refugee problem, but all of you, with but one exception—the Dominican Republic—refused to alter your immigration policies. You left us to die. And even when the truth of the camps was revealed, you did nothing."

"That's not true."

"You were asked to bomb the railways, the camps, but you did not."

"There were legitimate concerns about injuring or killing prisoners if bombing raids were sanctioned."

"Prisoners were being gassed and hanged and shot! Six thousand a day at Auschwitz alone in the summer of 1944!" Isha laughed, and Demers thought that she had never heard quite so much despair in the sound. "How much worse could bombing have been? Don't you see? All this is just too late. It won't bring the dead back. It will only allow you to sleep a little better in your beds at night."

Demers didn't know how to reply. Her head was thumping. She thought she might be sick.

"I'm sorry you feel that way," she said, and the words were so inadequate that she felt overwhelmed by a sense of their ridiculousness.

Isha gave Demers's arm a final squeeze.

"Sometimes, I don't know how I feel," said Isha. "Forgive me. You are a good young woman, and I am a foolish old one."

Demers said good-bye and walked to her car. She'd had failures in the past—they all had—but this one bothered her more than most, because she'd been so certain. Engel feared being returned to Germany, where he knew no one and would die a pariah. He wanted to save himself, yet he appeared to have lied.

And Isha Winter was partly right: Demers and her colleagues were motivated by an acute sense of justice, but their actions also represented a form of recompense, of atonement for the failures of the past; for the laziness and political expediency; for the parsimony that had deprived the hunt of resources for so long; and for the greed—for information, for new technology, for knowledge—that led American intelligence to join hands with men as terrible as Klaus Barbie and Friedrich Buchardt, whose *Einsatzkommando* unit was responsible for literally tens of thousands of deaths, making him the biggest mass murderer employed by the Allies after the war. Had the OSI been formed earlier—perhaps in the fifties, or even the early sixties—would the CIA have permitted Demers's predecessors to purge it of its Nazi connections? The depressing answer was that she doubted it.

Enough: she hadn't failed, not yet. Identification alone wouldn't have put Baulman on a plane back to Germany anyway. An obstacle had been placed in their way, and they'd simply have to find a way around it.

But it wasn't just about Isha. There was also her daughter, and Bruno Perlman, and the Tedescos. Perlman remained connected to Isha through Lubsko, and although doubts were now being raised about whether the mark on his orbital socket had actually been made by a blade, Demers was still convinced that he'd been murdered, if only because Lenny Tedesco, who appeared to be one of Perlman's few friends, had also been killed, along with his wife, and Demers wasn't about to buy that many coincidences.

Now there was Baulman, another potential Lubsko link in Maine, even if it had been almost severed by Isha Winter's inability to identify him as Kraus. No, this wasn't over. Pieces were missing, but they would find them.

On the drive to Bangor, the ticking of her watch grew so loud that she took it off and placed it in the glove compartment.

Yet still she thought she could hear it.

CHAPTER

XLVII

The ride from Bangor to Burlington, Vermont, was about six
hours—or more, since Louis was doing most of the driving.

"You drive like you got Miss Daisy in the back," said Angel,
as they made stately progress west. "I feel like I'm in a fucking funeral
cortege."

"And you know why I drive this way?"

"Because you're frightened?" suggested Angel. "Because someone
put a limiter on the car? Why?"

"Because I'm black. That's why I'm careful."

"You're not careful: you're just slow. The internal combustion engine is
wasted on you. You want me to get out and walk in front with a red flag?"

"Yeah, would you? Then I could run you over."

"You couldn't accelerate fast enough to run me over. By the time you
got up to speed, I'd have died of old age."

"Why don't you just count the number of black men you see driving
cars between here and Vermont? It's like a white supremacist road race.
And while you're counting, go find me a black state trooper. Around
here, they see a black man doing fifty and they're already writing his
name beside a cell door."

"At least if you get arrested in Vermont they might give you ice
cream, try to rehabilitate you."

Parker listened to them bicker. His back was against the door on the passenger side, his feet stretched out before him. He'd taken a pain-killer—just some Tylenol, not the prescription stuff they'd given him before he left the hospital. He wanted to keep a clear head.

He'd called Rachel shortly after they left Bangor, and told her he was on his way to see Sam, with Angel and Louis in tow. He assured her they wouldn't stop by until the morning, though. By the time they reached Burlington it would be nine p.m. at least, and he didn't want her to keep Sam up on his account. Rachel didn't sound too pleased to hear that he was heading to Vermont without giving her more notice, but he didn't care. Relations between them had been even more tense since Ruth Winter's murder. Rachel had driven from Burlington to Maine as soon as the call came in from the police informing her of what had happened on the beach at Green Heron Bay. She'd arrived at the Eastern Maine Medical Center to find her daughter in the care of a female officer, and Parker's internal injuries being treated on an oper-ating table. She'd then stayed with Sam while she gave her statement to the police, and they'd both been present when Parker had come out of the anesthetic. He hadn't been able to say much to either of them, but he could feel Rachel's anger, even through his drug-induced daze. He'd only spoken to Rachel once since then, when he'd called to check on Sam. She'd been pretty curt. He couldn't blame her.

Parker's side began to hurt after a couple of hours in the car, so they stopped at a Dunkin' Donuts to get some coffee and let him stretch his legs. He felt like a dog being exercised. They then drove on for a time before deciding to break up the ride at St. Johnsbury, where they checked into a chain motel and ate at Bailiwicks on Mill.

Over coffee, Louis told them the story of The Man Who Died Twice.

"You remember Bart Freed?" he asked Angel.

"No."

"Yeah, you do. He was a shylock out of Ocean City. Had a piece of some arcades far south as Cape May."

"Bodybuilder? Looked like someone had amputated his neck and stuck his head straight back on his shoulders?"

"That's him."

"Yeah, I recall him now. He died a couple of years ago, right?"

"Burst a blood vessel while bench-pressing four hundred pounds. Caved in his chest. So way back, there's a guy called Minimum Mike— got the name because he only ever pays the vig on his loans without ever denting the principal. But then Minimum Mike becomes Below-Minimum Mike, and crosses so many people who shouldn't be crossed that he's like a map of chaos, and these people decide it's time something was done about him. So they hire two guys out of Maryland to take care of him, and Bart Freed sets him up. Minimum Mike comes to Bart's house to talk about his debts, the two Maryland shooters are waiting inside for him, they quiet him down, and then they take him away. They don't drive him too far because, you know, nobody wants to be pulled over with some guy weeping in the backseat. They already have the hole dug for him in the woods so they shoot him, watch him fall in, then cover him up and drive off. They take the car to an all-night wash, get the full treatment for it inside and out, go have a burger and a beer, and figure they've done a good night's work. They crash at a motel and sleep like babies.

"Then, about four a.m., they get a call, and it's one of the guys who's picking up the tab for the night's work. He tells them that there's some problem at Freed's place, and to get their asses over there and sort it out, because Freed's hysterical, and it doesn't pay to have people hysterical after the event.

"So they drive back to Ocean City, and Freed answers the door. He's calmed down some, but he still doesn't seem happy. He doesn't even let them into the house, not immediately. He keeps them on the doorstep, and he says,

" 'So, Minimum Mike.'

" 'Yeah?'

" 'You did what you were supposed to do, right?'

"And the hitters say, yeah, of course they did, and they explain about the hole in the ground, and the gun, and covering up the body.

" 'So he's dead?' says Freed.

" 'Yeah, he's dead.'

" 'Well, if he's dead, why the fuck is he sitting at my kitchen table?'

"So the two hitters look at Freed like he's dropped a couple of screws, and he steps aside to let them in. They go to the kitchen, and just like the man said, Minimum Mike is sitting there. He doesn't look good. He's, like, covered in earth and dirt and shit, and when they make a closer examination they see that he has a hole in the back of his head and another close to his right eye, but it's definitely him. He's also got a glass of milk in front of him, and a cookie, although he hasn't touched them. They ask Freed why he has the milk and the cookie, and Freed tells them that he didn't know what else to give him.

"They figure what happened was that the bullet entered his skull, damaged his brain, came out under his eye, but didn't kill him. Somehow he woke up in the grave, managed to claw his way out, and had some vague memory in what was left of his lobe of being at Freed's house, so that was the first place he went to."

"What did they do?" asked Angel.

"They put him in the trunk of the car, drove him back to the grave, shot him again, and buried him. The second time, he didn't come back. The hitters, they didn't come back either. They retired. I think one of them had a breakdown."

Angel thought about it all.

"Is that true?"

"What I heard."

"Wow."

"Was a time," remarked Louis, "when you'd have said more than 'Wow' after a story like that."

"I guess it takes a lot to surprise me now," said Angel.

"Yeah," said Louis. "Takes a lot to surprise us all. We splitting the check?"

"No," said Parker. "I got it."

"Wow," said Angel. "That is—"

"Don't," warned Parker. "Just don't."

XLVIII

Baulman returned home from walking his dog. He was soaking wet, and the animal, an aging Weimaraner named Lotte, was shivering. Baulman had always had Weimaraners, and he credited them with keeping him relatively youthful until recent years. They needed a lot of exercise, and he had to be wary of walking them in the woods in case they caught the scent of deer and their hunting instinct kicked in, but they were intelligent, highly trainable, and immensely loyal. Lotte rarely left Baulman's side, but her muzzle was gray now, and he had fewer concerns about her running off after deer—stumbling off, maybe, but not running.

He removed her wet collar, and rummaged in the shoe basket for the towel used to dry her on such occasions, but Lotte was already gone, her tail wagging while she emitted uncertain little woofs of interest.

A light was burning in the kitchen, and Baulman was certain that he had only left on the lamp in the hall before leaving. He could see Lotte's tail wagging, and her rear end wiggling with delight. Someone was seated at the kitchen table, just beyond his line of sight—someone whom Lotte recognized, but who had no qualms about making his own way into a man's house while he was out walking his dog.

Baulman hung up his sodden coat and scarf, removed his damp shoes, and padded to the kitchen. Sitting in one of the pine chairs, facing the door, was the Jigsaw Man. Baulman glared at him for a moment before making his way to the stove, where he filled a pot with milk and set it to boil for hot chocolate. The damp was in his bones. Maybe later he would permit himself a Scotch, but for now hot chocolate would suffice.

"You might have made a less dramatic entrance," said Baulman.

"You're marked," said the Jigsaw Man. "I chose to be careful."

"Pah! Now you choose to be careful. You should have been careful when you killed Perlman. You should have been careful before you went off burning houses and murdering children."

The Jigsaw Man pointed out the irony of someone like Baulman objecting to the killing of children.

"It was not necessary," said Baulman.

"*I* deemed it necessary."

"Why, because you couldn't manage to make Perlman disappear? You, of all people, should have known about the tides."

Baulman found the jar of hot chocolate at the back of one of the kitchen closets. He'd bought it at the Trader Joe's down in Portland when he'd last visited the city. It was organic, and fair trade—not that these things particularly mattered to him, but it had performed well in taste tests, and Baulman was something of a connoisseur of hot chocolate. When Kathryn was alive they preferred to make their own from scratch, but it didn't seem worth the effort for just one person.

"It wasn't meant to happen that way," said the Jigsaw Man. "I thought he was unconscious, but I'd tied his shoelaces together, just in case. He was lying on the ground, and I was preparing to put him in the trunk of the car, and when I looked back he was standing. *Standing!* I'd taken out one of his eyes. Who knows what damage I did in there, yet he was on his feet. I approached him, and he simply stepped back and was gone, lost to the sea. I hoped that I might be lucky with the tides. I was not."

Baulman took the milk from the stove before it came to a boil, poured it into the cup of mix, and added a little cold milk to take off some of the heat. He took a seat opposite the Jigsaw Man. Lotte, knowing where her loyalties lay, came to join her master. Baulman dipped his finger into the cup, and allowed Lotte to lick the mixture.

The Jigsaw Man was an amateur—a gifted one, but an amateur nonetheless. He had provided good service in the past but now, like all of them, he was getting old. Yes, he was still decades younger than Baulman, but what did that matter? He was losing his edge, perhaps even his sanity. That business with the family over at the lake: what kind of sane individual would consider that an appropriate response to the problem of Perlman's body washing ashore?

"Aren't you going to offer me something to drink?" asked the Jigsaw Man.

"If you want hot chocolate, make your own."

"I'd prefer something stronger."

"You know where it is."

The Jigsaw Man rose. Lotte followed him with her eyes. When he returned, he'd poured himself a snifter of brandy. He swirled it before he drank. It didn't make much difference. It was poor stuff.

"Tell me about the Demers woman," he said.

Baulman went through the details of both encounters with Demers. He left nothing out, and resisted emphasizing what he perceived as his own cleverness.

"She visited Isha Winter," said the Jigsaw Man.

"I thought she might."

"So what does Demers do now?"

"She has nothing," said Baulman. "The doubtful word of a man trying to save his own skin, that's all. Without proof, she can't act."

"And yet they still haven't deported Engel."

"They will. He's of no use to them now."

"Not unless he tries naming more names. And a shadow still remains upon you."

"I have always had a shadow upon me."

"Not like this one."

"I told you: she has nothing to tie me to Kraus."

"But you say that she mentioned a discrepancy in paperwork."

"She was bluffing, trying to frighten me."

"You're sure?"

"The paperwork was good."

"Those were difficult times. Mistakes could have been made. A detail might have been missed."

"No, you must listen to me," said Baulman. "There is no problem with the paperwork, or nothing that would cause this kind of fuss. And let me remind you that we all received our documents from the same source. If there is a problem with one, there may be a problem with the rest, so why are you only giving me this *Scheisse*? I wasn't the reason Perlman ended up in the sea! It wasn't because of me that you thought you had to kill that family!"

"No, but you are the one to whom Demers has come. You're the one they're looking at."

"Ah!" Baulman waved a hand in dismissal. "It's done. By now she has gone back to Washington with her tail between her legs."

The Jigsaw Man looked into the depths of his cheap liquor, like a fortune-teller on the skids.

"Who else can Engel name?"

"What?"

"Who else can he name?"

Baulman sipped his hot chocolate. He wanted all of this to be at an end, but he was too careful to dismiss the Jigsaw Man's question out of hand.

"Hummel is the only one directly connected with Lubsko, but Hummel was close to Riese. Riese was not at Lubsko, but he and Hummel were friendly, and I cannot say what Hummel might have shared with him, and with Engel in turn. If Engel tries to sell anyone else out, it will be Hummel next, then Riese."

"Are you sure that these are the only ones Engel might give up?"

"He wouldn't dare name the last."

"You're sure of this?"

Baulman was suddenly tired. He felt the force of the past straining to emerge, like water behind a fracturing dam.

"No," he said, "I cannot be sure, but even Engel has his limits. Anyway, he will give them Hummel before he offers up anyone else, and who knows how long that will delay proceedings? But can't you get in touch with him and pressure him to remain silent?"

"We did, through his lawyer. Engel is angry that we wouldn't support him as far as the Supreme Court."

"Did you tell him that we can't shit gold?"

"He seems to believe that we have funds hidden away."

"For decades we have all enjoyed a life of comfort, of security. How does he think it was paid for?"

"I offered to put ten thousand euros into an account in Germany for his use. The lawyer says it's not enough. Even a hundred thousand wouldn't be enough to satisfy Engel. He wants to stay in the United States."

"If only he'd been more like Fuhrmann, and had the courage to take his punishment without complaint, and without betraying his comrades."

"Fuhrmann was an officer."

Baulman had suspected that this would be the Jigsaw Man's view. He was a snob of the worst kind. He had a point about Fuhrmann, though, who'd been their contact outside the camp. He'd remained silent, unlike Engel.

"But Engel," the Jigsaw Man added, "is a thug."

"We were all thugs," said Baulman.

"Even you?"

"Even me. I have no illusions. I was there."

The Jigsaw Man didn't contradict him, but Baulman could see him bristling. The Jigsaw Man didn't like such talk.

"Speak with Hummel and Riese," said the Jigsaw Man. "See what you can find out."

"Me?"

"Who else?"

"But they might be watching me."

"You told me they had nothing on you."

"I know, but . . ."

He bit his tongue. He didn't want to damn himself with his own mouth.

"What would be more suspicious?" asked the Jigsaw Man. "That you should continue to see your old friends or that you should suddenly stop seeing them for fear of drawing attention to them?"

"I have not spoken with Hummel in years. He lives in a home. I hear he's senile."

"Then I suggest that you renew his acquaintance before it's too late. And Riese?"

"We were never close, but I know him a little."

"So you find out if the Justice Department has been in touch with either of them, and apprise them of the importance of maintaining appearances."

The Jigsaw Man knocked back the rest of the brandy in one mouthful, and put the snifter on the table.

"If you hear anything more from Demers, be sure to inform me. And tell me how things go with Hummel and Riese. Remember, you're not the only one who has to be protected." He patted Baulman on the shoulder. "You're not even the most important."

XLIX

Gordon Walsh sat at the back of the conference room as Lieutenant Driver, the newly appointed commanding officer of Major Crimes Unit North, gave details to the assembled reporters of progress in the continuing search for Oran Wilde and the associated killings, which amounted to none at all. He tried to disguise it as best he could behind the usual platitudes about following a number of lines of inquiry, but the appeal for fresh information gave him away. Behind Driver, in a gesture of support, stood the commander of MCU South plus assorted uniformed officers and members of the Violent Crimes Task Force, along with a pair of FBI agents who were there simply to fill up the room and put some kind of governmental gloss on the whole mess. All present bore the expressions of men and women who wanted to be anywhere else but where they were. Walsh was reminded of those show trials in China, when everyone involved in a failure was paraded in front of the cameras before being hauled off and shot. They'd asked him to take his place up there with the damned, but he'd told them, in the most diplomatic way possible, to go screw themselves.

When the reporters had exhausted themselves by asking the same questions that they'd been posing ever since Oran Wilde vanished off the map, someone from NBC raised the Winter murder, and Driver gave a variation on the same theme: lines of inquiry, ongoing investigation, reluctant to compromise sources, any information gratefully received, and we'll even pay for the stamps. . . .

This led to Bruno Perlman, and the possibility that the case of the Tedescos down in Florida might be connected to his death. Driver gratefully ceded the microphone to Detective Louise Tyler, who was leading the Perlman investigation. Thank God they didn't put her buddy Welbecke up there, Walsh thought. She'd probably have punched someone out. Tyler threw the media a couple of bones, but they had little meat on them, and when she tried to suggest that Perlman's death might yet prove to be suicide it provoked open expressions of disbelief from the crowd. The Perlman question did allow the MSP to shift some of the heat to the FBI liaisons, one of whom told the room that because the results of the autopsy on Perlman were "inconclusive," a second, federal autopsy was in the process of being conducted. When asked about a connection to the murder of Ruth Winter, he said the investigation was still in progress. He gave the same answer when asked about the Tedescos.

While he was speaking, someone took the chair at the far end of the row from Walsh. He glanced over to see Marie Demers, who'd come nosing around following the Winter murder, and who was being copied on all relevant material. Walsh tried to recall if he'd ever been involved in a bigger clusterfuck, and decided that he hadn't. Maybe they should get T-shirts made for everyone once it was all over: I SURVIVED THE CLUSTERFUCK KILLINGS AND ALL I GOT WAS THIS LOUSY T-SHIRT— AND THE REMNANTS OF A CAREER.

The problem, from Walsh's point of view, was that the resources of the MSP were being fatally overstretched by the three investigations— Wilde, Winter, and Perlman—and, instead of alleviating the burden, the involvement of outside agencies was complicating the whole business still further. It was as though white noise was being pumped in over a piece of music, and now nobody could hear the tune.

But Demers interested him. He was the reason that she was in attendance at the press conference. He'd heard from Ross that she was back in Maine, staying at some hotel midway between Bangor and Boreas. He'd eventually succeeded in getting in touch with her the night before, and suggested that they meet, but she begged off with a migraine and offered to hook up after the press conference instead.

Mercifully, the conference started to wind up, and the whole sorry affair was brought to a close, the relief palpably emanating from those behind the microphone. Walsh sidled up to Demers. They'd met briefly in the aftermath of Ruth Winter's murder, and at her burial. This time he took Demers for coffee, where she ordered some kind of nonfat decaf which, to paraphrase the Tom Waits song, didn't even look strong enough to defend itself. In the spirit of the occasion Walsh resisted ordering something sweet and fat, and instead went for an Americano with so many shots that it practically counted as a giant espresso.

"Thanks for taking the time to meet," he said.

"SAC Ross told me that it might be worth my while speaking with you."

"That was nice of him."

"Ross doesn't do nice."

"No, he doesn't. I just said it for form's sake."

Walsh took a hit of his coffee, and the first of the caffeine lit up his synapses like fireworks on the Fourth of July. He thought his eyeballs might pop out.

"Well?" said Demers.

She wasn't much for small talk, Walsh thought. It might have been the aftereffects of the migraine, or it could be that she was always that way. He didn't much care which. It wasn't as if they were planning to get married.

"You're investigating a man named Marcus Baulman as a possible war criminal."

"Yes."

"This Baulman was at a concentration camp called Lubsko, of which Ruth Winter's mother was the sole survivor."

"It wasn't a concentration camp: it was officially an 'experimental colony' but otherwise, yes."

"And members of Bruno Perlman's family died at the same camp, which gives us a dotted line between Ruth Winter, Perlman, and Marcus Baulman."

"Again, all this is common knowledge."

"I have something that isn't," said Walsh.

"Really?"

Demers wasn't exactly on the edge of her seat, but he could see that he had piqued her curiosity for the first time.

"The man who killed Ruth Winter—the one we're calling Earl Steiger, in the absence of anything more conclusive—was a professional killer, possibly supplied by a man named Cambion."

Now Demers *was* interested. She even pushed her weird coffee to one side, as though it might impede the flow of information.

"Where did you get this?"

"It doesn't matter where, and it's not conclusive. I don't have any evidence to support it, but the source is good."

"You didn't share this with Ross?"

"I did."

"Ross didn't share it with me."

"You take that up with Ross. For what it's worth, he told me to keep it to myself, but I don't work for Ross—not officially, anyway, although sometimes he acts like I do. Plus I'm tired of seeing my entire department chasing its tail with no result. So I'm looking at all these pieces, but I can't make them fit together. Then you come along talking about war criminals, and suddenly I can see a picture."

"Go on."

"Bruno Perlman finds out something about Lubsko and Marcus Baulman that nobody else knows. He shares it with his friend Lenny

Tedesco, then heads north. Along the way, he lets someone up here know that he's coming—maybe even more than one person. Because of the Lubsko connection, I'm figuring one of them has to be either Isha Winter or her daughter."

"I spoke with Isha Winter," said Demers. "Perlman didn't say anything to her about coming back for a second visit, and I don't think he'd have been welcome anyway. Isha didn't care much for his attitude the first time they met."

"Then it's Ruth Winter he wanted to see. Perhaps he figures that an elderly woman shouldn't be approached directly about whatever he's discovered, and he might be better off going through her daughter. Baulman finds out that Perlman is coming, and hires Earl Steiger to take care of him and the Tedescos. Steiger could have killed all of them, but I'm leaning toward him farming out one of the jobs."

"Why?"

"The timing is tight—not too tight for it to be impossible for Steiger to have worked alone, but just tight enough to make it improbable. And also—"

He took a moment to risk another sip of coffee. This wasn't where he parted ways with Louis, exactly, but it was a leap that he still wasn't entirely confident about making.

"There's a chance," he said, "and only a chance, that the killing of the Wilde family might be part of the same picture, but designed to distract us."

Demers said nothing. He couldn't tell if it was disbelief, or if he had her.

"Everything about the Wilde case is off," said Walsh. "*Everything.* Oran Wilde should have been caught within hours, but he's still out there. His father's safe was locked when the house was examined, and we found charred bills in his wallet, so what's the kid doing for funds? And there's no motive. The more we find out about Oran, the more he seems like a regular kid—a little fond of wearing black, liked his shoot-

'em-ups, and not as smart as he thought he was, but no murderer. Just the opposite: his close friends had him pegged as a decent, sensitive guy. His yearbook photo should have read "Least Likely to Commit a Mass Killing." But somehow, his family ended up dead and we've committed huge resources to scouring the state for him, with no result."

"You're saying that someone slaughtered four members of a family, and abducted a fifth, as a diversion? From what?"

"From a body on a beach. From Bruno Perlman. Whoever put him in the water probably didn't know about the tides there, which are all screwy. Perlman wasn't supposed to wash up at Mason Point, but he did. I think someone went to the trouble of clogging up our system so Perlman would be overlooked and tagged as an accidental drowning, or a suicide, or would simply lie in cold storage until whatever else needed to be done could be completed."

"What about Ruth Winter?" asked Demers. "She doesn't fit into the same time frame. She dies later. Why not kill her along with Perlman?"

"Maybe because Perlman's killer knew that he hadn't shared his information with her yet. What if it was something physical, something that Perlman wanted to show her? There was no laptop in his car when it was found, and we know that he owned one from a warranty found in his apartment. Unless Perlman brought his computer with him for his last swim, then it, along with anything else that might be useful, was taken by his killer."

"Then why murder Ruth Winter at all?"

"That's where it all starts to fall apart," admitted Walsh.

"But you think Baulman may be the one who did the hiring," said Demers.

"Would he kill to hide his past?"

"He was responsible for murdering children at Lubsko, and apparently did without compunction. So, yes, I think he would—or, given his age, he'd pay someone else to do it for him."

"You have proof that Baulman is the one you're looking for?"

Demers drank some more of her coffee and scowled.

"Why am I even drinking this shit?" she said.

"I didn't want to ask."

She didn't wait for him to offer to get her something stronger, but went to the counter herself and came back a few minutes later with an espresso.

"Fuck it if I get another migraine," she said.

"That's the right attitude."

"Where were we?"

"Proof that Baulman is a war criminal."

"We don't have any."

"Jesus. For real?"

Demers shrugged.

"You know we have Engel awaiting deportation to Germany. Naturally, he doesn't want to go. The Germans don't want him either, because they say there's not enough evidence to try him, but that's not our problem. We'd prefer a trial, but getting him out of here is enough."

"Wait," said Walsh. "So why are we sending him over there?"

"We're deporting him on the basis of irregularities in his original visa application."

"Not because he was a war criminal."

"A suspected war criminal," she corrected. "No."

"I don't understand," said Walsh.

"Denaturalization and deportation is all we have," said Demers. "It's not ideal, and it's not enough, but it's better than the other option, which is to let these people live out their last years in the bosom of their adopted country. Because of a loophole in the system, we can even keep paying them their Social Security if they agree to go. Effectively, we bribe them to get the hell out of the United States. But Engel has a family here—a wife, children, grandchildren, great-grandchildren— and he wants to die surrounded by them. His wife still refuses to believe that her husband was a murderer who put bullets into the necks of naked kneeling men and women. She'll take him back, if he can stay. So Engel offered to give up another Nazi in hiding if we'd halt the deportation proceedings."

"Did you agree?"

"We told him it would depend upon the quality of the information. The truth is that he's going back to Germany no matter what he tells us. He could prove to us that Mengele didn't drown in Brazil in 1979 but is alive and well in Palm Beach, and we'd still want him gone. We're simply delaying packing him up and shipping him off until we've bled him for all we can get, and then his own people can have him."

"And Engel pointed you to Marcus Baulman?"

"He told us that Baulman was actually Reynard Kraus. He said he and Kraus served together at Lubsko. We looked into Baulman, and his paperwork had some gaps and inconsistencies in it—yet not enough to support a case against him, and they could be explained away by the chaos of war. But you get a sense for these people if you hunt them long enough, and Baulman is bad. What might have helped was a positive identification from Isha Winter, who knew Kraus by sight."

Walsh picked up on the words "might have."

"But you didn't get it," he said.

"Yesterday I showed Isha Winter a picture of Baulman as a younger man. She told me that Baulman wasn't Kraus."

"So Engel was lying."

"I haven't had a chance to put that to him yet."

"Unless he was right about Baulman, but somehow managed to connect him to the wrong name. I mean, all these guys must be as old as Methuselah by now. I have trouble remembering names, and I'm only fifty."

"It's also possible that Isha Winter is mistaken, but it's a long shot. She comes across as sharp as a tack. If she says Baulman isn't Kraus, then it must be true. I'm going to keep working the case, but I was banking on the positive ID to give us a push.

"It leaves you with problems too. Whatever information Bruno Perl-man had, it couldn't have been that Marcus Baulman was really Rey-nard Kraus, not unless he was as mistaken as Engel. Either way, why would Baulman go to the trouble of having Perlman and everyone con-nected with him killed if they were on the wrong track to begin with?"

Walsh swore. He'd been so sure that he'd found a way to connect all the pieces. It didn't take him long to regain his composure, though.

"Baulman doesn't matter," he said.

"Really?"

"The rest of it feels right. We just need another name, but Lubsko remains the common detail. Whatever is happening here, it goes back to there."

"Let's stay in touch, see what emerges," said Demers.

"And Ross?"

"I'm going to shout so loudly at him for keeping me out of the loop, his phone will melt."

"It sounds like a plan."

"Then he's going to shout at you."

"I have a plan too."

"Which is?"

Walsh abandoned the rest of his coffee. With luck, he'd manage to get a night's sleep sometime before Christmas.

"I won't answer my phone."

L

Rachel and Sam lived in converted stables adjoining the house owned by Rachel's parents, although a wood-and-glass conservatory furnished with overstuffed couches and chairs now connected it to the main building. Rachel's father, Frank, had recently retired, but continued to work as a freelance consultant in business realms in which Parker had no interest, even if Rachel's father had bothered to try to explain them to him. Parker had never gotten along with Frank Wolfe. He had been suspicious of the detective from the start, and everything that followed had only reinforced his conviction that Parker was bad for his daughter in almost every way. He made some small concession only for Sam, upon whom he and his wife doted, although Parker was certain Frank had somehow blocked from his mind the fact that Sam carried any genetic material from his daughter's former lover.

Thankfully Rachel's old man was absent when Parker, with Angel and Louis as escorts, arrived at the house. Frank had left the previous morning for a meeting in Seattle, and would not return until the weekend. It was doubly fortunate for all involved, because whatever doubts Frank had about Parker were multiplied manifold when it came to Angel and Louis. If he had his way, the two men wouldn't have been allowed into the state, let alone onto his property.

A white Mercedes CLS-Class Coupe was parked in the driveway outside the house as they pulled up, alongside Rachel's recently purchased used Prius.

"A white coupe," said Angel. "That's an asshole's car right there."

With that, the asshole himself appeared. Rachel's boyfriend, Jeff, was about ten years older than she was, and believed that if wealth was worth having, then it was worth displaying. He was all white teeth and prematurely white hair. If the lights went out in a mine, they could have sent Jeff to lead everyone back to safety using only his smile. Parker was self-aware enough to realize that he was still more than a little in love with Rachel, and therefore Christ Himself could have come down to date her and he still wouldn't have approved of the match. Still, the thought of Jeff and Rachel involved in any kind of intimacy—physical or emotional—caused his gut to tighten. Parker tried to be civil to Jeff for the sake of all involved, but the effort strained his diplomatic muscles to their limit. As for Angel and Louis, they made it clear—on the rare occasions when they were forced to spend time in Jeff's company— that if they could have gotten away with shooting him and dumping his remains in a swamp, they would have.

"The fuck is he doing here?" asked Louis.

"He doesn't look happy," said Angel. "Which makes me happy."

He was right. Jeff was red with rage, even beneath his year-round tan. He was wearing a yellow V-neck sweater over a pink shirt and blue pants, and was carrying a navy blazer in his left hand.

"He looks like the father of a groom at a casual gay wedding," said Angel.

Jeff paused as Parker got out of the car. He had to pass Parker to get to his own vehicle, but appeared reluctant to do so, as though he hoped the detective might instead just vanish into the ether, leaving only bad memories.

"Jeff," said Parker, by way of greeting.

Jeff managed to pull together a Frankenstein's creation of a smile, composed entirely of other unrelated emotions. It lived for only a moment before it collapsed and died.

"I heard you were coming," said Jeff.

"You didn't have to welcome me personally."

Jeff raised his right forefinger and pointed it in the direction of the house. His car keys dangled from his fist, catching the morning sun.

"They deserve better," he said. "That child deserves better."

"Better than what?"

"You know."

His eyes drifted past Parker to Angel and Louis, who remained seated in the car. Angel gave him a wave and a smile, and mouthed the word "fuckwad."

"And you bring these people here, these—"

"Careful," said Parker. "Their feelings are easily hurt."

Rachel appeared at the door of the house before Jeff could say anything more. Her arms were folded across her chest. She'd been crying.

"Jeff," she said. "Just go. Please."

Parker almost felt sorry for Jeff, but it quickly passed. Whatever had occurred before they'd arrived was serious, and possibly terminal. Now Jeff was suffering the added humiliation of retreating before the three men in the world he least wanted to see at that moment.

Jeff brushed past Parker, got in his shiny new car, and drove away. Parker watched him go. When he looked back at the house, Rachel was no longer at the door.

"Give us a minute?" he asked Angel and Louis.

"Sure," said Louis.

"Is it too early to start celebrating?" asked Angel.

Parker gave him a look that suggested he would be well advised to keep cracks like that to himself for the present.

"Okay," said Angel. "We'll celebrate on the inside."

Parker knocked on the door and called Rachel's name. He wasn't about to enter a house that wasn't his own without her permission, not even this one. She called to him from the kitchen, and he found her with her back against the sink, her head low and her shoulders shaking. He walked over and stood beside her, but he didn't touch her. He knew her better than that.

"Is there anything I can do?" he asked.

"Besides everything you've done already? You could shoot me. How about that?"

"I didn't bring my gun."

She gave a short laugh, then just cried harder.

"Why don't you go outside and borrow one? They must have a fucking arsenal in that car."

"I don't think they'd let me shoot you. They like you too much. But if you want someone else shot, I'm sure they'd be willing to oblige."

"Would they shoot *you* if I asked?"

"Possibly. You want to tell me what all that was about?"

Rachel wiped her nose on the back of her hand, disgusted herself by what she had done, and reached for a piece of paper towel.

"You know how mad I am at you?" she said.

"I figured. I saw it in your face at the hospital."

"She could have been killed, Charlie! That man on the beach, she saw him die. She watched him shoot a police officer. And if that dune hadn't collapsed, he'd probably have killed you, and her as well."

"I know."

She punched him in the arm.

"What were you thinking, putting her at risk—and yourself?"

"I—"

"You what? You couldn't stand by? You couldn't let someone be hurt? Christ, I know all that. But *Sam* was there. *She* was your priority. *She* was the one you should have thought about first."

There was no point in telling Rachel that he had ordered Sam to stay in the house. He should have guessed that she wouldn't stay. He was familiar enough with her nature by now. After all, it was so much like his.

"You're right," was all he said.

She stopped crying, although she still emitted small hiccupping sobs.

"I can say these things to you," she continued, "but Jeff can't—not to me, not to you, and certainly not to Sam. If anyone is going to drag you over hot coals, it's going to be me."

"I appreciate that. Kind of."

She wiped her nose again, and exhaled long and slowly.

"Go on," she said. "I know you want to ask."

"Ask what?" he said, with as much innocence as he could muster.

"Jerk. If it's over between Jeff and me."

"Is it over between Jeff and you?"

"I think so. I'm sure you're pleased."

"Damn. And I was just starting to like him."

She gave him another punch in the arm.

"I hate you. You ruined my life."

"Yeah, I'm sorry about that. You want some coffee?"

"Tea. And you can tell those other idiots to come in now, if you like. But if I catch them gloating, I'll ram their smiles down their throats."

"I'll be sure to warn them. Where's Sam?"

"My mom took her out to buy some pastries when Jeff arrived, and it all started getting heated. I'll let her know that it's safe to return."

Parker set some water to boil for her tea, put some grounds in the fancy coffee machine, then went out to tell Angel and Louis that the coast was clear.

"So it's over between them?" said Angel.

"Seems to be."

"I was just starting to like him."

"That's what I said."

"Are we allowed to gloat?"

"You can try, but she did say something about ramming smiles down throats."

"That's a no, then?"

"I'd take it that way."

A silver Volvo SUV turned at the gate and came up the drive. Parker could see Rachel's mother, Joan, behind the wheel, and Walter, the golden retriever—once owned by Rachel and him, but now very much a Vermont dog—occupying the passenger seat beside her. Then, as the car drew closer, he caught sight of Sam sitting belted in the back. As always, his heart lifted at the sight of her, but not as high as before. He was not looking forward to talking to her about what had happened at Green Heron Bay.

LI

Rachel's mother was significantly more tolerant of Parker than her husband was, although it was all relative. She was civil—bordering on polite—but it was clear that Louis and Angel were an added strain on her natural good manners. They behaved impeccably, which was like saying that a bomb behaved well by not exploding.

Sam, though, adored both of them, and even Louis tended to thaw in her presence. She chatted with them about school and TV, and scolded them halfheartedly for feeding scraps to Walter under the table. From a distance, they all looked like regular people.

But Parker noticed that Sam didn't say much to him. She'd hugged him upon leaving the car, and asked if he was okay, but beyond that she had devoted most of her attention to Angel and Louis, even more so than usual. It was as though she hoped to hide herself from him by pretending that he wasn't there.

But eventually she finished her milk and doughnut, and Parker suggested that they take a walk with Walter. Walter was more enthusiastic than Sam, but she didn't refuse, and together they strolled around the Wolfes' big backyard.

"How have you been?" he asked her.

"Good." She didn't look at him.

"I mean, after what happened at the beach. After what you saw there."

"Good."

Maybe, he thought, I should try bamboo slivers under her fingernails, or threaten to sabotage the cable box on the TV. He stopped and squatted before her. She peered up at him from beneath her bangs.

"Sam, do you think I'm mad at you?"

"No," she said, then offered: "Maybe."

"Why would I be?"

"Because I followed you when I wasn't supposed to."

"I'm not mad at you for doing that."

"Honest?"

"Well, I don't want you to do it again, but you're safe, and I'm safe. It could have ended badly, though. You could have been hurt, or worse. You know that, right?"

"Yes."

"So maybe in the future, if I tell you to do something, you might think about doing it?"

This time, she generated a small embarrassed smile.

"Okay."

"I do want to ask you something else about that night," he said.

Now they were coming to it. He was treading carefully, but he could already sense her retreating, as though she knew what it was that troubled her father.

"What do you remember?" he said. "I mean, from the time that you came to the dunes. What do you recall?"

She swallowed hard.

"I saw you kneeling down, and I knew you were hurt. I saw the man with the gun, and then the police officer stood up, and the man shot her."

"And after that?"

"He was going to shoot you."

"And were you frightened?"

A nod.

"Were you . . . angry?"

A pause. Another nod.

He saw her face again, lit by moonlight, and heard a sound like an exhalation as the dune collapsed.

"Did you maybe imagine something happening to him, something that would stop him from hurting me?"

She looked him straight in the eye.

"No."

"Sam, you have to know that I'm really not mad at you. I'm just trying to understand everything that took place. It's important."

"No," she repeated, more forcefully now. "I didn't do anything! I don't know what you're talking about. Leave me alone!"

She turned and ran, Walter at her heels. He let her go. He couldn't have chased her anyway. He wasn't strong enough. Now that he was down on his haunches he struggled to get back up again. Damn, that wasn't smart. He managed to get himself upright, but his side hurt, and he limped back to the house. He should have brought the crutch from the car after all, but he still hated the thing. He didn't want Sam to see him using it, so he'd hidden it in the trunk.

Rachel emerged from the back door of the house and walked toward him.

"You're pale," she said. "You need to sit down."

"I hate sitting down," he said. "It hurts. I'm better standing up. Did you see Sam?"

"Yes. She's gone to her room."

"I didn't mean to upset her."

"She wasn't crying, if that's what you mean. She had a face like thunder, but there were no tears. Can I ask what you were talking about?"

"The night that Earl Steiger died."

"She doesn't seem troubled by it," said Rachel. "We've had no nightmares, and no moods—or no more than usual."

"Does that bother you?"

"Some. I've tried talking to her myself, but she doesn't want to discuss it. It may emerge in time. I don't want to force it."

Parker was aware that they were having two different conversations about the same subject, but he didn't point it out. Rachel was discussing the aftermath, but he was interested in the event itself. Does she even see it, he wondered: the strangeness of their child?

Or maybe he was imagining it all, and was only projecting his own curse onto Sam. He was the troubled one. He was the one whose deceased child wrote messages to him on dusty glass, and crossed the boundaries between worlds, between what was and what once had been. He was the one tormented by memories of his own dying, of sitting by a glass lake while his dead daughter held his hand and his lost wife whispered words in his ear that he could not recall.

Dunes collapsed. Every year people died in accidents just like the one that killed Earl Steiger. The fact that no such incident had ever previously occurred at Green Heron Bay meant nothing. Steiger's death was not inexplicable. It was not even regrettable. His daughter had witnessed it, and no more than that.

But her face, her face . . .

Rachel broke into his thoughts.

"Are you leaving today?"

"I haven't discussed it with Angel and Louis, but I guess so."

"Why don't you stay?" she said. "There should be enough to keep those two occupied in Burlington for an evening, and I can get them a good rate at the Willard Street Inn. Sam has a sleepover planned, and my mom will catch a movie. I'll cook you dinner. We can talk."

"And where will I sleep?"

"We have space," she said. She placed her right hand against his face. "It'll do you good."

———

SO ANGEL AND LOUIS left, and he stayed. Sam came down from her room, and after circling warily for a time joined him to watch a Marx Brothers movie on TCM. Afterward they played checkers, and he fell asleep on the couch. When he woke, both Sam and her grandmother—who had not commented upon his continued presence beyond a mildly pained pursing of the lips—were gone, and Rachel was cooking chicken in a cream sauce. He showered in the guest bathroom, allowed himself a glass of wine, and they ate in the kitchen by candlelight while 1st Wave played in the background on Sirius. He helped her wash up when they were done, and then it was her turn to fall asleep beside him on the couch. He woke her shortly before eleven p.m., and kissed her good night.

He lay awake in the spare room. His side ached. He considered taking a couple of the prescription pills to help him sleep, but he hated the aftertaste of them, and the way they made his head feel clouded for hours after waking up. Thirty minutes, he thought. I'll give myself thirty minutes. If I can't get to sleep by then, I'll take the pills. He heard Rachel's mother come back and go to her room. After that, the house was quiet.

Fifteen minutes. Fifteen minutes more.

The bedroom door opened slowly, then closed again. Rachel came to him. She was wearing a short nightgown, and he watched as she lifted it over her head and let it fall to the floor.

"Does it hurt a lot?" she said.

"No, not a lot."

"Don't worry," she said. She eased herself onto the bed, and sat astride him. "You just stay still. I'll be gentle."

And he did, and she was.

LII

Rachel was gone when Parker woke. He had a vague memory of her getting up to leave during the night, but it seemed then as much of a dream as her sleeping presence beside him had been. He showered, and changed—he had just enough clothing in his overnight bag to remain presentable for another day. The rest of his wardrobe was divided between Scarborough and Boreas. His time as a resident of that northern town was coming to a close, but he had decided to return for a few more days at least. He had unfinished business there.

He went down to breakfast and caught Mrs. Wolfe sending bad juju his way, although at least she had the decency to include Rachel in her glare of disapproval. He figured that she'd heard Rachel heading back to her basilisk room in the stable annex during the night. At least Frank wasn't in the house as well. If he thought that his daughter had slept with her ex-partner under his roof, he'd have gone looking for his shotgun.

Rachel gave him coffee and a bagel, but refused to catch his eye for fear of confirming her mother's suspicions. It made Parker feel like a teenager again, and not in a bad way. Sam had gone straight from her sleepover to school, but it was a half day so he waited for her return. Angel and Louis appeared not long after she got back. Not wishing to strain Mrs. Wolfe's patience any further, they all made their farewells. Before Parker left, Sam hugged him and said, "Daddy, you should have used the crutch that they gave you." And he agreed that, yes, he should have, but he felt better now, and maybe he wouldn't need it at all.

Rachel kissed him on the cheek, and the affection of the gesture filled him with a tender sadness. The night before was lost to them now: it had been a small consecration, a minor epiphany, and no more than that, but sometimes such moments are all that we are given, and they are enough to fuel us, and give us hope that, somewhere down the line, another might be gifted.

Angel and Louis sensed something of his mood, and there was no mockery as they drove away, no loaded questions about how the night had gone. The sun shone, and a classical piece played on the radio, one that Parker thought he recognized but could not identify. He didn't ask its name, though. He simply listened, and let its waves break upon him.

And only then did he realize he had not told Sam about the crutch. It had remained in the trunk of the car, where she could not have seen it. He said nothing to Angel and Louis, but merely added it to his concerns about his daughter.

"What now?" said Louis, after they had been driving in silence for almost an hour.

"I'd like you to take me back to Boreas," said Parker. "I'd be grateful if you'd help me pack up my things. It won't take long: a couple of hours at most."

"And then?"

He'd read about the previous day's press conference on the *Portland Press Herald*'s website, and had followed up with a call to Gordon Walsh before he went down to breakfast. He was now clear on how slowly the investigation into Ruth Winter's murder was progressing. Steiger was one of the problems: a professional shooter meant a disconnect between the motive and the act, one that could only be remedied by forcing the killer to turn on whomever had hired him—not an option in the case of the late Earl Steiger. But as Louis pointed out, it also had to be recognized that, because Steiger could have been hired out by a third party—Cambion, in this case—he might not even have been aware of the original source of the contract. If they could get to Cambion, and make him talk, then they might learn something useful, but Cambion had hidden himself away. The solution, then, was to work backward.

"I'm going to find out who ordered the killing of Ruth Winter," said Parker.

Angel glanced at him in the rearview mirror. There was no doubt in the detective's voice, and although he was staring out the window, his eyes saw nothing of what passed before them.

Angel and Louis had spoken of Parker the night before. Yes, thought Angel, Louis was right: he is different. He has a certainty to him that was not there before. He should be dead, yet he is more alive, and more dangerous, than ever.

God help anyone who went up against him now.

God help them all.

LIII

Bernhard Hummel was currently residing in the special care unit of the Golden Hills Senior Living Community just outside Ellsworth, Maine.

Of the many ends that he might meet, Baulman had always been most fearful of dementia. The idea of slowly losing himself appalled him, and he had done all he could to ensure that such a fate was not destined to be his: he exercised regularly, ate well, and was never without a newspaper or a book. He played memory games—reciting the fifty state capitals, listing the names and numbers of beloved symphonies, or the German soccer teams of various vintages—and, although he was right-handed, he forced himself to perform many tasks using his left. His arthritis he could live with. His bladder was little better than a thimble, but he could calculate almost to the minute how long he had before he would need a men's room. He couldn't recall the last time he'd had a good night's sleep, but he'd learned to grab a nap whenever he could, and anyway, it left more time for reading.

But still he was troubled when he forgot the name of an acquaintance, living or dead, or couldn't bring to mind quickly enough a favorite film, or the title of a novel. Unlike poor old Bernhard Hummel, he had nobody around who might notice any deterioration in the quality of his mental functioning. He had to be his own guardian, his own monitor. He could only hope that, if it happened, he would recognize the symptoms before it was too late, giving him time to kill himself.

Golden Hills wasn't the worst such facility that Baulman had visited in his time. It did, at least, have hills of a sort, and the buildings and gardens were well maintained. One half of the property consisted entirely of apartments and small cottages for those individuals or couples who needed a little help with day-to-day activities, yet didn't require round-the-clock care, but Hummel was in a secure annex at the rear of the main building. Baulman was admitted without any trouble. He wasn't even required to show ID, and for an instant he considered signing in under a false name. But what if the people from the Justice Department were tailing him? He would only bring down suspicion on himself if they checked the visitors' register and found that he had signed in under an alias. He had grown increasingly paranoid about such surveillance—not without cause—and now found himself searching the faces of strangers for signs of excessive interest and monitoring the cars that followed him on both local roads and the freeway. He incorporated the routine into his memory games, filing away the license numbers, makes, and colors of cars. If they were keeping an eye on his movements, he had given them no cause to suspect him, and was not about to start today. He was entitled to visit his old friend Bernhard. What kind of man doesn't visit his friends in the hospital? To hell with them if they did question him about it.

He hadn't seen Hummel in two years, not since he'd been admitted to Golden Hills at the instigation of his daughter, Theodora. Baulman had never liked her. He hadn't liked Hummel's wife much either, but at least she had the decency to stop bothering people by dying. Theodora had always struck Baulman as too selfish even for mortality. She would outlive them all, like a cockroach. At the first sign of her father's deterioration she had packed him off to Golden Hills without a second thought, or so it appeared to Baulman. It made him glad that he would die without issue.

The receptionist gave him a four-digit code to get past the first door, but he had to press a button and wait to be admitted through the second. He smelled cooked food, and human waste, and disinfectant. No matter how well managed they were, all these places smelled the same. He tried to shut his ears to the wailing of an old woman somewhere to his left—"No!" she cried. "I don't want to! No, no, no, no, no . . ."—and barely glanced into the lounge where an assortment of residents younger than he sat slumped like zombies in chairs. He felt uncomfortable even being within these walls, as though one of the staff—a passing doctor, an orderly—might mistake him for a patient and refuse to let him leave. He had always hated confinement. It was why he would fight Demers and her kind until the end.

He found Hummel's room and paused on the threshold. He hadn't been sure what to bring. He had decided against hard candy or saltwater taffy—even he didn't care much for gnawing on such delicacies at his age—and opted instead for marshmallows and seedless grapes. He took a deep breath and entered the room.

Hummel was seated in a comfortable chair by the window, smiling beatifically. Outside was a line of trees, masking the wall of the property. Either he liked trees a lot, thought Baulman, or Hummel was communing with the birds. He had aged terribly since Baulman had last seen him. His clothes no longer fitted him properly, and his tiny bald head on its wrinkled neck poked from the collar of his shirt like the skull of some ancient tortoise.

Baulman coughed, but Hummel didn't react.

"Hello?" said Baulman. "Bernhard?"

Hummel's head turned slowly. The smile faded. He grew confused. Baulman wondered if he even knew who he was anymore. As far as Hummel was concerned, Baulman might as easily have called him by his wife's name and received something of the same response.

He moved into the room, but did not approach Hummel too closely for fear that he might frighten or distress him. It pained him to see his former colleague and friend this way. Hummel had always been so strong, so vital. At Lubsko, Baulman had watched him fight to the death with a Jew named Oppert, a former wrestler, just to prove that he could beat him. By then, Oppert had seen the bodies of his wife and children, and even though they promised to let him live if he won, Oppert knew better. He accepted the challenge because to do otherwise would be to accept a bullet in the back of the head, and he entertained the hope that he might go to his grave after breaking Hummel's neck. He was mistaken. Weeks at Lubsko had given Oppert back some of his strength, but he was still no match for Hummel, who had later been severely reprimanded for such a breach of regulations. Now look at him, thought Baulman: it's hard to believe that this is the same man.

A flicker of recognition ignited in Hummel's face, but still he did not speak.

"Bernhard, it's me, Marcus. Marcus Baulman."

The smile returned to Hummel's face.

"Kraus!" he said. "My friend, how good to see you!"

You have condemned yourself, thought Baulman. You are a dead man.

CHAPTER

LIV

It did not take them long to pack up most of Parker's possessions. He kept with him only toiletries, one canvas bag of clothes, some food and books, and his gun. Angel and Louis returned to Portland with the rest, leaving him alone in Boreas. It was as he wished it to be. They would come back if—or when—he needed them.

Night had already fallen by the time they were gone. He took the flashlight from under the sink in the kitchen, and slipped the gun into the pocket of his jacket. He walked north until he came to the house in which Ruth Winter had died. Crime scene tape sealed off the doors and the steps up to the porch. A printed notice advised anyone even thinking of trespassing that they would be subject to arrest.

He did not enter, but merely stood for a time beneath the window of Ruth's room. He had visited too many houses like this one, had stood at too many such scenes, not to feel that the building itself had suffered a form of psychic shock, that the crime committed under its roof had affected the physical space it occupied. Wood and brick had a kind of memory: blood seeped into their grain, their dust, and transformed them. Perhaps some people were just more sensitive than others, but he was willing to bet good money that it would be a long time before anyone settled easily into this place.

If he ever had any doubts about the sanity of such observations, he had only to remember the house in which his wife and their child died, and what he had witnessed there when he returned after many years. Some might have called them ghosts, or specters, but he didn't hold with such labels. They suggested incorporeality, and what he had seen in those rooms—and elsewhere too—had a substance to them, a lethality. Ethereal wisps couldn't write warnings to the living or draw blood from hunters and killers.

He pictured Ruth Winter's body on the bed, and the great arterial spray on the wall above. He felt no guilt for what had befallen her. He had tried his utmost to save her. He could have done no more. The stain of her death lay on the souls of others. One of them was already dead. He would find the rest.

He moved on until he came to the dunes. The place at which that great weight of sand had sheared off to bury Earl Steiger was still distinct from the rest, although the mound beneath which he died had been destroyed and scattered during the retrieval of his body. Parker realized that he was standing in almost the same spot his daughter had occupied that night. He thought again about their conversation in Vermont. There, with the backdrop of the Wolfes' beautiful old home, in warm light hazy with the advent of summer, he could convince himself that the culmination of the events at Green Heron Bay was a freak act of nature, one that had saved his life by snuffing out another's. But here, on this dark strand, the memory of those moments came back to him with a palpable force, and he knew that his suspicions about his daughter were not without foundation. He had glimpsed something in her face that night which was not entirely human, something he had never witnessed before—

No, that was not true. He had caught hints of it in others, in men and women who were—and this, too, was easier to deny in daylight than darkness—infested by entities, by supernatural agencies. They had an otherness to them, and he had caught a hint of that same essence in his own daughter as she caused the death of Earl Steiger. There: it was said.

It was what he believed. His daughter was not what she appeared to be. She was carrying something inside her of which she might not even be aware.

The realization numbed him, but he could already sense his emotions straining to break through. What was it? Was it evil? Was it some ancient, rotten spirit cast down to earth, burning as it fell, that had curled up amid rock and lava to wait until men arrived, enabling it to find a host among them? Or had it come from him? Had he infected his own child with a pollutant in his own nature, one that he himself had not yet been able to identify? So lost was he in his own fear and pain that it was some moments before he could bring himself even to consider the possibility of a more benign context for what he had witnessed.

A figure moved amid the dunes, dancing just beyond the reach of his flashlight, and he felt the presence of his dead daughter, and thought that he could hear her singing to him from the shadows. The numbness receded, and in its place came not anger and grief but a kind of solace that brought him back to the bench by a lake, where she had held his hand and promised him that all was not in vain, and if he returned to this life she would find a way to remain with him.

"Tell me," he said to the dark. "Tell me what she is."

The singing stopped, but no reply came. He passed the flashlight's beam around, trying to catch sight of her again, but what he could see of the dunes remained empty, and the only sound left was the breaking of the waves.

The flashlight flared, the bulb glowing gradually brighter and brighter until he could feel the heat of it, and it did not so much illuminate the night as burn a column of light through it; and just as the bulb exploded he caught a glimpse of his dead daughter at the very edge of the beam's reach, and all dread and doubt were banished as she was absorbed into the dark.

He turned away, walked back to his house, and did not fear the shadows.

IV

Had I turned into a soulless person, a wicked man, a murderer?
I went on plying my conscience with questions. Had I done
anything in the war but my duty and my obligations? Had I done
anything but remain loyal to my oath and obedient to my orders?
And my conscience answered me reassuringly. No, nothing else.
Had I killed defenseless people, or ordered them to be killed?
No, no, no. What in the devil's name did they want of me?

Extract from the memoirs of Adolf Eichmann, architect of the
Final Solution, published in *The People* newspaper, 1961

CHAPTER

LV

E ven by his poor standards, Baulman was enduring a difficult night. He replayed his conversation with Hummel over and over, the horror of it repeatedly unfolding before him. Baulman had been able to endure Hummel's company for only fifteen minutes, but throughout their entire conversation Hummel was unable to refer to him as anything other than "Reynard" or, occasionally, "my dear Kraus." It was a nightmare, and when at last Baulman had made his escape he felt physically weakened by the encounter. He sat in his car, and wondered how quickly Hummel could be put out of both of their miseries. While in the room he made a quick search of Hummel's belongings, just in case any mail might have arrived from the Justice Department, but there was nothing. Baulman thought Hummel's damned daughter had probably requested that all of her father's mail be redirected to her. What if the Justice people got in touch with her, and that bitch Demers came calling? Baulman could only hope that Theodora would be smart enough not to let Demers within fifty feet of her father.

He calmed himself, and tried to consider the problem logically. Theodora Hummel might have been as unpleasant as shingles, but she wasn't stupid. Who knew what Hummel, in his dotage, had let slip to her about his past? Even after only a quarter of an hour with him, Baulman was convinced that he had regressed to his wartime service.

Every word from Hummel's lips had concerned his time in uniform and, stirred by the presence of his old comrade, their time together at Lubsko, although Hummel spoke only of the flower beds, and the good food, and the relaxed regime, excluding from his memory entirely the walking corpses that justified the camp's existence. Sometimes he even forgot that he was now Bernhard Hummel and corrected Baulman when he called him by that name. . . .

Slowly, Baulman became convinced that Theodora must have some awareness of what her father had really done during the war. Hummel's cover story was that he had been persecuted for trade union activism, and forced to wear the red inverted triangle of a political prisoner. He claimed to have been incarcerated, first in Kuhberg and Flossenbürg, and then in Dachau. This story had initially caused him some difficulties with the Americans, due to the inevitable Communist connotations of trade union activism, but the supporting documentation from various sympathetic members of the clergy, as well as his American sponsors, had made it clear that Bernhard Hummel was as anti-Communist as it was possible to be, and had, in fact, become involved in workers' rights as much to fight against unwelcome Marxist influences as fascism. By now Theodora Hummel certainly knew this to be a lie, but she had remained silent, as any good daughter would.

And what if Demers did manage to interview Hummel? The ravings of a demented man would not stand up in court. But did they have to stand up? Again, it came down to the burden of proof required for deportation. Maybe even Hummel's ramblings would be enough to damn Baulman. If, as he believed, Engel had betrayed him, then Hummel would give them the confirmation Demers needed to continue her investigation. Once they began pulling threads, some unraveling was inevitable.

He went over all this again as he lay sleepless in his bed, Lotte snoring peacefully on her cushion under the window. He concluded that Theodora Hummel's instinct for self-preservation, and her desire to maintain her status in the community—she was an assistant principal at an elementary-middle school—meant that she had decided to conceal whatever she might have learned about her father's true identity. He could approach her, of course, and sound her out to confirm this, but it seemed inadvisable, just in case she actually did not know the truth about her father, or had decided to leave it unacknowledged even to herself, and because she had no more love for Baulman than he had for her. There was another way, though, another person to whom he could speak about Hummel, one who was closer to him than Baulman had been: Riese. Yes, just as he had been instructed to do, Baulman would consult with Riese, and on the basis of what he learned he would be able to gauge the best way of dealing with Theodora.

With that, Baulman's body and mind began to relax at last, and he fell asleep.

———

HE WOKE SHORTLY BEFORE seven. He fed Lotte, made himself some poached eggs on toast, and took the dog for a short walk before driving to Harrington to see Ambros Riese. He introduced himself to Riese's daughter-in-law as an old acquaintance, and asked if he might be permitted to visit with him for a time. She seemed pleased, and Baulman guessed that Riese didn't receive many visitors. None of them did. Most of those who might have visited them were dead.

Riese's son and daughter-in-law had converted their two-car garage into living accommodations for the old man. He had a separate bedroom, his own bathroom, and a kitchen-cum-living room. He was sitting in an armchair watching CNN when Baulman was admitted. Unlike Hummel, Riese had not shrunk. He was still a big man, and his blue eyes gleamed with the clarity of prime gemstones. An oxygen tank was positioned behind the chair, a plastic cannula feeding the gas into his nostrils. A walker stood at the ready to his right, and a mobility scooter was charging in a corner by the door.

Riese didn't appear particularly surprised to see Baulman, although he was less pleased than his daughter-in-law had been. Baulman immediately felt a combination of deference and resentment in Riese's presence. Riese was not like him, although both had entered the United States from Argentina within weeks of each other, and the same source of funds had helped them to escape and settle in this new land. Although Baulman knew relatively little about Riese's past, the contrast between their respective methods of flight from Europe indicated that he had once been a figure of some importance.

Baulman had escaped Germany via the "Iberian Way." Through the offices of the Nazi sympathizer Bishop Alois Hudal, the rector of an Austro-German church in Rome, Baulman had traveled by boat from Genoa to Barcelona, his left arm still aching from the procedure to remove his blood-group tattoo and sew up the wound. From there he traveled on to Madrid, where he had waited two months before securing passage to Argentina. He recalled Madrid fondly, even though he had lived in one room of a dark, cluttered apartment owned by a half-blind Falangist who slept in his clothes and stank of piss and wine. He remembered the voyage west with less happiness, having spent most of it lying seasick in a shared cabin.

It was on the ship that he first saw Riese, who occupied his own cabin in first class and liked to smoke cigars from his vantage point on the upper deck. Through gossip, Baulman learned that Riese had been spirited out through the "Roman Way," the escape route of choice for senior Nazis, and Monsignor Draganović himself had personally seen him off from San Girolamo, the Croatian monastery in Rome that functioned as de facto headquarters for the operation to smuggle Nazis out of Italy.

Baulman had only seen Krunoslav Draganović once, and then from a distance, but he had conceived an immediate dislike for the Croatian cleric, and nothing he had learned about him in the decades since had caused him to modify his opinion in the slightest. As a veteran of

Auschwitz and Lubsko, Baulman had no illusions about the capacities of his own regime, but the excesses of the Croatian Ustasha Catholic nationalists who had formed their own independent state after the Axis invasion of 1941 made even him feel ill. Baulman couldn't stand by and let an animal suffer unnecessarily, never mind a Jew or Gypsy child, but the Ustasha reveled in sadism, and their camp at Jasenovac was notorious for the cruelty of its methods of dispatch: hacking, stabbing, suffocation, burial alive—the list of torments went on and on. It was from Jasenovac that the Ustasha's leader, Ante Pavelić, once received a basket of eyeballs as a tribute from his admirers. And who was the chaplain at Jasenovac? Monsignor Krunoslav Draganović, who appeared to have found in the mysterious Riese something of a kindred spirit.

Yet Baulman's fate had become intertwined with that of Riese and Hummel, who was also on that same ship. Each had been supplied with an identity card signed by Alois Hudal, which allowed him to apply for a Red Cross passport. That organization was too overburdened even to check the identities of applicants, and a Red Cross passport was the first important step in establishing a new identity. Once obtained, the escape route typically sent fugitives to Genoa, and from there to greener pastures. Baulman and Hummel had boarded the ship together at Barcelona. Hudal had secured Hummel's release from the internment camp at Miranda de Ebro south of Bilbao, but only after Hummel had promised to convert to Catholicism, a promise he never bothered to keep. Riese had already been on board when the ship left Italy for Argentina.

Once settled in Salta, Riese had brought his young wife over, then entered the United States with her as German-Argentines of long descent. Both subsequently became naturalized US citizens, and raised their family in Maine. Baulman and Hummel had followed shortly after, their admission into the United States delayed when the INS wanted to know why they had not applied to enter the country directly as displaced persons instead of first traveling to Argentina and making their application from there. It was Hummel who had come up with the perfect answer: they had, he told the Americans, not realized how many ex-Nazis would be with them in Argentina.

Engel arrived a year later: his refusal to countenance a new name troubled the others—Riese most of all—but it quickly became apparent that nobody was interested in them. They were not being hunted, not then. Only later did the pursuit begin.

Baulman still did not know Riese's true identity, and none of the others had been made aware of it either, as far as he could tell. Riese might have told Hummel, he supposed. Their friendship had always struck Baulman as curious, and even inadvisable. Baulman had kept his distance from all of them, meeting with the others only once or twice a year—less, if he could manage it, especially in the case of Engel. Baulman was solitary by nature, and had no need of their company. Also, if one of them came under suspicion from the Americans, the rest would be at less risk of exposure if few ties of intimate friendship could be established between them. He still regretted allying himself with Hummel during that US immigration business, but he had been far from home, and Argentina had proved an unpleasantly alien environment.

Sheila, Riese's daughter-in-law, offered to make coffee, and Baulman and her father-in-law exchanged small talk until she returned with a pot and cookies, before announcing that she would leave them alone to talk. She smiled at them as she left, like a mother approving of children on a playdate. Baulman poured the coffee, the hiss of Riese's oxygen like an aural manifestation of his host's disapproval. Nevertheless, Riese muted the sound on the television so they could speak. He kept his voice low, though, as did Baulman. Old habits.

"Why are you here, Baulman?"

"Some problems have arisen. *Die Kacke ist am dampfen*." The shit is steaming: the old expression came to his lips before he even realized what he was saying. It happened when his brain knew before he did that the English language would not suffice. "I need your advice."

Riese's icy demeanor didn't quite melt, but there was the hint of a thaw.

"Go on."

Baulman quickly explained everything that he could about Perlman, the Tedescos, and Ruth Winter. He chose not to mention the Wilde family. They were connected, but not entirely relevant to the present situation. Finally, he confessed that he was being investigated by the Human Rights and Special Prosecutions Section of the Justice Department.

"The OSI?" said Riese. To their generation, it would always be the OSI that hunted them. "And you come here, to me?"

"I had no choice. We are so few now. But I've been careful, and they've been thrown off the scent."

Those bright eyes fixed themselves on Baulman, like an owl preparing to snatch a mouse and eat it.

"How did they find you?"

"We believe that Engel has been talking in an effort to save himself."

"Fucking Engel. I never trusted him. I would not allow him into my house."

Baulman had never cared much for Engel either. Unfortunately, they were bound together by shared history.

Baulman sipped his coffee. It was strong, but tasted cheap. He set it down again. Drinking it wasn't worth the trouble to his bladder.

"I went to see Hummel yesterday," he said.

"And how is Bernhard?"

"He has lost his mind."

"It's a shame. When last I saw him, he was just forgetful. His *Fotze* daughter barely gave him time to pack his bags before she had him locked up."

"Hummel," said Baulman carefully, "has not forgotten everything."

"What do you mean?"

"When I visited him, he insisted on calling me Kraus, and talked only of the war."

"Christ."

"If his mind has gone to such a degree, I may not be the only one whom he—"

"I'm not a fool, Baulman. I understand."

Riese nibbled on a cookie. His jaws were more gum than teeth, and he scattered crumbs on his lap as he ate.

"About his daughter," said Baulman.

"Yes?"

"Does she know?"

Riese stared down at his hands. Baulman noticed that the right had a slight but persistent tremor.

"I think so," he said. "Before she put Bernhard away, she said something odd. She told me that it would be the best thing 'for all of us,' then added 'for all of you.' So, yes, I believe that she knows."

"If Engel is talking to the Justice Department, it can only be a matter of time before he gives them Hummel. And even if Engel were not to feed you to them, Hummel might do so accidentally if he were approached by the Americans. My relations with his daughter have never been good, but it would be best if someone could talk with her, and find out if she or her father has been contacted. If they have not, she can be forewarned."

"She may have to fight them in court," said Riese. "I am no lawyer, but I'm sure they have the power to interview a suspect, even if he is old and demented."

"And if he starts naming names . . ."

"Yes. That would be regrettable." He pointed to the tray. "You're not drinking your coffee."

"No."

"I don't blame you. She buys discounted garbage. She has a good heart, but no taste."

Riese began fiddling with his cannula. The tube had slipped out from behind his left ear. Baulman asked permission to help. He tightened it in place, and saw that the area behind Riese's ears had been rubbed almost raw. His nostrils, too, were dry and irritated. God, thought Baulman, I've been lucky.

"Hummel talked with me about you," said Riese, as Baulman returned to his seat.

"Really? He was always discreet about you."

"Huh. Good. He told me that you killed a man before the war."

It had been so long since Baulman had thought of it. He had not spoken of his youth in many years, and there had been so many other killings after that. But it was the first that had set him on his path, he supposed. The first is always the hardest.

"That's right," said Baulman.

"Who was he?"

"A criminal. A burglar. My father ran a clothing store. Sometimes he kept money in the house. He did not have a safe. He said that if he had one, people would start asking why he needed it, so better to do without.

"It was close to Christmas. He was busy, and there was more money than usual in the drawer in his office. He and my mother were at a party. I was alone in the house—well, I had Britta for company. She was a little mongrel, but a good dog. She heard a noise in the kitchen, and went to investigate. Seconds later, I heard her yelp, and when I went to see what was happening there was a man holding her up by the collar. He had a scarf around his mouth, and a hat over his eyes. He put a knife to Britta's throat, and he killed her, right in front of me, and told me that I'd be next if I didn't show him where the money was.

"So I led him to my father's office. I remember crying because of what he'd done to Britta, but I was also so angry. It was a cold rage. I recall it clearly.

"The man began searching the desk, but my father kept his money in a concealed drawer. There was a lever under the desk, and you had to know where it was to open the drawer. I told the man that I could do it for him, and he stepped back. He was not frightened of me. I was only thirteen, and still small for my age.

"I found the lever with my left hand, and released the drawer. I knew that my father kept a little Mauser pistol there, a 6.35 mm auto. He'd had it since the war. It was in my grasp before the man realized what I was doing. I held it up and pointed it at him. I can remember that my hands didn't even shake, and I thought that they should. He raised his own hands, and he started to laugh. He told me that I was brave, but I should hand over the gun before I hurt myself, that it was hard to kill a man, no matter what I might have thought or heard."

Baulman swallowed. His mouth was dry. It was like telling a story about a stranger. This was not Baulman's history; this was Reynard Kraus's. Only the memory of Britta's death made it real to him.

"And I said to him, 'Is it harder than killing a dog?' and I pulled the trigger. The bullet hit him in the chest, and he fell back against the wall. There was a chair, and somehow he managed to sit down. He put his hand to the wound, and it came away red. He asked me to call a doctor, and I shot him again, and I kept shooting until the pistol was empty. Then I called my father at the party and told him what I had done.

"The police came. I explained everything. I didn't lie. There was talk about charging me with murder because I'd shot the man so many times, but it never came to anything. Eventually I joined the SS, and, because I was considered bright, and was good with numbers, I was recruited for the Economic-Administration Main Office, when the Inspectorate of Concentration Camps was incorporated into it in 1942. That was how I eventually came to Lubsko."

Riese nodded, as though somehow Baulman made a kind of sense to him now.

"I was at Mittelbau-Dora," he said. "First under Förschner, then Baer."

Mittelbau-Dora, sometimes referred to simply as Nordhausen, was a subcamp of Buchenwald, where prisoners worked on tunnel excavations for the production of V-1 and V-2 rockets. It was slave labor of the worst kind: twenty thousand died of exhaustion, disease, starvation, in accidents, or at the end of a noose. In 1947, the Americans tried nineteen former Nordhausen guards and kapos at Dachau, of whom fifteen were convicted and one executed. In an act of gross hypocrisy, the Americans also recruited Arthur Rudolph, one of the Nordhausen rocket scientists, under Operation Paperclip, and he went on to enjoy a distinguished career at NASA before being thrown out of the country in the 1980s.

Riese said no more, and Baulman did not pursue the matter. He wondered who Riese really was. He had worked as an engineer in the United States, so perhaps he had been a scientist. No matter. Like Baulman, he had lived under his false identity for longer than his true one. He was more Ambros Riese than anyone else. Pressure had been placed upon them to provide funds for his escape. Hudal and Draganović together had asked, and Baulman and the others could not refuse, because the clerics were supplying the paperwork. Money was no good without papers.

"Do you regret anything that you did, Baulman?"

The question took Baulman by surprise. It was not that he had never considered it, merely that he had never heard it asked aloud.

"I cannot connect it to myself," he replied. "When I recall everything that occurred, it seems to be the work of another man."

"It's so long ago now," said Riese. "It is to me like a bad dream."

On the television, the news shifted to some godforsaken part of the Middle East, where bodies lay in the dust—civilians, Baulman thought, although it was hard to tell in these conflicts.

"Why do they continue to pursue us?" asked Riese. "Why all this effort for old men and women who can no longer hurt anyone, when all they have to do is turn on their televisions and see more worthwhile outlets for their self-righteousness? The world has no shortage of war criminals, no end of mass slaughter, yet still they focus their attentions on us."

"They perceive no moral complexity in us," said Baulman, "no shades of right and wrong. They can show pictures of us to schoolchildren, and they can say, 'See? This is what evil looks like.' But show them men and women with machetes in Africa, show them Syrians fighting a dictatorship and then flying the flag of Al-Qaeda, show them Israeli tanks and Hamas gunmen, and all they see is confusion. It is easier to torment us than to try to unravel the knots of outrageous human behavior that they witness every day. That is what I believe."

Yet Baulman had never thought of himself as evil. He had done what he had to do. If he had not, others would have taken his place. He had tried to make sure that the children did not suffer. He put them to sleep the way his vets had put a succession of Weimaraners to sleep. He had not wanted the children to feel pain and fear at the last any more than he would have wanted his dogs to die in distress.

"What will you do about Hummel?" asked Riese.

"Our friend will take care of him. It will be a mercy."

"He will be discreet?"

"Yes."

"If Engel has named Hummel, they will investigate his death."

"Let them. Old men die. It's what they do."

"What *we* do," Riese corrected.

"No, not us. Not yet."

Riese reached out and placed his left hand on Baulman's leg.

"Do you know how Harry Houdini died?" he asked.

"What?" said Baulman.

"The escape artist, Houdini. Do you know how he died?"

"No." Baulman was confused.

"He would boast that punches could never hurt him," said Riese. "A university student—Whitehead I believe was his name—came to Houdini in his dressing room at a theater in Montreal and asked if this was true, that he could not be hurt by a fist. Houdini said that it was. This Whitehead asked permission to strike Houdini in the stomach, and when the great escapologist assented, Whitehead hit him hard repeatedly, just below the belt. The blows ruptured Houdini's appendix. You see, he had been reclining on a couch at the time due to a broken ankle, and so could not brace himself properly to receive the blows. He died of peritonitis as a result of the injuries he had received. What is the lesson of that story, Baulman?"

"That one should always be on one's guard?"

Riese's fingers dug painfully into Baulman's thigh.

"No," said Riese. "The lesson is that, in the end, nobody escapes."

He picked up the clicker, and raised the volume on the television.

"Go now," he told Baulman, "and don't come here again."

LVI

Amanda Winter was playing with a small white mongrel dog in the yard of her grandmother's house when Parker arrived. Like his temporary home in Boreas, Isha Winter's house overlooked the sea, but it was separated from the beach by a road. A gap in a fence opposite gave access to a wooden path that led through the dunes to the strand. The Winter residence was painted white with blue trim. The paintwork was fresh, and the garden was neatly tended.

Amanda seemed not to recognize him at first, and he thought that she looked thinner than when he'd last seen her, even though only a short time had passed. The dog barked at him, but not in a threatening way. As far as the dog was concerned, he was simply another potential playmate. The gate was closed, and it pressed its muzzle between the bars, its tail wagging.

Amanda squinted at him. The sun was behind him, and shone in her eyes.

"Hello," she said.

"Hi. Do you remember me?"

She nodded. "You're Sam's dad."

"That's right."

He leaned against the gatepost, but did not enter.

"How are you doing, Amanda?"

"I'm okay," she said. She couldn't hold his gaze, so she knelt down and patted the dog instead.

He didn't want to offer her platitudes. They wouldn't have meant anything to her anyway. Instead he asked, "Who's the dog?"

"Milo."

"Is he yours?"

She shrugged. "Not really. He belongs to the Frobergs. They just got him yesterday."

"Who named him?"

"I thought of it, but everyone had to agree."

"It's a good name. He looks like a Milo."

An elderly woman appeared at the door of the house, flanked by a younger couple. The man stepped past the two women and came down the drive toward Parker. He was in his forties, and already had a small belly that strained against his polo shirt. He was wearing cargo shorts, even though it was still a little cold for them.

"Can I help you?" he asked.

"I'm here to see Mrs. Winter. My name is Charlie Parker."

Recognition dawned on the man's face.

"Please," he said, opening the gate, "come in. My name is Christian Froberg. Amanda is living with my family now."

They shook hands. Amanda held on to Milo to prevent him from jumping up, or making a break for freedom through the open gate. Froberg made the introductions to his wife, Cara, and to Isha Winter. It appeared that the Frobergs were about to leave—each day they brought Amanda to sit shiva for a time with her grandmother—but they felt obliged to exchange some stilted small talk with Parker, made more awkward by the fact that Mrs. Winter appeared unable to speak to him. She just stared, and wrung her hands as though trying to clean them of a stain.

"Whose idea was it to get a dog?" asked Parker.

Christian Froberg smiled at his wife. "Our kids have been nagging us to get one for the last year, but we'd resisted. Then, when we took in Amanda, we thought it might be good for her."

"I heard that she was staying with foster parents."

"We're in touch with Child and Family Services," said Cara. "We're hoping to start the adoption procedure next month."

"We don't want to rush anything," said Christian. "For Amanda's sake."

Again, Parker avoided platitudes. They didn't seem like stupid people. They'd know how hard it was going to be for Amanda—and for them. What had befallen her mother would never leave her, and there would be difficult times ahead.

"I wish you luck," was all he said.

The Frobergs made their farewells, gathered up Amanda and Milo, and headed for their station wagon, which was parked in the drive. Amanda put Milo on a leash, and he trotted along at her heels. Something in Parker broke away at the sight of her, a fragment of his heart that went out to the girl. It was in the way that she walked, and how she held her head, like a boxer who has taken a ferocious blow and is trying only not to fall. Now he wished that he could have found the right words, some consolation to offer. The certainties that he had felt at Green Heron Bay slipped away. If only he had been able to run faster, if only he had not been injured . . .

Behind him, Isha Winter spoke her first words to him since "Hello."

"Thank you for coming," she said. "Thank you for what you tried to do."

Then she began to cry.

———

HE SAT WITH HER in the kitchen. It still bore the remains of the food that she had shared with the Frobergs. He accepted her offer of some water, but declined anything more. She told him to call her Isha, but could not bring herself to address him as anything other than Mr. Parker. It was like being with the Fulcis' mother.

"I thought of visiting you in the hospital," she said. "But there was so much to do—the funeral, taking care of Amanda. I'm sorry, I—"

"It's not necessary," said Parker. "Really."

"No," she insisted, "it is. You risked your life for my daughter, and my granddaughter. You were hurt for them. I wanted to thank you for it. I'm glad that you have come."

She took his right hand in her own, and squeezed it briefly before releasing it.

"I know that you've spoken to the police," he said.

"They have been very good. They asked many questions, but some of them I could not answer."

"Such as?"

"I could not tell them why my daughter was murdered."

She appeared to be on the verge of tears again, but she forced them back.

"All I could explain to them," she continued, "was that there have always been those who hate us, and I think there always will be."

"By 'us,' you mean Jews?"

"I told the detectives—I told them at the cemetery, and I told them again here, at this table—that they will never leave us in peace."

"Have there been incidents in the past?"

Only after he spoke did he realize the absurdity of what he had said. Adding "apart from the Holocaust" wasn't really an option. Isha guessed his thoughts. He saw her smile.

"You mean recently?" she said. "You mean here?"

"Yes."

"Not so much. Someone once sprayed a swastika on the wall, but that was years ago, and we would sometimes find literature in the mailbox—vile letters and pamphlets. But the men and women who do that, they are cowards. They can't even find the courage to face an old woman during the day. They sneak by at night to spread their hatred."

"The man who killed your daughter was a professional," said Parker. "I don't think he was the kind to paint swastikas on walls, then run away."

"I know this. The detective told me."

"Detective Walsh?"

"Yes."

"He's a good man."

"He said the same thing about you."

"Did he have to grit his teeth first?"

"*Na, na!*" Isha Winter looked appalled at the thought. She slapped his hand gently, scolding him. "He meant it."

"Did he also tell you that a connection might exist between your daughter's murder and your time in the camp at Lubsko?"

"He said this, but I could think of nothing."

"What about the man the Justice Department is investigating— Kraus?"

"But I looked at the photograph, and it was not who they said it was. They wanted me to say that it was Reynard Kraus, but it was not!"

He let it go. Perhaps he was coming at this from the wrong angle. Could Ruth Winter have discovered something independent of her mother's past that had then brought her into contact with Bruno Perlman? It seemed unlikely.

He asked Isha about Perlman, and she described again her only encounter with him, at that same kitchen table. From what she told Parker, Perlman was fascinated—even obsessed—by Lubsko, and by the hunt for the last surviving Nazi war criminals hiding in the United States.

"He told me," she said, "that he had helped to find Nazis in the past. He said that he had provided information to the government."

Parker didn't know if that was true. He suspected it wasn't. Epstein had said nothing about it, and neither had Walsh.

"He showed me the tattoos on his arm," said Isha.

"The Auschwitz numbers?"

"Yes, the numbers." She shook her head. "I don't think he understood why I found it such an odd thing to have done. He knew so
little of his people, only their names. It was not done for commemoration by him. I think he was looking for something to be angry about. I
think"—she tapped a forefinger to her right temple—"in his mind, he
had almost convinced himself that he was there with them, at Auschwitz and Lubsko."

"Did he meet your daughter while he was here?"

"Yes, but just for a short time."

"Your daughter and granddaughter used to live with you, didn't
they?" he asked.

"For many years, yes. My husband owned all of this land." She gestured through the walls at unseen fields. "He built a guest cottage so
that friends could come and stay with us, and enjoy the sea, but not
many ever did. We rented it out, but after he died it seemed like so
much trouble. I just left it empty, but then Ruth came back here with
Amanda, and it was a good place for them to live."

"And Amanda's father?"

"He was not her husband," said Isha, answering another question
entirely, but one that was apparently important to her. "They were not
married."

"What did he do?"

She leaned forward, and lowered her voice.

"He beat her."

"I meant for a living."

"Oh, he worked in a *garage*," she said, putting all of the contempt
she could muster into the last word. "But really, he was a criminal.
Ruth told me. Stolen cars, drugs. He was a *Kriecher*. You understand
Kriecher? A lowlife. She almost lost the baby once, he hit her so hard.
When he died, it was a blessing."

"As I understand it, he didn't just die: he was murdered."

"The police said it was over drugs. He was shot."

Her tone suggested that it was the least he deserved.

"And so Ruth came to live with you?"

"Not immediately. But it was hard for her with the baby, and money was a problem. Why would she live in a dirty apartment when she could use the house here? It was just common sense."

"And why did she then move to Boreas?"

Isha began wringing her hands again.

"Because I am a nosy, demanding old woman. Because even in separate houses, there was not enough space for us. I think she felt that I was always looking over her shoulder, always criticizing."

"And were you?"

The tears came again.

"I think that I was. And now she is gone."

———

THEY SPOKE FOR A short time longer. Isha Winter talked to him of Lubsko, of her first sight of it with her parents—"the little houses, the gardens—there were even bathtubs!" They arrived with four other families, each of them unable to believe quite what they were seeing. Within days, pressure was being placed upon them: discreet at first, then more insistent. Lubsko was not free. A life there had to be paid for.

"My father did not trust them," said Isha. "But he paid up, like the rest. He was an art dealer in Aachen before the war, and he had hidden paintings in two vaults in Düren, the old cemetery. One of them was a Bellini Madonna; another was a nude by Rubens. These are the only ones that I can remember. The other families, they offered money, jewelry, diamonds, whatever they had put away in the hope that they might be able to come back for it after the war.

"I know now that most families lasted a month, but we were given only two weeks. Before us, the Nazis had taken their time in the hope that more hidden treasures might be revealed to them, or so they could convince men with secret wealth to name others with the promise that they, too, would be brought to Lubsko. But it was 1945, and they knew that the end was coming. Lubsko was to be closed, so they were in a hurry to bleed us dry and be gone. They held on just too long, though, because they were greedy, and by then *die Russen* were almost at the gates."

Although she remained a presence in the room, a part of her was now elsewhere, lying in a shallow grave beneath a layer of dirt.

"I saw Kraus take the children away first," she said. "Then the shooting started. They were going from hut to hut. My father told me to run and hide. I did not even have time to say good-bye, and when I saw them again they were dead.

"I think I heard the shots that killed the commandant and his wife. I was near their house, and I heard the sound of a pistol firing twice. Later, I could smell their quarters burning.

"And then I found the grave. They must have opened it that morning, or the night before, so that they could save time and bury us quickly. I remember the smell, and the sight of the bones, and the bodies that had been revealed by the digging. I took off my clothes so that I would look like all the rest. I threw myself in, and covered my body with dirt, and I lay there and waited.

"Soon everything went quiet, but I stayed in the grave until it was dark. That was when I saw all of the bodies: not just our people, but the Germans too. They had turned on their own, like animals. They had not even bothered to hide what they'd done. The Russians found me two days later. I was sitting by the bodies of my mother and father. They tell me that I was eating an apple, but I don't remember this. I was the only one left alive. The only one. I was dirty, and in shock. I looked younger than I was. I think that was the only reason they did not rape me. Then one of their officers came, and he made me tell my story. I think he realized that I had some propaganda value, and he made sure I was protected until his superiors had spoken with me. Finally, I made it out of Poland into Germany. I told my story again to the Americans, and they let me come here."

"When did you arrive?"

"Nineteen fifty-one."

"Can I ask how you came to Maine?"

"I was a Jew helped by a Lutheran: Pastor Otto Werner of Boreas reached out to me. He found me a job, a place to live. He even introduced me to the man who would become my husband. David was working on the pastor's house at the time, painting it inside and out. In the end, I found some peace, Mr. Parker. I found it here."

There was nothing more to say. Parker stood, thanked her for her time, and prepared to leave. As he passed the dining room, he saw cards piled on the table, and envelopes sealed and addressed, and a fountain pen.

"Is there anything that I can do for you?" he asked.

"You know, you could take these to the post office, if it is not too much trouble," she said. "I received many cards, many letters, and I am trying to reply to them all. They will need stamps."

She counted the sealed envelopes carefully, made a calculation in her head, then found her purse and gave him the exact amount in bills and coins. Only as he was about to leave did she notice that she had paused in the act of addressing an envelope. She picked up the pen and wrote the rest of the address. He noticed that she was forced to hold the fountain pen awkwardly, for she was left-handed and did not want the ink to smudge. She returned to her purse for more change for the last stamp. He tried to tell her not to go to the trouble, but she wouldn't hear of it.

She walked him to the door.

"The detective, Mr. Walsh, he told me that you might come here," she said. "He told me you might want to help find the ones who killed my Ruth. Is that true?"

"Yes."

She nodded.

"Then *auf Wiedersehen*, Herr Parker," she said. "*Und machs gut*. Take care . . ."

He bought stamps at the post office in Boreas. He did not recognize any of the names on the envelopes, although most of the addresses were local. Before he mailed them he made a note of each addressee, then went to look for Bobby Soames.

LVII

Soames blanched when Parker appeared at his office door. His receptionist was taking a late lunch, and Soames was left alone to take care of business. Not that the phone was ringing off the hook anyway, or not as far as anywhere in Boreas was concerned. Nothing was more likely to smother the tentative growth of a local property market than a killing. Soames thought that it might actually be years before he managed to rent or sell either of the properties on Green Heron Bay again. Sometimes Google was a curse.

"Are you here to renew your lease?" he asked the detective, and he wasn't sure which answer he wanted to hear more. A "yes" would guarantee his clients—and, by extension, Bobby Soames—some income from one of the properties. A "no" would mean that he'd see the back of the detective, who still made him nervous, and whom he secretly regarded as having cursed Green Heron Bay by his presence.

"No, I hope I'll be leaving before the month is out."

Soames felt relief, and realized that he'd wanted peace of mind more than money. He wondered if he might be coming down with something.

"I do have a question for you, though," Parker went on. "I want to find out more about the area. Who's the best person to turn to for a history lesson?"

Soames leaned back in his chair and folded his hands over his belly. Now that the detective had confirmed he was leaving, Soames was feeling a certain warmth toward him.

"Well, there's no shortage of old farts who'll make you wish you'd never asked," he said. "But if you want it concise and to the point, I'd talk to Pastor Werner over at Christ the Redeemer Lutheran. His father was pastor here before him. It's a family business."

"What's he like?"

"Between us?"

"Sure."

"Never married. Might be gay. Nobody asks, nobody cares."

"Are you Lutheran?"

"No, I'm Catholic, but it doesn't worry me."

"Being Catholic?"

"Being gay." He frowned. "Or being Catholic, now that you mention it. I'm a once-a-year-at-Christmas kind of churchgoer. I guess I'm in a state of disagreement with a lot of the rules."

"You're a one-man schism."

"Yeah, but don't tell anyone. I don't want to attract followers. Last I heard, you were in the hospital."

"I'm all better now."

"You'll pardon me for saying so, but you don't look all better."

Parker had caught a glimpse of himself in the mirror outside Soames's office. He'd more or less ignored the surgeon's advice about taking it easy, and it was showing on his face.

"Is this how you attract clients?"

"Again, you'll pardon me for saying so, but I'm kind of happy that you're leaving, so I don't want you as a client. I admire what you tried to do for that woman and her child, but the sooner you're gone, the sooner you'll be forgotten here, and the sooner I can find someone to take those houses off my hands."

"You're a practical man, Mr. Soames."

"As are you. The police any closer to finding out what happened up there?"

"I don't know."

"And you?"

"I'm still looking."

"If I can help, you have my number."

"Because if you help me, it might speed me on my way?"

"That's part of it," said Soames. "The other part is that I was there when the cleaning crew wiped the blood from the walls. I didn't like it."

"Well," said Parker, as he turned to go, "there's not a lot about it to like."

———

HE STOPPED BY THE Boreas Police Department after leaving Soames, and was just in time to hear the tail end of an altercation between Sergeant Stynes, who was acting chief while Cory Bloom recovered from her injuries, and a gray-haired man who must have topped out at six-five or six-six, and was wearing a blue windbreaker with the words BOREAS PD in white letters on the back over tan pants and black shoes. They were standing in the chief's glass-walled office, the door of which stood open. All activity had ceased around them as two officers in uniform—one of them Mary Preston, the other a youngish man—and a receptionist listened to what was unfolding.

"You don't tell my people how to do their job, Mr. Foster," said Stynes. "Do I have to remind you that you're officially retired?"

So this was Carl Foster, thought Parker. He'd heard all about him from the locals. The former deputy chief looked like a hard man. Parker was glad that he had been able to deal with Cory Bloom instead of him.

"They should have brought me back!" shouted Foster. "I know this town, damn it. I know it better than you ever will!" He emphasized his point by slamming the palm of his right hand on the desk. "And I can tell you that these people"—he now waved the same hand behind him at the listening figures without even deigning to glance at them—"aren't worth shit."

"Get out of this office," said Stynes.

Unlike Foster, she didn't shout, didn't swear. Her authority was enough to carry her voice. She was handling herself well.

"This isn't over," said Foster.

"Yes," said Stynes, "it is. And I'd be grateful if you'd leave that windbreaker here when you leave. That's department property."

"You want it, you'll have to take it off my fucking back yourself," said Foster.

He stomped out of the office, passed between a pair of desks, and exited through the door beside the reception desk, only coming up short when he almost ran into Parker. He took a step back when he realized who the newcomer was, glowered, and then used the basest of epithets to describe Stynes, pointing his thumb in her direction so that Parker could be under no illusion as to whom he was referring. He appeared to be seeking an ally, but Parker simply turned his head away.

"Fuck you too," said Foster.

He brushed past Parker with enough force to cause him to move his feet, but not to stumble. When he was gone, Parker went to the desk.

"Do I need to put my name down to shout at someone," he asked the receptionist, "or can I just go straight through?"

Preston appeared behind her before she could answer. She was one of those who had come to the hospital to hear Parker's statement after the deaths at Green Heron Bay, and their encounter had been civilized.

"I guess you can go right to the head of the line," said Preston.

She opened the door, and led him to the chief's office. Stynes invited him to sit, but he told her that he preferred to stand. His injured side was plaguing him. He was about done for the day.

"No offense meant," he told her. "It's more comfortable for me to stay on my feet, and if I sit down I may not be able to get up again."

"How are you feeling?"

"Alive. How's Cory Bloom?"

"They're letting her out of the ICU tomorrow."

"I'm glad."

Stynes turned to look out the window, where Foster's Jeep was pulling out of the parking lot.

"I'm sorry you had to hear that."

"I've heard worse."

"Did he say something to you on the way out?"

"He might have used a rude word. I tried not to look offended."

"He's a jerk."

"Still, he hides it well."

"I was wondering if you'd come back here," said Stynes.

"I'm going to stay around for a few days."

"To recuperate?"

"To ask some questions."

"Bangor is handling the investigation."

"Does that mean you object to my asking questions?"

"Would it make any difference if I did?"

"Yes."

"I'm not sure I believe that."

"It strikes me that you have enough people making life difficult for you. I'm not planning to add to your problems."

"I'll hold you to that," she said. "I had an idea that you might be taking what happened up there personally."

"Just as you are."

"Cory's not only my superior, she's also my friend. Who were you planning on talking to?"

"Anyone I can. I've already spoken to Ruth Winter's mother. I also mentioned to Bobby Soames that I'd be hanging around for a while. I'm sure I can think of a few more."

"Bobby Soames leaks like the *Titanic* after the iceberg hit."

"Really? A chatty Realtor. Who knew?"

She nibbled at her bottom lip.

"If you were anyone else, I'd tell you to turn around and keep driving until you hit Portland," she said. "But I'll make an exception, if only because I know that my objections wouldn't be worth a damn. If you find out anything, you share it with Bangor—and me."

"Agreed."

"You still have your weapon?"

"Yes."

"Don't use it."

"Anything else?"

"Just one. I have feds crawling all over this, and our department is a virtual outpost of the MCU. If this goes to hell, and I'm asked, we never had this conversation."

"I get that a lot."

"I'll bet. You take care, Mr. Parker."

"You know, you're the second person today who's told me to do that?"

"Only the second?" said Stynes. "I'm shocked. Just make sure I'm not the last."

————

MARY PRESTON JOINED STYNES in her office after Parker had left.

"I'm starting to like him," said Preston. "But is it okay to say that he makes me nervous?"

"He has blood on his hands," said Stynes. "And, you know, I think he may be almost fearless."

"Why do you say that?"

"Don't you see what he's doing? He's announcing his presence here, letting people like Bobby Soames know that he's taking a professional interest in what happened to Ruth Winter, and by extension Bruno Perlman, and the Tedescos down in Florida. Whoever ordered their deaths is going to hear about it, and is going to know that Charlie

Parker isn't like the cops, or even the feds. He's single-minded, he follows things through to their conclusion, and he won't give up. I don't think he ever gives up."

Preston still looked confused.

"He's staking himself out, Mary," Stynes explained. "He's going to bring whoever was responsible for those deaths down upon himself."

"And then?"

"I believe he's going to tear them apart."

LVIII

In any given situation, the most difficult step is to reach a decision. Once a decision is made, control can be asserted. Baulman and Riese were old soldiers, and they knew that, in war, any decision was better than none. To allow Hummel to remain alive, and wait to see what unfolded, would have been intolerable to them. It would have handed control of the situation to others—to Marie Demers, to the Justice Department, and to all those who wished to deprive them of a peaceful death.

And so the Jigsaw Man arrived at Golden Hills. He had been there on many previous occasions, and was familiar with the names of at least half a dozen patients at any one time, but he had never before traveled there with the intention of ending a life.

At the front desk, he gave the name of Beate Seidel, who had been a resident at Golden Hills for more than four years, and was now in a state of terminal decline. The Jigsaw Man doubted that Beate was capable of any kind of coherence in word, deed, or memory. Her mind was a series of baffling images, and all he saw in her face that afternoon was fear. He stayed with her for half an hour, attuning himself to the rhythms of the staff. The evening meal had just been served, and a calm of sorts reigned, punctuated by the sound of competing televisions from various rooms. The orderlies and nurses had retreated to their stations to catch up on paperwork, and grab something to eat or drink.

The Jigsaw Man left Beate in her bed, staring at the ceiling, and stepped to the door to check the hallway. It was clear, so he walked quickly down to Bernhard Hummel's room, slipping on his coat as he went, as though preparing to leave. The old man was snoozing on his bed, his slippers still on his feet. The Jigsaw Man left the door slightly open, advanced to the bed, and pulled the curtain halfway across, concealing them from anyone who might choose to peer in.

He stood over Hummel, and the old man opened his eyes. In his final moments, Bernhard Hummel was gifted with clarity.

"I knew you'd come," he said. "Ever since Kraus visited, I knew."

"I'm sorry," said the Jigsaw Man.

"Don't be. I'm tired of being afraid."

Hummel closed his eyes and began to whisper.

"Please hear my confession and pronounce forgiveness in order to fulfill God's will," he said. "I, a poor sinner, plead guilty before God of all sins. I have lived as if God did not matter and as if I mattered most. My Lord's name I have not honored as I should; my worship and prayers have faltered. I have not let His love—"

The Jigsaw Man had considered the best way to get rid of Hummel. Suffocation would have been easiest, but he knew that all deaths by suffocation or smothering were automatically treated as suspicious. Even a relatively gentle method, such as covering Hummel's face with a pillow, would leave traces: bloodshot eyes, bruising around the nose and mouth, and high levels of carbon dioxide in the blood. It was important that Hummel's passing should appear natural. Unfortunately for Hummel, that meant a difficult death.

"In the stead and by the command of my Lord Jesus Christ, I forgive you all your sins—" said the Jigsaw Man, talking over Hummel.

It was Baulman who had given the Jigsaw Man the idea. The grapes he had brought for Hummel were still in a bowl by the bed. The Jigsaw

Man had also brought a small bag of them with him in his pocket, just in case Baulman's gift had already been removed, but now they would not be needed. He gently gripped Hummel's lower jaw and pulled down, exposing the interior of his mouth. Hummel's eyes opened again, but the Jigsaw Man shook his head.

"No," he said, and Hummel squeezed his eyes shut.

"—in the name of the Father and of the Son and of the Holy Spirit," the Jigsaw Man continued, as he plucked three large grapes from their stems and dropped them down Hummel's throat. "Amen."

The grapes lodged perfectly, and Hummel began to choke. The Jigsaw Man put the slightest of upward pressure on Hummel's Adam's apple to make sure that he could not swallow. Tears rolled down Hummel's cheeks. He clawed briefly at the Jigsaw Man's gloved hand, and spittle flew from his mouth. The Jigsaw Man counted the seconds until Hummel's body arched violently, and he smelled the dying of him. It had taken less time than expected. The Jigsaw Man was glad. He had always liked Hummel, and had no desire to see him suffer.

"Go in peace," he concluded.

He pulled back the curtain, returned to the door, and listened. He heard no footsteps, no voices. He risked a glance out, and saw only the retreating back of an orderly. He stepped into the corridor, walked to the exit, and pressed the red button that unlocked the door. The receptionist looked up from his desk.

"Good-bye, Pastor Werner," he said.

"Good-bye," Werner replied. "And God bless you."

CHAPTER

LIX

Werner stood in the bathroom, his body dripping from the shower. He was hosting a soup supper that evening in the hall beside the church, to be followed by a short prayer service. He didn't want to arrive there with the smell of Golden Hills still on his clothes and body.

He remained a lean, muscular man, even in his fifties. He kept weights and a bench in his basement, and exercised every morning. There was a good gym on the outskirts of town, with a better selection of weights and machines, but he rarely used it, and when he did he was careful to change before going, and to shower at home.

Now, naked before the mirror, he saw the hairless body of the Jigsaw Man. The child, Amanda Winter, used the name when she was being interviewed by the police after her mother's murder, and Werner was amused when he heard about it—for few events in a small town, especially not the details of a murder investigation, could ever really be kept secret. The Jigsaw Man. Looking at himself, it made a kind of sense.

Werner's entire torso was covered with tattoos, as was his lower body down to his thighs. They had begun as a single small *Balkenkreuz*, the iron cross emblem of the *Wehrmacht* found on the side of German armored vehicles and aircraft during World War II. It was a shadow of the pectoral cross that he sometimes wore as a cleric. The *Balkenkreuz* had always fascinated him, even more than the swastika. The latter, he felt, had been hijacked by ignorant men—although his back was emblazoned with the *Parteiadler* of the Nazi Party, the stylized eagle atop the swastika—but the *Balkenkreuz* was the icon of soldiery. He'd had it placed in the center of his chest when he turned eighteen, then had slowly added more crosses over the years, creating an interlocking pattern, a gridwork, interspersed with other symbols, including the twin Sig runes of the SS, the *Wolfsangel* of the 2nd SS Panzer Division, and even the sword-and-hammer symbol of Strasserism. He had also supplemented the ornaments with appropriate quotations from Hitler and others. The first, written on his back, read "It is thus necessary that the individual should finally come to realize that his own ego is of no importance in comparison with the existence of the nation, that the position of the individual is conditioned solely by the interests of the nation as a whole." The second, across his stomach, read "Parallel to the training of the body a struggle against the poisoning of the soul must begin." All of the work had been done by the same sympathetic tattooist in Bangor. He was now an old man who, if he was aware of Werner's vocation, gave no indication of it. So, yes, Werner was a Jigsaw Man, but the pieces came together to form a representation of something far greater than himself.

As far as he was aware, the police had largely dismissed Amanda's description of the man at her window as a nightmare, and Werner supposed that was what he was. He still wasn't sure what had brought him to the Winter house that night, although he suspected that one element of it was the desire to spare Earl Steiger the trouble of doing the job, and to save a little money in the process.

A kind of madness had overcome him as he approached the dwelling. He wanted Ruth Winter to see him as he truly was, to witness his glory in her final moments. He stripped in the car, and walked through the darkness to her home. Only the sight of Amanda Winter asleep in her bed had saved her mother, for Werner sensed that, if he entered the house, the child might hear him and take fright, and then he would be forced to kill her too. He even thought, as he watched her, that she might already be half awake. He didn't want to kill Amanda. That wasn't part of the deal by any stretch of the imagination.

Sanity returned to him after he had watched the girl for a time, or perhaps it was only a different kind of mania. He heard the sea call his name, and it spoke in the voice of Bruno Perlman. He almost thought that he could see Perlman standing amid the surf, beckoning to him, the hollow of his ruined eye like the gateway to the void into which Werner must ultimately, and inevitably, descend.

And he thought that it might not be the worst way to die, even as Perlman took solid form, the waves breaking against him, the stink of him sharp even against the salty tang of the night air. Werner barely felt the intense cold of the water as he entered it. Let oblivion come, he thought. Let the old horrors deal with the residue of their sins; I have watched over them for long enough. I will take this peace. I will lose myself in blackness, and I will sleep.

Only as the waves closed over his head did he realize that the voice that spoke to him was not his own. Salt water flooded his mouth and nose. He opened his eyes and saw Perlman floating before him, his teeth bared in rage as he recognized that he was about to lose his prize. Werner broke the surface, his body already going into shock. He fought his way back to shore, uncertain that he had the strength to make it, kicking all the while at surf and seaweed, and at the hands that he felt clawing at his legs even unto those final seconds when he crawled to the beach and lay shivering on the sand. He barely recalled returning to his car, and since then he had kept his distance from the water.

One memory of that night remained beyond dispute: he had watched over these old Germans for long enough, and mortality could not come soon enough to those that remained.

But Baulman was still a problem. Werner wasn't sure that he could be trusted to remain silent if the Justice Department put further pressure on him, yet Baulman was one of those whom Werner had sworn to protect. Then again, he had sworn to protect Hummel, but he viewed his death as a kind of mercy killing. Baulman was different. Werner would have to consult on the matter, if it became an issue, although he was already certain of the answer he would receive.

Do it.

It would not be quite as much of a blessing as Hummel's death, but it would be close. All Baulman had left was his dog, and even she was old. Werner would send them on their way together.

At least Oran Wilde was dead and buried. Werner had kept him alive for longer than was wise, but it had been necessary. He had required the boy's blood to sow doubt and confuse investigators, and he didn't know enough about pathology to be certain that analysis of the fluids wouldn't reveal if the boy had been dead or alive when it was taken from him. Instead Werner locked Oran in the basement, and made sure that he didn't suffer at the end.

Werner dried himself, put on a fresh shirt and pants, and attached his clerical collar. He was just combing his hair when the doorbell rang.

He answered it to find the detective, Charlie Parker, standing on his doorstep.

———

PARKER'S FIRST REACTION TO Pastor Werner was that Soames had been wrong in thinking him gay. There was an asexuality to the man, but at first Parker could not pinpoint the source of this impression. As their conversation continued he concluded that Werner had directed his sexual impulses away from both males and females, channeling them into his belief system. Parker had seen the pastor around town, but they had never spoken until now. Like most of the inhabitants of Boreas, he had appeared content to leave Parker in peace.

Werner was doing his best to hide his shock. The threat posed by Parker, and recognized by Steiger, was now upon him.

"Pastor Werner?" said Parker. "I'm—"

"I know who you are."

It came out sharper than Werner would have liked, so he tried to moderate its impact by adding, "I'm sorry. We have a soup supper at the church hall this evening, followed by prayers. I was about to leave."

Parker checked his watch. "It's at six o'clock, right?"

"Yes."

"It's not even five yet, and I won't keep you long. I just have a few questions."

"What kind of questions?"

"About the town, and your father."

"You sound like a policeman."

"Old habits die hard."

"Are you engaged in an investigation, Mr. Parker?"

He said it casually, but he saw the light change in Parker's eyes. Be careful with this one, thought Werner. Be very careful.

"Of a kind," said Parker. "I'm trying to understand what happened here—to Ruth Winter, maybe to Bruno Perlman as well. I was involved, at least as far as Ruth Winter is concerned, so it's personal as much as professional."

"But nobody has hired you?"

"No. This one's on my own dime."

"In that case," said Werner, "your time is like money. I can spare you half an hour, but then I will have to go. Come in, come in."

He stepped aside, and welcomed the hunter into his home.

LX

Marie Demers came out of a meeting in the Justice Department on Pennsylvania Avenue to find Toller rushing down the hallway toward her: Thomas Engel, who was being held in the Metropolitan Correctional Center in Manhattan, had just been moved to Lower Manhattan Hospital following what was believed to be a stroke.

The meeting she had left was convened to discuss five war crimes cases at various stages of investigation, Engel's among them. In attendance were the chief of the Human Rights and Special Prosecutions Section, two deputy chiefs, and two other investigating attorneys. Demers had gone through with them, in detail, her experiences with Marcus Baulman and Isha Winter, and recounted her conversation with Detective Gordon Walsh of the Major Crimes Unit of the Maine State Police. She had also discussed the deaths of Bruno Perlman, Ruth Winter, and the Tedescos in Florida, along with what was known—or suspected—about Ruth's killer, Earl Steiger. She also mentioned to them Walsh's theory that the murders of the Wilde family, and the disappearance of their son, could have some connection to everything else that was happening.

"Can you offer us a conclusion?" one of the deputy chiefs inquired.

"Somebody is lying," was Demers's reply. "And I think it may be Engel."

"What do you want to do with him?"

"He's wasted enough of our time," said Demers. "Put him on the next flight to Germany, and let them find somewhere to dump him. "

"Engel's case remains problematic for them. We've given them all we have on him, but they still feel it's not enough to support a prosecution."

"We'll accept deportation. They know that."

"But they don't want him, not yet. You know how they are about the optics of these things. Without a trial, they feel that they leave themselves open to accusations of providing state support for criminals, and they already have their hands full with Fuhrmann. How about you talk to Engel one more time, just in case?"

God, thought Demers: the Germans and their optics. They were obsessed with appearances, with procedure, with keeping their hands clean, yet their language and speech was peppered with casual references to shit and excrement. During one visit to Berlin, she had even heard a German lawyer refer to her behind her back as the *Klugscheisser*: the intelligence shitter. Toller, who dealt with them more regularly than she did, and was himself half Jewish, was of the opinion that the majority of Germans had never seen or met a Jew in their own country, so that when he visited he was an object of careful curiosity, like a living fossil. Most of the German Jews were gone. They were an abstraction. The Germans could think of them only in terms of victimhood.

Demers took a calming breath. She was tired and angry, which wasn't conducive to making wise decisions. Tackling Engel one last time was the smart thing to do, but she did not want to look at him again. She was sick of him. Engel was playing with them, doing all that he could to cling on in the hope of a reprieve. His lawyers were now trying to argue that an error had been made in the recording of Engel's date of birth on certain relevant paperwork, and he had actually joined the SS as a minor. It smacked of desperation, but a 2003 decision in the case of Johann Breyer, suspected of being a guard at Auschwitz, found that someone who enlisted in the SS as a minor could not be held legally responsible for his actions. It was another delaying tactic to eat up money, resources, and time—both her own and Engel's. The longer he stayed in the United States, the closer he came to dying on its soil.

"Of course," she said. "I'll talk to him tomorrow."

"Is there anything else we should know?" she was asked by the second deputy director.

"Just this: the INS records show that Baulman came to the United States from Argentina with another man, Bernhard Hummel. I ran him through the system, and I see some of the same irregularities in his paperwork that we found in Baulman's. Hummel settled in Maine, not far from Baulman. Toller made a telephone call to Hummel's home, but there was no reply. I overnighted a letter, requesting that he call us to schedule an interview."

"You're sure he's still alive?"

"There's no record of his death."

"Ask Engel about him. See what he says."

"I will. Thank you."

———

NOW HERE WAS TOLLER informing her that Engel was lying incapacitated in a hospital bed. She asked him how bad the old bastard was, and learned that he was conscious, but entirely paralyzed along his left side.

"Nyman is screaming blue murder," said Toller.

Barry Nyman was leading Engel's legal team. He was determined to convince Demers that he was defending Engel on principle, but if he was, then it was a principle with zeros and a decimal point after it. This was another aspect of the case that bothered her. Nyman didn't work for free—he could take his protestations that he was working pro bono and stick them up his ass—but Engel's financial resources were limited, and somehow Nyman was still being paid: possibly in cash, and certainly under the table, but paid nonetheless, even though Demers figured that the funds were almost bled dry, or else Nyman might have made a bid for a Supreme Court hearing for his client.

Meanwhile, Nyman had unsuccessfully argued that Engel should be allowed to remain in his own home pending deportation. Engel had suffered a series of minor strokes over the previous years, and Nyman tried to convince the US magistrate that his frail health would be put at risk in a prison environment, probably so that when Engel was back in his own bed, a by-the-hour expert physician could be found to swear that moving him again might prove fatal. The magistrate had disagreed, but Demers knew that Nyman was certainly already making an application to have the original decision reversed on the grounds of Engel's emergency hospitalization, if the magistrate had not already done so himself. A bail application would immediately follow, and was likely to be granted.

"I'm going up there," Demers said.

"Now?" said Toller.

"Yes, now. Do me a favor: just get me on the Delta Shuttle. I'll pick up an overnight bag on the way."

LXI

Werner didn't offer Parker anything to drink. It was just as well. The detective felt as though his lone kidney had probably dealt with enough liquids for the day. They sat in a corner of the living-cum-dining room that Werner had converted into a home office, Werner in an old recliner by his desk and Parker on a chair pulled from the small dining table. A crucifix hung on the wall behind Werner: Christ set in bronze against dark, angled wood.

"I wanted to ask you about your father," said Parker. "I believe he underwent a Damascene conversion."

"An apt metaphor," said Werner. "My father was involved in anti-interventionist circles before Pearl Harbor. He was not alone in that. A great many people believed that the United States should not get involved in another European war."

"As I understand it, your father was more than anti-interventionist: he was a leader of the Bund."

Werner shrugged.

"Are you asking me for a history lesson, Mr. Parker? I can give you one, although it will, of necessity, be brief. There has been a German community here in Boreas since the last century. During—and after—World War I, that community, like German communities through-out the United States, found itself the object of suspicion and hatred.

German music was banned, German-language books burned. In 1918, a German coal miner named Robert Prager was lynched by a mob in Collinsville, Illinois. This experience made German Americans insular and defensive, and not without justification.

"Then, after the war, another wave of German immigrants arrived here, my father among them. They were intelligent men and women, some of whom had fought the Communists on the streets of Berlin, and they wanted no part of the new Germany. They saw it as humiliated, flawed, and unstable."

"How many of them were fascists?" asked Parker.

Werner smiled.

"Quite a number, I should imagine!"

Parker smiled too, just to be polite. "Was your father one of them?"

"No," said Werner. "But he was angry and bitter. When Hitler came to power in 1933, my father rejoiced. He was by then a US citizen, and became a founding member of the Friends of the New Germany, which later morphed into the German American Bund. But the Bund never really gained much of a foothold in Maine—the German community here was just too small—and my father also grew increasingly uneasy about its activities. He was not interested in indoctrinating youth with Nazi policies, or marching through the streets in brown shirts and jackboots. He welcomed the revival of Germany, he was angry about the Jewish boycott of German goods here—and why would he not be, as the pastor of a German congregation?—and he wished his adopted homeland to remain neutral, because he did not want to see it come into conflict with the country in which he was born. These were not unreasonable sentiments at the time."

"Didn't he show propaganda films in your church hall?"

"You *have* been doing your homework," said Werner.

"One of the benefits of being a member in good standing of the Maine Historical Society, and having friends at the University of Southern Maine. They e-mailed me what they had on him."

"I hope that not all of it was bad. But yes, he showed German propaganda films to sympathetic groups, both in Maine and New Hampshire, including *Campaign for Poland*, *Victory in the West*, and *Feuerstaufe*, or *Baptism of Fire*. I know all these names because I found the original films in the basement some years ago. I handed them over to the National Archives. I couldn't think what else to do with them. I simply recognized that they were very rare. Reprehensible now, but rare."

"Why did he show them?"

"In part because he wanted to believe the truth of them, I think, but he was also under some pressure from the Bund. It was growing increasingly extreme, and had begun to infiltrate cultural organizations and German churches. German Americans were reluctant to speak out against it, though. Many could still recall the persecution they had endured after the last war, and believed it was important that they remain united. My father, as a pastor and a community leader, felt deeply conflicted. But by 1938, I think, anti-Nazi sentiment—and, by extension, anti-Bund sentiment—was growing so strong that most German Americans felt they had no choice but to reject it. My father was particularly vocal in his rejection of the Bund. It made him some enemies, but he never regretted it.

"And then, after the war, when the scale of the Nazi atrocities became apparent, he wanted to make recompense. He wrote submissions to the Citizens Committee on Displaced Persons, worked with the Lutheran World Federation on the issue, and petitioned public representatives to support Truman's efforts to accommodate refugees. When the second DP Act came into force in 1950, he was heavily involved in finding sponsors for German immigrants, but he made no distinctions, and worked just as hard for other races and ethnicities."

"He found a sponsor for Isha Winter, didn't he?"

"I did not know that," said Werner.

"It's what she told me."

"He certainly wrote many supportive letters on behalf of displaced persons, and assisted them once they arrived here. It does not surprise me to hear that she was one of them, although I knew nothing of her past until the recent unfortunate events brought it to light. But I would not have thought that Isha Winter's case was especially problematic for the US government. She was the sole survivor of an experimental concentration camp. The decision to admit her can't have been difficult."

"Did your father make mistakes?"

"In what sense?"

"Did he provide sponsorship or support for war criminals?"

"I can't say. If he did so, it was unwittingly. Why do you ask?"

"Because two men from the Northeast, Engel and Fuhrmann, have been in the news lately. You can't have missed them. Fuhrmann has been extradited and Engel is awaiting deportation, both for crimes allegedly committed during World War II. The Justice Department believes that there might be others hiding in this state. It has assigned an investigator named Marie Demers to the case."

"You're very well informed."

"As I told you, I've taken an interest. Could Engel and Fuhrmann be among those helped by your father?"

"I can't answer your question, Mr. Parker. I don't know the names of every man and woman my father assisted because there were hundreds of them. I just know how hard he worked to make up for the sins of other Germans. And I sense that you're trying to besmirch his legacy, which I find objectionable. I think we're finished now."

Werner stood, and Parker stood with him.

"This is a sensitive issue," said Werner. "You must understand that."

"People are dying, Pastor," said Parker. "You must understand *that*."

Werner didn't argue. He wanted the detective gone from his house. He needed space in which to think. He followed Parker to the door.

"I see you wear a cross," he said, indicating the old pilgrim's cross that the detective wore around his neck. He didn't want the detective to leave angry. Concessions had to be made to avoid it.

"I find it gives me consolation," said Parker.

"So you have faith?"

"No."

Werner looked confused. "But why wear it if you do not believe?"

"That wasn't your question," Parker replied. "You asked if I had faith. I don't. Faith is belief based on spiritual conviction instead of proof. You could say that the nature of my convictions has changed recently. Faith is no longer an absolute requirement."

"If that's true, I would not wish to be you," said Werner. "I don't want proof, not of what I now believe through faith. If I had proof, I would have no need of faith, and it is faith that sustains me. And, in my experience, people may say that they want proof, but the last time God gave it to them, they nailed it to a tree."

They shook hands, and Parker left. Werner returned to his desk and switched off the lamp.

He would have to move Oran Wilde's body.

———

WERNER'S SOUP SUPPER WAS well attended, and everyone stayed on for the short prayer service. Afterward, as he was making his farewells, he noticed a bottleneck at the door of the hall, and went to investigate.

The detective was there, handing out business cards.

"My name is Charlie Parker," Werner heard him say. "I'm a private detective. I found Ruth Winter's body out at Green Heron Bay. If you think of anything that might help in the investigation, anything at all, please contact me or Detective Gordon Walsh at . . ."

Werner turned away.

CHAPTER

LXII

Demers arrived at Engel's bedside. As anticipated, the magistrate had reversed his decision and granted bail. Nyman had filed a new appeal against Engel's deportation based on health grounds. At the very least, deportation would now be delayed further.

Engel's wife and daughters were still on their way down to Manhattan from Maine, but their arrival was imminent. Demers didn't have much time.

Engel's left eye was half closed, and his mouth hung open. His face resembled a rock formation that had collapsed on one side. His right eye swiveled in her direction.

"How are you feeling, Mr. Engel?" she asked.

His reply was slurred, but it wasn't hard to pick out the words "Like you fucking care."

"I spoke with Isha Winter," she continued. "She denied that Baulman and Kraus are the same man. You lied to me."

Engel started to gurgle, and the gurgle became a laugh. His body shook with the effort.

"Don't care," he said. "Going home. To Augusta. You lose."

He stank, she thought. He reeked of vomit and corruption and old sins. He had participated in murders untold, and was about to cheat the law at the last.

She leaned in closer to him. She had intended to ask him about Hummel, but she knew she would get nothing out of him now.

"I've spoken to the doctors," she whispered. "You're dying. You can expect another stroke in the next six to twelve hours. If it doesn't kill you, it'll leave you in a vegetative state, but even that won't last very long. You're never going to see your home again, you bastard. You lose."

And his howls of rage followed her all the way down the hall until the elevator doors closed and silenced them.

LXIII

Werner visited Theodora Hummel the next day to offer his condolences on the sad death of her father. She was a moderately unattractive woman who had never married, and was her father's only child. Some work colleagues were with her in the family home when Werner called. She seemed surprised to see him. Her father had been a member of his congregation, but she had not set foot in his church—any church—in many years. She introduced Werner to her friends and offered him a drink. He then participated gamely in the commemoration of the foul old man who was her father, although he did not struggle to come up with anecdotes to amuse them, for—whatever his past—Bernhard Hummel had been something of a character, even if much of his wit, and many of his pranks, came at the expense of others, and were underpinned by petty cruelty.

Eventually the friends began to drift away, until Werner and Theodora were left alone. He helped her clean up, and saw that she had done a lot of work on the house since her father was shipped off to Golden Hills. The kitchen, once dark and oppressive, with oak closets stained almost to black, had been extended and modernized, just as the living room was less forbidding than he remembered. Yet the changes were strangely characterless, and Werner felt as though he had wandered into the pages of a design catalog, and a poor one at that. It wasn't that Theodora Hummel had bad taste: rather, she appeared to have no taste of her own at all.

Finally, Werner resumed his original seat, and waited for Theodora to join him. They sat on uncomfortable chairs, and pretended that they were celebrating the memory of a man who, in reality, would not be missed. It seemed about time to shed the pretense.

"It must be hard for you," said Werner, "living here surrounded by so many memories of your father."

He didn't even try to disguise his sarcasm. No trace of Bernhard Hummel remained in the house, as far as he could see, not unless the first floor was a trap to fool the unwary and Theodora had preserved the second as a kind of mausoleum, all set to receive her father's ashes.

"What do you want, Pastor?" asked Theodora.

"To ask what you knew of your father's past."

"I knew enough."

"Enough?"

"Enough not to speak of it—to him, or to others."

So there would be no games, Werner realized. Good.

"I take it that you wish me to conduct the funeral service," he said.

"I'm sure that's what my father would have wanted."

"We have to be careful at such times," said Werner. "We are consigning a soul to its maker. There is, in the view of some, the requirement of an honest accounting. We cannot speak ill of the dead, yet we cannot whitewash their failings either. But perhaps, in this case, a private acknowledgment of them between ourselves may suffice."

"My father was a Nazi war criminal."

"So it might be said."

"He was helped to make a home in the United States by your father."

"My father, like yours, made mistakes in his life."

"But that was not one of them."

"I couldn't comment."

"I thought we were acknowledging sins."

"We are: the sins of Bernhard Hummel. We need not trouble ourselves with those of others."

Theodora wet her lips. They were too large for her face, the lower lip in particular. It hung, pendulous and dark-blooded, like a slug.

"I have a reputation to protect," she said.

"I hear that you may be about to become principal of your school. Congratulations."

"I've worked hard for it."

"I'm sure that you have."

She rose and went to the kitchen. When she returned, she was holding an envelope. She handed it to Werner. It was addressed to Bernhard Hummel. The letter inside bore the seal of the Justice Department, and came from the Human Rights and Special Prosecutions Section at the Main Justice Building, Pennsylvania Avenue, Washington, DC. Werner read it through. It requested that Bernhard Hummel present himself for an interview over possible irregularities in his original immigration paperwork, and advised him to make contact with the section to arrange a suitable time and venue for a discussion of the same. It was signed by Marie Demers.

"When did you receive it?" asked Werner.

"This morning."

"Unfortunate timing—for the Justice Department."

"My father had not had contact with Thomas Engel for many years," said Theodora. "They had a falling-out over money, and my father refused to speak to him again."

"Did someone call to warn you that Engel might be talking?"

"Ambros Riese. He and my father were once close. Riese hates Engel."

"Have you seen the news today?" Werner asked.

"No, I have not."

"It appears that Thomas Engel died of a stroke early this morning."

"Should I pretend to be sorry?"

"Not on my account, or even his. I doubt that he would have wished it."

Werner folded the letter, replaced it in the envelope, and returned it to Theodora.

"Your father suffered from dementia in his later years," he said carefully.

"That's right."

"Sometimes such people may not know to whom they are talking, or speak of the past as a thing of the present. Was your father such a man?"

"He was."

"Was he careless?"

"He was very paranoid, even before he entered Golden Hills," said Theodora. "I think his illness reinforced that paranoia, but I also did my best to make sure that he did not speak out of turn. I drummed the potential consequences into him. I think he was afraid to speak to those whom he did not know."

"The Justice Department may be in touch with you again when they learn of his passing."

"I don't see what help I can be to them."

"Your father did not keep records, or old documents, that might interest them?"

"I threw out boxes of his old junk when he left for Golden Hills. I don't think I even looked at what was inside. Anything that remains, I may burn tonight. I feel a chill in my bones."

Werner stood. He was satisfied.

"Then your father's passing was, I think, fortunate," he said. "A man should not have to live in such a state of distress."

Theodora stood too. She was the same height as Werner, and could look him in the eye. She handed him his coat, and helped him put it on.

"They are investigating my father's death at the home," she said.

"Really?"

"An autopsy is to be carried out. I think it's standard procedure—not that there should be any cause for concern. His death was an accident."

"Yes. He choked, I believe."

"On grapes," said Theodora. "That's the only odd thing about it."

"Odd?" asked Werner. "How?"

Theodora smiled.

"My father didn't like grapes."

———

THAT EVENING, MARCUS BAULMAN poured himself a large celebratory snifter of brandy, and drank it while watching German soccer from the Bundesliga on his computer. Hummel was dead, and now Engel, too, was gone. Had he been a religious man, it might have been enough to make him send up a prayer of thanksgiving. Instead he watched Bayern Munich score again against Kaiserslautern, and was glad that he seemed assured of living out his final days in this great country.

But as is often the case with those who manage to escape punishment for an offense of which they are actually guilty, Baulman's relief was tempered by rage at his persecutors. Baulman had lived a blameless life after the war. He was a loving husband, a good citizen. He paid his taxes. He contributed time and money to charitable works. But the Justice Department dogs smelled on him only the blood of seven decades before; for them, Baulman's actions during the war defined him. Yet if he was the monster that they claimed, why had he not continued to kill when the war was over? He had never even considered hurting a child since the end of the conflict. The very thought was repugnant to him. The war had transformed him, but not utterly, and not permanently. Instead, the circumstances in which he had found himself caused aspects of his personality to metastasize into strange forms, and a man who had once thought of becoming a vet instead found himself euthanizing children, just as it was said that the devotional aspect of Klaus Barbie's personality might have seen him become a priest had the war not intervened. Baulman was not Reynard Kraus: Kraus had vanished with the surrender, along with all that he represented, and all the sins he had committed.

Marcus Baulman was a blameless man.

———

DETECTIVE GORDON WALSH ARRIVED at Golden Hills shortly after eight, when many of the home's residents were already asleep. The call had come just an hour or two before from Marie Demers, asking for a favor. He supposed that he could have done it over the phone, but he preferred to take care of these matters in person. Besides, he had loved war movies as a child, and the thought of hunting Nazis appealed to him. He identified himself over the intercom, showed his badge to the orderly on duty, and asked to see the visitors' book for the day of Bernhard Hummel's death. He went through the list of names, then asked if there was a photocopier he could use. He was shown to a small office, where he copied the relevant pages. None of the names meant anything to him, but they might mean more to Demers, he supposed.

Walsh was about to leave when a thought struck him. He turned back to the orderly, who had already returned to his puzzle book.

"Does every visitor have to sign in?" Walsh asked.

"Physicians who make regular visits usually don't get asked," said the orderly. "Priests and clergy too, I guess, once we get to know them. Basically, if you've been coming here for a while, and you're trusted, we let it slide."

"Do you know who was on desk duty that day?"

"I can check."

The orderly came back with three names, one of whom happened to be working elsewhere in Golden Hills that evening. Walsh spoke to him in person, and called the other two from his cell phone in the lobby.

When he was done, he had added four more names to the list of visitors.

LXIV

A light burned in the detective's house, but Werner could see no sign of Parker. With Engel and Hummel dead, and Theodora Hummel revealed to be her father's child in her capacity for self-preservation, Werner felt that they were almost out of danger.

Baulman still concerned Werner, but with Engel's death the threat to the old man had receded. Of course, there might be more inconsistencies in Baulman's paperwork if they dug deeply enough, but it would take them a long time to assemble a workable case against him, if they could manage it at all. They still had allies in Germany, the last vestiges of the *Kamaradenwerk*, and files were easily lost, even in this computerized age. It would be less complicated than getting rid of Baulman, especially with the Justice Department still circling him, at whatever the distance. But if it came down to it, he would find a way to remove Baulman from the picture, one that wouldn't draw too much attention. It would have been difficult in the past because Baulman was the amateur accountant, the *Geldscheisser*, but now the money was reduced to small change at the bottom of the jar, and Baulman's importance to them had vanished with it.

That left only the detective. His continued presence in Boreas was unfortunate, and his visit to Werner's house had left the pastor deeply disturbed. He had decided against moving Oran Wilde's body. It was too risky. Maybe once all this was over . . .

Werner knew that he might have to kill the detective. It wasn't just that Parker would keep looking, for that alone would not necessarily bring him down upon them. No, it was the fact that he had a kind of luck. It was a function of his perseverance, Werner supposed. What was that old Woody Allen line: 80 percent of success is showing up? Well, Parker showed up, and once established, he didn't go away. If a man had the patience to wait and watch for long enough, something of the world would reveal itself to him, especially if he already knew what he was hoping to see.

But Werner also admitted to himself that he *wanted* to kill the detective. Had he been alive to see it, Steiger might have acknowledged that he was mistaken, at least to a degree, about Werner's nature. Killing might not have given him pleasure, but it did endow him with a sense of vocation, beyond paying lip service to a god in whom he often struggled to believe.

A figure appeared on the beach, emerging from the shadows to the north. It was the detective. He was wearing sweatpants and an old T-shirt, with a hooded sweatshirt hanging open over it. Werner had heard that the detective walked regularly on the beach as part of his efforts at rehabilitation. It appeared that he had resumed this habit. Werner checked the time. Was the detective a man of routine? Possibly, but Werner decided to allow an hour either side for safety.

A day or two, he thought. I will give it a day or two in the hope that fortune intervenes. If not, I'll kill him.

LXV

P arker ate breakfast at Olesens the next morning before beginning a door-to-door canvass of stores and businesses on and off
Main Street. When he was done, he drove west to the small town
of Cawton, parked in the municipal lot, and took a window table at a
coffee shop called Ma Baker's, where the coffee was terrible and the pastries worse, but which gave him a clear view of a neat house with flow-
ering planters on the windowsills and a car in the drive.

After an hour, an elderly man appeared at the door of the house,
holding a Weimaraner on a leash. Parker left the coffee shop, and intercepted him as he headed for a pedestrian access between two buildings
that led down to a pebbled beach.

"Mr. Baulman?" said Parker.

"Yes?"

The dog looked to its master for some clue as to how to behave
toward the newcomer.

"My name is Charlie Parker. I'm looking into the death of Ruth
Winter."

Baulman barely reacted. He might even have been expecting Parker
to appear, so unperturbed did he seem, and he did not give any of the
answers that might have been anticipated in such a situation. He said

only, "I can't help you." Beside him, the dog stared up mournfully at the stranger who had interrupted the routine of their walk.

Parker extended a card.

"In case you think of anything."

Baulman took the card, tore it in two, and threw the pieces to the wind.

"I told you: I can't help you."

Parker watched the halves of his card blow away.

"Well, thank you for your time," he said.

Baulman continued on his walk. The sun was starting to set. Parker walked to his car, and returned to Boreas to wait.

LXVI

Cambion's decline was accelerating. He drifted between consciousness and unconsciousness, and was not always able to identify those in the room with him, even though only Edmund and the woman attended him. He spoke to figures that were not present except as memories, and argued with gods that had no name. He was a being in absolute torment, his physical and psychological pain mingling until one became indistinguishable from the other, so that even dosed up on morphine he remained in a realm of confused agony.

The only events to have roused him from his sufferings were those taking place far to the north in Boreas, Maine. During the hour or so each day when he was semicogent—Cambion tended to be more alert in the morning—he would ask Edmund to show him the newspapers on his laptop computer, the reports magnified to such a degree that just a sentence or two filled the screen. When even seeing these grew beyond him, the news stories were read aloud to him, though the space allotted to them grew smaller and smaller as progress in the investigation slowed, then stopped.

That very afternoon, Edmund had heard Cambion—half awake, half asleep—talking with one of his specters. This time, it was Earl Steiger.

"You came up against the wrong man, Earl," Cambion was saying. "This one has the breath of God upon him. This one bleeds from the palms of his hands. . . ."

But now Cambion was silent. The bedroom stood at the back of the house, on the first floor. It had a single small window, which Edmund had nailed shut. The only ventilation came from a grating in a corner. The room stank, but it remained reasonably secure.

Edmund could see that Cambion was already half gone from this world, with one foot in the beyond. It would not be long now. He sat by his master's bed, and gently bathed his brow with a damp cloth. Cambion was no longer eating, but Edmund forced him to take water mixed with a little protein powder. Sometimes Cambion managed to keep it down.

Edmund and the woman had fitted Cambion with a catheter. A plastic sheet placed on the bed made it easier to clean him when he soiled himself, and prevented the sheets and mattress from being ruined. It was Edmund who wiped him, and Edmund who fed him. The woman kept her distance unless it was absolutely necessary to approach him. Her hatred for Cambion added a further pollutant to the atmosphere of the room. For a time Edmund had wondered why she had even agreed to take Cambion in. Initially he thought her need for money was so desperate that she could not bring herself to refuse, but he had come to recognize the pleasure she derived from bearing witness to Cambion's final sufferings, a pleasure complicated still further by the memory of the love she once bore for him. In a terrible way, she now shared his torments.

None of this was spoken aloud by Edmund. He was not mute: he had simply made a decision not to speak, for no words could describe what he had seen during his years with Cambion. He had not killed for him, but he had watched others do so, although in later years he had refused even to do this. He would transport Cambion to wherever he needed to go—an opulent bedroom, a quiet basement, a disused garage—and leave him to his pleasures or, as his condition worsened, to live vicariously through the pleasures of others. Sometimes Edmund would still be able to hear what was happening, so he grew to be a connoisseur of noise-canceling headphones, which helped. He disliked listening to music to disguise the sound of suffering and dying, though. He found that the melodies became tainted by the knowledge of what they had been used to obscure. Slowly, surely, he began to speak less and less, until eventually he did not speak at all. He feared that if he tried to do so, the only sound to emerge would be a scream.

Yet, like the woman who hovered in the background, waiting for this man to die, he had a kind of love for Cambion, and a deep loyalty. He loved him because it was too easy to hate him. He was loyal to him because there was so much to betray.

Edmund used the cloth to wipe Cambion's mouth. It came away with blood on it, and the water turned pink when he dropped the cloth in the bowl. He set it aside, found the balm, and used it to moisten Cambion's dry lips. At no point did Cambion open his eyes.

Edmund walked to the bathroom and emptied the bloody water down the sink, then refilled the bowl. His eyes itched. He suffered from lagophthalmos, a partial facial paralysis that prevented his eyelids from closing, depriving the eyes of effective lubrication. He tilted his head back and tipped some drops into them. His vision had just cleared when he heard a sound at the front door of the house—the squeak of the handle being tested.

He put down the bowl, drew his gun, and moved into the hallway. Only a lamp burned there. He stayed very still, watching the door. The handle did not move. Still, he was certain of what he had heard.

Then Cambion cried out in alarm.

Edmund rushed to the bedroom. Cambion's eyes were open, and one ruined hand was pointing at the window.

"Something there," said Cambion. "Something bad."

Edmund stepped carefully to the drapes, and pulled them away from the wall at one side. It gave him only a peripheral view, but it was enough.

A face stared back at him. It reminded Edmund of a piece of gray, rotting fruit that had decayed almost to white, an impression strengthened by the wrinkles around its mouth and at the edges of its empty eye sockets. Then it retreated, and he might have begun to doubt that he had ever seen it were it not for what happened next.

A cigarette burned briefly in the yard next door. The house was empty and boarded up, the lawn a wasteland of trash and weeds, but now a man stood among them. In the glow of the cigarette, Edmund glimpsed his lank receding hair, and a white shirt buttoned to the neck.

The Collector, the claimer of souls, had found them: the Collector, and the empty husks who walked with him.

And Edmund was afraid.

"Edmund," said Cambion, and when the giant looked to him he saw his own fear reflected in Cambion's eyes, but also a depth of awareness that had not been present in them for many months, like the last flaring of a candle before its flame dies out forever. Cambion knew who—and what—was out there.

"The phone," said Cambion. "I want you to dial a number for me, then put me on speaker."

A cheap, untraceable burner phone lay on the bedside locker. Only Earl Steiger had used it to call, but now Earl Steiger was dead. Cambion dredged up the number from memory. It never changed, and few had it.

Louis answered on the second ring.

"Who is this?"

"A dead man," said Cambion. "Do you know me?"

"Yes," said Louis. "I know you."

"The Collector has found me."

"Good," said Louis.

Cambion coughed. It took Edmund a moment to realize that it was the ghost of a laugh.

"I think you may have fed me to him."

"I tried, but you slipped the noose. Looks like he didn't give up."

"He is persistent. It's almost admirable."

Cambion's mouth was drying up. He gestured for water. Edmund placed a straw between his lips, and squeezed the liquid into his mouth from the plastic bottle.

"Are you calling to say good-bye?" asked Louis. "If so, consider it done."

"I'm calling to give you a gift," said Cambion.

"You've got nothing I want."

"I have information."

There was silence on the other end of the phone, then Louis said, "Earl Steiger. He was one of yours."

"Very good. But he was more than one of mine: he was the last."

"And Charlie Parker buried him."

"No, God buried him."

"I didn't think you believed in God."

"I feel His presence. I stand at the crossing of worlds. I await His judgment."

"You're raving."

"No, I am offering a trade."

"To me?"

"To God. I'm asking Him to decide what a soul is worth, what *my* soul is worth."

"I can tell you that in nickels and dimes."

"It's not for you to determine."

"So you're trying to save yourself? You're deluded."

"No, I see with absolute clarity. Here it is, my parting gift to you: Earl Steiger was hired by a preacher named Werner to kill Ruth Winter, and Lenny and Pegi Tedesco. It wasn't the first time that Werner had used him. Werner's nature is corrupt. He is a fanatic."

"Why did Werner hire him?"

"I didn't ask. I rarely do. Steiger told me a little of him. Werner is a neo-Nazi, but the ones he guards are the real thing."

"Did Werner kill the Wilde family?"

"Yes, according to Steiger. He was also holding the boy, Oran, but he's certainly dead by now. Werner was the one who tortured Perlman, before he went into the sea. He kills to protect."

"Do you have proof? Without proof—"

Again came that hacked laugh.

"Now you know where to look," said Cambion. "The proof you'll have to find for yourself. Good-bye, Louis. You were right to decline my offer of employment. I think you would have turned on me in the end."

"This won't save you," said Louis. "You think you're going to avoid damnation with one phone call?"

"Not damnation," said Cambion. "Just a form of it."

He nodded at Edmund, who killed the connection. The light was already fading from Cambion's eyes, to be replaced by the pure terror of the final darkness. He stared at the closed drapes, as though he could pierce through to what waited for him beyond them. Edmund heard a scratching at the glass, as of nails picking at the window, and from the hall came the low creak of the doorknob being tried again. The woman screamed from somewhere upstairs. Perhaps they were already in the house.

"There is still money in the bag," said Cambion. His gaze lit briefly on a brown satchel lying at the top of the bedroom closet. "Some jewels too, I think, and a handful of Swiss gold francs. Take it."

Gently, Edmund lifted a pillow from beneath Cambion's head. The old man's eyes turned to him, lost in his distorted flesh.

"I am grateful to you," said Cambion. "For all that you have done."

Edmund placed the pillow over his master's face, and held it there until his struggles ceased. Then he went to the closet and took down the satchel. He searched inside, and his fingers found the cloth bag of gold coins. He removed two, and laid them on Cambion's eyes.

The woman was waiting outside the bedroom. She was crouched in a corner, seemingly frozen in place, her face raised to the stairs. Edmund heard movement above his head. He walked past her to the front door, paused for a second, then unlocked it.

The Collector stood on the doorstep. His cigarette was gone, and in its place he held a filleting knife. Edmund stared at him. He was still carrying the gun, but he dropped it at the sight of the Collector, and held up the empty hand. Shapes drifted past the woman in the hall, wraiths with pits for eyes, as the Hollow Men converged on Cambion.

The Collector sniffed the air. He bared his yellow teeth as his face was transformed by rage.

"I wanted him alive!" he said.

Edmund found the first words that he had spoken in years.

"Too bad," he replied.

And then the Collector was on him, the thin, curved blade thrusting into Edmund again and again in a blur of frustrated wrath, and the giant had never felt such pain.

At last the Collector was sated. He took a step back, his right hand red to the wrist. He barely glanced at Edmund as he slumped to the floor and the last of the life gushed from him, but the Collector did find it in himself to impart some final words to the giant.

"It was not enough to block your ears," he said. "It was not enough to do nothing. You should have known that we would come for you as well."

Edmund shuddered, and the flow of blood began to slow as he died.

The Collector looked beyond him to where the woman was now curled into a ball in the hallway. The noises from above had ceased. She was alone in the house. Her eyes traveled to the blade in the Collector's hand, but she did not plead or cry out. She was too far gone for that.

The Collector wiped his knife clean on Edmund's bright yellow jacket, now bibbed with scarlet, and restored it to the sheath on his belt. He picked up the satchel and examined its contents. He took one of the Swiss francs and dropped it into a pocket of his coat. It would suffice for his collection. He wanted nothing more from Cambion, or from anyone else in this place. He tossed the satchel to the woman, and left her.

CHAPTER

LXVII

arker stood by the shoreline, near hypnotized by the waves, lost
in their rhythm, the ascending moon his witness. Although he
had long resided by Scarborough's tidal marshes, and had grown
to love their intricate silver tracery, he understood why those who lived
their lives within sight and sound of the sea found themselves unsettled
when they were away from the ocean, salt calling to salt.

Despite his injuries, he had managed to walk farther than he had
previously done, even though his bag of stones had disappeared and he
had been forced to guess the distance. It was more progress, and progress was all that mattered, although the pain in his side said otherwise.
A single white earphone was inserted in his right ear. The other hung
loose over his shoulder.

He did not hear the footsteps on the soft sand until they were almost
upon him. He turned slowly, his hands outstretched, Christ waiting
to be taken. Werner stood before him. He was not wearing his clerical garb, but instead was dressed in paint-flecked jeans and a baggy
sweater, and his white sneakers were so old that they had turned to
gray. Disposable clothes, Parker thought: Werner would burn them
when he was done. The gun in his right hand shone a cold blue in the
moonlight.

"Pastor," said Parker.

"You don't seem surprised."

"I knew that someone would come, eventually. You, or another—it makes no difference. Now that it's come down to it, I'm glad you came yourself. But then Steiger is dead, and I don't think you have anyone left to call upon for help."

Werner looked puzzled.

"I've been watching you for a while," said Werner. "You were like a statue by the sea."

"I hadn't realized how much I loved it."

"The tide will soon be coming in," said Werner. "It'll cleanse this place of all trace of you."

"Will you send me out with it, or did you learn from your mistake with Perlman?"

"I'm not here to answer your questions, Mr. Parker. That only happens in the movies. I'm here to kill you."

"That's a pity," said Parker. "I had a lot of questions."

Werner raised the gun, and slowly, almost sadly, Parker closed his fists. He heard the shot at the same moment that the left side of Werner's head spat a cloud of blood, bone, and tissue as the bullet exited. There was hardly any wind. The evening dimness apart, it had probably been an easy shot. Parker's only regret was that Werner wouldn't talk. He had seen it in his eyes. He knew from the moment it had begun.

Parker reached beneath his sweater, killed the connection on his phone, and removed the earphone with its little mike attachment. Louis emerged from the dunes to the south. He had already disassembled the rifle, and was carrying the case in his right hand. Moments later, Angel—who had been watching Werner for most of the day—drove down from his perch above the bay.

Parker stepped over Werner's body, which was staining the sands red, and went to join the others. He didn't want their footprints on the beach, even with the tide coming in. The police would have to be called, and his story had no hope of standing unless the only steps visible were Werner's and his own.

"I was hoping you could have shot to wound," said Parker to Louis.

"Like the man said, that's just for the movies."

"I don't suppose it matters," said Parker. "He would have told us nothing."

"What did you want to know?"

"What everyone wants to know about anything: why."

"We could search his house," said Angel.

"No. You don't know what you're looking for, and you'd need more time than I can give you. Just get going. Don't drive through town. Head north, then cut southwest. Don't stop. Just keep going."

"What will you tell them when you call it in?" asked Louis.

"Everything, except who fired the shot."

"Walsh will know."

"Did you write him a confession?"

"Yeah, I signed my name on the sand, and left my card under a stone."

"Then let Walsh think what he wants."

He handed Angel the burner phone. Louis did the same with his. Their use was at an end.

"You're going to be real popular here," said Angel.

"It's okay," said Parker. "I was leaving anyway."

———

HE MADE THE CALL from the porch of the house, and returned to wait by Werner's body for the first of the cars to arrive. The bullet had distorted Werner's face. He was not the same man who had served soup and said prayers only a few nights earlier. Then again, he had never really been that man.

Stynes arrived first, Preston close behind. The sea was already lapping at Werner's feet. They stared down at his body, then Stynes told

Parker to raise his hands while Preston searched him. He was not carrying a gun. He had always had faith in Louis and Angel. Preston went to get some plastic sheeting from the car, in order to preserve whatever evidence might be left on Werner's body.

"Tell me what happened," said Stynes, and Parker did, or most of it.

"And you want me to believe that you don't know who fired the shot?" she asked, when he was done.

"I've no idea."

"You set yourself up as bait, and then you trapped him."

"Have you secured his house?" asked Parker, ignoring her.

"Answer me."

"I've told you all I know. Now: have you secured Werner's house?"

"Yes, we have an officer out there. What kind of amateurs do you think we are?"

"You'll need to search his property with ground-penetrating radar."

"Why?"

"I think Oran Wilde is buried there."

"Did Werner tell you that?"

"Call it an educated guess."

Stynes was visibly reddening.

"You might not have pulled the trigger, but you had this man killed."

Parker leaned in closer to her.

"Even if that were true, you knew what I was doing, and you let me use myself as bait for whoever came."

Stynes produced a pair of cuffs and told Parker to turn around.

"I'm placing you under arrest," she said. "You have the right to remain silent. Anything you say can and will be used against you. . . ."

He looked out at the sea. He breathed in the salt air. His side still hurt, but he didn't care. He wondered if his conversation with Baulman had been the final spur for Werner to move against him. Had all this been about Baulman? Ruth Winter, Bruno Perlman, Oran Wilde and his family, Lenny and Pegi Tedesco, all killed to protect one old war criminal who might well have died before he could be punished for his sins?

Another car arrived, followed by an ambulance. Soon the detectives from the MSP would join them, and the feds, and then the real fun would start. He was in for a difficult couple of days. It didn't matter.

For he could smell the sea.

LXVIII

Parker was put in one of the holding cells at the back of the Boreas Police Department. They were clean, and mostly used for DUIs and the occasional out-of-control student during the summer months. He closed his eyes and tried to create a narrative that would satisfactorily explain all of the killings. He kept coming back to Lubsko. That had to be the connection, but Ruth Winter's death didn't fit comfortably into the chain of events. Even though she was linked to Lubsko through her mother, her murder still made no sense to him. He remained convinced that Perlman had told her something to bring Steiger down on her, but what?

Gordon Walsh appeared after a couple of hours, trailed by Tyler and Welbecke, the two female detectives out of Belfast. Parker knew Tyler by sight, but not well. He was aware of Welbecke by reputation, mainly because she was one of the few people who could put the fear of God into Walsh.

The Boreas PD had one interview room, which, as in many small departments—and some larger ones—doubled as storage space for boxes of paperwork and broken chairs that might yet be repaired and salvaged. The room didn't have built-in recording facilities, so Walsh and Tyler both used their phones to record the interview. Tyler looked surprised when Parker waived his right to have counsel present, but

Walsh didn't. They had very little on Parker: a man had been shot and killed with what appeared to be a high-powered rifle at Green Heron Bay, but unless the private detective was capable of bilocation he hadn't pulled the trigger. On the other hand, they only had Parker's word on what had been said in the minutes before Werner's death. A Lutheran pastor, a respected member of his community, was dead, and Parker was the sole witness to his killing. Walsh decided that, for now, Parker didn't need to know that Werner had been at Golden Hills when Bernhard Hummel, another suspected war criminal, had apparently choked to death.

So Walsh said little, leaving most of the talking to Tyler and Welbecke. Walsh had been in this situation before with Parker. It was getting to be uncomfortably close to a habit, and he already knew what he was likely to hear: the truth, but not the whole truth, and maybe even nothing like the truth. He sat back and let Tyler and Welbecke go through the motions while he tried to spot the lies and omissions.

After listening to the back-and-forth for an hour, and watching Welbecke come close to an aneurysm on at least one occasion, Walsh arrived at two conclusions. The first was that Parker was lying when he said he hadn't known for sure that it was Werner who would be coming for him, although he had his suspicions. Walsh couldn't say why, exactly, but he was convinced that Parker had been forewarned.

The second conclusion arose from Parker's acknowledgment that he had put himself out there as bait by approaching both Werner and Baulman, yet he also claimed not to have been armed when Werner finally confronted him on the beach. Parker wasn't angling to be a martyr, and he wasn't a fool. Werner had been fixed in a rifle sight from the moment he set foot on that beach, and Walsh believed that he knew exactly whose sight it was. Despite his denials, Parker knew too.

"Why did you tell Sergeant Stynes to search Werner's property for Oran Wilde's body?" Tyler asked.

"A theory," he said.

"Based on what?"

Parker looked over her shoulder to where Walsh was seated.

"Based on a belief that the killing of the Wilde family, and the subsequent hunt for their son, was a distraction, a means of drawing attention away from the drowning of Bruno Perlman, and from the town of Boreas."

Parker waited to see if Walsh would be drawn into saying something, but he remained silent.

"And Werner gave no indication that this might be true before he was killed?" said Tyler.

"As I told you, he wasn't in the mood to talk. But check his gun: I think you'll find a match with the bullets used to kill the Wilde family."

"So you're saying that he came to murder you, but before he could, he was shot."

"Yes."

"Why?"

"I guess we'll never know."

"You seem certain that the mystery of his death is destined to remain unsolved."

It was Welbecke. Parker had to admit that she had a nice line in withering sarcasm.

"Since he was about to shoot me," he replied, "you'll understand if I have a natural sympathy for his killer, and wish him—or her—every success in the future."

Tyler began going back through the same questions again for form's sake, although Walsh could tell that she still hoped to trip Parker up on the details of Werner's killing. Walsh admired her tenacity, but Parker wasn't going to make any slips. There was not a single person in the room who accepted that he didn't know the identity of Werner's killer, but it was also true that none of the three detectives believed Werner's shooting was anything but a last resort. That didn't make it right, but they had more hope of charging Parker as an accessory to the rising and setting of the sun than they had of linking him to the shooting.

Tyler was almost done when there was a knock on the door. Walsh opened it, and Parker caught a glimpse of a small, dark woman in a gray suit. She radiated seriousness. Parker figured her for a fed, or maybe Justice Department. She couldn't have screamed government more if her face had been stamped with the seal of the President. She struck him as vaguely familiar, and he wondered if their paths had crossed before. Walsh went outside to speak with her, and when he returned he whispered something in Tyler's ear that made her wrap up the interview there and then. She thanked Parker for his time, even if she didn't sound like she meant it, and left the final word to Welbecke.

"Sometime soon your luck is going to run out," Welbecke told Parker.

"I'll know it's happened when we start dating."

Tyler hustled her partner out before the interview descended into actual violence. Walsh retrieved his phone and ended the recording.

"Really?" he said. "A dating joke?"

"I was under pressure."

"Huh." Walsh pocketed the phone. "Right now, I'd like to feed you to Welbecke and let her chew on your bones for what went down on that beach."

"I don't know what you're talking about."

"Spare me," said Walsh. "When they eventually come for you, just remember that you brought it on yourself."

"Is that all?" said Parker. "I'd like to leave now, if I'm free to go."

"You can stay where you are," said Walsh. "That was just the warm-up. The good stuff is next."

He admitted the woman in the suit. She took a seat across from Parker, and asked Walsh if he wanted to stay.

"No, I've heard enough," said Walsh. "I'm going to get some sleep."

He already had the door open when Parker called to him.

"Walsh?"

"What?"

Parker wanted to tell him about Cambion's call to Louis, and his confirmation that Werner had been behind not just the Wilde killings, but the deaths of Perlman and the Tedescos as well, but to do so would effectively negate his earlier statement, and put Walsh in a position of knowing for certain that it was untrue.

"Somehow, Werner knew the Wildes. He didn't pluck them from thin air. He was familiar with the family. He killed them, and then he put Oran Wilde in the ground."

Walsh nodded.

"We found a D ring fixed to the wall of his basement," he said. "The house is empty, but we'll start searching the grounds at first light."

———

MARIE DEMERS INTRODUCED HERSELF, and at the mention of her name Parker realized who she was. He'd seen her in the TV news reports about Engel and Fuhrmann. She didn't produce any recording devices more sophisticated than a yellow legal pad and a pencil. For the next two hours, Parker recounted in detail all that had occurred during his time in Boreas, including his dealings with Ruth and Amanda Winter, and his conversations with Isha Winter, Pastor Werner, and lastly, Marcus Baulman. He left out only matters pertaining to Angel and Louis, and his daughter and his private concerns about her. By the end, he was exhausted, but he also felt a certain satisfaction. It was the first time that he had been able to properly assemble a coherent version of events from start to finish and recite it aloud, both to himself and another. It enabled him to hear the places where it rang hollow.

"I don't believe that Werner's father underwent any kind of conversion during or after the war," he told Demers. "I think he used his position to arrange for war criminals to enter the United States under the guise of immigrants and displaced persons. When he died, his son took on the responsibility of protecting them. Somehow Bruno Perlman discovered the truth, and it involved Lubsko. He made contact with the Winter family, but Werner found out, and so it began."

He had been sitting for too long. He felt as though he were being repeatedly lanced in his side. He wanted to lie down and sleep.

"What I don't understand," he finished, "is why Ruth Winter was targeted, but not Isha. As the last survivor, Isha had to be the one with dangerous knowledge, even if she didn't know that she was in possession of it."

"Maybe Perlman thought Isha Winter was too old to be able to do anything about it," said Demers, "and, for the same reason, Werner didn't perceive her as a threat."

Now that he had acknowledged his desire to rest, Parker was overcome with weariness. He couldn't think clearly. He could barely keep his eyes open.

"Yes," he said. "That must be it. I think I'd like to rest now."

"One last question."

"What is it?"

"Did you have Werner killed?"

Parker summoned up his last reserves of energy. He had almost begun to relax. He looked at her across the table: so small, so neat, so threatening.

"I wanted him alive," he replied.

"You're not answering the question."

"No," said Parker, "I just did. There is no more. I'm done." He rose from his chair. It fell backward as he pushed it away. "You know where to find me."

"Yes, I do," said Demers, and this time the threat was audible. "Sleep well, Mr. Parker."

He left her sitting at the table, pages of her legal pad filled with penciled notes. Preston gave him a ride back to Green Heron Bay. He dozed all the way, and when he woke the next morning he could not remember how he had managed to get from the car to his bed. Through his window he saw gray clouds heavy with the promise of rain. Just as Werner had said, the tide had washed the beach clean of all traces of his presence. Over in the dunes, a forensic team searched for traces of a shooter they would never find.

Parker made a pot of coffee, put the last of his possessions into two boxes, and prepared to leave Boreas at last.

CHAPTER

LXIX

O ne of the more useful aspects of mortality, from an investigator's point of view, is that the dead can't object. They have no privacy. By noon that day, the detectives sequestered in Boreas had obtained Werner's telephone records, and some, but not all, of his bank details.

The call came through to Parker while he was putting the boxes in his car. He was grateful that most of his stuff was already gone. There was a limit to what a Mustang could hold and still be driven safely, and lifting boxes hurt like a bitch.

"Are you leaving us?" asked Walsh.

Parker glanced to his left. One of Stynes's officers was sitting in an unmarked car on the road above the dunes, watching the house.

"I was planning on saying good-bye."

"I'm sure you were. We're going to arrest Baulman."

"On what grounds?"

"It looks like you panicked him when you got in his face yesterday. He called Werner from his home telephone. It was careless of him. Demers recognized the number. We're going to ask him the purpose of the call, just as we're planning to ask him why he has made cash transfers totaling almost twenty thousand dollars over the past three weeks to one of Werner's accounts."

"Protection costs money," said Parker.

"Although some folks get it for free. Is the forensics team still out on the dunes?"

From what Parker could see, the search of the area was drawing to a close.

"They're almost done. I don't think they've left a grain of sand untouched."

"You could have saved them a lot of trouble."

"You want me to go through it all again? It was growing dark. I didn't see anything. I just heard the shot and hit the sand."

"Unfortunate."

"Yeah."

"There's something I didn't tell you last night: Werner was present at a nursing home called Golden Hills when a patient named Bernhard Hummel choked to death on grapes. Hummel knew Baulman: they'd come to this country together. Hummel suffered from dementia, and didn't eat unless someone fed him with a spoon."

"Werner was afraid that Hummel might let something slip."

"Whoever's work he was doing, it wasn't God's. It seems that Marcus Baulman also visited Hummel shortly before Werner did."

"So Baulman raised the alarm, and Werner did the killing."

"We're planning to ask Baulman about that, along with everything else."

"What about Werner's property?"

"We've started looking, but nothing yet. As for the gun, we're not 100 percent sure, but it looks like the same one that was used to kill the Wildes. I still have some folks who want to believe that Werner was Oran Wilde's accomplice and protector, but a body will shut them up. We found the link between Werner and Oran, by the way: Oran won an essay competition organized by the Lutheran churches in the Northeast. Werner was one of the judges. We have a picture of him presenting Oran with a certificate and a check. Oran won a hundred dollars, and it cost him and his family their lives."

"Where are you?"

"Outside the Boreas PD, taking the air."

"There's a bookstore called Olesens in the center of town, with a parking lot at the back. I'll see you there in about fifteen minutes."

"For what?"

"God, Walsh, just be there, okay?"

———

IT WAS UNFORTUNATE THAT Marcus Baulman opened his front door to take his dog for a walk just as the two unmarked cars pulled up outside. He didn't recognize the women who stepped from the first car, but he made them for police. When Marie Demers appeared from the second vehicle, he was certain that they had come for him. Werner was dead, and who knew what they had subsequently discovered about him— about all of them?

Baulman darted back inside and closed the door. Lotte, primed for her walk, looked confused. He patted her on the head. He would miss her. He pushed her into the living room and closed the door. He did not want the police to panic and hurt her.

The doorbell rang, followed by three heavy knocks. An unfamiliar female voice called his name, and the woman identified herself as a detective, but by then Baulman was already heading for the stairs. Lotte started barking, and Baulman caught sight of a shape passing by the kitchen window, making for the back door of the house. He was in his bedroom when he heard the sound of glass breaking, and he had the gun in his hand by the time the first footsteps sounded on the stairs.

He tasted oil in his mouth as he pulled the trigger.

———

WALSH WAS WAITING FOR Parker in the lot. He hadn't driven over. The Boreas Police Department was only a short walk away. Parker pulled up beside him and got out of the car.

"Do I need to make it okay with Stynes and Demers before I leave?" Parker asked.

"I'll let them know. They'll be heartbroken."

"About Oran Wilde."

"Go on."

"Louis told you that Steiger might have worked for a man named Cambion. Now Cambion is dead. He was killed in a house in Queens the night before last. It made the papers, although they haven't formally identified him yet, or the man who died with him. The woman who owned the house is in a catatonic state. Before he died, Cambion confirmed that Werner killed not only the Wildes but stuck that blade in Perlman's eye, and ordered Earl Steiger to kill Ruth Winter and the Tedescos."

If Walsh already knew this through Ross, then he gave no sign.

"Who did Cambion tell?" asked Walsh.

"I can't—"

"Fuck you. Who did he tell? You? Louis?"

"It doesn't matter."

"You know, you're right: it doesn't. You set up Werner, you and Louis and that other son of a bitch. You lured him out, and then you killed him."

"He didn't come to that beach to give himself up."

"He didn't get the chance!"

"He murdered children, Walsh. He kept Oran Wilde alive for just long enough to use him, and then he killed him too."

"Maybe if you'd left Werner alive, we could have asked him ourselves."

Parker leaned against his car. His face was expressionless. He knew that he had put himself at risk by telling Walsh about Cambion's call. If Walsh chose to do so, he could arrest him on suspicion of accessory to murder. Parker would deny having said anything at all, of course, and Walsh knew it, but Walsh's word would be worth more in a court of law, and accessory charges brought a sentence of up to three years. Conspiracy to commit murder, meanwhile, was twenty-five to life.

"I've turned a blind eye in the past," said Walsh. "But this is different."

"Is it?"

"This is murder! Look at yourself. What happened to you?"

Parker's blank visage stared back at him.

"I died," he said. "And then I came back."

"This is—" Walsh began.

"Did you enjoy your meal, Detective?" asked Parker.

"What?"

"Your meal in Augusta. Did you enjoy it?"

He did not sound triumphant, just sorrowful.

And Walsh understood. He had shown Steiger's body to Louis and Angel, and afterward he ate and drank with them. He was complicit. He had made himself so, step by step, ever since he had taken sides with Ross, but Ross would not protect him. To turn on Parker, and by extension on Angel and Louis, was to initiate the destruction of his own career.

And to what end: for a killer of children?

Walsh's anger began to ebb, to be replaced by a sense of vertigo, of a spinning, nauseating world. He believed in good, in morality, but so too did the man standing before him, and Walsh found himself unable to balance the two perspectives. Was this how it had to be? To eradicate a little of the evil from the world, did you have to sacrifice something of your own goodness? He had thought that he could consort with men like this, yet keep a moral distance. He had been wrong.

Walsh's cell phone rang in his pocket. He answered it, listened, and said only "I'm coming down there" before he hung up.

"Baulman is dead," he said. "He shot himself before they could get to him."

He stared at the phone in his hand, as though expecting another call that might explain everything to him.

"I'm going home," said Parker. "It's time."

———

THE FULCIS HAD DONE a good job, even in the few days allowed them. The plywood over the busted window in the kitchen door was gone, and there was new glass in its place. The holes left by bullets and shotgun pellets had been filled in, and the kitchen repainted. His office had a new door. They had even bought milk, bread, and coffee, and put a six-pack of Shipyard Export in the refrigerator. Two bottles of wine stood on the kitchen counter. A note, signed by both of them, wished him well, and advised that they had one or two small tasks to finish up whenever it suited him.

And here, in the place in which he had almost died, the home that he had once shared with Rachel and Sam, he felt suddenly overwhelmed by emotion—rage, gratitude, guilt, regret. He sat in his office chair, buried his face in his hands, and did not move for a long time.

CHAPTER

LXX

Werner's property was searched with radar to detect anomalies in the soil. Three holes were dug as a result, but only an old tarp and some animal remains were found. On the second day, the compost pile was noticed. Werner had built himself a wooden composting unit and placed it at the end of his yard beneath a copse of trees. There was concern that the heat from the pile would play hell with the equipment, so it was decided to make an exploratory dig once the unit had been moved.

They discovered Oran Wilde's body buried just two feet below the ground.

———

SOMETIMES CONVICTIONS COME FROM meticulous police work, from thousands of hours of effort. Sometimes a witness emerges. Sometimes a confession is made.

Sometimes you get a break.

One week after Werner's death, a letter arrived at Bruno Perlman's old address from a mailbox company located two miles from his house, notifying him that his two-month rental agreement was about to expire, and offering him one year for the price of six months should he choose to extend. A court order was obtained to open the box, which was found to contain paperwork relating to the late Bernhard Hummel, aka Udo Hoch, a former guard at Lubsko concentration camp; and another Maine resident named Ambros Riese, tentatively identified by Perlman as Anselm Trommler, an *Obersturmbannführer* and engineering specialist at Mittelbau-Dora concentration camp. Perlman, it seemed, had not been such a fantasist after all, although it was not clear at first how he had come to find these men. Eventually it was established that his was the most basic kind of investigation: in the aftermath of Engel's arrest, he had used voter records to create a short list of German Americans living in Maine whose ages corresponded to Engel's. He then appeared to have surreptitiously begun photographing them, and comparing them with available photographs of men and women who had served on the staff at Lubsko by using a fairly simple piece of face-aging software.

Perlman's mailbox also contained two high-quality copies of photographs that were neither from official Nazi Party identification documents nor taken by Perlman himself. One showed a woman in profile, her face almost entirely hidden by her blond hair, her left hand raised to fire a pistol. She was surrounded by a small crowd of SS officers and men. It was unclear at what exactly she was firing, but when enlarged, two shapes on the ground to her right were revealed to be the bodies of naked men.

The second photograph showed another woman standing at a chalkboard, pointing at some writing with a piece of chalk held in her right hand. Her light hair was pulled back in a bun. In front of her were two rows of teenagers, the first standing, the second kneeling. The writing on the board read: "*Der Jahrgang 1938, Klassenlehrer Fraulein Górski.*" It was a picture of the graduating students of 1938, with their homeroom teacher, Isha Górski, later Isha Winter, at the Bierhoff Jewish Private School in Aachen. On the back of the photo, Perlman had written down the names of each of the students, and the camps to which they had been taken.

None had survived the war.

———

MARIE DEMERS CALLED ON Charlie Parker as she was heading to Portland Jetport to catch her flight back to DC. Ambros Riese had been questioned at his home, and denied all knowledge of Anselm Trommler. But Demers had unearthed a labor requisition form from Mittelbrau-Dora with Trommler's name signed on the bottom, along with photographs and documents that traced his journey from Germany to Argentina, and on to the United States, during which time Trommler became Riese. Trommler's photograph on his Nazi Party membership documents was almost identical, a little less weight in the face aside, to the picture on his INS paperwork. There was enough evidence, Demers believed, to begin denaturalization and deportation proceedings against him, assuming he lived long enough. All this was explained to Riese as he sat in his chair, the oxygen hissing into him, while his son advised him to say nothing until they hired a lawyer, and his daughter-in-law looked on in silent shock.

And then, just as Demers and Toller were leaving, Riese confessed. He didn't do so out of shame, or guilt, or even some strange relief.

He did it, Demers thought, out of pride.

———

THE PRIVATE DETECTIVE INTERESTED Demers. She was content to discuss the details of the case with him, and what had been discovered in Perlman's rented mailbox. It was all about to become a matter of public record anyway.

"But you found nothing about Baulman?" asked Parker.

"No, just Riese, and Hummel, and the photographs. We're still working on identifying the second woman, but we think it's almost certainly

Magda Probst, wife of *Obersturmbannführer* Lothar Probst, commandant of Lubsko Experimental Camp."

She pulled a file from her bag and showed him the photographs.

"That's him on the right," said Demers.

But Parker was not looking at the picture of the woman with the
gun. He was looking at the photograph of Isha Górski.

And he knew.

V

[We] will pursue them to the uttermost ends of the earth and will deliver them to their accusors in order that justice may be done.

From "Concerning Responsibility of Hitlerites for Committed Atrocities," October 30, 1943, signed by Roosevelt, Churchill, and Stalin

LXXI

He had not expected to be heading north again so soon. He did so with a certain peace, and a kind of assurance. He had no proof— or none that would stand up in court—but he had certainty. Perhaps he should have told Demers immediately, but it was one thing to have faith in one's own convictions, and another to encourage others to share it. And he held fast to another truth: that there was not one form of justice, but many.

It took Isha Winter a while to answer her doorbell. He thought that she might have been watching his arrival from an upstairs window, for he saw a shadow move against the glass. She appeared reluctant to admit him, as though she already knew why he had come. As they sat across from each other in the living room, the sun spearing light through a gap in the drapes, he felt like one who had come to bring news of a death.

"You were there," she said, "when the pastor was killed."

"I was."

"The police came. They told me about him, about Marcus Baulman, about the buried boy. . . ."

Parker said nothing. He sat back and let her speak while he watched, barely listening to the words that came from her lips, seeing them only as black seeds that dropped to the floor, slipping between the boards to germinate poisonously in the darkness that lay beneath, until at last sound became silence. He took in once again the old wood, the stained boards, the low ceilings. It reminded him of an animal's lair, a place to hide from hunters.

"Why have you come here?" she asked.

"Because you are not who you claim to be."

"Then who am I?"

"I don't know, not for sure, but you are not Isha Górski. I think you probably looked a little like her in your youth, or enough to pass for her among those who knew her only from photographs. Like you, she was fair-haired. Surgery may have helped, but mostly the deception succeeded because everyone who had once been close to Isha was dead. If I had to guess, I'd say that you were once Magda Probst, who calmed children as they were led in to die at the point of one of Reynard Kraus's needles. Like you, she was left-handed. I've seen a photograph of her firing a gun. Isha Górski wrote with her right hand. I've seen a photograph of her too, but she was holding only a piece of chalk, surrounded by children who didn't know they were already dead.

"I think you colluded with Kraus and Udo Hoch and Thomas Engel to escape justice, although I've been trying to figure out what part your husband, Lothar, played in what happened. Maybe he was noble enough to sacrifice himself so you could get away, but I think that you and your accomplices killed him. I've read up on him. He was older than you, and walked with a limp. He'd only have been a burden, even if he'd agreed to become involved. His body wasn't as badly burned as Isha's—because that was who ended up in his bed at the end, I think, although I imagine she was charred flesh before she was even put there—and confirmation of his identity would have led to an assumption about the remains found in the house with him: a murder-suicide involving husband and wife, with the Russians at the gates. Anyway, nobody was going to look very closely at a pair of blackened bodies in a gutted house, not with Germany on the verge of collapse and plenty of the dead and dying to occupy the Allies, and not with one courageous survivor left alive to tell a tale of how she hid in a grave while SS guards disposed of the evidence of murder, and the commandant and his wife ended their lives together. I still don't know why you didn't flee with the others. Maybe you were ill, or injured, or perhaps you just knew that a whole lot of problems could be avoided if Magda Probst was believed dead, and Isha Górski alive. The Allies didn't put dead people on wanted lists.

"Of course, for that story to work you had to pretend to be a Jew. Not that it bothered you. You weren't an anti-Semite, and neither was your husband. That's why you were chosen for Lubsko. You were just mercenaries at heart. Still, I suspect you hoped it would only be a temporary arrangement until you could get to the money and disappear—because that's what it was all about, right: money? Those poor souls who thought they could buy their lives from you gave up the hiding places for whatever wealth they had stashed away, and I'll bet that, toward the end, not all of that information was making its way to Berlin.

"But because of the story you had created for yourself—the Sole Survivor, the Last Witness to Lubsko—you were stuck with Isha's identity for the long term. It worked out well, though: what better place to hide than among those you'd tried so hard to wipe out, with a husband who was Jewish by birth but not by observance? I hear that Werner had a quotation from Goebbels tattooed on the small of his back. Werner had lots of tattoos, but I think this one had a particular meaning for him: 'If you tell a lie big enough and keep repeating it, people will eventually come to believe it.' You were the big lie. Your life was the lie."

The woman who called herself Isha Winter remained very still. Her eyes were bright, and he remembered reading that the eyes did not age. They did not grow, nor did they change. He wondered if this was true. In appearance Isha Winter was an old woman, a Jew who had suffered and survived, but the truth of her, the essence, lay in those eyes. Her mouth was fixed in the faintest of smiles, as though she were listening to a tale being told by a child.

"I wondered about the other guards as well," said Parker. "Some of them must have been good, loyal Germans, and couldn't be trusted with what you were planning to do, so that was where Engel and Hoch came in: a pair of killers who were prepared to murder their own in return for money and protection when the war was over. Kraus was different: he was good with figures, and Demers believes that he looked after a lot of the paperwork for the camp. I wondered at first if you might even have been sleeping with him, but now I don't think so: you didn't hook up after the war, and you both married other people. The arrangement was purely financial, and so much the better for it. What did you do: split the records of hidden wealth that you'd obtained during your time in Lubsko, or did you just trust each other?"

But the woman before him gave no reply.

"Anyway, they fled, and you remained in Europe, and the assets you stole paid for everyone's paperwork, and ultimately bought passage to the United States, helped by Werner's father. When he died, his son took on the duty of watching over you all. I'm sure that you paid good money to the Werners in the beginning, although I doubt there's much left now. Baulman, or Kraus, or whatever you called him in private, might even have used the last of it to cover the cost of hiring Steiger—because twenty thousand isn't much for three killings, not for a man of Steiger's quality, although he was probably past his prime when he died—but you were also fortunate that Pastor Werner turned out to be a fanatic. Fanatics work cheap.

"Which brings us to why Steiger was hired to begin with, and why Werner had to get his own hands bloody: Bruno Perlman. He found out that members of his family had died at Lubsko, and he became a man with a mission. He wanted to discover all that he could about the camp, which ultimately meant talking to the only eyewitness left alive: Isha Górski, now Isha Winter. I don't think he suspected anything then. I think he just wanted to know more. But he was perceptive, and somehow he spotted what I did, because he mailed those two pictures to himself, one of Isha Górski, and the other of Magda Probst. The more he looked, the more convinced he became that the woman who claimed to have survived Lubsko was not who she said she was.

"But Perlman was also a fanatic in his way, and an egotist. He didn't trust the authorities, and I think he wanted to claim the credit for exposing the truth. He only had one close friend, Lenny Tedesco, and he confided in him.

"And then he made the first of his mistakes: he called your daughter. I don't know why—he strikes me as having been a lonely man, and maybe he felt they had made some connection after his visit to you— but whatever the reason, he contacted her, and shared with her something of what he suspected. What he told her took root, because there was a tiny part of your daughter that knew it to be true. She confronted you, and saw in your eyes what I'm seeing now. There might have been threats made, words spoken in anger, but what it came down to was that Ruth left, took your granddaughter with her, and told you that they wanted nothing more to do with you. Then she had to decide what to do with the information Perlman had given her. Did she give him away then? Did she tell you that he was coming, that he thought he had proof against you? And did you, in turn, contact Werner, who somehow managed to convince Perlman to meet him while Steiger stayed in Florida and took care of the Tedescos?"

The smile never wavered. The stillness remained. He felt as though he were conversing with a simulacrum of a human being, an imperfect imitation. He supposed that was exactly what she was.

"Whatever the chain of events, you made the decision to sacrifice your daughter. You might have been under pressure from Werner or Kraus to acquiesce, but ultimately the choice was yours, because you always had the final word. You assented to her murder, but on one condition: your granddaughter was not to be harmed. Your daughter had disappointed you, but you weren't about to lose your grandchild because of her. You know, now that I consider it, you might even have had Amanda's father killed years before. Werner would have arranged to have it done for you, if you'd asked, or even taken care of it personally. Alex Goyer wouldn't have been much of a father to Amanda anyway: a petty criminal, a beater of women. He'd almost made Ruth lose her child. You told me so yourself. You gave your own daughter to the knife, so I don't think you'd have blinked at the thought of having her boyfriend murdered."

His mouth was growing dry. The sunlight departed from the window as if in shame. He wanted to be gone from this house, and from this woman's presence. Just a little longer, he thought. Just a few more minutes.

At last she spoke.

"All this, from a photograph?" she said. "Even if it were true, which it is not—I watch TV, Mr. Parker: I know of wires, of recordings, of trickery—who would believe it?"

"I'm not recording you." He lifted his shirt, and then showed her his phone. It was powered off, and the battery had been removed.

"I don't care," she said. "These are all lies, fabrications. And even if they were to be believed, how could they be proved? Not with a picture of a woman in a schoolroom. Not with invented stories."

"We'll see."

"Perhaps. I can't stop you. Let them look. Let them begin a search that will take years to complete. I will be long dead. I am past the evening of my life, and the dark closes in on me."

"Aren't you afraid?" he asked.

"Of what?"

"Of what waits in that night?"

"Of God?"

She laughed at him, then covered her mouth to hide it. It was a curiously girlish gesture, and he found it repellent.

"Do you know how many people cried out to God at the end in Lubsko, in Birkenau, in Dachau?" she asked. "Can you imagine all

those voices screaming together, begging for rescue, for mercy, for
an end to pain, for the annihilation of their tormentors? And do you
know how many of them were answered? Tell me. Speak the number.
No? Then let me say it for you: none. There was no answer. There was
no mercy. From that, what can we say of God? Either that He does not
exist, or He turned away from His own creation, and would not listen
to their cries. What have we to fear from a being like that, even if He is
real? How could He even look us in the eye and pass sentence upon us?

"But I do not believe in that God, or any god. I do not believe in a
world beyond this one. I will close my eyes, and I will cease to exist, and
laws and justice will have no further meaning for me. Leave now, Mr.
Parker. Whatever satisfaction you seek, whatever answers you desire,
won't be found here."

He got to his feet. He had what he wanted: not a confession, but confirmation. She had given him enough. He had stared in her face as he
told his story, and had seen the truth of it reflected there. He said nothing more before he left, and did not look back at her. He called Demers
from his car, and told her of the woman who had addressed her cards
with her left hand, but years earlier had apparently written her name in
chalk with her right. Let Demers do what she wished with the information, for he had other work to do, and the old horror in there was right:
she was beyond the reach of Demers, and beyond any written law, any
human justice.

But that was not the only justice.

LXXII

Parker returned to the Scarborough house. As night fell, he poured a glass of red wine and went outside to sit on the porch and wait.

At some point he must have fallen asleep, for when he woke the glass was lying on the ground, and his dead daughter was watching him from behind an old oak. Her singing had roused him. He could not see her ruined face: as always, she tried to keep it hidden by turning away and allowing her long hair to conceal the damage.

He no longer feared her. He understood something of what she was, and knew that she loved him enough to move between worlds in order to be closer to him. He thought of what Werner had said to him: that he did not wish to know the truth about life after death, that he did not want proof of another existence. He recalled the conviction of the woman who wore the mask of Isha Winter: that law and justice could not get to her in time in this world, and the rest was sleep.

But Parker knew the truth, and it was not so terrible, not for him. The difficulty for some might lie in remaining engaged with this world after such a revelation, but it presented no obstacle to Parker. There was work to be done here.

"Hello, Jennifer," he said.

hello

The voice less like a whisper than the memory of one, the sound of it

coming from so close by that he could almost feel the words as a coldness against his skin, even though the dead daughter remained behind
the tree.

"How long have you been there?"

a little while

"Are you alone?"

yes

The other was not with her now, the entity composed of residues of
hurt and anger that took the shape of his dead wife.

will you be staying here?

"For a while."

good

"Do you like it here?"

you like it here

"Yes." He smiled at her, and tried to hold it for as long as he could
before he let it fade. "Jennifer, what can you tell me about Sam?"

nothing

"She's special. I know that now."

i can't say

"Why?"

i'm not supposed to

"Who told you not to?"

sam did

"Do you have to do what Sam tells you?"

yes

"Are you frightened of Sam?"

A pause.

yes

"Jennifer, is Sam—?"

please daddy stop you have to stop

And he did, because he could hear the terror in her voice, but also a
kind of awe, the wonder that one might feel at being forced to confront

a force of nature capable of immense destruction: a storm, a tornado, a tsunami. He took a deep breath.

"There's something I want you to do for me, Jennifer."

what is it?

He told her, and she understood. He bent down to collect the glass, and when he looked up again she was gone. He placed the glass in the kitchen sink, then went to the storage shed at the back of the house and unlocked it. He took a spade from inside, walked to a patch of ground not far from where his dead daughter had been standing, and started to dig. The ground was hard, and the effort pained him, but what he wanted was not buried deep. The spade struck something solid after he'd dug about eighteen inches down, and shortly after he had uncovered the waterproof Lexan box.

Inside was a rectangular package secured in a sealed pouch. He refilled the hole and took the box back to the house. He opened it next to the sink so as not to spread dirt, then brought the pouch into his office and set it on his desk. He made a cup of coffee, unzipped the pouch, and removed the sheaf of papers that it contained.

In the glow of his computer screen, he began to read the list of names.

CHAPTER

LXXIII

I sha Winter had not eaten since her conversation with the private detective. Neither could she sleep. She was not afraid of him, nor of the bitch Demers, but she burned with fury at both of them. If only Werner had managed to kill Parker. If only her *blöde Fotze* daughter had kept her distance from him . . .

Now she was entirely alone, and there was no one to help her. Even the vile Riese was gone, although she had no concern that he might imitate Engel and try to buy his own freedom by selling out others. Riese would endure his sufferings in silence. Contact between them had always been limited, but from Baulman she knew that Riese had few regrets. If he could, he would have worn his full SS regalia for Bangor's Veterans Day Parade, and cursed anyone who objected.

The letter from the Justice Department had arrived, and soon Demers would come. There would be more questions. Isha would deny everything. The search for evidence would begin. She wondered how long it would be before someone leaked information to the newspapers or the TV people. She liked being able to go out. She liked being greeted in the stores and going to the senior center to play bridge and bingo. She did not wish to become an outcast in her own community. But if that was the worst they could do, then let them persecute her. She had enough unread books to last a decade at least, and she would be long dead before then. *Fick euch!*

Isha. Isha, Isha, Isha . . .

In a sense, she had possessed Isha Górski by inhabiting her form and appropriating her past. She had every right to all of it now. It was hers, decade upon decade of it. Most of the time, she was no longer even conscious of herself as the hidden other. She had married as Isha Górski, but made love as Isha Winter, and become a mother as Isha Winter. She had believed herself unable to conceive—had not even wanted a child—and then, in her midforties, she had given birth to Ruth. It wasn't quite as miraculous as Sarah bearing Abraham a son in her twilight years, but it was close.

And she had cared for Ruth, in her way, although it was always David who truly loved their daughter. Perhaps if she had felt more strongly about the child, things might have been different. How strange, too, that Ruth should only have given birth in her late thirties, and that Isha should have loved her granddaughter more than her daughter. Maybe it was because David had not lived long enough to become a part of Amanda's life, and so she became her grandmother's child, like a figure from a folktale. Everybody said so.

But she had loved David, too. The detective was right: even in her old life, she had borne the Jews no particular hatred, and had married one because that was what the real Isha would have done, but she had surprised herself by her affection—and desire—for David Winter. She knew that Riese in particular had despised her for it, and considered her imposture the deepest form of degradation for an Aryan woman, but he kept his own counsel because the embezzled Lubsko wealth, carefully secured by her in the aftermath of the war, had paid for his passage from Europe to South America, and on to the United States, and had protected him as well as the others. When the Jews came sniffing after Riese in the early 1960s, seeking files related to Mittelbau-Dora and Anselm Trommler, it was her bribes that ensured the relevant paperwork went missing from the Bundesarchiv.

Kraus, by contrast, had taken a more pragmatic, even romantic view, of Isha, regarding her as essentially sacrificing herself for the sake of her comrades. "What man offers in heroism on the field of battle, woman equals with unending perseverance and sacrifice," he had once told her, quoting one of Hitler's maxims, and conveniently forgetting that Isha had blooded herself in Lubsko, leading children by the hand to the surgery before aiding Kraus with the final injections. Of course, she'd had to do it discreetly: killing was men's work, and although she had euthanized physical and mental defectives at Grafeneck, it was still deemed inappropriate for a woman to engage openly in acts of murder, even against Jews and other enemies of the state.

And Axel Werner? Werner had adored her.

She was suddenly aware of a chill in the room, as though the temperature had plummeted in a matter of seconds. She drew the blankets around her, but it did no good. Damn it, she would have to turn on the heater again, and to do that she'd have to get out of bed, as the control unit was on her dressing table. She grabbed her robe from a chair and put it on before she left her bed. The cold hurt her feet as she walked past the window. The drapes were open. She rarely closed them. She never slept much beyond six a.m. anyway. She liked having the morning sunlight streaming into her room, and looking out upon the beach and the sea. It was coming on for high tide, and she could see the waves peaking and disintegrating.

It was only now that she noticed her bedroom door was slightly ajar. She always closed it before she went to bed because it creaked if there was a breeze, and she was a light sleeper. She was still considering the peculiarity of the situation when she heard footsteps in the hall outside. They were not heavy, and reminded her of the sound of Amanda running around the house in her stocking feet when she was younger.

"Who's there?" she shouted. "I have a gun."

Isha heard the footsteps descending the stairs, but they paused about halfway, inviting her to follow. She knew that she should lock the door and call the police. She also had a personal alarm hanging around her neck in case she should fall or be taken ill. If she activated it, an ambulance would come, and maybe the police too.

But she did not use the phone, and she did not activate the alarm. The child laughed, and it sounded so like Amanda's laugh that Isha left the bedroom and stepped into the hall. Could Amanda have come? Maybe there had been some problem with the Frobergs and she had fled to her grandmother's house.

"Amanda?" she asked the darkness. She advanced down the hall until she could see the stairs, and was just in time to catch sight of a girl skipping off the last step and disappearing through the open front door.

"Amanda?" said Isha again. "Is that you?"

She found herself descending the stairs, heedless of the chill air, moving less of her own volition than impelled by an unseen force that had taken control of her limbs and was urging her on, sending her out to find the child. She saw the girl at the gate, her long blond hair trailing behind her, like a figure glimpsed floating beneath the sea, and then the girl was crossing the road and heading toward the beach, and Isha was following her, the gravel drive cutting at the soles of her feet, the night air pricking her flesh. There were no cars on the road, and the moon was a pale smudged fingerprint behind the clouds, like the mark upon creation of a god in whom she did not believe.

Blacktop became stone, and stone became sand. Isha was on the beach. The girl had stopped walking, and was facing the sea. Isha looked down at her own faint shadow, and realized that the girl cast none. Isha wanted to turn back now, but she was frozen in place. And though the girl still had no umbra, other shadows were moving around her, cast on the beach by unseen figures that emerged from the sea, spreading like ink from the dark ocean, moving closer and closer to Isha, reaching out to her, touching her: tens, then hundreds of them— men, women and children who had conspired to make their absence palpable, like silhouettes cut from card. They surrounded her as the sands released her, and she fell to her knees. They called her by her true name, over and over—chiding, regretful—until their voices became one with the sound of the sea, and the cold water touched her knees, then her toes, soaking her nightgown and her robe.

And the girl joined them, and Isha was permitted to look upon her face at last.

———

ISHA WINTER WAS FOUND hours later when a milk truck driver caught her hunched figure in his headlights. She was soaking wet and barely conscious, and could not stop shivering. He wrapped her in his coat, then carried her to the cab of his truck and kept her warm while he waited for the ambulance to arrive. She lapsed into unconsciousness on the journey to the hospital, and woke only once more in the days thereafter, when she asked to see not a rabbi but a Lutheran pastor, and make her final confession. She was, said a nurse who was present, weeping with fear.

By the time the minister arrived, she was dead.

LXXIV

Ross, special agent in charge of his own unique section of the Federal Bureau of Investigation, arrived at Maxwell's on Reade Street, his usual Friday lunchtime haunt, to be told that his guest was already waiting for him. This was unwelcome news, since Ross always enjoyed reading the *New York Times* with his Friday lunch, and also something of a surprise because he wasn't expecting a guest. Nevertheless, if he was going to be killed it probably wasn't going to be over the spinach dip at Maxwell's, so he thanked the host and followed him to the table. Wine was waiting, along with his guest.

"I ordered you a glass of white," said Parker, "seeing as how it's Friday and all, and the waiter tells me that you usually order the fish."

Ross took a seat across from the detective. They hadn't seen each other in some time, although Parker was rarely far from Ross's mind. They were not close, and they were not friends, but Ross thought that he knew more about Parker than just about any man on earth.

"You're looking better than I expected," said Ross.

"I'm recovering well."

"And keeping yourself busy, I see. Buried anyone else in sand lately?"

"It was an act of God."

"I'll bet his insurance company will be pleased to hear it."

Ross picked up a menu, but only for form's sake. The waiter was right: he always had fish on Fridays. It was a hangover from his Catholic upbringing, but he also just liked the fish at Maxwell's.

"You eating?" he asked Parker.

"No, I'm not staying."

"Then what can I do for you?"

Parker handed over a sheaf of papers, held together with a black clip. Ross read the first page, and looked bemused. After reading the second, third, and fourth, the expression on his face suggested that he might need something stronger than wine.

"What the fuck is this?"

"It's an agreement," said Parker. "The Federal Bureau of Investigation is going to hire me as a freelance contractor and adviser on cases linked to your office. Basically, you're going to put me on retainer. You can feel free to play with the language a little, but I'd appreciate if you'd run the final version by my lawyer, Aimee Price, before signing it. I don't want you stiffing me in the small print."

"And why would I want to retain you?"

"A number of reasons: because I have work to do, and I can do some of it more easily by flying your flag when convenient; because the income will be useful, as I'm tired of asking my friends to help me in return for beer money; because I realized how easily I took on the role of the sacrificial lamb up in Boreas, mainly as I've been playing the same role for you, and you may as well pay me for the risk involved. Oh, and finally, because of this."

He handed Ross two more sheets of paper, stapled together. They contained a list of typewritten names, most of them with sums of money beside them.

"Those came from a plane that crashed in the Great North Woods of Maine in 2001. I think you know what they are, but in case you haven't been keeping up with events, they're the names of compromised individuals, men and women who, for want of a better term, have struck deals with the devil. They're either corrupt or they can be corrupted. They're ticking time bombs waiting to be used against you—against all of us."

Ross went down the list of names, running an index finger under each one. On two occasions he whispered the word "Jesus." When he was finished, he placed the papers facedown on the table.

"Some of these names have been redacted," he said. "Did you do that?"

"They're people I'm personally curious about," said Parker. "For now, they don't concern you. If I think you should be worried about them, I'll pass on the information in time. Consider it part of our agreement."

"We don't have an agreement."

"Yet."

"Are there more of these pages?"

"Lots."

"When do I get them?"

"When do I get my first check?"

"Jesus."

"You said that already."

A waiter approached, but Ross waved him away.

"I'm not running an employment agency," he said.

All trace of good humor vanished from Parker's face.

"Listen to me, Ross: you're hunting, and you've used me in your hunt when it suited you, but whatever is happening here, whatever is approaching, I'm tied up with it, and I'll be there at the end. You need me, and I'm offering to cooperate."

"And the rest of the pages?"

"Those should keep you occupied for now. I'm working my way through the list. I'll pass on more names at regular intervals."

"No deal. I want them all—immediately."

"I said 'cooperate,' not 'capitulate.'"

"I can get a court order. I can tear apart your house. For God's sake, I can have you locked up!"

"And I guarantee that you'll never see any more of the list than you already have. Come on, Ross. My retainer is about what you spend on printer ink in a month."

Ross looked at the page of names. He looked at the contract. He stopped just short of putting one in his right hand, the other in his left, and weighing them against each other.

"I'll be in touch," he said.

Parker stood.

"Talk to Aimee," said Parker. "Oh, and I told her you'd take care of her fee. Enjoy your lunch."

Ross watched him leave. When he was gone, he took out his cell phone and dialed a number. Epstein answered on the second ring.

"We have Parker," said Ross.

LXXV

C hristian Froberg smelled something burning as he worked on the busted leg of a chair in his garage. The smoke had an acrid tinge, and he heard Milo barking. He stepped into the yard and saw Amanda standing beside the barbecue, a plume of smoke rising before her. He didn't shout, didn't make a fuss: he had learned to be careful where Amanda was concerned, especially in recent days as the truth about her grandmother had become known.

Slowly he approached her. He saw photographs burning, faces curling in the flames; and books; and a pair of soft toys that she had brought with her to their home—all of them given to her by her grandmother. Amanda's shoulders were heaving as she consigned them to the flames. He did not speak, but simply drew closer to her. After a moment, he put his arm around her, and felt her lean into him.

Together they watched her past burn.

CHAPTER

LXXVI

Sam came to stay the next weekend. Parker met Rachel in Concord for the pickup on Friday evening, and assured her that he'd have Sam back at the same spot for collection by late on Sunday afternoon. He and Sam caught a movie at the Nickelodeon in Portland, and ate garlic bread with prosciutto followed by pizza at the Corner Room. Afterward they walked along the waterfront before driving back to Scarborough. Sam brushed her teeth and waited for her father to kiss her good night. As he leaned over, she hugged him tight, and whispered in his right ear.

"You have to stop asking about me, Daddy," she said.

He froze against her. He tried to push her away so that he could see her face, but her grip was viselike around his neck.

"How did you know?" he asked.

"Jennifer told me," she said. "She told me after she brought the sad people to the lady by the sea."

My God, my God . . .

"You can see Jennifer?"

"I've always been able to see her."

"Sam, I don't—"

"Listen, Daddy. Please. We can't talk about it. We just can't."

"But why?"

"Because it's not time, not yet."

He recalled what Ruth Winter had said to him on the beach at Boreas—*Sometimes I think we're only put here to watch over our children until they're ready to take care of themselves*—and he understood.

Sam released him, but only so that she could watch him, so that she could put her hands to his face and consider his reaction, and he thought that he had never looked in the eyes of one so beautiful and yet so ancient.

"And because they're listening," she said, and her tone almost stilled his heart. "They're *always* listening. We have to be careful, Daddy, because they'll hear. They'll hear, and they'll come. . . ."

ACKNOWLEDGMENTS

As always, I rely on the goodwill and knowledge of a great many people to make me appear better at what I do than I actually am. *Hunting Evil* by Guy Walters (Transworld, 2009) proved an invaluable resource in the writing of this book, and a trove of anecdotal and statistical details. *Hitler's Furies: German Women in the Nazi Killing Fields* by Wendy Lower (Houghton Mifflin Harcourt, 2013) was a fascinating insight into the female killers of the Nazi era, while *Boomerang: Travels in the New Third World* by Michael Lewis (W. W. Norton & Company, 2011) inspired some of Marie Demers's views on elements of national character. *The Years of Extermination: Nazi Germany and the Jews, 1939–1945* (Harper Collins, 2007) became a crucial tool in the cross-checking of information. The *United States Attorneys' Bulletin* (Vol. 54, No. 1, January 2006), detailing the work of what was then the Office of Special Investigations, provided much of the background to cases and procedure used in this book. I am also deeply grateful to Eli Rosenbaum, the director of Human Rights Strategy and Policy at the Human Rights and Special Prosecutions Section of the Department of Justice, for taking the time to answer my questions. I should stress that any opinions expressed in this book are largely my own. I don't want to make the job of the HRSP any harder than it already is. Thanks, too, to Dr. Robert Drummond for guidance on medical issues, and to Rachel Unterman for casting an eye over particular details of the story.

I'd be all at sea without my editor at Hodder & Stoughton, Sue Fletcher, and Emily Bestler, my editor at Atria Books/Emily Bestler Books, so my thanks to them both and to everyone at Atria and Simon

& Schuster, including Judith Curr, Megan Reid, David Brown, and Louise Burke; and everyone at Hodder and Hachette, including Swati Gamble, Kerry Hood, Carolyn Mays, Lucy Hale, Breda Purdue, Jim Binchy, Ruth Shern, and Frank Cronin. Darley Anderson and his angels in London remain the best agents a boy could ask for. Clair Lamb, minion beyond compare, acts as a voice of reason and friendship, and Madeira James and all at xuni.com keep me connected to the digital world, and try to explain concepts like the Internet to me without raising their voices. Meanwhile, Kate O'Hearn, author and good soul, took care of clearances, which sounds much easier than it actually was.

Finally, love and gratitude to my partner and fellow author, Jennie Ridyard, and to Cameron and Alistair. I mean, what would be the point without you all?